THEY WERE DRIVEN BY DREAMS FORGED IN VISIONS OF A WESTERN PARADISE . . .

EMMALEE—An intelligent, headstrong beauty, she longed for land and independence, convinced that a man's love demanded surrender.

GARN—A reckless adventurer, gambler, and wilderness scout, he offered Emmalee his love and protection, but pride prevented him from offering more than once.

RANDY—The passions Emmalee aroused troubled him; he swore to wait for their marriage vows. But waiting worked changes . . . and then there was another woman he wanted for his wife.

LOTTIE—Cunning, clever, she knew Emmalee was her most dangerous rival. She would have to use every wile if she hoped to win Garn's love. And she used them.

TORQUIST—Leader of the farmers' wagon train, he believed passionately in the Pure Land. But he was swept up in a desperate race with the ranchers, and he, too, would succumb to the lust for wealth and power.

THE PASSIONATE AND THE PROUD

Books by Vanessa Royall

FLAMES OF DESIRE
COME FAITH, COME FIRE
FIREBRAND'S WOMAN
WILD WIND WESTWARD
SEIZE THE DAWN

THE PASSIONATE AND THE PROUD

Vanessa Royall

A DELL BOOK

Published by
Dell Publishing Co., Inc.
1 Dag Hammarskjold Plaza
New York, New York 10017

To Kathryn Falk and *Romantic Times*

ISBN: 0-440-16814-7

Printed in the United States of America

First printing—November 1984

Author's Note

THE PASSIONATE AND THE PROUD is a story about the American frontier, a time of struggle and triumph that will never be seen again upon this earth. It is also a story of tempestuous love between Emmalee Alden, a proud but dispossessed young woman, and Garn Landar, who is just as prideful and just as ambitious. Emmalee and Garn learn many things as they seek their destinies, and from each other they learn the most valuable knowledge of all: Love is not surrender.

The driver of the wagon swaying through forest and swamp of the Ohio wilderness was a ragged girl of fourteen. Her mother they had buried near the Monongahela —the girl herself had heaped with torn sods the grave beside the river of the beautiful name. Her father lay shrinking with fever on the floor of the wagon-box. . . .

She halted at the fork in the grassy road, and the sick man quavered, "Emmy, ye better turn towards Cincinnati. If we could find your Uncle Ed, I guess he'd take us in."

"Nobody ain't going to take us in," she said. "We're goin' on jus' long as we can. Going West! There's a whole lot of new things I aim to be seeing!"

She cooked the supper . . . and sat by the fire, alone.

—***Arrowsmith*, Sinclair Lewis**

Runaway

It was just a creaky old logsled drawn through the wintry woods of southern Illinois by two huge, plodding horses. But to Emmalee Alden, bundled in blankets, half buried in piled hay, and pressed close to her beau, it might as well have been a royal sleigh.

"It's too bad the others felt sick," said Val Jannings, "but finally we're alone together. It seems that I've been waiting forever for a day like this."

"Ummm." Emmalee smiled, closing her eyes, inviting him to kiss her again, which he did. She let herself drift with the kiss and its warmth, savoring the slow excitement building in her body, enjoying the tender pressure of Val beside her in the hay. She wanted to enjoy every moment of this January afternoon.

Indeed, Emmalee had feared that the Cairo Lutheran Orphanage's annual sleigh ride would not take place at all. There had been no snow through December, and right after New Year's Day everyone at the home began to come down with the grippe. But she hadn't gotten sick, and when a sudden blizzard came howling down the Mississippi Valley, turning the whole world brilliantly white, Emmalee implored the Reverend Bowerly to let her take the horses out.

"I know it'll be just Val Jannings and me," she'd told the orphanage's superintendent, "but I've wanted so much to have a bit of free time. And you know how generous the Jannings family has been to us here at the home."

The superintendent, a gentle, careworn man, had smiled and given his approval. He respected and trusted Emmalee, who had been living and working at the orphanage, caring for the younger children, for almost two years. She had come limping into Cairo, Illinois, in the spring of 1866, a fourteen-year-old waif mumbling dazedly about "going west." She had buried her father near Springfield, had lost possessions, wagon, and horses trying to ford the swollen Sangamon River. She hadn't the strength to go a step farther, and so the Lutheran orphanage had opened its doors to her. She had been there ever since, gaining strength, growing up, and becoming almost indispensable. Here also she'd learned to read and write, acquired a knowledge of the country she meant to traverse someday.

"Of course you can have an afternoon off, Emmalee," the reverend had said. "And I know you and young Mr. Jannings can be trusted. Just make sure that you're back here by sundown. It can get mighty cold out there in the woods."

True, the woods were cold, but it was warm and cozy in the sleigh and in Val's arms. The sun was dropping swiftly now, a glowing reddish ball falling toward the prairie west of the Mississippi River, and the horses had turned toward home. Emmalee and Val kissed fervently, as she imagined that these two plowhorses were Arabian stallions, that this jouncing logsled had glistening silver runners, and that the sweet hay which covered them was a rich fur blanket, glossy and soft.

But most of all, she wished she was not an "orphanage girl," with nothing to her name. Val Jannings, son of a wealthy merchant, didn't seem to mind that, but Emmalee did.

"Em, Em," he said, breaking off from the kiss and laying his cheek against hers. "Pretty soon you'll be sixteen and free to leave the home. Free to do anything you choose. Tell you what. Pa is going to put me to work in his lumberyard, I'll be making some real money of my own, and I was thinking . . . well, maybe *we* might start thinking about getting engaged. . . ."

Reverie forged of sunset, sleigh ride, and slow kisses spun away in a flash.

"What?" she asked, drawing away to peer at Val. He was a strong-looking, sandy-haired boy with blue, serious eyes, which widened when he saw the way that Emmalee was studying him.

"Why, what's wrong, Em?" he asked. "You look startled. All I said was that maybe we should think about getting married, seeing as how we get on so well. Haven't you thought about it? I mean, hasn't it . . . crossed your mind?"

"Well, I don't know, I'd always thought . . ."

"Tell me, Em. You can tell me anything."

She told him. "I guess I just always saw my future somewhere out west," she declared. "It's an . . . it's an urge I've always had."

Val laughed. "Oh, I know that, Em. You've talked about the west often enough. But there comes a time in this life when grown people have to settle for what's best. Why, there's no place on this earth that's better than good old Cairo, Illinois. What grander future is there? And you know my parents adore you."

Emmalee sat up and pulled slightly away from him. The horses plodded on, back toward the home. Stripped black trees cast long shadows on the snow; high, thin branches shivered in the wind.

He reached for her, and she let herself be drawn back to him. He was a good boy and she knew he loved her, but here he was talking about marriage, talking about his forthcoming job in the lumberyard, while she was dreaming of adventure and faraway places.

"Well, what *are* you going to do when you turn sixteen this April, Em?" Val demanded. "You say you want to go west. How? Do you have any money? That's what it takes, you know. And what do you want to do out there, anyway?"

"I want to get some land. I want to have a farm, just like we did when I was growing up in Pennsylvania. If Ma and Pa hadn't died on the trail west, I imagine we'd have that farm already."

She spoke with such intensity that Val softened his tone. "I'm sure you would have, Em. And I'm just as sorry as you about what happened to your parents. But it did happen. We all have to make some compromises in this life. That's what my father always says."

"I—I guess I'll have to think about it," Emmalee said. It was always difficult to speak of one's private dreams. So few people really listened, and even fewer understood. It was not that they were uncharitable; it was simply that visions were just so damned difficult to communicate to others.

Emmalee fell silent. Val believed that he'd convinced her about finding a glorious future in Illinois, a future with him. He pulled her to him for another kiss, and Emmalee responded. But Val was too much in love with her, with the Emmalee he thought he knew, to sense the great distance between them, a distance that Emmalee herself was beginning to ponder seriously.

It was not a regal sleigh but only an old logsled that pulled up in front of the stables at the Lutheran orphanage.

* * *

Val jumped down from the sled onto hard-packed snow, turning to offer Emmalee his arm. She grasped it and let him lower her. They stood there awkwardly for a moment of farewell.

"It's Sunday evening," Val whispered. "Ask the Reverend Bowerly if you can come to dinner at my home. My parents would love to have you."

"I'd like to," she said, "but a lot of the children are ill. I'm afraid I'll have to get back to work. Maybe next Sunday, though? We'd better turn the horses over to Peter and say good-bye."

Val looked disappointed. Emmalee turned away and started walking toward the stable door.

"Peter?" she called. "Peter?"

Peter Weller, the stableboy, usually came running out to take charge of the horses as soon as he heard their hoofs on the roadway. The big beasts were stomping in the snow, anxious to get to their stalls for oats, hay, and a rubdown, and the temperature was dropping by the moment.

"Peter?" Emmalee asked again, entering the stable. She saw the stableboy lying on a pile of straw, shivering in his heavy coat. "Peter, what's the matter?"

"I—I think I've got the grippe, Em. I feel just . . . terrible."

Emmalee had felt plenty of feverish foreheads during the past days and nights, and had carried more than enough basins and compresses and bowls of soup. She knew the symptoms of grippe, just as she knew that, after a few suffering days, the victims would gradually be restored to health. But she noticed on Peter's face a couple of blotchy scars similar to those she'd seen on the children with the highest temperatures.

"I'm afraid you've got it pretty bad," she said gently. "Think you can make it as far as your dormitory bed? Val and I can see to the horses, and I'll tell the Reverend Bowerly—"

"Oh!" exclaimed Peter, with what would have been urgency had he been fully alert. "The reverend wanted to see you as soon as you . . . as soon as you came back."

"What's going on in here?" asked Val, sticking his head in the doorway. "These horses are about to freeze. What's wrong?" he demanded, alarmed, as he caught sight of Peter.

"He's taken sick," explained Emmalee. "I'll walk him over to his dormitory. Val, would you lead the horses to their stalls, please?"

As Val went to bring the horses inside, Emmalee tried to help Peter to his feet. He groaned in agony and sagged against her.

"I'll never make it to the dorm," he said. "Just let me lie down. *Please*."

Aware that she couldn't carry him—indeed, she could barely support him—Emmalee eased him back down to the straw.

Val had unhitched the big Belgian horses from the sled. He led them into the stable, and they clomped eagerly to their stalls, to warmth and hay. He removed their harness, hung it, saw that they had water and oats. Then he joined Emmalee. They stared down, with growing alarm, at Peter Weller.

"He looks *strange*," said Val. "I think the two of us can carry him, though."

"Peter, are you awake?" asked Emmalee.

It seemed, at first glance, that the stableboy had fallen asleep, but his face was oddly discolored and his breathing came in alarming snorts. Emmalee bent toward him, feeling the same combination of fear and knowledge that she had experienced once on the banks of the Monongahela River and again in a rain-soaked grove outside Springfield,

Illinois. She could not rid herself of the feeling that, if she had not been afraid, Death would not have come to claim her mother and her father. Now she steeled herself, so that this time Death would not arrive to take Peter away with him.

"Emmalee!" exclaimed the Reverend Bowerly, ducking into the stable out of the frosty twilight. "You're back. Hello, Val. What's wrong with Peter?"

The superintendent pulled the stable door shut and strode quickly to the pile of straw upon which Peter lay.

"I think he passed out," Emmalee said. She watched as the reverend bent to examine the young man. Superintendent Bowerly usually looked concerned about one thing or another, what with the lives of eighty-odd parentless children on his mind. But Emmalee had never seen him so starkly frightened.

"Miss Alden," he said, standing up and addressing her formally, "have you felt ill of late? Fever? Chills? Anything like that?"

She shook her head. "Why, no. . . ."

"I'm afraid we have something very serious on our hands here, and I have summoned Dr. Legatt from town. Seven more children in your dormitory fell ill after lunch today, and some of them are in an awfully bad way. They have—"

He decided not to say anything more. "I'll look after Peter. Please go to your dormitory. Dr. Legatt and I will be there shortly."

"Is there anything I can do to help?" asked Val.

"I don't think so, son," said the Reverend Bowerly. "You'd best get home and see to your own health."

Outside the stable, Emmalee and Val said a hasty, half-frightened good-bye.

"Maybe I should stay with you, Em," he suggested.

"No. The superintendent is right. You go home. There

isn't too much anyone can do except take care of the sick, and I don't want you coming down with the grippe. It'll be bad enough if I do.''

Val started to protest but Emmalee shushed him with a quick farewell kiss. Their lips were cold.

''Go, now.'' She smiled. ''I'll see you tomorrow.''

Reluctantly, Val left, waving. She could hear the crunch of his boots in the snow.

Emmalee waited until he had disappeared into darkness, then turned away from the stable and dashed across the drifted snow on the orphanage grounds. Peter's condition had upset her, and the reverend's reaction to it had alarmed her even more. Night had fallen now, the hard, iron winter night, and all above her blazed sharp, cold, pitiless stars. For once Emmalee was glad of the dormitory's close warmth.

The dormitory where Emmalee was in charge was a long, narrow wooden structure sheltering little girls, aged four to twelve. Bunks ran along the walls and a wood-burning metal stove crouched on a brick platform in the center of the room. During summer, with the windows open and cool air blowing, the dorm was pleasant enough. But in winter, with the stoked fire hot and roaring, the atmosphere became oppressive, the air dead and stale.

Emmalee entered, hung up her scarf and coat, and heard the sniffling, coughing, and crying of the sick children.

''Oh, Emmalee!'' exclaimed Louise Bunyon, one of the older girls. ''Somethin' is fearfully wrong with little Tessie, and I'm askeerd.''

''Don't worry, Louise. Dr. Legatt will be along shortly. Why don't we go and comfort Tessie? Could you bring me a basin of cold water and some clean rags?''

Louise went to fetch those items, as she was told, while Emmalee made her way down the long line of bunks. Tessie Bailey, five years old, had been a favorite of

Emmalee's since her arrival at the home. Her parents had been drowned in a riverboat accident north of Hannibal, Missouri, when the little girl was still a baby. The only life she'd known was here at the orphanage, and Emmalee was almost like a mother to her.

Emmalee reached Tessie's bunk, looked down at the girl, and stifled a cry of alarm that rose instinctively. Tessie's eyes were open and she appeared to be conscious, but Emmalee could tell that her little pet was delirious. Tessie spoke soft, disjointed nonsense words, a reddish foam lined her dry, scarlet lips, and on her face were the same ugly blotches that Emmalee had seen on Peter Weller's skin. The terrible sight triggered a memory. Now Emmalee knew what it was, understood what was happening and all that it meant. . . .

Louise Bunyon came hurrying up with the basin and rags. Emmalee had just placed one of the cool cloths on Tessie's forehead when Superintendent Bowerly and Dr. Legatt, the Cairo physician, strode into the dormitory. Dr. Legatt, a heavyset man with a red walrus mustache and a luxurious set of the newly fashionable sideburns, passed quickly from bed to bed, peering at each of the children. He grinned reassuringly at those who shrank away from him. They were afraid he might give them some foul-tasting medicine, and thus they were too alert to be truly ill. But he masked with a gentle smile the deep concern he felt upon examining children who were too weak even to respond to his presence. When he reached little Tessie Bailey's bunk, he dropped quickly to his knees and studied her grimly. The Reverend Bowerly stood beside him.

"All right," said the doctor quietly, rising wearily to his feet. "Reverend, we must talk. In private. Who has been tending these children since the first case of grippe?"

"Why, Miss Alden, sir." The Reverend Bowerly indicated Emmalee with a gesture. "Is everything all right?"

"No," said Dr. Legatt. "Miss Alden, you come with us."

Puzzled and a little jittery, Emmalee followed the doctor and the reverend through the dormitory and outside into the cold vestibule. They stood close to one another. Three frosty clouds rose in puffs as they exhaled.

"What is it, Doctor?" Bowerly asked. "What's going on here?"

Dr. Legatt stared intently at Emmalee, pulling on his great mustache. Then he faced the Reverend Bowerly.

"It's smallpox, Reverend. I hate to say it, but that's what it is, and it looks as if you're on your way to having a horrible outbreak here. You've seen those splotches on the faces of some of the children? By tomorrow those sores will be open and suppurating. Beware the pus, it's deadly. You're going to need—"

"But what about Tessie?" cried Emmalee. "What about Peter Weller?"

Dr. Legatt's voice was gentle, soothing. But his words were blunt.

"The strong will survive," he said. "Some will be scarred for life, some not, depending upon how severely they are stricken. But"—he lifted his strong, well-cared-for hands and let them fall—"many will die. It's in God's hands now. There's little medicine can do. As I was about to say, you're going to need help. I'll contact people in town who've survived the disease. Some of them will help you out, I'm sure. Of course, they'll have to live here. The orphanage will have to be quarantined until late spring, at least."

"Dear lord," the reverend said. "And what about Emmalee? She's been in close contact with the sick children for almost a week now, isn't that right?"

Emmalee nodded her corroboration. One of the doctor's

phrases kept running through her mind: *The strong will survive, the strong will survive, the strong will survive . . .*

"Ever have smallpox, Emmalee?" demanded Dr. Legatt, scowling at her. He saw her peerless, fair winter-tinted skin, ruddy in the cheeks, her face framed by thick, dark-blond hair that was like ancient gold. He held her violet eyes with his gaze, expecting the truth.

"I—I think I had it . . . when I was a child," Emmalee told him. "That's what my mother told me. But it was a mild case."

"It certainly was. *If* you had it at all. There's not a mark on you. By the way, how old are you?"

"Sixteen in April."

The doctor's eyes widened. "Forgive my surprise," he said. "You look at least twenty. Forgive me, again. We gruff old doctors lose our manners faster than . . . but I assumed you were an employee here? A nurse or teacher, perhaps?"

"No," Superintendent Bowerly corrected, "Emmalee is one of our charges. She looks and acts more mature than her years suggest, and thank God for that. She's been a tremendous help to us."

Dr. Legatt shrugged resignedly. "Well, she'll have to be quarantined like all the rest," he said. "You haven't had any contact with individuals outside the home recently, have you?" he asked Emmalee.

Instantly Emmalee's eyes met the Reverend Bowerly's, and in shocked unison they pronounced the name.

"Val Jannings!"

The Lutheran orphanage was situated on the crest of a wooded, gently sloping hill that rose on the eastern bank of the Mississippi River. Chapel, stables, sheds, and dormitories sparkled white in the April sunshine, white against the green of new grass, and the even brighter green of budding trees and bushes. Emmalee took from the orphanage's pantry half a loaf of bread, a chunk of salami, and a small stone jug full of cow's milk, and went out onto the lawn to celebrate her sixteenth birthday. For distraction, she brought along a copy of the Cairo *Bulletin*, freshly printed and dated April 12, 1868.

Emmalee celebrated alone. She had toiled and prayed through the long months of winter, had cared for the stricken from long before dawn until past midnight, until she fell into fretful, exhausted sleep. But to little avail. She picnicked alone because she walked now like a living ghost in a lost house emptied of blood and brood. Tessie was dead, and Peter Weller. Louise Bunyon and the Reverend Bowerly were gone. Dozens of others, dead too, were resting down there in the grove of trees below the hill, where the new white crosses stood, mutely admonishing Emmalee for the temerity of having survived.

Val Jannings did not lie beneath one of those small, neatly carpentered pine crosses. His family had afforded him a mausoleum in the fashionable cemetery outside Cairo, with a big stone angel guarding the door. Emmalee had been asked not to attend Val's funeral, but she had visited the mausoleum. The Jannings family blamed Emmalee for having transmitted smallpox to Val. It did not matter that she had suffered and acquired immunity to the disease at an early age. Nor did they wish to hear with what selflessness she had cared for the afflicted during the winter nights. She was the cause of Val's death; that was the only way they could see it.

Heavyhearted with this knowledge, Emmalee walked out and sat down on the lawn, wondering what to do. Today, according to the laws of the country, she was a woman. Today, according to the rules by which the Lutheran home was governed, she was free—indeed, she was admonished—to go out and find her way in the world.

That world lay bright and shining across the sparkling Mississippi. Sidewheelers and sternwheelers plied the ceaseless thoroughfare, and barges laden with all manner of men and goods fought their way upstream or drifted with the current. Across the river, as far as Emmalee could see, were the green hills of Missouri. And beyond them was the great west, always a part of Emmalee's dreams, but which, for months, she had been too troubled to contemplate. Even today, on her birthday, she felt too dispirited to think about the future very much.

Fighting a sorrow she could do nothing to dispel, Emmalee lay down on the sun-warmed grass and closed her eyes. Flickering patterns of light, red and blue and amber, burst and reburst and danced behind her eyelids. Old earth held and cradled her. The sun was warm and loving, bathing her strong, young body in its gentle glow. She heard, down on the river, the calls of pilots and boatmen, the lowing of cattle transported to market on the barges, and the constant splash and slosh of the big paddlewheels. She smelled the coalsmoke of the steam engines that drove the paddlewheels.

My life is marked by graves, she thought.

But self-pity made her angry with herself. Emmalee sat up, bit into the strongly spiced salami, ate a chunk of bread, and took long swallows of the stone-cooled milk. Then, squinting against the sun, she began to scan the Cairo *Bulletin*. The rest of the world was teeming and fighting and scheming, getting on with life.

President Andrew Johnson, reeling from the twin burdens of incompetence and impeachment, stood no chance of reelection. General Ulysses S. Grant, hero of the triumphant Union army, would save the nation again, this time from the White House.

The new transcontinental railroad would revolutionize America, would bind the farflung seaboards even more effectively than the telegraph had advanced communication. All manner of immigrants had worked on the railroad, even Chinese. Emmalee had never seen any Chinese, nor any of the far places mentioned in the news.

The old spirit of her wanderlust rose again inside her. That same powerful yet obscure drive that had caused her parents to leave their comfortable little farm in the Pennsylvania hills was her heritage, and she felt it surge in her soul again as she gazed westward across the Mississippi.

She turned the page of the newspaper and found herself staring at dozens of advertisements for travel to the west.

> SOUTHWESTERN COMPANY FOR CALIFORNIA
> The company is putting out a train of good wagons, for the purpose of carrying passengers to central California. We will take a man through for $150, starting from Kansas City on the 12 of May, 1868. . . .

Emmalee felt a small thrill. There was certainly no place farther west than California, at least none to which she could aspire, and there was time to get to Kansas City in a month. But then she read the notice again, with its inevitable and depressing particular: the trip would cost $150 per man or, presumably, per woman. She had perhaps ten dollars to her name, painstakingly saved from the small allowance the Reverend Bowerly had given the older children. But, as yet undaunted, she read on.

> OFFICIAL ANNOUNCEMENT OF THE GOVERNMENT OF THE UNITED STATES OF AMERICA: Territorial offices hereby inform all interested citizens of a land rush to be held in the Territory of Olympia, beyond the Rocky Mountains, on October 1, 1868. All able-bodied citizens who have reached majority may lay claim to no more than one hundred sixty acres of land per family. Prospective

claimants must register their intent to claim land with U.S. agent Vestor Tell in the town of Arcady, Territory of Olympia, on or before commencement of the land rush.

Land! Emmalee studied the announcement carefully. She had always loved to study geography and received something like a physical thrill from the examination of maps. They spoke of distant places, always more exciting than wherever she happened to be. And she had read of land rushes as well. Horses and wagons and people lined up as in a race, and at the sound of a starter's pistol shot, they went out to claim the best land they could find. Land rushes were a device to attract settlers to distant regions, and from what Emmalee had been able to learn, they were very successful in accomplishing that goal.

But how on earth was she going to get beyond the Rocky Mountains by October? Another advertisement caught her eye.

HO FOR OLYMPIA OVER THE WESTERN MOUNTAINS
Mr. Burt Pennington is now preparing an outfit for passage to Olympia starting the 1st of May. Those with an interest in ranching cattle are sought. Experienced guides will be with the company. All possible care will be taken of persons sick on the trip, and proper medicines kept in readiness. Persons wishing passage should contact Mr. Burt Pennington at the Schuyler Hotel on Market Street in St. Joseph.

Emmalee scanned the notice a second time, feeling a small surge of hope. Pennington must be a gentleman. None of the other notices, she saw after further examination, mentioned medicine, but all of them mentioned money. The cheapest fare listed was $120 per person, but that applied only if the passanger brought along his own horse, mule, or ox, none of which Emmalee owned or had any immediate prospect of owning. But perhaps she might strike some sort of arrangement with this Mr. Pennington. At any rate, all the wagon trains seemed to be leaving from Kansas City or St. Joe.

She began to think seriously about leaving the home and making her way to St. Joe. The town lay in the northwestern part of Missouri, over three hundred miles as the crow flew. Emmalee had desire, strong legs, a young body, and ten dollars. Would they be a match for three hundred miles of Missouri?

Emmalee pondered this, doubtful one moment, confident the next. Then little Sarah Shedd came running toward her across the lawn. Sarah was all of seven. She had survived the smallpox, one of the twenty-three orphans fortunate enough to have done so, but the malady had pocked her poor little face for life.

"Em, Em!" she cried, racing toward the older girl. "Preacher Task wants to talk to everybody right now. Hurry up or you'll be late."

Preacher Task had been appointed the home's new superintendent and had arrived only this morning to take up his responsibilities. Emmalee had not yet seen him, but she hoped he would turn out to be as good and dedicated as the Reverend Bowerly had been, even though she had no intention of remaining at the orphanage. She got up, folded the newspaper, picked up the remains of her lunch, and accompanied Sarah to the chapel.

Most of the children, with a mixture of curiosity and apprehension, had already taken their seats in the chapel pews, and Preacher Task was standing in front of the altar when Emmalee entered with the little girl. In appearance and demeanor, Preacher Task stood in stark contrast to the late Reverend Bowerly. He was tall, thin, and brittle-looking, as if his whole body were nothing more than a collection of stiff joints. His face was long, thin, and pale. He appeared to be a man who had known little pleasure or comfort in life, but Emmalee could not tell if that had been the result of self-denial or bad luck.

"Let me tell you about myself," Preacher Task said then, beginning his presentation, "and tell you, likewise, what I shall expect of each and every one of you during my tenure as your superintendent. . . ."

He proceeded to tell the children how he had found Christ and was reborn, after which he enumerated a dizzying list of rules and restrictions. Emmalee watched the little faces fall into boredom and gloom. The Reverend Bowerly, at least, had believed that children ought to have a little fun. The home was obviously going to be rather dour from now on.

"You may now go to your chores and your studies," Preacher Task concluded, dismissing them. "But I should like to see Emmalee Alden forthwith."

The children filed out of the chapel and Emmalee approached the altar.

"You are Miss Alden?" asked the preacher, gazing at her with some surprise.

"That's right."

"I had . . . I guess I had expected a more *teacherly* sort of girl, from what I've been told of the help you've given the home. . . ."

His voice trailed off as he studied Emmalee, radiant in the prime of young womanhood. Her thick, darkly golden hair fell softly to her shoulders, framing an astonishingly striking face with high, widely spaced cheekbones. Her eyes, also widely set, were violet in color and intelligently watchful, full of spirit and curiosity. They seemed to look through the preacher to distant places. Her mouth was straight and firm, a woman's mouth with full, gentle lips.

Her nose was small and straight; her chin slightly rounded. The shape of her high breasts pressed against a calico dress, as did the perfect swell of her hips. She had a strong body, the preacher noted, and she was at least five and a half feet tall.

Preacher Task was a bit nonplussed; Emmalee did not look like any teacher he had seen before.

"Come with me," he said. "We shall go to my office."

Wordlessly, Emmalee followed him across the orphanage grounds. She judged him to be a serious, well-intentioned man, but his personality seemed devoid of spark or fire. So vibrantly alive herself, so responsive to others who shared her spirit, Emmalee felt vaguely sorry for the preacher.

"Sit down, Miss Alden," he told her when they were inside his office. "I want to discuss your responsibilities with you. I am, you see, placing you in charge of the children's studies and discipline—"

"But, sir, I am leaving the home. Today is my sixteenth birthday, and—"

"It is?" asked Task, looking perplexed. "No one told me about that. I was counting on you to—"

"I'm sorry, but I've already made my plans."

That was not entirely true, of course. Emmalee's plans were still indefinite. But she saw that Preacher Task was a stubborn man and that he did not take kindly to the possibility of his own plans being thwarted.

"*I* must sign the papers that approve your leaving," he pointed out.

"That is true, but I am sixteen now and free to leave."

The man's eyes narrowed as he considered this.

"How do you know you're sixteen?" he asked. "Do you have proof?"

"I was born on April 12, 1852, in Lancaster, Pennsylvania."

"That's not proof, is it? Now, if you had a written record of birth from your home parish, or a certificate of baptism, perhaps? You are free, of course, to write for one. . . ."

Emmalee thought of the time that such an exercise would require. She considered too the wagon trains that were now being outfitted to leave St. Joe.

"And where would you go if you left here?" Preacher Task was asking, a grave, concerned expression on his long face.

"There's going to be a land rush in Olympia," she answered enthusiastically. "I'm going out there and see if I can stake a claim. That's what my folks planned to do and—"

"Come now, my dear," he interrupted gently. "We must all aim high, mustn't we? But aren't you being just a tad unrealistic? I can see that you're a strong, ambitious young woman, but you'll have to cross the Great Plains with a wagon train, you'll be in the company of adventurers and charlatans and perhaps even thieves. I'd advise against it."

Emmalee fumed. What was wrong with being in the company of adventurers? She looked forward to it. But she held her tongue. Preacher Task was obviously not a man who readily countenanced contradiction. She decided to keep her own counsel and make her own plans. She was going to leave the home, no matter how he felt about it, no matter what he said.

"Let us wait until you have your proof of age," he told her. "Then I'll help you make a reasonable arrangement for the future."

Emmalee spent the afternoon mapping strategy. Since she would have to be present for supper, she would not be able to leave until it was almost dark. With neither doubts nor second thoughts, but with a bit of trepidation, she saw herself trudging along a nighttime roadway, maybe catching a few hours of sleep beneath trees. She could not risk asking for shelter in a home anywhere near Cairo, on the chance that Preacher Task would notice her absence and send out some sort of alarm. And she certainly could not spend any of her pathetic little treasury except in a case of dire emergency.

Then, as she was folding and packing her few worn dresses and her pretty white Sunday-go-to-meetin' dress in the portmanteau Val Jannings had given her for Christmas, Emmalee suddenly thought of a new plan, so obvious that she was amazed it had not occurred to her before.

First she visited the storeroom, where the clothing, toys, and trinkets that had belonged to the children who'd died during the winter were kept. Then, taking thread and needle from her little sewing kit, she sat down on her bunk and set to work. By suppertime Emmalee had completed her task and had hidden her portmanteau in the hayloft above the stable.

She wore her oldest, baggiest, loosest dress to supper, a gray, sacklike garment that might once have been blue. It had two very large pockets that, at the conclusion of the meal, were stuffed with every portion of biscuit, piece of cornbread, or baked potato the children did not eat.

At twilight, when the children were in their beds, Emmalee stole away to the stable, still wearing the gray dress. Poor Peter Weller had not yet been replaced so there was no one hanging around the stable, but she surprised the big Belgian plowhorses, who nickered and stomped nervously until she gave them each a wedge of sweet cornbread from her cache of food. Then she climbed to the hayloft, slipped out of the gray sack, and put on the white go-to-meetin' dress. But it was no longer the plain, simple garment of prayer and hymn. At cuff and hem and neckline,

Emmalee had sewn ruffles fashioned from discarded cloth. A sash made from ribbons she'd been saving encircled her waist, and around her throat she clasped a string of imitation pearls that Tessie Bailey's mother had once worn. Seen from up close, flaws in her handiwork would not withstand clever scrutiny, but to any casual observer, Emmalee now wore the dress of a lady. Only her footwear would truly give her away: a pair of well-worn slippers. But the ruffles at the hem of her dress hid them adequately, she thought.

The horses were startled again by her billowing garment as Emmalee climbed down the ladder from the loft, and when Emmalee hurried out of the stable she saw Preacher Task poking his long head out of a window to see what the disturbance was.

Damn it! she thought, walking as fast as she could, lugging her portmanteau down the road toward the river. *Oh, damn it and damn it again!* Task saw my white dress for sure. After a few minutes of running and walking and running again, she stopped for a minute and listened.

Fast footfalls followed her, and an angry cry: "Miss Alden! Miss Alden, you come back! I shall summon the authorities if you don't come back! I thought the two of us had reached an agreement."

For just a moment, for the shred of a second, Emmalee considered giving up her flight. After all, it wouldn't take much more than half a year to get her baptismal certificate from Pennsylvania. She'd have it by October, most likely. *If* mail came through.

But in October, in Olympia, the government would be giving away land.

"I mean to have me a piece of that land!" she vowed aloud, and began again to run, away from Preacher Task and toward the Mississippi River.

A Gambler

Emmalee had two big advantages in her flight from Preacher Task. In the first place, she was young and fast and sure-footed. She fairly flew along the narrow, steeply inclined streets leading to the wharves, while he hobbled along, hindered by his years. Second, Task was a stranger to Cairo, whereas Emmalee had gone walking and exploring numerous times in the town and along the river.

Still, she was in danger of being caught. Her plan was to inquire along the wharves about the price of a passenger ticket upriver to Hannibal, and to board the boat if she could afford the fare. But making inquiries and finding a northbound steamer would take time. Meanwhile, she would be conspicuous on the wharves. Her newly decorated dress was designed to make her casually acceptable on the deck of a boat, not to conceal her on the rough and brawling docks. With her long hair flowing and the white dress displaying her figure, she had no idea how lovely she looked, nor how out of place.

Cairo, Illinois, was a major riverport, a center of commercial trade and passenger travel. Wharves and warehouses lined the riverbank. Rich, strong smells of merchandise rode the air: tobacco, raw cotton, and hemp; the dusty scent of wheat; bayleaf, pepper, thyme; the strange, sharp odor of kerosene. To this were added the smells of leather and men and horses, and the perfumed fragrances of women aboard the passenger steamers.

One such vessel, the *Queen of Natchez*, was docked at riverside now, and in spite of her haste Emmalee could not but slow down a little to admire it. She had seen it on the river many times before, and she especially enjoyed watching it at night. With three tiers of decks, lighted by multicolored lanterns, it seemed from a distance to be a huge, many-layered birthday cake floating along the Mississippi. The sounds of music rose from the *Queen* on a summer's night, as did the laughter of men and women at play. It was rumored that even a woman could get a drink of hard liquor on board, and desperate men gambled vast sums with knives in their belts and loaded pistols on the table next to stacks of gold coins and ingeniously marked playing cards. To the more pious of the boys and girls at the Lutheran orphanage, the *Queen of Natchez* seemed sin itself.

Emmalee drew near the *Queen* and halted. Passengers were boarding, their tickets being examined at the foot of the gangway by a uniformed man wearing epaulets and a tiny cap with a polished leather visor. Negro footmen scurried up and down the dock, up and down the gangway, carrying luggage. The boat was getting ready to depart!

Should she attempt to buy a ticket from the man with the little cap? After all, she did have ten dollars and she looked like a legitimate traveler carrying the portmanteau. But the *Queen* was intimidatingly grand. Emmalee hesitated.

"Stop that girl!"

Preacher Task had made his way down the hill now and was trying to hurry through the milling swarm of people on the dock. She caught a momentary glimpse of him—and he of her—but he disappeared behind a horse-drawn lorry. He'd reach her in a minute. There was no time to buy a ticket. She'd have to run, try to find a place to hide. Already she anticipated the humiliation of confronting him there on the crowded wharves.

"Permit me to assist you, miss."

The voice was resonant and sure, mildly amused. It was a voice of extraordinary character and timbre. Emmalee responded to it as immediately, as directly, as she did to the grip of the strong hand at her elbow.

"Just come with me and you'll be fine," the voice advised her then, with just the merest touch of urgency, and Emmalee felt herself moved slowly but deliberately toward the gangway of the *Queen*. She looked up and saw to whom the hand and voice belonged, noting by waning twilight and the flickering lanterns of the boat that she was in the company of an elegant young roughneck. The chiseled, dark planes of his face were strong but not threatening, and his mouth had a self-certainty that hinted of a high-spirited recklessness. Emmalee realized that he was quite young, twenty-one or two, in spite of his expensive dove-gray suit and his fashionable broad-brimmed hat with an odd-looking band of silver pieces around it.

"Who *are* you?" she demanded, trying to pull free of his grasp.

"You'll never find out if we stop for proper introductions. Your friend back there on the wharf is going to be here in no time. Stop talking and just smile now, all right? We're going aboard."

The man reached for her portmanteau and took it from her, guiding her toward the foot of the gangway. Emmalee felt an impulse to spin away from him, to flee. She could have done it, but she realized that, for whatever reasons, he was helping her escape Preacher Task. Besides, what could happen to her on the *Queen*, with all those people around?

"Evenin', Mr. Landar." The uniformed official at the gangway grinned. He tipped his shiny-visored cap to Emmalee, studying her with an unsettling frankness. His grin widened. "I see that you . . . ah, have a companion," he added, with a leering wink.

"Observant of you, Kuffel."

Emmalee's self-appointed rescuer hustled her up the gangway and onto the *Queen*. There, taking her hand, he led her quickly up a staircase to the crowded second deck, at one end of which a small band was playing. Emmalee felt confused and increasingly alarmed. She was trying to sort out the various features of this strange, sudden, and not entirely comfortable experience. The dazzle of the *Queen of Natchez* dulled her senses, as had that big roll of bills in this Mr. Landar's hand, but she was able to recall quite well the smirking words of the uniformed man at the gangway: *"I see that you . . . ah, have a companion."*

Emmalee had *heard* of things like this, of loose women who were used by men for . . .

That's not going to happen to me! she vowed.

Landar was standing at the railing, looking down at the dock. He'd positioned Emmalee behind him, and he still held her hand. She tried to yank it free, but his grip tightened and he turned toward her. She could see his face much more clearly here under the lanterns of the second deck. He really was as handsome as she'd thought moments earlier, but his gray eyes did look a little dangerous.

"You can let me go now," she told him, surprising herself with the calmness in her voice. "I think you've mistaken me for someone else."

He grinned down at her. "I doubt it," he said, leaning toward her, bringing his face close to hers. She had to tilt her head backward to look up at him. "I doubt it, and by tomorrow morning you'll realize that meeting me was the best thing that ever happened to you, not to mention the most pleasurable."

Emmalee's eyes widened in astonishment at his casual boldness. She was trying to think of something to say, attempting to find words that would smash his outrageous presumption, when a steward walked up to them.

"Your cabin is made up and ready, sir," he said to this incredible Mr. Landar. "Cabin twelve, deck three. Will there be anything else?"

"Yes." With a quick motion, he pulled the portmanteau from Emmalee's hand and gave it to the steward. "Take the lady's bag up to my cabin."

The steward gave Emmalee just the tiniest glance of appraisal, then left to do as he was bidden.

Emmalee was still alarmed, but her substantial temper flared. "Who do you think you *are*?" she demanded, pulling her hand out of his grasp.

"Garn Landar," he replied, with a slow, amused smile. "At your service." He took off his elegant hat. Those strange silver pieces that made up the hatband glinted in lamplight. He had dark, thick hair, and when he removed his hat a lock fell down across his forehead. He wore high-heeled western boots but even without them he was well over six feet tall. Emmalee sensed a lithe, hard-waisted body beneath his elegant suit, a muscular body, square-shouldered and taut. Leaning over her, he seemed like a sleek animal crouched to pounce. His gray eyes gleamed lazily, crinkled and slightly slanted at the corners. He had straight black brows, a proud nose, and a strong mouth that hinted, when he smiled, of recklessness and a touch of self-indulgence. In spite of his unconscionable behavior, Emmalee felt the presence and attraction of male beauty far more directly than she'd ever felt it before.

Such a feeling, in her predicament, was dangerous. She sought refuge in a legitimate, explicable anger.

"Call that steward back immediately!" she ordered Garn Landar. "I want my portmanteau. I wish to leave this boat!"

"But you've only just boarded," he replied, putting his hat back on with an indolent movement of his arm. "We'll dine, perhaps gamble a bit in the casino, and then go to my cabin. As I said a moment ago, you won't regret it."

"You'll regret it if you continue to speak to me in this manner. I do not wish to be with you. I do not wish to be *here*." Her anxiety was mounting.

Garn looked faintly puzzled. "A well-dressed lady, alone and carrying baggage on the docks, would seem to be traveling. And no lady should travel alone. I can certainly make your journey safer and much more interesting."

He winked at her and touched her cheek, an intimate, proprietary gesture that gave Emmalee an unexpected thrill. Because it did, her anger rose still more.

"I am perfectly capable," she told him, "of getting where I want to go *on my own*. And I assure you that I would *never* countenance a man who approaches a woman the way you have done to me. . . ."

"What?" he asked, laughing aloud. "Most women in my experience have found my forthrightness refreshing. We understand each other from the start. Here," he added, taking her arm, "let's have a drink in the lounge and I'll permit you to get to know me better."

"I will not. . . ."

Emmalee was about to dash away from him, but suddenly he grabbed her by the arm, spun her around, and turned toward the railing of the *Queen*, looking down at the wharf.

"Let me *go*!"

"Would you be quiet?" he snapped, that rich, melodic

voice as sharp as a whiplash now. "Don't make a scene. I want to hear this."

He let her go and leaned over the railing. Emmalee caught a glimpse of Preacher Task there on the dock. She ducked behind Garn and peered over his shoulder to find out what was going on.

Preacher Task, in shirt-sleeves, his long, bony arms gesticulating wildly, was speaking to the man in the visored cap.

". . . a runaway," he was screeching, "from the Lutheran home up there on the hill. She would have been wearing a plain white dress, like a dress for church on Sundays. I know she's down here somewhere. You've got to help me find her. I'm afraid for her soul."

"It ain't her soul I'd be worried about, Reverend," came the reply. "Leastways not down here. But I can tell you for sure that not too many a Sunday school girl is gonna be found on the *Queen*. Run along now, we're about to cast off."

Greatly relieved, Emmalee saw Preacher Task walk away from the boat, his head moving this way and that, looking, looking.

Garn turned to her then with a rather amazed expression on his tanned face. "You ran away from an *orphanage*?" he asked. "I thought perhaps you were fleeing a bad lover, or even a husband, God forbid. How old are you, anyway?"

"I'm sixteen. And I didn't run away, not exactly. I was free to leave, but that man wanted me to stay awhile longer."

"Sixteen?" he asked. She could tell he didn't believe her.

"It's true," she declared. "My name is Emmalee Alden, I'm free, and I'm sixteen years old. My birthday is today."

Garn's look softened, and then he said, "Well, happy birthday, Emmalee. We must do something to celebrate."

His voice held no trace of the teasing or irony. In truth, he was amazed and impressed. This beautiful young woman not only talked with spirit, she *had* spirit. He excused himself for misjudging her age—anyone could have made the same mistake—and decided to act like a gentleman.

"Let's go have dinner, shall we, Emmalee?" he offered politely. "Tell me about yourself, where you're headed, things like that. I might be able to help."

But Emmalee, even though free of the threat of Preacher Task, was still furious at Garn for the way he'd approached her.

"Get me my portmanteau!" she snapped, crossing her arms over her breasts and glaring at him. "I'm leaving! I don't need your help and I don't want to talk to you anymore. I want to see the captain. I want to get off."

Then the *Queen*'s big foghorn blasted dolefully and the powerful sternwheel started up, moving the vessel out into the Mississippi's current. The sudden motion caused Emmalee to sway against Garn. He put out his arms to steady her. She felt again, and against her wishes, the shock of his touch. It seemed to charge her body with a subtle current.

"Too late to get off." He smiled easily. "You're a stowaway now. Do you know what happens to them if they're discovered? Shall we call the captain and find out?"

Damn! she thought. Trapped. But then she noted that his tone had changed. He was friendly now, even gentle. Don't relax, she told herself. It's some sort of trick on his part. He has you captive on the boat. He can afford to be gallant now.

"Well, how about dinner?" he was asking.

Emmalee regarded him warily, calculating. "I'm afraid I'm not hungry," she said.

"An orphan who's not hungry? Emmalee, you are even

more unusual than I'd already judged you to be. Let's go to the casino then and do a little gambling."

He *is* reckless, she thought with disapproval.

"If I had any money," she told him, "I certainly wouldn't throw it away."

Garn just laughed. "I'll worry about that. You just come along and be my good-luck piece."

Against her better judgment, Emmalee took Garn Landar's arm. He couldn't do anything to her—and she well knew what "anything" encompassed—if they were seated in a crowded gaming room.

They walked along the second deck, which held a restaurant, a lounge with a small dance floor, and the casino. A band in the lounge began to play "Aura Lee," a ballad from the war years. Men in suits of black velvet with gleaming white collars, in suits of ivory, burgundy, or powder blue rose from deck tables laden with crystal and silver and led to the dance floor splendid, languorous women in gowns of silk and satin and lace. Emmalee, in her homemade garment, felt like a country cousin and stole a glance at her benefactor, who was watching the women dance. *He* could probably have any of those women if he wanted. He might well have had some of them already! She wondered how the other women responded to him, how they answered his frank, good-humored, utterly self-confident propositions. And, without intending to, consciously trying not to, she wondered how those women felt when they were in his arms.

"So," he asked as they strolled toward the casino, "I know what you're running from. But where are you going?"

His voice still held that new note of concern, as if he truly cared about her. It was just a ploy, Emmalee decided, since he hadn't gotten anywhere with her by using the direct approach. She would make sure that this genteel strategy didn't work either!

"St. Joe," she told him.

"Is that right? Why, so am I. May I inquire as to your purpose?"

"There will be a land rush in Olympia. In October. I want to sign onto a wagon train that will take me there."

He glanced at her sharply. He looked startled. Emmalee thought she knew why.

"You don't think I'll make it, do you?" she asked. "Well, don't tell me. I don't want to hear it. I *will* make it."

Garn Landar suppressed, with difficulty, an impulse to say, Yes, that was exactly what I was thinking. I don't believe you will make it.

Perhaps she'll get as far as St. Joe, he thought. But, good God, does she have any idea of what lies ahead? He decided to make the point gently, to warn her.

"Traveling alone all the way?"

"Yes."

"And you're figuring on claiming land out there?"

"That's right. For a farm."

With difficulty, Garn kept from shaking his head in disbelief. "Miss Alden, I know Olympia," he said instead. "Believe me, making a land claim will be the easy part. First you have to get there. I've crossed the Great Plains quite a few times. . . ."

Emmalee could not help laughing.

"Did I say something funny?"

"You may brag if you like, but I seriously doubt your story. You're not old enough."

"It's true, though. I know the high plains well, and the difficulty of surviving with bad food, little water, lame horses. Not to mention the problem of eluding Indians. Let me see your hands."

"What?"

"Your hands. Let me see them."

He stopped walking, took her hands, and held them palms-upward.

"Well, I see that you have done some work."

"Of course I have."

"That'll help. There's no end of hard work on the trail. The weak and the fainthearted either die or turn back long before a wagon train gets as far as Denver. Then there are the mountains to cross. Do you have any money?"

"I don't answer questions like that," she snapped, thinking of her poverty.

"I guessed as much." He sighed and started walking again, leading her toward the casino. It was clear to Garn now that Emmalee was not what he'd thought her to be when he'd first seen her running along the Cairo dock. He still wanted her, just as he'd desired her on sight, but she was too young, she would be too unrealistic about the temporary liaisons he enjoyed. There was, of course, still a chance that he could bend her to his will on the journey upriver, but what then? She might want to cling to him. She might even fall in love. Young girls were like that. And, as much as he craved the pleasure her body had obviously been created to give, Garn Landar did not wish to sacrifice one iota of his freedom nor surrender a speck of his will.

He decided to make sure she arrived in St. Joe safely. Then she could fend for herself, which was what she claimed to want.

Walking beside him, rather excited now at the prospect of visiting an actual casino, Emmalee tried to read Garn's mood. He was no longer insulting her with unsavory suggestions, that was true, and he was undeniably attractive. But she sensed in him a carelessness, an insouciance that could only spell trouble. He was, she thought, one of those men who simply used women, paralyzed them with charm and pleasure until they were all used up, until he owned them.

She decided that he was the height of risky business. Still, it did seem an adventure to be visiting the casino with him. I'll be fine if I stay on guard, she thought.

Entering the casino, Emmalee glanced warily about. She'd half expected a circle of ragged, wild men crouched gloomily over clattering dice, knives in their teeth and desperation in their bloodshot eyes. But to her surprise, the gambling casino of the *Queen of Natchez* looked eminently civilized, almost like the parlor of the Jannings home back in Cairo.

"Here again, Mr. Landar?" asked a suave-looking, waistcoated man at the doorway. "Glad to see you're going to give us the opportunity to win back some of our money."

"Not a chance, Jason. I've brought real good luck with me this time. Miss Alden, this is Jason Bascomb, treasurer here on the *Queen*."

"A pleasure, Miss Alden. Care for refreshments?"

"A mint julep for me, thanks. Bring the lady one too. Emmalee?"

"I guess so," she said. A mint julep sounded like a very good thing.

Bascomb twirled his finger in the air and a huge ebony fellow appeared, carrying a tray laden with all manner of drinks.

"Thanks, Brutus, don't mind if I do," said Garn, helping himself to a julep in a frosty glass.

Brutus proffered the tray to Emmalee. She shrank back slightly. The man was about seven feet tall. His face was totally devoid of expression. He looked intimidating just standing there.

Garn and Jason Bascomb laughed. "You need not fear

our Brutus,'' Bascomb told Emmalee. ''He is here to maintain order in the casino, something that he can do effortlessly. No one has ever taken a swing at him. I don't know what would happen if anyone did. Have a drink, please. On the house.''

Emmalee took a mint julep and sipped it tentatively. It was very good.

''Mr. Landar, may Brutus take your hat?'' Jason asked.

''No, sirree. Might need this hat if I get in a pinch.''

Bascomb smiled thinly. ''I most fervently wish it,'' he said.

Garn led Emmalee across the floor of the gaming room. Several varieties of card games were going on; dice rattled in cups and upon the taut green-felt tops of tables surrounded by equally taut men and women. At still another table, a large clattering wheel spun and ceased, its every cessation followed by mingled cheers and groans.

''That's what I want,'' said Garn, taking a long swallow of his drink. ''Let's try roulette. What do you say?''

''I don't know anything about . . . what is it? Roulette?''

''Easiest thing in the world.''

''What did Mr. Bascomb mean about your hat?''

Garn looked at her, then removed the headpiece and showed her that unusual band. ''See these pieces in the hatband? Hammered silver. Hopi handiwork. Each of these pieces is worth fifty dollars.''

Emmalee counted frantically. There had to be at least twenty pieces of silver in the hatband. Garn nonchalantly put the hat back on.

''This hatband is my insurance. I'll never gamble it.''

''I should hope not,'' said Emmalee. But she did not entirely believe him. His reckless streak was too apparent.

But he certainly was handsome, she had to admit. That long swatch of rich, black hair curled down across his forehead when he removed his hat. An almost perpetual glint of amusement around his eyes and mouth softened his strong, young face. And when he spoke, whether to her or to someone else, Emmalee could not help but thrill to a voice that seemed to have the range and flexibility of a musical instrument. She wondered how it would sound if he whispered.

The setting, too, enhanced his attractiveness, as well as Emmalee's growing sense of enjoyment and adventure. The casino was on the port side of the *Queen*, with walls of windows overlooking the dark, irregular outline of Missouri, as well as affording a glimpse of the majestic white paddlewheel to the stern, which drove the big ship through the roiling waters of the Mississippi, upriver into the night. Perhaps for the first time since she'd left Pennsylvania with her parents, Emmalee felt completely free. All America waited for her now, wild as wind or time or tempest, and anything could happen.

"Dealer. Chips, if you please," commanded Garn, easing into a space at the edge of the table and positioning Emmalee beside him. His gray eyes gleamed with anticipation.

"Hey, Mr. Landar! Nice to give us your trade again," said the man in charge of the roulette table. Several dozen men and women surrounded the table, either gambling or watching, and they, too, called out greetings to Garn. Obviously he was not a stranger there. Emmalee did not fail to notice the frank, appreciative glances given Garn by many of the women—who somehow contrived not to notice Emmalee at all—and she was irritated with herself when she discovered just the smallest twinge of jealousy way down deep inside her. How incredibly ridiculous! She barely knew this Garn Landar, planned to get away from him as soon as the boat docked in Hannibal, and already realized that he was not at all what a man should be. Namely: responsible, reserved, and sober. Garn was the exact opposite: carefree (if not careless!), flamboyant, and self-indulgent.

She hoped he wouldn't lose too much of his money though. In the orphanage, she'd been told many times that gamblers always lost. So Emmalee was very surprised when Garn won. Sipping her drink, she watched as Garn exchanged greenbacks for piles of colored chips, which he placed on numbered squares. Then the dealer spun the big wheel, everyone waited breathlessly, and—*voilá!*—Garn won money. Gambling, Emmalee reflected, was not at all dangerous, or difficult, and it was a lot of fun too.

But then Garn began to lose. It happened gradually. At first, he lost a bet only now and then. As the evening progressed, though, he lost more frequently, until, at around midnight, he was losing almost every time he made a wager. Despite herself Emmalee had begun to feel a certain proprietary inclination toward Garn, especially after she'd overheard a couple of men murmuring about what a fool he was, but her mood was composed equally of concern and disgust.

"You'd better stop now," she told him during a break in the gaming, while Brutus and a score of stewards served more drinks, succulent sandwiches, and other delicacies Emmalee couldn't identify.

"Splendid advice," Garn responded, wolfing a sandwich of rare roast beef, "but I can't."

"Why not?"

"Because I'm behind. When I catch up again, I'll quit."

"You mean you've lost all that money you had?" She couldn't believe it.

"More. I'm in the hole."

"But I don't understand."

"All right," called the dealer, "play will resume!"

"But what will happen," Emmalee asked, "if you keep losing?"

"I won't. I'll win. You're my good-luck charm, remember? You just have to try harder." He started toward the roulette table, ransacking his pockets for spare bills. Then he did something so cavalier, so idiotic, that she was too appalled to do anything but observe.

He removed his splendid gray hat, unclasped the band of silver pieces, slipped them from the thin leather thong to which they were bound, and held them out for all to see. "More chips!" he ordered the dealer. "Let's get that wheel spinning!"

Over the heads of the people around the table, he tossed one of the hammered silver discs to Emmalee.

"Alms for the goddess!" he called expansively. Instinctively Emmalee caught the piece as it flew toward her through the air. Everyone cheered.

Garn began to win again. Action at the craps table ceased, poker and blackjack players ended their games, waiters and stewards and everyone else drifted over to watch Garn duel with the roulette wheel. Jason Bascomb, in charge of money on the *Queen of Natchez,* stepped over and said something to the dealer. Emmalee could see a fine film of sweat on his forehead.

"All right." The dealer grinned, after Garn raked another particularly large pile of chips to his end of the table. "All right, you've got your money back. Congratulations. The wheel's closing for the night."

"Hell, no," cried Garn. "Keep the damn thing rolling." He was supported by the onlookers, who let out a refined chorus of protest. They wanted to see more action.

"You can't do this *now,*" Garn complained. "Jesus!"

"Come now, Mr. Landar," Jason Bascomb said, "the rules are the rules. Closing time."

"It's not fair," said someone in the crowd. "Let him get a little ahead or even go behind again, but you can't end it this way."

"Damn right," agreed Garn, swaying slightly. "And let's make it interesting. Double or nothing." He'd been drinking mint juleps all night and his words were a bit slurred.

An excited gasp rose from the spectators. Bascomb looked at Garn to see if he was serious. He was. The dealer and Bascomb conferred in whispers.

Emmalee found her way to Garn's side. He was painstakingly stacking piles of chips.

"What on earth is the matter with you?" she hissed. Emmalee knew that this was none of her business. She had no right or reason to be angry with him in a personal way. Yet she was.

"What?" he asked. "I'm perfectly fine."

"No one who's 'perfectly fine' would risk a bet like this. How much money does it amount to, anyway?"

He shrugged. "Somewhere in the neighborhood of nine or nine fifty."

"*Nine hundred and fifty dollars?* Oh, my God."

"No. Nine thousand dollars, or maybe nine thousand and five hundred."

Emmalee felt herself grow lightheaded.

"I can double it," he told her. His eyes were shining.

"You could lose it all."

"If you never take risks, you don't get ahead. Look, let me give you some money, if that's what you're worried about. That silver piece should easily get you as far as St. Joe, but a little extra . . ." He grabbed a handful of chips and handed them to her. "Just cash these in at the window over there. Bascomb'll redeem them for you."

"I don't want them!" Emmalee flared, pushing his hand away. "You don't have to take care of me."

"Hey! But I want to!"

"You can't even take care of *yourself*! Don't worry about me. I'll make it on my own!"

He grinned at her. "I like that spirit," he said. "I like to see that in a gal. But, hell, you're just a little kid."

"Well, at least I know not to throw money away!"

"I'm going to double it."

"You don't even *care*!" she accused him.

There in the crowded room, his expression and tone changed. Just for a moment, he looked deeply into her eyes. So intense was his gaze that she was alone with him in a private world of meaning. It was as if the rest of the people no longer existed.

"That's right," Garn told Emmalee then. "I don't care. But there will come a time when I do, and when that time comes, you can bet money, body, and soul that I will not lose whatever it is that I choose to care about."

"All right, Landar," Mr. Bascomb called. "Double or nothing, just as you wish."

The crowd cheered, pushed close to the table, then quieted. Even mighty Brutus, whose disdain for everyone and everything had persisted throughout the evening, strode over to watch the spin of the wheel.

"Let's see," said Garn, glancing at Emmalee. "Tonight's a special occasion. I'm putting all my money on number sixteen."

"As you wish." The dealer shrugged, setting the wheel in motion.

The entire casino and everyone in it were caught in a hush. In the distance, foghorns sounded on the river. Outside, the paddlewheel churned and water splashed. And, on the table, the roulette wheel spun and clattered, fast at first, slower, more slowly still, until, notch by notch, the numbers passed, each lingering for what seemed an eternity. Nine. Ten. Eleven. The wheel coming down to the end of its spin now. Twelve. Thirteen. Fourteen. "Come on, come on!" cried Garn, now on his feet. *Come on!* prayed Emmalee. She felt as if her heart was slowing like the wheel, as if her heart would surely stop forever when the wheel did. Fifteen. Barely moving, just one more, just one more . . .

Sixteen!

The crowd let out a wild, exuberant howl.

Emmalee suppressed an impulse to give Garn Landar a congratulatory embrace. He would be insufferable enough as it was.

Click!

"Seventeen," called the dealer in a bored voice. "You lose, Landar."

The quiet in the room was now as deep as it had been while the wheel was spinning, but the character of that silence was completely different. Then it had been filled with the tension of risk. Now it was colored by the imminence of danger.

"Funny thing," said Garn. His voice was as taut and certain as he was, filled with an imminence of its own. "I swear I never saw a roulette wheel behave the way this one just did. Maybe it's got a busted spring or something. Or maybe an *extra* spring. Surely you won't mind if I have a look?"

Sensing trouble, people started backing slowly away from the table, the men shielding the women. Garn stood on one side of the table, the dealer and Jason Bascomb on the other. Brutus looked on, impassive and glowering.

"I'm sure we can settle this without incident," said the suave Bascomb.

"Sure we can," replied Garn, his voice clear and tense now. "Sure we can, as soon as I have a look at the workings underneath that roulette wheel."

"I'm afraid that's not permitted, Landar. There is no law providing for such an examination."

Garn put his hands beneath the edge of the table and started to lift it. Chips and coins slid as the table tilted.

"Stop it, Landar, or you'll be sorry," Bascomb threatened.

"No," replied Garn. "You'll be sorry at the next port if I find that this wheel's been doctored."

The dealer stepped toward Garn and grabbed his shoulder. Garn dropped the table, spun around, and sent the dealer to the floor with a straight right jab. He lay there moaning and twitching.

Bascomb made his decision. "Brutus, get Mr. Landar out of here."

The black giant had biceps larger than country hams and a breadth of shoulders two axe-handles across. He was monstrous. No man had ever dared challenge him.

Please, no, prayed Emmalee, as Brutus came around the table toward Garn, who stood his ground.

"Come quiet and no get hurt," rumbled the giant.

"Stay where you are!" Garn told him. "Don't come a step nearer." The danger of his situation had cleared Garn's head. He showed no traces of alcohol now.

Astounded and bewildered, Brutus stood there for a moment, then looked at Bascomb for instructions.

"I don't want a fight," Garn said.

Bascomb made a sound that was like a laugh and a groan. "I bet you don't. But you're the one who's provoked this. Brutus, get him out of here."

The black giant strode forward again, toward Garn. His tremendous arms reached out.

Garn stepped to one side, drew back his fist, and smashed Brutus right in the nose.

Emmalee heard herself scream, which was quite a feat since everybody else was screaming too. Brutus, unused to pain, not to mention defiance, let out a roar that filled the casino. With his eyes on the slowly retreating Garn, he reached down and lifted the roulette table from the floor . . .

"Brutus! No!" yelled Bascomb, thinking of his elegant casino.

. . . and lifted the massive rectangle of mahogany and felt above his head, scattering wheel and chips, coins and greenback and gold. Garn was backed against the wall of windows on the port side of the ship.

"Brutus! Wait!" shouted Garn. He knew he was in trouble, and his clever gray eyes darted here and there in search of an escape route, but his calm was almost insouciant. "Brutus! I bet I can jump through this glass window before you can throw that table at me!"

Garn made a move toward the window.

The ebony behemoth hurled the roulette table at that magnificent wall of sheer glass.

Garn flattened himself to the floor as the table sailed above him, crashed through the glass, out into the night, and down into the Mississippi.

"Thanks, Brutus." Garn smiled, standing. "I really didn't want to have to swim all the way to Missouri on a night like this."

He leaped through the great open space where the window had been and dived to the water below. Emmalee and the others pressed as close as they dared to the rent and riddled side of the casino and peered down at the dark river. For a long, long moment Emmalee held her breath, able to see nothing but the reflected, multicolored lights of festive lanterns on the black, fast-moving current. Then, with a great sucking, plopping sound, the huge gaming table bobbed to the surface, and in another moment Garn Landar could be seen swimming strongly toward it. It was very dark on the river and already the table was drifting away from the *Queen of Natchez*, but Garn had slipped out of his jacket. He was quite visible in his expensive white shirt, and Emmalee saw him clearly as he climbed aboard the table. He was alive anyway, if not totally safe. She realized that she'd been holding her breath and exhaled now in a rush.

Most of the people were cheering and waving at Garn, which they continued to do until he floated out of sight. The ruined casino was filled with excited, milling people. Some of the men were remonstrating fiercely with Jason Bascomb. Brutus stood at the broken window, gazing sullenly down upon the river. Emmalee made her decision and left the casino, climbing to cabin twelve on deck three. There, bothered by no one, she spent the rest of the journey to Hannibal. She slept, she looked out at the changeless river and the ever-changing countryside. She nibbled at the food she'd taken with her from the Lutheran home, and she wondered what further exciting adventures lay in store for her. The world outside Cairo, Illinois, had certainly supplied her with a tantalizing prelude.

Also, while on board the *Queen,* she thought of what Garn Landar had said: "*You can bet money, body, and soul that I will not lose whatever it is that I choose to care about.*"

She had no idea what he'd meant by that, and for a moment she wished he was there so she could ask him. It was a most unusual thing to have said, but then Garn Landar was obviously an unusual man. She smiled to herself, thinking of him floating away on the roulette table, waving. And she remembered, with a small shudder, the way his very touch had made her feel. Garn was a man; despite his reliability and sweetness, Val Jannings had been but a boy. Yet Garn seemed flawed, his immense attractiveness notwithstanding.

One of the things Emmalee wanted most was to control her own destiny. Garn, with the freedom given by money, appeared to enjoy such control, but he was squandering it! Again, Emmalee wished that he was there so that she could tell him, warn him. It was distressing to think that a man as interesting as he would come to no good end and have nothing but his undisciplined extravagance to blame it on.

So maybe it was better that he was not there after all: Emmalee did not want a reckless person distracting her from her own goals. But her mind roamed inevitably back to his words: "I will not lose whatever it is that I choose to care about."

"Good luck," she said aloud, thinking of Garn. "Good luck, and I'm glad it's not me you're going to choose. There'd be no end of trouble then."

Once she arrived in Hannibal, Emmalee went to a bank and traded the piece of hammered Hopi silver for fifty real dollars, less a one-dollar "transaction fee." Now, with nearly sixty dollars to her name, she felt positively rich.

She bought a canteen, a bedroll, two bright, durable calico dresses, a jacket, and a pair of boots for the trail, and a train ticket to St. Joe, Missouri. The future had arrived. Fortune would take care of itself.

Getting Where You Want to Go

The place was camping ground, way station, overnight stop for thousands of pilgrims heading west. It was a vital, tawdry, raucous, sprawling frontier town on the banks of the mighty Missouri. The maps called it St. Joseph, but to those who lived there and to those who passed through on their way to someplace else it was just St. Joe.

Emmalee thrilled and her heart beat fast as her train chugged into town on a bright spring morning. The dowdy buildings of clapboard and stucco and brick had been washed clean by an overnight shower, settling the dust in the streets and giving St. Joe a bright, snappy look. A white cloud of steam from the engine drifted into a peerless prairie sky; daffodils, violets, and sunflowers blossomed in the tall, wind-bent grass across the Missouri.

"Where you bound for, ma'am?" asked the old conductor as he helped Emmalee down from the train. St. Joe was a place where, it was assumed, one would not be staying long.

"Olympia," she replied proudly.

He did not tell her how difficult the trip would be, or discourage her at all.

"Good luck," he said, with a smile that made her feel happy and gave her an extra jot of confidence. Good weather and good wishes: Emmalee felt blessed.

Studying the advertisement she had clipped from the Cairo newspaper, Emmalee made her way to the Schuyler Hotel on Market Street and inquired at the desk as to the whereabouts of Mr. Burt Pennington, wagonmaster.

"That's him over there at the table in the corner of the lobby," said a bored, young clerk who was trying without conspicuous success to raise a mustache. "He's busy now. Better wait your turn."

Emmalee walked across the lobby and took up a position beside a marble column, from which she could discreetly overhear what was going on. Burt Pennington, seated at the table, was a bald, bullet-headed, vigorous-looking man. Next to him was a very pretty redhaired young woman, who wore a frilly lavender frock that Emmalee envied on sight. The girl was sighing and yawning, obviously bored. Pennington was in conversation with a rangy fellow standing in front of the table. He had the look of a renegade about him.

". . . full up and nigh on ready to roll out, Mr. Pennington," the renegade was saying.

"Good work, Otis. Damn good work. Ever' day counts. We got to get a head start on Horace Torquist and his party. Damn farmers. If they get to Olympia 'fore we do, they'll get the best land."

"Don't think there's any need to worry, Mr. Pennington. From what I hear downtown and around, Torquist won't be ready to roll for a while yet."

Emmalee's ears perked up. *Damn farmers?* What was going on here? Why were these people going to Olympia, if not to farm?

"Otis, did that new scout we hired show up yet?"

"Landar? No, sir. Ain't seen hide nor hair of him."

Landar? thought Emmalee, startled. *Garn* Landar? Perhaps. He had said that he was headed for St. Joe.

"Hell," said Pennington, "if he can't even make it here on time, we can sure get along without him. I didn't care for the idea of hiring him sight unseen anyway. I like to look a man in the eye."

Otis shrugged. "Too bad he ain't showed. Had good recommendations on him, and he's crossed the Rockies eight times with wagon trains."

Eight times across the Rocky Mountains? Emmalee reflected. If they were indeed talking about Garn, her estimation of him increased. Slightly.

"Well, he should have been here by now and he's not," Pennington pronounced. "It was in his contract. If he shows up, fire him."

"Pay him travel expenses?" Otis wanted to know.

"Hell, no. It wasn't in his contract."

Poor Garn, thought Emmalee. He was already broke. Well, it was his own fault. He ought to have been here on time, not off on the Mississippi causing trouble and . . .

Suddenly she was aware of eyes on her and looked to find the redhaired girl staring her up and down. It was an arrogant, measuring look.

"You want something?" the girl asked, as if Emmalee could not possibly be important enough to bother with.

"I'd like to see Mr. Pennington."

"About what?" the girl snapped.

Burt Pennington looked over and saw Emmalee. "Lottie, I'll handle this," he said. "Otis, that'll be all."

Otis tipped his hat to Emmalee, looking her over too, a glance of cool male appraisal, then strode away, the heels of his high, western-style boots clacking on the floor.

"Come over here and sit down," Pennington ordered

Emmalee, in a manner that was both businesslike and courteous. "What can I do for you?"

Emmalee approached the table and showed Pennington the newspaper ad. Lottie looked over, saw the ad, and dismissed the whole subject with a stifled yawn.

"I want to sign up for your train west, sir," Emmalee said. "Are there any places left?"

"Just for yourself? You alone?"

Lottie showed signs of life now. "You're not married or *anything*?" she asked.

"Lottie, mind your manners for once. This is my daughter, Lottie Pennington. And you are?"

"Emmalee Alden. And, no, I'm not married. But I want to travel west."

"Well, I probably could squeeze in a few more fares. You got relatives out there, or what?"

"No, sir. I plan to claim land in the Territory of Olympia."

Burt Pennington's incredulity was too great to be concealed, although for the sake of good manners he made an attempt to mute it.

"Pretty ambitious for a girl your age," he said. "You *are* serious?"

"Oh, yes."

"Well, it's a free country since Honest Abe let the slaves loose. What you want that land for?"

Emmalee recalled Pennington's derogatory remark about farmers and remembered that his ad in the paper had addressed itself in particular to those with an interest in ranching. "Naturally, I'd fit right in with the other people in your group," she said.

"I wouldn't count on that," Lottie said.

"I told you once to be quiet," her father warned. Then he said to Emmalee, "You intend to *ranch* in Olympia?" This time he was frankly disbelieving.

"Oh, yes," she lied.

"Where you from?" Pennington inquired suspiciously.

"Pennsylvania. That is, originally."

"Lots of ranches there," he said dryly. "What's a dogie?" he demanded abruptly.

"A-a what?"

"A *dogie*. You say you grew up on this ranch in Pennsylvania, so you must know what a *dogie* is."

It must be some kind of ranching word, Emmalee realized. Pennington was testing her.

"I think I used to know but I forgot," she said.

Lottie laughed, and this time her father did not chide her.

"Look, young lady," he advised Emmalee. "They got *farms* in Pennsylvania. But it don't matter anyway. You got no business going out across Kansas and Colorado by yourself. Wagon trains are tough stuff, and the trip is even worse. Then you got to cross the mountains . . ."

If Garn Landar did it eight times, I can do it once, Emmalee was sure.

". . . and then you got to claim and settle your land. And there won't be any farms in Olympia anyways."

"Why not?"

"On account of us ranchers is gonna get there first and take the place over. We got to. Farmers tear up land, beat it down, *ruin* it. Land is the only thing that counts, and farmers destroy it. Look, take a piece of advice from a man who's seen a bit in his time. Find yourself a nice young fellow—"

"If she can," Lottie said, snickering.

"—and settle down here in St. Joe. You must have read too many books or heard too many stories. You'll *never* make it out to Olympia."

"Someone else thought so too," said Emmalee, thinking of Garn. Maybe she would have a test of her own.

Those who told her she should settle down here and get married, those who said she wouldn't survive the trek west, well, they would just *fail* her test, that was all there was to it.

"Thank you for your time," she said to Pennington.

He stood. "Sorry I couldn't be of more help," he said, not ungallantly. "I stand behind the advice, though."

Lottie could not restrain herself. For whatever reason, fate or chemistry or bad bile, who knew? Lottie Pennington had taken an instant dislike to Emmalee, a feeling that was reciprocated.

"If I owned me a calico dress like that," Lottie oozed, assaying Emmalee's serviceable but unstylish garment, "I just bet I could find me a man real easy."

"It seems you do have that virtue," replied Emmalee sweetly.

Lottie looked puzzled. "What do you mean?"

"Finding things easy. I understand it is a virtue in some women."

Burt Pennington could not restrain a snort of laughter. "Lottie," he said, shaking his head, "I think you met your match for once."

The redhead fumed and glared at Emmalee.

"Good luck, Miss Alden," Pennington said, "and if anyone else ever asks you, a *dogie* is a stray calf."

A stray calf! Emmalee thought, back outside the hotel on Market Street. Well, how was I to know? Would Pennington know what a harrow was? Or when to plant the corn? She thought not. Anyway, it was probably just as well that he'd rejected her outright. They hadn't even gotten around to discussing the price of the fare! In the long run, it didn't pay to go where you weren't wanted.

But it was absolutely essential to get where you wanted to go, and for Emmalee that place was Olympia. She stood outside the Schuyler Hotel for a moment, watching the horses and wagons roll by, enjoying the swarm of women and children, men and cattle and dogs. Then she set out to find this Torquist fellow. Pennington had implied that he was organizing a wagon train composed of farmers.

She found that train on a green plain outside St. Joe, although few observing the chaotic swirl of random activity would have called it a train. There were many Conestoga wagons, true: high-wheeled, canvas-covered vessels built to sail a sea of grass. There were scores of tethered horses, oxen grazing beyond the wagons, and piles of bedrolls, foodstuffs, and other supplies. Children ran all around, shrieking at their play. Harried men and women dashed this way and that, to no particular purpose that Emmalee could discern.

She put her bedroll and bulging portmanteau down on the grass and looked about, trying to catch the eye of someone who might tell her where to locate Horace Torquist. But everyone rushed past her without paying the slightest bit of attention. The Torquist people, she decided, were very energetic, if not entirely observant.

Picking up her gear, she began to walk toward a group of women who were folding and stowing blankets in one of the wagons. In order to reach them she had to cut between a smithy's forge—she could see the burly, sweating blacksmith hammering a glowing chunk of metal—and a wheelless wagon undergoing repairs. She heard hoofbeats close by, but thought nothing of them until, coming out from behind the wagon, she caught a glimpse of horse and rider bearing down on her.

"*Whoooaaa!*" the rider called sharply, jerking frantically at the reins of a big dapple-gray, which reared and veered sideways, just missing Emmalee. She dropped her gear and leaped backwards, tripped and sprawled in the dirt beneath the wagon. Her head struck one of the blocks supporting the wagon, and for a few moments all she felt was pain and all she saw were stars.

Then, slowly, her world recomposed itself, her vision cleared, and Emmalee found herself gazing into a pair of worried blue eyes. As her consciousness returned, the expression of concern in those eyes lessened, and she was aware of their startling beauty. They were shining, cornflower blue, with glints of golden light, conveying an effect that was at once intelligent and gentle. Then, with her mind beginning to function normally again, Emmalee saw that those wonderful eyes belonged to a strong, square, open face, ringed with damp blond curls that pushed out from beneath the brim of a battered felt hat. She watched as a sparkling smile of relief appeared on the face, and Emmalee knew she had almost been run over by an archangel riding a dapple-gray.

"You all right?" the young man asked. "You seem to be all right, but don't get up too quickly. You want some water or something?"

"No, no, I'm fine. Really." Emmalee sat up. She did feel all right.

The man helped her up. He was tall, and broad in the shoulders and chest. His waist was trim and narrow; his hips were lean in denim trousers.

"You got to watch out around this camp," he warned her with gentle severity. "I didn't have the foggiest notion you were going to jump out at me from behind that wagon."

"I didn't exactly jump out at you. . . ."

"Sorry. Just a figure of speech. Say, I don't think I've seen you around here before. I'm Randy Clay."

He offered his hand, which was well shaped, with long, strong fingers.

"You haven't," Emmalee replied. "I just got here. In

fact, I was looking for Mr. Torquist. I want to sign up for a place on the train."

She waited, expecting the half-disbelieving, half-derisive response to her plans that she'd received from Val Jannings, Garn Landar, and, most recently, Burt Pennington. But Randy Clay just grinned and asked what her name was.

"Sounds fine to me, Emmalee," he said then. "But where's the rest of you?"

"What do you mean?"

"The others. Ma. Pa. Husband, cousins, kids."

"There aren't any. I'm alone."

This news did not seem to alarm Randy Clay either, but he did inform her that the Torquist wagon train was composed of people who wanted to claim land in Olympia for the purpose of farming.

"So do I," she said. "That's why I'm here."

He smiled again. He had a wonderful smile. It made her feel happy and wanted, like a friend.

"Well, let me take you to Mr. Torquist then. He's the one who can tell you exactly how things stand. I'm signed on as a scout, but I'm really aimin' to get land of my own once we reach Olympia."

He helped her up onto the big gray horse, which Emmalee could tell was a sturdy beast, respectable but without lineage. It was the horse of an honest man who needs an animal not for the sake of appearances but for good, hard work. In fact, the dapple-gray wore no saddle, so when Randy swung up on its back behind Emmalee and put his arms around her so that he could hold the reins, the two of them were mounted close together. Emmalee was very conscious of the warmth of Randy's body behind her.

"My gear—" she began.

"Leave it," he said. "Nobody'll touch it. We've got decent people on this train. Not like some others I could name."

He kicked the horse lightly with his heels and the beast lumbered into a trot.

Emmalee indulged in a small measure of satisfaction. Things seemed to be progressing fairly well. Randy had said that good people belonged to this company, and that was nice to know. Moreover, he would personally introduce her to the leader, Mr. Torquist. That was ever so much better than having to stumble up on one's own, a stranger out of nowhere. There was just one small matter, however, which had yet to be resolved.

"What is the fare on this train?" she asked, trying to assume an air of casual confidence.

"A hundred and thirty dollars."

Her heart sank. After the train trip and the purchases in Hannibal, she had four dollars and twenty cents left.

"Less than most," he said.

"Oh, yes. I shopped around. What is Mr. Torquist like?" she asked. "As a person, I mean?"

"Well," said Randy Clay, hesitating, "that's sort of a hard question to answer."

"What I mean is . . . well, is he a good man?"

"Oh, definitely good."

"Has he taken a wagon train out west before?"

"No, but he's a strong leader, that's for sure. I doubt there are any stronger."

"Somehow you don't seem especially enthusiastic about that."

"Oh, I am," replied Randy. "It's just that Mr. Torquist is *very* sure of everything. Sometimes this causes him to have trouble with other people. Not serious trouble, mind you, but . . ."

Emmalee decided to approach Horace Torquist warily. "And he is a farmer?" she asked.

"You bet! He had a huge farm in Ohio, near Galena. That's where I'm from. But his wife died, he turned sour on the people there, and so he sold out. For a big profit, I might add."

"Turned sour on the people?" asked Emmalee.

"That's the only way I know to describe it. You see, the Civil War changed a lot of things. People passed through, settled, started businesses and such. Galena changed. Mr. Torquist wants to go out to Olympia and set up a pure, simple farming community of God-fearing people. To start all over again, in a manner of speaking."

"Then I bet he's pretty particular about who gets on his train?" guessed Emmalee.

"You're right quick, Emmalee Alden." Randy laughed.

"I guess I'm God-fearing," she said. "I read almost the whole Bible at the—" She was about to say "at the Lutheran orphanage," but that didn't exactly suggest that she possessed the price of a fare. "Why did you decide to leave Galena?" she asked.

Randy guided the gray horse past a well at which men were busy filling barrels with water and hoisting them onto a flat-bedded wagon. Emmalee could see, just up ahead, a fine, new Conestoga with a large tent set up next to it.

"My family's got only a small farm there," he said matter-of-factly, "and I have five brothers. No way to make a living if the land is split six ways, or even two ways, actually. And the price of land is too high for me to afford an Ohio farm. I'm on my own. Sold my share to my kin to get up money for this trip. I hated to leave home, but I just know everything's going to turn out fine."

He sounded wistful and confident at the same time.

"Then you're alone too?" she blurted.

" 'Cept for my horse." He laughed and reined the dapple-gray to a halt in front of the tent. "Mr. Torquist?" he called. "You available for a minute? Got a young lady out here wants to discuss something important with you."

Emmalee slid down from the horse and adjusted her

skirt and her hair. "Thanks for the ride," she said, looking up at Randy. Then the tent flap was thrown abruptly aside and a man stepped out of it and into the sunlight, shielding his eyes with his hand.

"What is it?" he demanded, glancing from Emmalee to Randy.

"This is Emmalee Alden, sir. She wants to talk to you."

"About what?" Horace Torquist demanded peremptorily, looking at Emmalee. It seemed as if he were glaring, so forceful was his manner, so imposing his bearing. Torquist was only of medium height, but he carried himself with such fierce erectness that he seemed tall, an effect enhanced by a mane of wild white hair that appeared incapable of being tamed by brush or comb. That unkempt head of hair seemed incongruous to Emmalee at first, but then she realized that it suggested some immense inner drive on Torquist's part, a single bizarre feature on a man otherwise fastidiously groomed. His wild hair rendered the wagonmaster singular and prophetlike.

"I'd . . . I'd like to talk to you about a place on your train," Emmalee said, managing to sound reasonably crisp and businesslike.

Torquist's troubled gray eyes showed interest.

"I do hope you've some room left," Emmalee pressed.

"Just yourself?"

"Yes. Sir." He was the type of man to whom one instinctively felt a need to say "sir."

"What's your background?" he demanded.

"I'm a farm girl from Pennsylvania. My parents died on the trail. . . ."

"You a churchgoer, Emmalee?"

"Yes, Lutheran," said Emmalee, thinking of the chapel at the home.

Horace Torquist thought it over, making judgments and

calculations Emmalee could not assay. "Be off about your business, Clay," he ordered Randy then. "Miss Alden, you come inside with me and I'll explain a few things to you."

Randy gave Emmalee an encouraging smile and jerked the gray's reins, trotting away. Emmalee followed the dour wagonmaster into his spacious tent. Its furnishings were austere, like the man himself, but of excellent quality. A narrow bed with a mahogany headboard and a thick, quilted coverlet rested on a rich rectangle of carpeting. The washstand, also of polished mahogany, bore a pitcher and basin of the finest porcelain. Two ornamentally carved straightback chairs flanked a sturdy desk that gleamed dully in the subdued lighting. The tent was clean and cool.

"Sit down, Emmalee."

It was an order, not an invitation. Emmalee sat down.

"My fare is a hundred and thirty dollars, payable in advance."

Emmalee was about to explain that she didn't have a hundred and thirty dollars, but Torquist took a seat behind the desk and went on speaking.

"First there are certain matters to consider," he said. "Matters much more important than mere money."

"Yes, sir." More important than money? This set of priorities sounded encouraging.

"Do you know why I am making this mighty venture, Emmalee?" Torquist demanded. "This great trek west?"

Emmalee decided to use the information she'd learned from Randy Clay. Torquist might be pleased to know that she was aware of his ideals.

"Yes, I do," she responded briskly. "Parts of the eastern United States have grown oversettled and—"

The wagonmaster nodded, put up his hand, and interrupted. He wanted to do his own explaining. "Jefferson and God," he said. "I'm taking this community of souls out across the Rocky Mountains because of Thomas Jefferson and God Almighty."

Emmalee decided to keep quiet.

"What do you know about Thomas Jefferson, Miss Alden? That he was our third president, a Founding Father, a great man?"

Emmalee nodded energetically.

"Of course. Everyone but the most benighted fool knows those things. But Jefferson was more. He was a *prophet*, Miss Alden." Torquist thumped the big desk with the flat of a powerful hand. "He was a prophet *scorned*!"

Nothing Randy Clay had told her about Horace Torquist prepared Emmalee for this kind of display. The white-maned leader was as different from blunt, businesslike Burt Pennington as any man she could imagine.

"Jefferson," Torquist railed, "believed that America—the idea and the reality of America—could be preserved only if our country remained true to its agrarian roots, true to the *land*, Emmalee. He was a farmer, do you see what I mean? The farmer is close to the soil, gives to it, receives from it, and both are made strong. But people here in the east have forgotten that purity, that essential nobility, in the pursuit of crass wealth. Moneychangers have invaded the temple. Do I make myself clear?"

"Oh, yes, indeed," said Emmalee.

"God knows it too, Emmalee. Mark my words. God knows what has become of our country. And that is why He is showing us the way to a new, unsullied horizon. The west. It is our last chance to make good the bounty He has lain before us, and it is my conviction that this time, *this time* He will not permit corruption and decay and degradation to ruin His handiwork. We shall have to fight for it, of course, and fight hard. But we shall be victorious."

Torquist paused a moment, savoring his rhetorical flight.

"Are you a fighter, Emmalee?" he asked quietly.

Emmalee hesitated. Was this some sort of a trick? Torquist had said that "hard fighting" might be required in the settling of the west. But he was also a man of God, whose followers had been admonished to turn the other cheek.

"I stand up for myself when I have to," she said, truthfully but cautiously.

Torquist was pleased. "That's what I like to hear, Emmalee. Stand up for yourself, and for the rest of the community. We've got to stick together if we want to beat Burt Pennington to Olympia and, even more importantly, to claim the best land out there for farming purposes."

"But Mr. Pennington is ready to leave St. Joe almost any day now," Emmalee said.

The wagonmaster, who seemed to have been in the process of warming up to her, now grew instantly suspicious. And angry.

"What do you know of Burt Pennington?" he snapped. "And how did you come by such knowledge?"

"Well, I'd . . . I'd seen his advertisement in a newspaper and when I reached St. Joe I looked him up. I didn't know he was a—"

"A rancher?"

"Yes. In fact, that's why I'm here. Mr. Pennington mentioned that the people on your train are farmers and—"

"So he wouldn't take you on, eh?" Torquist was studying her with narrowed eyes. "And how do *I* know that you're interested in the land? How do I know that you're not just using me to make your way out west? Yes, you're strong and young. I can see that. No doubt you'll make some man a fine wife before too long, and a community needs sound marriages . . ."

Emmalee chose not to respond to that remark.

". . . but do you really know anything about farming?"

She recalled Pennington's query about the "dogie."

"You might ask me some questions," Emmalee said.

Mr. Torquist leaned forward. "All right, I will. What do you plant first in the spring, corn or oats?"

"Oats. It has a shorter growing season and must be harvested before frost in the fall."

"Hmmm. And how do you shock oats?"

"Three bundles on one side, three on the other. Two on the ends as braces, and one on top to keep the rain off."

"What's a stanchion, Emmalee?"

"A couple of bars that serve as a neck-yoke to keep cows in the barn."

"You had milking cows on your farm in Pennsylvania?"

"Yes, sir."

"What breed were they?"

"Jersey."

"Black and white, eh?"

"No, Jerseys are brown."

The wagonmaster seemed satisfied that she knew something of farming. "All right," he said, "you strike me as a girl who might fit into my plans. You're willing to fight if you have to—and, mark my words, we'll have to face down Pennington sometime—and you come from farm stock. Something else bothers me, however, and don't get the idea that I'm being insensitive, but I'd be remiss in my responsibilities if I didn't bring it up."

Torquist almost sounded as if he were hemming and hawing, which was uncharacteristic of him.

"Just go ahead and say it," Emmalee invited.

He frowned. "It has to do with your . . . ah . . . with your nature or . . . ah . . . your circumstances."

"Yes?" This must be where the money part came up.

But he surprised her. "Miss Alden," he said, not quite meeting her eyes, "you are . . . you are a, well, a handsome young woman. . . ."

"Thank you, sir."

"But you're not attached to any man. What I'm getting

at is that . . . is that, while I assume everyone to be moral and righteous until I find out differently, there *are* a number of single men on the train. It is a hard and tedious journey, and if they were to be distracted by . . . well, you can see what I mean, can't you?''

Emmalee could see quite clearly. Torquist meant that *she* had better not ''distract'' those unattached men, or any other men. He was putting the burden on her, as he would certainly place the blame on her as well.

''Any troubles of that kind,'' he warned, shaking his thick finger at her, ''and I'll be forced to leave you in Denver. We stop there for a couple of weeks to reoutfit the train before crossing the Rockies. Do I make myself clear?''

''Yes, you do. You won't have any trouble from me.''

''It's not only you, of course. I require the highest comportment from everyone, at all times. Myself included. Now, you wish to travel with us and sign on as a member of our group. The fare is a hundred and thirty—''

''I'm afraid I don't have that much.''

''How much do you have?''

Emmalee told him.

''Four dollars! Why on earth are you here? I admire pluck, but this is business, not charity.''

''I'm not asking for charity. That's the last thing I'll ever want. It was just that I thought . . . well, maybe some sort of arrangement could be made. . . .''

Torquist hadn't thrown her out of the tent yet, so Emmalee felt there was some hope left. ''I could work,'' she offered.

''Miss Alden, everybody on my train works. It is a condition of passage.''

''Perhaps something extra?''

Torquist's gray eyes glinted shrewdly. ''Situations like yours are not unknown to me,'' he said. ''So I will make you the only offer possible under these circumstances, and only because you appear to be an upright Christian girl who wants to better herself. I will take you to Olympia without fare . . ."

Emmalee listened.

". . . if, in return, you agree to work for me for a period of two years."

"Two years?"

"Take it or leave it, Miss Alden."

To a girl of sixteen, two years seemed an awfully long time. Emmalee thought it over. If she was fortunate enough to claim land, this commitment might prevent her from working her own farm. Torquist might demand most—if not all—of her time. On the other hand, the land would grow in value, and she might be able to borrow money using it as security.

"If I'm able to . . . to get some money together, couldn't we agree?"

"That you could buy your way out of the two-year commitment? Yes, I'm amenable to that. Let's say two hundred and fifty dollars a year?"

Emmalee's spirits sank. All that money seemed more formidable than two years. Nevertheless, Emmalee reasoned, this deal with Mr. Torquist was probably the only way to get where she wanted to go. If she stayed in St. Joe, it would take her months to earn the fare, and then, by the time she reached Olympia with another wagon train, all the land would be long since snatched up. The important thing was to reach Olympia. I'll get by somehow, she vowed.

While Torquist took from his desk an inkwell, an old-fashioned quill pen, and a piece of thick, yellow paper on which to inscribe the terms of his contract with Emmalee, she could not help but think of all the money Garn Landar had squandered while gambling and of the silver pieces he'd so cavalierly thrown away. At Torquist's rates, two hundred fifty dollars a year, he'd blown a whole lifetime in the space of an hour.

"I assure you that agreements such as ours are as old as America, Emmalee," Torquist told her, proffering the contract for her signature. "Even in colonial times, indenture was a respectable way for poor, unpropertied youths to make their start in the world."

Reluctantly, thinking of time and bondage, Emmalee signed her name.

"Good, good." Torquist studied her signature, then put inkwell, pen, and contract back into his desk, locking the drawer with a small key. "Now, what skills have you that may be of use as we traverse the Great Plains? Ever drive a team of oxen?"

"No, sir. I've handled teams of horses though."

"Might come in handy. What else?"

"I sew. I've taken care of sick people."

"Oh, where was that?"

"In . . . different places." She didn't want to breathe a word about smallpox.

"That might prove very useful, Emmalee. Now, you must go and find a woman named Myrtle Higgins. She's in charge of assigning people to wagons, as well as overseeing the daily tasks of women and children on the train. She's out in the camp somewhere. Can't miss her, either. She'll be riding a mule or yelling at someone, probably both. And a word of advice. Don't get on her bad side, or you'll have a very unpleasant trip."

Emmalee felt the troubled, unsettling eyes of the wild-maned wagonmaster on her as she walked away from his tent in search of Myrtle Higgins. The nature of his gaze was penetrating but difficult to interpret. It was obvious that he saw her as a woman, and that fact seemed to threaten him. True, if people did not behave themselves on an enterprise as dangerous as a wagon train traversing a thousand miles of raw land, the consequences could be devastating. Self-discipline was required of everyone. Yet Torquist had made it sound as if she might, with her mere presence, cause troubles within the party. That assumption was completely unfair. Yet he *had* accepted her as a passenger, so she had reason to be glad.

I guess Randy Clay was right, she thought. Horace Torquist is a very hard man to get a handle on.

The farther from his tent she walked, the better she felt. Then, scanning the bustling encampment, she spied her portmanteau aboard a sleek black horse. It was tied to the saddlehorn, bouncing rhythmically as the glossy beast cantered gracefully alongside a column of Conestoga wagons. She also spied her other gear in a bundle stowed behind the saddle.

''Hey!'' she shrieked. ''Stop!''

Randy had told her that no one would touch her things, and here somebody had gone and stolen . . .

She began to run after the horse, yelling again: ''Wait! Stop!''

The rider reined his horse to a halt and turned to see who was shouting.

And Emmalee saw Garn Landar grinning down at her from beneath the broad brim of his hat. Around the hat was the band of hammered silver pieces, with one piece missing.

She ran up to him and stopped, breathless and bewildered. The horse was a magnificent animal, the finest Emmalee had ever seen. Its rider, however, looked slightly the worse for wear in the rough, rawhide jacket of a plainsman. A large, irregular bruise discolored his left cheekbone, and there was a touch of blood on his lip, the result of a cut broken open when he'd flashed Emmalee that grin. He looked happy to see her, but surprised as well.

''You made it here!'' he said, jumping down from the horse and walking toward her.

"Of course I did. You had doubts?"

Actually, Garn had entertained some misgivings, and even after diving from the *Queen of Natchez* he'd worried that Emmalee, an unpaid passenger, might have gotten into trouble on the boat. Now he realized that she was fully as ambitious as she seemed and a lot more capable than he'd believed.

"Didn't doubt it for a second," he told her, smiling widely, unfazed by his battered appearance. "First time I laid eyes on you I knew you were my kind of—"

Abruptly, yet not ungently, he took her by the shoulders, swung her into the shadow behind a nearby Conestoga, pulled her to him, and kissed her. Emmalee was too startled to know what was happening until she felt his mouth on hers. He held her very close to him and a delicious quiver ran all through her body. Emmalee found herself kissing him back.

It required as much effort of will as it did physical strength to tear herself away from him.

"I'm glad that you're happy to see me." He grinned as she smoothed her dress and collected her wits.

Emmalee was irritated by his presumption, but secretly even more appalled at her reaction to the kiss. Her breath was coming fast. She couldn't think of a single thing to say.

"Sure I figured you'd get here," he was saying, looking into her eyes, standing so close that she could feel the heat of his body. "From the time we started talking on the *Queen*, I had a feeling you'd be able to do whatever you set your heart on. I like that in a woman. I really do."

"What on earth *are* you doing here?" she demanded, stepping a little away from him and putting her hands on her hips, so that anyone watching might get the impression that this conversation was entirely proper and detached. "And would you be so good as *not* to kiss me again?"

He put on a wounded look. "But that's why I came here. To kiss you. I never got a chance when we were on the *Queen*."

"Would you be *serious* for once?"

"I *am* being serious." His voice, which had been light and teasing in a way Emmalee found both amusing and infuriating, suddenly changed. The words came out like beats on a subtle drum.

"I wandered into camp," he went on, "saw your bag, and knew you'd be around somewhere."

"You just 'wandered in'?" Emmalee responded. She'd noticed his horse, clothes, and battered face. Now she took a complete look. Bulging saddlebags hung from both sides of the black horse, along with two leather scabbards, from which the polished wooden stocks of high-powered rifles protruded. And from a thick leather cartridge-laden belt partially concealed beneath the drooping rawhide jacket hung an unholstered revolver with a barrel the size of a club. Yes, this was indeed a man who might have crossed the Rocky Mountains eight times.

Knowing that Garn must by now have been fired from his job as a scout for Burt Pennington, Emmalee decided to give him a little rope and see if he'd hang himself with it.

"So you just happened to be passing through St. Joe?"

"That's right."

"And it occurred to you to look around for me?"

"No other reason, angel."

"Don't call me 'angel.' "

"All right. What shall I call you?"

"Miss Alden will do."

"Fine with me, Miss Alden will do."

"Ride along now," she said. "Give me my things and go."

"Why? I just got here."

"I'm very busy now. I've just bought a berth on this train."

Garn laughed. "What'd you buy it with?" he asked sharply. "Was that ungainly old joker chasing you down the Cairo docks because you absconded with orphanage funds? Or were you lying to me about that whole orphanage business in the first place?"

"I wouldn't talk about lying if I were you," Emmalee responded. "I know you were supposed to work for Burt Pennington. I know you arrived here in St. Joe late . . ."

"That would never have happened if I hadn't tried to impress you at the roulette table."

". . . and I also know that Pennington *fired* you, so there!"

Garn's black eyes widened. "You know all that? Miss Alden, you continue to surprise me. I figured that, with luck, you might get as far as St. Joe. But if you plan on traveling across the Great Plains, you're going to need my help. So since I'm here I'll just sign on as a scout for Horace Torquist."

Emmalee laughed, trying to sound brave and nonchalant. But she was beginning to understand, from the things she'd heard, that passage overland might prove more difficult than she'd anticipated.

"You don't think you need my help?" He grinned.

"Thank you, no. But that's not what made me laugh. You see, I've just come from a meeting with Mr. Torquist, and I don't think you'll quite fit into his plans. You're not the kind of man he's looking for."

"He may not know it yet, but I'm exactly the kind of man he desperately needs."

"It seems that you figure *everybody* needs you, don't you?"

"Well now, since you seem to know so much about it, what kind of man *is* he looking for?"

"Mr. Torquist wants men *and* women who are *responsible* and *respectful* and of *high moral character*."

"I couldn't be described more succinctly. Torquist took you on just because you happen to have the same virtues?"

"Well . . . no." Emmalee faltered. "That is, not exactly. I made an agreement with him. . . ."

"You don't seem too happy about it. What were the terms of agreement?"

"Actually, it's a fairly standard thing. In return for passage, I agreed to work for him. For two years."

"What?" cried Garn, astounded. "You signed away two years of your life?"

"It's not that bad," she told Garn. "I can buy myself out of the agreement for five hundred dollars."

He seemed relieved. "Look," he said readily, reaching into his pocket, "let me give you the money. You got yourself into a no-good deal."

He pulled out a thick wad of greenbacks, wet his thumb, and started to peel off twenty-dollar bills, one by one. Emmalee was, once again, astounded by all the cash, and as Garn bent over his counting, she noticed again the band of silver discs around his hat.

"How did you get your hatband back?" Emmalee asked him suspiciously. "When you jumped from the deck of the *Queen*, you were broke, weren't you?"

Garn stopped counting and looked at her. The cut on his lip reopened when he smiled. "A resourceful man—or woman, possibly—is always rich. The morning after that incident in the *Queen*'s casino, I managed to win a few games of poker in a Cairo saloon. Then I bought passage on the next steamer for Hannibal, where I boarded the *Queen* and politely requested a return of my money and silver."

"So that's where you got beaten up?"

"To some extent, angel . . . forgive me, Miss Alden

will do. But I sure won't be having any more altercations with Brutus, and I have my hatband back . . . minus a piece of silver, of course."

Emmalee looked at the one vacant section on that strikingly extravagant hatband and felt guilty, both for having accepted the silver from him and for having exchanged it for money. Now he was offering her a handful of bills.

"Take the money," he said. "Buy your way out of the contract now. Pay me back whenever you can, or don't pay me back at all."

"And what would you expect me to do in return for this 'gift' of yours?" Emmalee asked.

"What would I *expect* of you? Why, nothing that you aren't already prepared to give me."

"You misjudge me greatly, sir."

"Sir? *Sir?* I thought we were friends."

"Keep your money," Emmalee pronounced, drawing herself up to her full five feet seven inches and assuming as dignified a stance as she could manage. "I have been prepared from the start to make my own way, and that is what I shall do."

Garn looked genuinely startled for a moment, an expression quickly replaced by an intelligent assessment of the young woman who stood, shoulders back, chin up, and lovely chest out before him.

"So you weren't kidding after all," he said. "I didn't think so, but you can see that I wanted to be sure."

"All you wanted," Emmalee said to Garn, uneasily conscious of the appraising way his eyes were moving from her breasts to her mouth to her eyes and back to her breasts again in a way that raised heat in her body, "all you wanted was a feather to stick in that empty place in your hatband!"

Garn put the bills back into his pocket and smiled broadly, leaving a scarlet touch of blood on an incisor.

"No, Miss Alden," he said, his magnificient voice turned too tender now to be believed, "no, that may have been what I thought I wanted at first, but now I *must* have you."

"Lord, spare me!" Emmalee said. Thank God Horace Torquist was the manner of man he was; he would never accept onto his train a cavalier desperado like Garn.

"Just remember, Miss Alden," Garn was saying as he took her gear from the back of his black horse, "it's the prerogative of each of us to decide what we want."

"That is *very* true," Emmalee agreed.

"And when I decide what that is, I go after it. If somebody takes it away from me"—he touched his silver hatband—"well, I make it a point to get it back."

"I'm so glad," said Emmalee.

Garn handed Emmalee her portmanteau. "You're different, Emmalee," he told her. "Really different. That's why I'm going to protect you on the trail from Indians and bandits and your own stubbornness."

"Thank you so much, Mr. Landar," she replied crisply, taking her gear from him. "Just watch out for yourself. That ought to keep you busy enough. Now, good-bye."

Garn mounted, tipped his hat, and cantered off easily on the elegant black, passing on his way a long, rangy woman with a thin face, a wispy gray bun of hair, and hooded, clever eyes. The woman rode up to Emmalee and looked down from her stolid mule.

"You're the Alden girl, ain'tcha? I'm Myrtle Higgins. Come along. I got work for you. And, by the way, what the hell was *that* all about? Who was that young fellow you were jawin' with? I ain't seen him around."

"His name is Garn Landar."

"Hmmm. Handsome-looking man. What'd he want?"

"Well, I signed a contract with Mr. Torquist—"

"Yeah, so I heard."

"And Mr. Landar wanted to give me money to buy myself out of it."

Myrtle Higgins shrugged. "I saw all that cash he was offering you. Thought it might be another kind of deal entirely."

"Never! I'm not that kind of a . . . person."

"Hmmm."

"I'm going to make my way on my own. I've learned that it's the only way to be certain that I control my own life. I wouldn't let a man like . . . like Garn Landar maneuver me into a situation where I'd be beholden to him."

"Sure, sure," said Myrtle Higgins.

"Why, to have taken Garn Landar's money would have been like *selling* myself," Emmalee raged. "And he's the type of man who just loves having everything he wants, having things his way."

"Maybe he just fancies you," Myrtle suggested.

"I'm *not* going to sell myself," Emmalee declared again.

"But honey," said Myrtle Higgins, gesturing toward Horace Torquist's tent in the distance, in front of which Garn Landar's black horse was tethered, "but honey, ain't that exactly what you've already gone and done?"

Emmalee had no answer.

"Sure is a prime piece of stallion," Myrtle said.

"What? Oh, yes, an excellent horse."

"I'm talkin' about Garn Landar," Myrtle said.

Sea of Grass

The Torquist train rolled out of St. Joe, Missouri, on May 8, 1868, wagon after wagon after wagon, and struck off upon the grassy heart of the windswept Kansas plains. All morning long citizens of the town waved, calling God-speed and farewell as the slow column passed, exuberantly but solemnly too, down Market Street and westward: 178 Conestoga wagons, 311 horses, 256 oxen, 88 head of dairy cattle, 29 dogs, 424 people. The Torquist company was not particularly large. Burt Pennngton's train, which had departed two days earlier, was almost twice as big, and raised a mighty cloud of dust that could be seen, swirling like a pillar of smoke, against the western sky. That cloud of dust was Torquist's constant goad and bane; in order to overtake it, he drove his people hard, and drove himself harder.

Everyone had known that the trek would not be easy, yet all were stunned at the random suddenness with which life and nature attacked their high dreams of destiny. The tall, sweet grass bent flat and died beneath wheel and hoof. Dust of dry earth, fine as powder, rose into the air and settled down upon the travelers, coating eyelids, lining nostrils of men and animals alike, forming a constant rind of grit around their panting mouths. The water wagon, driven by diligent but excitable Lambert Strep of Tennessee, was mobbed all the time, until Torquist, fearing a depletion of the precious supply, decreed strict rationing and made it stick by the force of his will. Thirst never ceased, nor did dust, and after a day on the trail, horses and oxen and men were coated with whitish-gray powder. The once-white canvases of the Conestogas, rippling, billowing in the wind, were coated too, and from a distance, in spite of the sunlight, it appeared as if a procession of ghosts and ghostly wagons had set out upon a journey into disintegration and shadowy nothingness.

The first horse collapsed thirty-seven miles outside St. Joe. Horace Torquist shot the floundering beast between the eyes, cursing ill luck. He and a half-dozen other men dragged the dead animal to the side of the trail and set to work cutting hide from the carcass, cutting horseflesh into thin strips for drying. The trail to Olympia, across Kansas, Colorado, and the Rockies, was long, hard, and unpredictable, and edible meat of whatever kind could not be discarded. Horseflesh, salted and dried, tasted like beef jerky, except that it was slightly sweeter if the horse—unlike this hapless beast—was not too old.

The first person died on the eleventh day out of Missouri, a six-month-old girl fallen victim to dehydration and the heat of the ceaselessly burning wind. She was buried in haste, with scant ceremony, beneath thick Kansas sod. The wails of the child's heartbroken parents could be heard all along the line of the train. In time the cries diminished, becoming part of and indistinguishable from the sobbing of the wind itself, and the wagon train moved out once more, past a makeshift cross of wooden sticks.

Emmalee, trudging along beside the wagon to which she

had been assigned, forced herself to stare straight and hard at the tiny cross, remembering similar crosses on the banks of the Monongahela and outside Springfield, Illinois, recalling all the other crosses in the grove above the Mississippi. Death preyed first upon the fearful. It would not get her.

"I'm going to live a long time," she told herself. "A very, very long time. I'm going to make it out west and get land and—"

"Talking to yourself already, Emmalee? It's a bad sign."

Emmalee looked up to find Randy Clay riding along beside her. She had been walking next to a team of horses pulling one of the Conestogas—adults, unless ill, walked in order to spare the beasts additional burden—but he was on his dapple-gray. Randy had been assigned as a scout and outrider, sometimes reconnoitering ahead of the train, sometimes riding up and down the line of march to check up on the progress of the company.

"Here. Swing up behind me for a minute," Randy offered. "Give your limbs a rest."

Emmalee suppressed a smile. Randy was so correct. She remembered how appalled Mrs. Jannings had been when she'd complained of a sore hip once. Polite people did not say arm or leg or—God forbid—hip. They said "limb." Emmalee decided that Randy was really quite sweet. He was probably even blushing under his sunburn.

"Hoist me up," she told him. "It wouldn't hurt to take a load off my legs at all."

Randy reached for her and his powerful arms plucked her from the ground as if she were a feather. She twisted her body in midair, straddling the gray horse, and swung into a position behind Randy. She put her arms around his waist lightly, adjusting herself to the slow, swaying motion of the horse, which smelled of sweat and saddle leather. Randy smelled dusty but vital, a slight band of perspiration streaking the faded blue shirt that strained against his big shoulders. The horse felt warm between Emmalee's thighs.

"Things look a lot different from up here," said Emmalee. While walking, she hadn't been able to see much more than the few wagons ahead of her own and the few wagons behind. But now, seated behind Randy atop the big horse, she saw the immense length of the column and sensed the human dimensions of hope and risk and wonder. These high-wheeled, creaking Conestogas were ships that sailed a sea of grass, wagons that held within their wooden boxes the worldly goods of all who ventured forth upon the sea, crude but sturdy vehicles that cradled and sustained a firmament of dreams. This was a voyage, and a hard one; Emmalee felt deeply proud to be part of it.

"How are you making it, Emmalee?" asked Randy, over his shoulder.

"Oh, pretty well. The boots I bought in St. Joe are holding up all right. So far."

" 'So far' is about as good as the news gets on a trip like this. Or so I'm told."

Emmalee laughed. "That's good. Who told you that?"

"The new scout. The one Mr. Torquist hired just before we left Missouri."

Emmalee stiffened slightly. "What new scout?" she asked. In the frenzied bustle of getting the wagon train ready to roll, of carrying out the hundred and one tasks Myrtle had levied, Emmalee hadn't had the time to reflect very much upon scouts of any kind. She'd simply assumed that the shrewd and suspicious Horace Torquist would immediately perceive Garn for what he was—an irresponsible adventurer!—and throw him out of the encampment forthwith. Also, Garn was violent, while Torquist claimed to be a man of God. Guns and ideals did not mix too well.

Emmalee had confessed to herself, however—confessed

only briefly, and then absolved herself quickly—that Garn's kiss back in St. Joe had actually been quite pleasant. And she'd found herself flattered in response to his remark that she was "different." Well, I am, aren't I? she thought. Making my way west, all by myself!

But she'd also figured—or rationalized—that the touch of his lips had been nice only because she hadn't kissed anyone since Val Jannings last January. It had nothing to do with that arrogant Garn Landar.

Emmalee wondered if Randy Clay thought she was "different" in a compelling or attractive sort of way.

"What new scout is that?" she heard herself asking Randy.

"You don't know? Why, he's the talk of the train! Apparently he showed up just a couple of days before we pulled out of St. Joe and convinced Mr. Torquist that there were all kinds of disasters lying in wait for us on the trail. He also promised Torquist that he'd see to it that we get to Denver and Olympia before Burt Pennington does."

Randy hadn't mentioned the name of this scout, but Emmalee already knew that it was Garn Landar. She recognized without effort the form and substance of his insouciant braggadocio. And she was amazed that Torquist had fallen for it.

"He's quite a guy," Randy was saying. "It's rumored that he's crossed the Great Plains fifteen times. Eight times across the Rockies. Supposed to be marked cards and weighted dice in his saddlebags. And it's said that he had to get out of Missouri on the quick because he killed and gutted some black man on board a riverboat in Hannibal."

Oh, God! thought Emmalee. She shuddered.

"Hey! What's the matter?" Randy asked.

"Just slipped a little. I'm fine."

"Well, Mr. Torquist made it plain to him, just like he does to everybody. The new scout's got to toe the line, or he's out. I admire Mr. Torquist for his ideals, don't you? He's the glue holding us all together. Once we reach Olympia, the ranchers will begin fighting among themselves as they always do, but Mr. Torquist, with his personal strength and his command of virtue, will see us through to stability and success. We farmers are different."

Randy sounded absolutely convinced. Nor could Emmalee doubt the inner conviction she'd perceived in the wagonmaster. The only thing that surprised her was that the rigid Torquist had actually hired Garn Landar!

"You said this . . . this new scout . . . ?"

"Landar," offered Randy helpfully.

"He's promised to get us to Denver ahead of Pennington? I thought the important thing was to reach *Olympia* first?"

"That too. But we have to re-outfit in Denver. Who knows how many wagons and animals we'll lose by the time we get there? Supplies are limited. The train that reaches Denver first will best be able to climb the Rockies."

There was a long silence, during which Emmalee sensed that Randy had not come here to tell her about hardships along the trail. The wagon train rolled along, dust rose and fell. Emmalee, with her hands linked around Randy's waist, felt his breathing quicken slightly.

"Em," he said, "there's a big meeting around the campfire tonight. Mr. Torquist wants everyone to be there."

"Sure," she said. "Thanks for telling me."

He turned to look at her. "Would you . . . would you sit with me? I'd like to spend a little time with you."

There was a touch of sweet shyness to his request. Emmalee was charmed.

"Maybe we can . . . talk a bit after Mr. Torquist is through," Randy said.

Emmalee was more than pleased. She remembered her first glimpse of Randy, the tender concern she'd seen in his eyes on the day he'd accidentally run her down. And everyone spoke highly of him. She wouldn't mind spending time with him at all.

"Sounds *grand* to me," she responded enthusiastically. "I'm getting *so* tired of plodding along beside these . . . these *damn* horses. . . ."

"You ought to try driving oxen if you think this is bad. What else has Myrtle got you assigned to?"

"At night I'm supposed to be a seamstress. Did you ever try to sew anything in campfire light?"

"No, ma'am. I never tried to sew anything at all."

"Well, Myrtle said she might have another job for me real soon. I hope so. It can't be any worse."

Randy didn't say anything for a little while. Then he half-turned, looked her in the eyes, and asked, "Is it true that you signed some sort of two-year deal with Mr. Torquist?"

"That's right. Why do you ask?"

"Oh, just curious," Randy replied, with a rather woebegone expression. "Well, I guess I got to be riding on. Have to tell everybody about the meeting tonight."

He helped Emmalee down from the horse, and she returned to the trudging grind beside the Conestoga. How far had she walked already? A hundred and fifty miles, for sure. That meant a little less or a little more than a thousand to go, not counting the additional effort required in crossing the mountains. Some people, she knew, sneaked aboard the Conestogas and slept as the wagons rolled. Myrtle Higgins usually routed them out, to their considerable humiliation. Well, human beings could stand quite a lot of humiliation, particularly if they got a little shut-eye in the trade-off.

Myrtle Higgins, on her mule, came riding down the line from the head of the train. Emmalee's wagon was approximately in the middle of the march; Horace Torquist's led the way; driven cattle and laggard Conestogas brought up the rear.

"Horace wants to see you, girl," Myrtle announced through the scarf she wore over her nose and mouth to keep out the dust. "Jump up on Ned here and I'll take you up to see him."

Myrtle was one of the very few people on the train who called Torquist Horace even to his face.

"What does he want?" Emmalee asked, pulling herself up on the ornery animal, who kicked out at her and even tried to turn and give her a nip as she mounted, a protest against the added burden it would have to carry. Myrtle slapped it in the jawbone for discipline and jerked the bit back into the beast's mouth, sawing hard on the reins. Ned had no choice but to defer to her wishes, and began to plod lugubriously on toward the head of the train.

"Did Mr. Torquist say what he wanted?" Emmalee asked again, somewhat more anxiously. In spite of all the respect he commanded, Emmalee felt uncomfortable with the wagonmaster.

"He didn't say. But I expect it's that new job I was telling you about. I don't want to gab about what I think, but I reckon, if you play your cards right, there might be a little money in it for you."

"Oh, really?" Emmalee's apprehension lessened, and her enthusiasm increased.

"Don't count no chickens. Wait and see. Bye-the-bye, I met Randy Clay as I was riding down to fetch you, and he looked just about as happy as a clam. Couldn't be that he's meetin' you at the campfire tonight, could it?"

"Oh, I doubt that."

Myrtle snorted derisively. "You know," she said, "I ain't much to look at anymore, but I wasn't all that bad, so quite a bunch of men were wise enough to tell me, and

I was even your age once. But don't you think you have a chip on your shoulder?''

''Myrtle, I don't know what you're talking about.''

''You don't. Then you're in worse shape than I figured. You think you're all alone in the world, or what? There's men on the train complainin' that you won't even give 'em the time of day.''

''That's not true. I try to be polite to everyone. And as for being alone, well, I guess I am. I've had a pretty hard time. . . .''

''Sure. About your pa and ma dyin' and all. Well, I'm sorry. But you know young Randy Clay has eyes for you. I figure he's gonna do more than all right for himself when we get to Olympia, claim land, and get settled.''

''I know that, but—''

''And there's this scout who signed on. . . .''

''Garn Landar? Myrtle, never! You have no idea what he's like!''

''Do you?''

''I certainly do. Do *you*?''

''Well, not hardly. I don't claim to. But what I'm tryin' to tell you is that it don't hurt to give these things a look-see. Don't be so fast to say no, even if the horse looks like it can't go the mile, get my drift? Things look a damn sight different at my age than at yours. Keep it in mind. Bein' alone in this world is no picnic.''

''I guess I've had to learn to be.''

''Sure. I understand that. But keep your options open. You know, when I was about your age, this was in Indiana, I had me a choice. There was Sven, this really fine man, honest as the day is long, owned his own farm, and everybody liked him. And there was William, worked as a clerk in the county courthouse and read law on the side. Girl, he was a man with words, sharp as a whip, he could talk your petticoats off. They was both of them madly in love with me."

"What did you do?"

"I anguished and I agonized; I agonized and I prayed. Sven or William, William or Sven."

"Which one did you finally choose?"

"Neither. Sven got tired of waitin' an' got hitched to Sally Bundrem from South Bend. Got him a huge farm and seventeen grandkids now. William, he went on to be elected governor and married a rich girl from Memphis. Later on I married a real charming charlatan who gambled most of his money away, and what he didn't gamble he drank away. Died two years ago. That's why I'm here, to start over. Oh, he was a sweetheart in some ways, but I lost a better life because I didn't make a choice."

"Well, I'll be sure to keep that in mind," said Emmalee.

They were catching up to Torquist's wagon now, and Emmalee could see him leaning forward in the wagon seat, his very posture suggesting a vast, implacable impatience.

"There you are, Emmalee," he called. "Climb up here next to me for a minute, would you?"

Myrtle swung the mule in close to the wagonmaster's Conestoga. Emmalee grabbed hold of the seat and pulled herself onto the moving vehicle. Torquist lent her a hand.

"Thanks, Myrtle," Emmalee called, as the old woman turned the mule and rode away.

"Well, Emmalee," said Torquist. "You're a little bit dusty but otherwise no worse for the wear."

Even Torquist had to face the dust raised by his own horses. But being first in the column had distinct advantages. Across the Great Plains, Emmalee could see the swirling dust of the Pennington train. And far out ahead of the Torquist company she saw the scouts riding. Garn would be among them. He breathed less dust than Torquist. Emmalee indulged herself in a moment of resentment.

Scouts also got extra rations. Garn! A man like that always found a quick, cheap easy way to get a better deal than anybody else!

"You'll recall our conversation in the tent, Emmalee?" Horace Torquist was asking. "I inquired if you'd had any experience that might prove useful to us and you said you'd taken care of sick people?"

"Yes, sir."

"The reason I bring it up is because, riding in the wagon just behind us, there's an old acquaintance of mine from Galena, Ohio, days, Ebenezer Creel. He and his wife joined the train late, and for tragic reasons, I'm afraid. She's very ill, and they hope that the clean, pure air of Olympia will help her to get better. At any rate, Ebenezer is too old to take care of her all the time, and I want you to do it."

Torquist was not asking her; he was telling her. Emmalee wondered what malady afflicted Mrs. Creel. She hoped it wasn't anything contagious.

"Do you want me to start taking care of her today?"

"Thank you, Emmalee. I knew you'd be cooperative."

"Well, I am working for you now," she said.

"Oh, no," disagreed the wagonmaster. "Your term of indenture begins once we reach Olympia. That's clearly stated in the contract we both signed. . . ."

Emmalee recalled, with sharp rue, her hasty signing of the contract. She'd been too distracted by the prospect of two year's worth of bondage to scan the details.

"I see," said Emmalee coldly. There was nothing she could do. "I'll go and make myself known to the Creels now," she began, getting ready to jump down from the wagon and recalling Myrtle's hint that there might be some reward in this new job. She wondered now just what Myrtle had meant.

"Hold on just a second!" cried Torquist, interrupting

her and grabbing her shoulder before she had a chance to leave the wagon. "Can you make out what's going on up there?"

Emmalee followed his eyes. Up ahead on the green, rolling Kansas prairie, the mounted band of scouts was galloping back toward the wagon train.

"Looks like the scouts are heading back this way," Emmalee replied. She felt faintly excited. For a moment, she thought that her reaction was due to the prospect of something interesting or unusual about to happen. Then she realized that she was anticipating a glimpse of Garn Landar. *You've grown dull-witted marching along with this train,* she scolded herself. *Don't be a silly goose.*

The scouts came riding hard and reined their prancing mounts to a walk alongside their boss's wagon. The glossy flanks of the beasts rippled and quivered. Emmalee studied the scouts with interest: four hard, lean men whose eyes held few illusions. Their job was to keep wagon trains safe, and to do so they'd have to survive innumerable crossings of the Great Plains. Those treks had taken their toll: The scouts were flinty and cold-blooded.

Randy Clay, who sometimes rode with them, was not present. Neither was Garn Landar.

"What is it, men?" asked Torquist, betraying a touch of anxiety. This was unusual for him. In order to keep his followers calm, he invariably projected an air of paternal confidence.

One of the scouts spat out a greasy brown streak of tobacco juice and pointed toward the horizon.

"Burt Pennington and his train've swung north off the trail, boss. We can't figure out why he'd want to do a thing like that. It's gonna delay him, no doubt about it. It's rougher country up there."

Horace Torquist, Emmalee, and the scouts all studied that moving cloud of dust in the distance. It was indeed drifting to the north. Since the wind hadn't shifted direction, the obvious conclusion was that the ranchers were on an inexplicable course that would slow them considerably.

"Got any surmises on that, Cassidy?" Torquist asked.

"Mebbe Pennington run into some trouble we don't know about. He could be striking north toward Belleville. It's the only town hereabouts. Still, it don't make sense."

"Where's Landar?" the wagonmaster asked.

"He wanted to ride on ahead and see what was up," said a second scout, somewhat sarcastically. "Could be he wants to fix himself up a deal with Pennington."

The scouts laughed mirthlessly, a hoarse, guttural snicker. Emmalee realized that they did not care for Garn.

"I'm sure he'll be back when he finds out . . ." said Emmalee, without thinking. All eyes turned toward her, toward this inexperienced young girl who was, without apparent reason, defending Garn. She was surprised at herself too. ". . . when he finds out what he wants to know," she finished weakly.

"Yuh!" Cassidy grunted, and spat some more tobacco juice.

Torquist shot Emmalee a quick, odd glance. Then his characteristically somber expression gave way to a look of cautious optimism.

"Well, we'll hear from Landar in due time, I suppose," he said. "But this may be the break we've been waiting for. Pennington is going to fall behind, mark my words. I want you to ride down the line and tell all the drivers to pick up the pace. We're pushing on. We'll discuss our situation tonight at the campfire."

Ebenezer Creel was a crotchety, bony seventy-year-old whose first words to Emmalee when she climbed into his Conestoga were: "So you're the one who sold her soul to Horace Torquist!"

"I beg your pardon?" said Emmalee, startled not only by the old man's query but also by the interior of the wagon itself. Arranged as if it were a small house or cabin, with binlike shelves built into the sides of the wagonbox, this traveling home also had two hammocks, a bureau with a real mirror attached to it, and a bust of Jefferson Davis bolted to the top of the bureau. Likenesses of the former Confederate President had been pretty hard to find since the Civil War ended in April of 1865.

Ebenezer caught her staring at the bust. "So I picked the losing side." He cackled. "So what?"

"Oh, don't go feeling sorry for yourself, Ebenezer. We got other problems now. Is that the girl who's come to take care of me? Bring her over here so's I can have a look."

The voice was coming from a dark bundle in the nearer of the two hammocks. Emmalee felt Ebenezer's dry, talonlike fingers close on her arm as he guided her back into the wagon, which, even at midday, was dimly lighted. But Emmalee's eyes adjusted and she saw Mrs. Creel, piled with blankets, looking up at her.

Emmalee could not stifle a gasp. The woman's face had most likely once been full, but now folds of gray skin hung from the stark structure of facial bones and her pallor was unearthly. She was wasting away.

"What's the matter with you, girl?" Ebenezer cackled. "This here's my wife, Bernice. She's a bit under the weather, but she'll be fine once we get to that good air over the mountains."

Didn't the old man realize—or didn't he want to admit—the seriousness of his wife's condition?

"I'm Emmalee Alden, Mrs. Creel. How do you feel?"

"Pretty tired all the time. But as long as I get my medicine, there isn't too much pain."

"Medicine?" asked Emmalee.

"I'll tell you all about it," Ebenezer said quickly. "Let's step to the back of the wagon."

"You're keeping things from me again," whined the woman.

"Now, you know that ain't true, Bernice. Not a'tall." He took Emmalee's arm again with his bony hand, leading her away. Throwing open the Conestoga's canvas flaps, he let down the tailgate, which provided a wide, wooden platform.

"Have a seat, Emmalee," he said, easing stiff-jointedly down. Emmalee joined him, her legs swinging free over the edge of the platform. Following Creel's Conestoga was Lambert Strep's water wagon, its great weight dragged along by six yoked oxen. Emmalee blinked in the sudden sunlight, noting that Ebenezer appeared quite spry for a man of his years. He wore a white shirt, old but well-tailored trousers, and a wide leather belt of peculiar thickness.

"I like you, girl," he said, putting a claw on her shoulder. "I like you right well. Now, let's talk turkey. Obviously, Bernice is real sick. She's got her a cancer"—he swatted his concave abdomen with his sticklike hand—"down here, an' there ain't much hope. But I don't want her to know that, see?"

"I understand."

"You do a real good job and"—here he fumbled with his belt, which Emmalee now saw to be notched with narrow, pocketlike openings—"an' this'll be yours." He withdrew a piece of folded paper from one of the slots in his belt and waved it under Emmalee's nose. It was a one-hundred-dollar bill. This must be what Myrtle Higgins had been hinting about!

"I'll do the very best I can," promised Emmalee, wondering how many notches were in the belt, and how many more bills.

"All you got to do," he went on, putting the bill away, "is talk to Bernice when she wants, read her the Bible—she likes the Psalms especially—and give her the medicine when she starts complainin' about the pain. It's opium. Got it from an apothecary in Kansas City. It ain't goin' to cure her, but it holds the pain down. It's in a bag in the wagon. I'll show you. Just mix a spoonful into a glass of water and make her drink it."

"I will."

"So far, the opium does the trick. But if we ever get a time when it don't, or when Bernice gets too sick to swallow the stuff, then we're in big trouble."

Emmalee was touched by this hard old man's devotion to his wife. She imagined the Creels as they might have been when they were young, and thought of all the years they'd been together, caring for each other. Perhaps Myrtle Higgins had had a point. Being alone was no picnic, and it got worse as one grew older.

"There's one more thing you have to do," Creel was saying, "and it's for me."

"Just ask."

"You know how Horace is by now, I suspect? He's pretty much a man of the straight and narrow."

"Pretty much."

"Well, I'm gettin' on in years, and I've gotten used to a little nip now an' then. Strong waters is what I'm referrin' to. I promised Horace that I wouldn't touch a drop—that was one of his conditions for takin' me an' Bernice along—but I got a barrel of it stowed on board. Don't worry. I ain't gonna get bent out of shape and scream and carry on. But I am gonna drink it. You got to promise not to tell nobody."

"I won't. You have my word."

"Good. Ain't nobody on this train drinks liquor anyway,

not that I know of. 'Cept one of the scouts. He's damn good company for an old codger like me."

"Mr. Cassidy?"

"Hell, no. I'm talkin' about that smart young feller, sharp as a whip."

"I don't think I know who you mean," lied Emmalee.

"Landar's his name. He'll be around from time to time. But he won't pay you no never-mind. You ain't his type at all."

"I'm not?" asked Emmalee, startled. The elderly sometimes took the liberty of making gratuitous judgments, but Ebenezer's casual dictum caught her off guard.

"Naw." Ebenezer cackled. "Landar's pa was an outlaw an' his ma was a hoor. So I heard. He's bright and tough, an' he's goin' on to be a big man in this country one of these years, like Jefferson Davis."

"Oh, Davis was *splendid*," said Emmalee. "He was fortunate not to have been hanged!"

"Just had bad luck, that's all. He was a great man. I'm talkin' 'bout great men. An' you're the sweet, innocent kind of female who ought to marry one of these farmers on the train, settle down, and have a passel of kids."

Emmalee was a little offended; Ebenezer Creel was reading her wrong. He didn't even *know* her. Who was he to think about marrying her off?

"Now I'll show you where Bernice's medicine is stashed and then you can read her a little something from the Bible."

Emmalee went to the chuckwagon and carried a tin of rabbit broth back to Bernice Creel. The sick woman didn't want any supper at all, but Emmalee convinced her to swallow spoonful after slow spoonful, and even a few bits of broth-soaked bread. Then, with Mrs. Creel asleep and Ebenezer nodding over a tin cup full of *his* medicine,

Emmalee set off toward the campfire, anticipating with pleasure the company of Randy Clay, looking forward with curiosity to the meeting Torquist had called.

During the nights, the wagons were drawn up into three concentric circles on the prairie. A huge campfire was kindled in the center. No Indians had been encountered as yet, and everybody prayed that none would be, but the tribes that roamed the high plains of Kansas and Colorado were as untamed as they were unpredictable. Ten or fifteen or twenty trains might make the passage west with complete safety, with nary a glimpse of the Red Man, and then for no apparent reason, without provocation, the next expedition would be attacked and decimated. The most-feared predator in these regions was an Arapaho chieftain Fire-On-The-Moon, whose warriors crushed the skulls of children, roasted men over slow flames, and carried women away into violation and servitude.

So it was rumored, at any rate. Emmalee didn't believe a word of it. Things that horrible just wouldn't happen in modern times.

Anyway, this was not a night designed for rapine or plunder. The sky was cloudless, bedazzled with stars, and a three-quarter moon rose, slowly bathing the plains and the low purple hills in luminous glow. The hint of a fragrant breeze came out of the west, down from the far Rockies, and Emmalee smelled—or imagined that she smelled—a hint of pine in the very air. She walked softly through the dreamy half-darkness and experienced a formless yearning, a tender desire, that quickened her body as pleasure might and shot her soul through with wonder. She remembered—her body remembered—what it had felt like to be pressed close to Val Jannings in the hay-piled sleigh, and—

"Em! Em, I'm over here!'

Randy. He had washed up and put on a new blue shirt. Without his hat, long blond curls fell almost to his shoulders.

He was seated near the campfire, two mugs of coffee on the ground in front of him. He gave Emmalee one of the cups when she joined him.

"Thought you weren't goin' to make it."

"I had to wait until Mrs. Creel went to sleep. I'm taking care of her. Thank you for the coffee."

"Don't mention it."

"Did anything happen yet?" asked Emmalee, sipping the coffee. It was cold. She smiled as she realized that Randy had arrived early, so as not to miss her.

"No. I heard that Mr. Torquist and the other scouts are waitin' on Garn Landar. He rode off and hasn't come back yet."

"Is that right?" asked Emmalee, wondering what Garn was up to now.

"You know, Em, I was thinking. . . ."

"Yes?"

"It's too bad about that two-year contract you signed with Mr. Torquist."

"Don't I know it!"

"That's a heap of money. You know it had occurred to me that if *two* people were to claim sections of land right next to each other, that would be three hundred and twenty acres. And that'd be the foundation of a very substantial farm. It'd produce a big cash crop."

"It certainly would," said Emmalee, turning to look at him. She thought she knew the two people he had in mind, a suspicion he confirmed when he met her gaze with his serious blue eyes.

"You know, Em," he said, "I think what I want even more than land is a good solid home and a family."

"I think most everybody wants those things."

"Do you, Em?" He was looking at her intently. "Do you want them?"

"Of course I do."

There was no mistaking Randy's intentions. He wanted to see if she shared his kind of dreams, ambitions, desires. And Emmalee did, but . . . but not yet. He was sitting there next to her, holding his coffee cup, half smiling, his physical presence very appealing and even comforting. She liked being with him, felt flattered by his attentions, and, yes, she sensed that he would be a loving husband and a good father. But, she thought, I'm not ready yet to be a wife or a mother. I've barely had time to be a girl, much less to grow into womanhood. A husband, a home, children: These were pleasing but shadowy insubstantialities in a vague, glowing future. She wasn't as ready as Randy for those things, but she didn't quite know how to say so without discouraging his interest in her.

"After Mr. Torquist gets through talking to us," Randy was saying, "why don't you and I take a little stroll out onto the prairie? It's a real nice night. . . ."

Emmalee considered her response. A stroll in the moonlight with a man who looked like a young blond angel would not be hard to bear, and it was a wonderful night. . . .

"I reckon everybody's here who could make it," proclaimed Horace Torquist then, striding in front of the campfire. "Let me discuss with you a few important matters so you can get to your bedrolls for a good night's sleep."

The crowd, which numbered upward of four hundred people, quieted to listen. They were good, decent, hardworking people—the women in bonnets and kerchiefs, the men in overalls or rude trail garb—and obedience to authority was a part of their creed. Torquist, by virtue of will, money, bearing, and education exerted upon them a natural dominance, which they both welcomed and required.

There was Lambert Strep, of Tennessee. And Jasper Heaton, an Indiana farmer down on his luck. Virgil Waters and his wife, Elvira, formerly of Maine, regarded Torquist almost as if he were a man of the cloth. Elvira held their two-year-old son over the heads of the people for a moment, so he could see Torquist there at the fire. Lawrence Redding, the blacksmith, was present, and so were Wayne and Mildred Reed, failed Kentucky pig farmers, and Willard Buttlesworth, who dreamed of founding a sawmill in Olympia to replace the one that had burned in Wisconsin. All these people, and many more, had come to St. Joe from across the eastern United States, and now they stood, past lives cast off, the future beyond grasp, on a patch of the Kansas prairie, their dreams, frail or vibrant, pinned to the destiny of Horace Torquist. If he had "gone sour" on the people of Galena, Ohio, as Randy Clay had suggested, then over four hundred people whose lives had gone sour in one way or another were here with him on a quest to forge a better world, to build a singing dream.

"First off," called Torquist, "I want you to meet our scouts. We had to leave St. Joe in such a hurry that getting to know each other wasn't possible."

The four men Emmalee had seen earlier that day stepped forward, and Torquist gave their names. Red Cassidy and Hap Ryder, J. C. Steele and Tip Mexx. Each man nodded grimly, outlined against sundown, reddened by flickering campfire light.

"Randy Clay also scouts for us," said Torquist, locating Randy by the fire, showing a certain surprise when he spotted Emmalee there too, "and another of our scouts, Garn Landar, is out there somewhere on the plains, doing his job even as I speak. I've called you all together," Mr. Torquist said, "for the purpose of making our journey a success. And, as we are all aware, success means beating Burt Pennington to Olympia."

The people gave a small cheer. They were not the kind, by nature or training, to show emotion readily. The cheer was a show of fortitude and spirit.

"First of all, water is getting to be more of a problem than it was. Until we reach the Smoky Hill River, which should only be three or four more days, there will be no bathing."

A small groan arose, but the wagonmaster waved the protest aside.

"The horses and oxen need the water," he pointed out. "If they don't get it, none of us survive. Also, beginning tomorrow, we will no longer be stopping for a midday meal. We can't afford the time. Burt Pennington, you see, has swung north off the trail into rough country, and this is a God-given chance to overtake him. We'll get first crack at supplies and fresh animals in Denver, and after that—"

Torquist was interrupted by the sound of hoofbeats on the prairie. The sound grew louder and louder—a powerful horse urged onward at top speed—and then Garn Landar came galloping into camp astride his magnificent black. He pulled up at the campfire, reined his horse to a prancing halt, and leaped down from the saddle. The horse gleamed with sweat, and so did Garn. He nodded to Torquist.

"Horace, we better talk," Garn said.

Emmalee saw that Garn had removed his buckskin jacket. His tight, black riding trousers were soaked with the sweat of the horse, and his expensive, ivory-colored shirt stuck to his own sweat-soaked skin. The single vacant space stood out starkly in his silver hatband.

"What's it about?" Torquist demanded.

"If I could just have a private word . . ." Garn suggested.

"This is a community," Torquist preached. "And it is as a community that we stand or fall. I have just been describing the providential boon with which we have been visited. I refer, of course, to Burt Pennington's alteration of route. . . ."

"All right," Garn said, "but the community better

know that Pennington pulled off the trail because Chief Fire-On-The-Moon and his Arapaho are lying in wait for us up ahead."

"I don't believe it!" Torquist cried, as the scouts looked at one another in alarm and the people exchanged expressions of consternation.

"It's true," Garn said.

"Hold on just a minute here, Landar," interrupted Tip Mexx, who wore a long knife in his boot and a longer one at his belt. "Did you actually *see* any of these here Indians?"

"Yes, and so did Otis, the guy who scouts for Pennington. We can't get to Olympia, first, last, or in between, if we're dead. I recommend we head north and avoid a clash with Fire-On-The-Moon."

"No!" cried Horace Torquist. "This may be our one and only chance of overtaking Pennington!"

Emmalee noticed that Cassidy had squared off, facing Garn, and that his hand hovered just above the butt of his revolver. "It was well known in St. Joe that you were going to scout for Pennington. I smell something fishy about what you're saying."

"Is that true?" Torquist asked Garn. "You were planning to scout for Pennington? Why didn't you tell me?"

Garn kept his eye on Cassidy. "A man looking for a job doesn't exactly advertise his firings," he told the wagonboss. "But what I say is true. I've observed Arapaho. They're up ahead, all right."

"He's a liar," Cassidy said, making the accusation that no man could allow to stand lest he forfeit his right to honor. "Me an' the boys guarantee there ain't no redskins up ahead."

Cassidy's hand dangled over the handle of his gun. The other scouts nodded.

Emmalee felt the tense silence of the crowd, sensed also the acute tension of Randy beside her. He said nothing.

She was afraid of what would happen. Garn was young, fast, and no stranger to violence. He would draw his weapon and blow Red Cassidy's head off.

But he did not.

"We've got enough problems as it is without fighting among ourselves," he said. "I've done my job. I've warned you about the Arapaho. They may leave us alone. You know where to find me if they don't."

With that, he turned and led his horse away into the gathering darkness.

"Damn coward," muttered Cassidy, grinning.

"I believe the matter has been settled then," decreed Torquist. "We'll push on. Go to your wagons now and get some rest. But just to be on the safe side, make sure that no one wanders away from the wagons. Not for any reason."

His followers complied, but a pall of fear hung over the encampment.

"Landar won't dare stay around after what happened," observed Randy. "It was incredible the way he backed off when Cassidy faced him down."

"He probably just didn't want to hurt anybody," suggested Emmalee.

"Come on, you know better than that. Why would he let Cassidy call him a liar unless he is one? And a coward to boot."

He was walking Emmalee back to the Creels' wagon. She wanted to check on Mrs. Creel before going to her own bedroll. In truth, she was puzzled. She'd already judged that Garn was different from other men—more recklessly daring than most, certainly—thus his retreat from a situation in which reckless courage ought to have served him well was more than a little puzzling. Once again she had an inkling that there was more to him than he let on, something she'd sensed earlier when Garn had spoken of finding something to care about.

"What if there really are Indians up ahead?" she asked.

"Don't worry, I'll protect you," Randy said. "And, as I was . . . sort of saying earlier, with two sections of land, why, I bet we'd have enough security to borrow five hundred bucks and pay off Mr. Torquist. . . ."

"There are so many things to think about," replied Emmalee.

They approached the Conestoga. Moonlight flooded the area around them, half as bright as daytime. Randy eased Em into the shadow of the wagon. She could hear the gurgle of a cup being filled from the spigot of a barrel. Ebenezer was having more than a little nip tonight.

"Em, whyn't we just take that little walk out on the prairie?" Randy suggested. "It's such a nice night."

"Oh, I don't think we'd better. Remember what Mr. Torquist said."

"Let me kiss you then, Em."

Emmalee held back a sigh. She would have enjoyed kissing Randy Clay, enjoyed it very much, but his apparent intentions toward her went far beyond her plans for her own future, plans that were predicated on her independence. Once she secured her own world, *then* she might be ready for Randy or someone like him. Moreover, he had *asked* her for a kiss. Men didn't understand anything. If she kissed him, after all his hinting around about two adjacent farms and paying off Mr. Torquist and the rest of it, he would take the kiss as a kind of promissory note on the future. Although she had given him no assurances of any kind, he would interpret the kiss as a seal of mutual unity and affirmation.

Anyway, men ought to just go ahead and kiss you if they wanted to. You could let them or you could turn aside, as you wished.

Of course, Garn Landar had gone right ahead and kissed her before she had a chance to turn aside, but that was just Garn. It hadn't meant anything to him.

"Come on, Em!" Randy was coaxing.

He had her pressed close up against the side of the Conestoga now, his body holding her gently there in dark shadow. She felt the evidence of excitement through his trousers, and she felt her body stir in response. A sweet warmth took hold of her then as she saw him bending toward her for the kiss. Why not? she thought, closing her eyes. His lips were gentle at first, and she responded, putting her arms around his shoulders, holding on to him, letting herself drift in easy pleasure. But the spark, so casually struck, flashed suddenly upon the tinder of mutual need. Emmalee felt his strong arms pull her even closer. A shudder ran down the length of his body and transmitted itself to her. He was kissing her hungrily now, and Em was beginning to lose her breath. This was getting far too serious. He might think that she *was* ready for the home and family he'd mentioned. The last thing she wanted was to lead him on, to hurt him. . . .

With difficulty, both because of his strength and because she wouldn't have minded continuing the kiss, Emmalee broke away.

"No, Randy—" she began.

"Please, Em . . ."

There was a sound of movement from inside the wagon, and then from the back of the Conestoga came that unmistakable voice, husky, amused, conspiratorial: "Go ahead and kiss him, Em, and get it over with. People in camp are trying to get to sleep."

Garn! What was he doing in Ebenezer Creel's wagon?

Randy edged away from her. He and Emmalee turned toward the back of the wagon. Garn had stepped down from the endgate and stood in the moonlight, grinning.

He'd put on a clean white shirt, which gleamed in the pale light, and he'd found refreshments too. There was a mug in his hand.

Randy, embarrassed, went on the offensive.

"What were you doing in that wagon?" he demanded angrily. "And at this hour?"

"Mr. Creel's a newfound friend of mine." Garn's voice was calm, rational. "He said I could stop by any time and share his blessings." He lifted the cup slightly, in parody of a toast. "What are you doing out *at this hour*, my friend? Corrupting the morals of our fair youth?"

"It's certainly nothing like that. . . ." Emmalee said.

"I'm a little amazed that you're still around," Randy said, "after that humiliation."

"Really?" asked Garn. "What humiliation was that?"

"Would you two stop this?" Emmalee pleaded, realizing that she was the reason for this unpleasant exchange. Two men and a woman. Bad combination.

"If you don't know," Randy was saying, "it'd be no use telling you."

"As you wish." Garn laughed. "Now, go away and see if you can get Emmalee to kiss you somewhere else. I want to have a drink in peace."

"Let's go, Randy," Emmalee said. "It's late and I have to get to my bedroll."

"Ah! Sounds intriguing," said Garn.

"Landar!" Randy warned. "Watch your tongue."

"Forget it, Clay. Cool down. You're one of these intrepid farmers, not a fighter. You even strike me as a decent man. Let's shake hands and forget about this."

"Backing down again, eh, Landar?"

"Randy!" cautioned Emmalee, who knew by Garn's tone that, whatever his motives, he hadn't truly truckled before Cassidy, and he certainly wasn't doing so now.

Emmalee stepped between the men and took Randy's arm. "Let's go, Randy."

"All right," Randy agreed. "Don't expect we'll be seeing you around here much longer, will we?" he called over his shoulder to Garn as Emmalee led him away.

"Yes, you will, I'm afraid. I've got to protect this train against itself."

"Well, don't you worry about Emmalee! I'll take care of her."

Garn laughed again, low and throaty. He'd enjoyed the whole exchange. "But Emmalee's told me that she's totally capable of looking out for herself," he said.

"Be quiet out there!" shouted somebody from one of the wagons. "People around here are trying to get some sleep."

In spite of her fatigue, sleep came hard to Emmalee. The wagon was close and stuffy, and her bunkmates, three daughters of former Arkansas sharecropper Festus Bent, tossed and sighed and wheezed. They suffered from hay fever and from desperate dreams of men. Emmalee took her bedroll and laid it underneath the wagon. Soon she began to drift away, regretting but trying to forget the scene between Garn and Randy, remembering how her body had felt with Randy pressed close to her. . . .

"Emmalee!"

A husky whisper. She awoke to a hand clasped over her mouth. Her first impulse was to scream, but then she saw Garn beside her, silhouetted against the moon.

"Can we talk?" he whispered.

The first time she'd heard his voice, Emmalee recalled, she'd wondered what it would sound like when he whispered. Now she knew. Velvety and insidious. She nodded, and he took his hand away. She was excited against her will, by his nearness and the night.

"You shouldn't be here," she said.

"I had to come. I wanted to see you."

Emmalee recalled that he'd been drinking, but he sounded perfectly lucid and sober to her.

"See me tomorrow," she said.

"No, now. You gave your time, and more, to Randy Clay."

He was leaning over her. By shifting his weight just a little, he could easily pin her to the blankets on which she slept.

"All right," she said, "what do you want?"

"To make love to you."

"What?" she cried aloud, trying to jerk upright. But he clasped his hand over her mouth again, shifted his weight, and pinned her down.

"You want it as much as I do," he said.

Then he took his hand away and replaced it with his mouth. It was like a shock. His kiss came so suddenly, so surprisingly, that at first she could not resist. She tried to get her hands up to his chest to push him away, but he was close on top of her and his lips were beginning to have an effect, an entirely unwanted effect, on her whole being. A quiver of heat shot up and down her body. His kiss was not hard or magisterial, but rather tender, almost reverent, completely different from what she might have expected, given her knowledge of him.

The kiss charmed her, dazed her, stunned her. She sensed rather than felt his hands move beneath her nightdress, loosening the tie-string at her throat and slipping the garment down slowly across her shoulders and breasts. Cool night air touched her skin and might have brought her to her senses, rescued her from this great, slow fall into which she was so deliciously descending, but Garn's shirt was open and when the skin of his chest met her nipples she jolted in response to the shock and he crushed her to himself. Her mind was dazzled by sensation. She fought to think clearly but could not. In fact, she could not think at all. Her whole body seemed to be on fire with a timeless flame that kept flashing brighter and brighter but yet did not consume, and she was spinning slowly in a ravished space between heaven and earth. This was truly passion, to which love was supposed to lead, real passion and not childish snuggling in a sleigh or the slow, almost brotherly kisses evoking hearth and home. There was a dangerous power present here. If Emmalee surrendered, she would be lost. . . .

Sporadic waves of heat flashed in her body now, sourceless, questing, careening through her being from one place to another, random tracers in search of a target. In the first moments, she'd tried to escape his kiss, but now she could not. A hot hollow grew beneath her breasts and the very air became thin and rare, rivers of heat flowing down into her abdomen now, and down . . .

. . . kissing him back now, hard, as fiery tributaries became rivers of flowing heat moving toward confluence, then into a great channel of aching need, nightdress torn away, his hands gentle on her breasts, on her quivering thighs, sweet fingers searching to find . . .

"*Stop!*" She moaned, gathered herself, straining, and tearing herself away from the sorcery by which he sought to bewitch her. Emmalee wrenched herself free of him and sat up, pulling nightdress and blankets around her shoulders and bare, tingling breasts. Above, inside the wagon, one of the Bent sisters murmured in her sleep. Across the camp, a dog barked. Emmalee heard two people panting and realized that they were Garn and herself. She slowed her breathing with an effort of the will.

"Why . . . did you stop?" He gasped.

Because I can't allow something or someone to have

such control over me, she thought. "Because I don't want to," she said.

"That's a lie. You've never wanted anything as much."

"Not with you."

"Another lie. We're alike. We're out of the same mold. You need me."

Emmalee was beginning to collect her wits.

"I don't," she said. "And you only want me. There's a big difference."

"How would you know?"

"I know."

"When I first saw you on the pier," he said, "I knew you were made for a man to want, but as I've learned more about you, your ambition, your independent spirit, I've come to realize that you're exactly what I need."

"I suppose I should be flattered—"

"You should," he interrupted. It was the kind of remark so characteristic of him.

"But I'm not. Besides which, you might get me into a lot of trouble here on the train."

They were whispering. No one seemed to hear them.

"Only if you tell someone," he said, with a quiet laugh. He reached out and touched her cheek. She felt herself leaning instinctively into his hand, then moved away.

"Why are you giving me such a hard time?"

"Because I don't trust you. I don't respect you. We're not alike at all. I've seen how you drink, gamble, show off instead of face problems. . . ."

"You mean that business with Red Cassidy?" he asked, laughing quietly. "What would you have done?"

"I'd have—" Emmalee faltered.

"Shot him. Sure, I could have. But then I'd have been run out of camp, if not lynched on the spot, and you'd be defenseless."

"Look, I don't *need* your protection. That's another kind of need you can spare me."

"Oh, angel . . ."

"Don't call me 'angel.' "

One of the Bent sisters coughed and rolled over. "Shhh!" Emmalee said.

"You know what I think I'll do," Garn threatened. "I'll raise a big ruckus, people will come running, and Torquist's notions of morality will force him to throw us both out. Then you'll have to stick with me."

"I wouldn't count on that."

"Or maybe Randy Clay would come running to save your honor. What is it with him, anyway? Can't he see that you're not at all his type of woman?"

"Randy is an honorable and decent man," Emmalee flared. "He's certainly not like you."

Garn drew away from her slightly. His voice was thoughtful and serious. "And what exactly *am* I like?"

"I believe that I've given you some indication of what I think about that, haven't I? You're reckless and opportunistic and irresponsible. I don't think you'd see a difficult thing through to the end, and I'm sorry to say this but I really can't visualize much of a future for you."

"Well, well. That's quite an indictment. Not too charitable of you either. I thought I explained all that to you back on the *Queen of Natchez*. When I find something worth caring about, then I might just reveal virtues more to your liking."

He was deadly serious, speaking without jest. For the first time since she'd met him, Emmalee had the impression that she was close to touching the real Garn, unsuspected until now, who existed beneath that magisterial, swaggering, insouciant facade.

"Maybe I was a little uncharitable," she admitted. "It's just that the way you've acted, the manner in which you carry yourself, well, you don't make it easy for a woman to let down her guard with you. And then there are the stories that you're the son of an outlaw. . . ."

"Sure. I know that one. And you've heard that my mother was a prostitute as well?"

Emmalee nodded.

"Untrue, both tales. I was born in Laramie, Wyoming. My father was framed and hanged as a cattle rustler. The good, Christian people of Laramie turned against my mother and me. I was just a kid at the time. The only people who would take us in were 'ladies of the night,' I suppose you would say. They raised me, since my mother died when I was five."

"Is that true?" Emmalee asked, surprised at his story.

"I may be many things, but a liar is not one of them, Red Cassidy's opinion to the contrary. So you see, with a few variations our pasts are not that different."

"Well, I'm not a gambler," Emmalee said. She recalled Myrtle's story about having married a charming gambler and how it had changed her life for the worse. "I don't gamble with *my* life."

"You've got to take some risks. I really gamble money only for amusement. I'd never do it over something serious."

"Such as?"

"I think we're talking about it now."

Slowly, the moon had been descending as they talked, and now a glowing rind of dawn had appeared in the eastern horizon.

"Oh, my God," Emmalee exclaimed. "It's almost sun-up and I haven't gotten any sleep at all."

In the wagon, one of the Bent sisters awakened, plodded to the rear of the Conestoga.

"Please leave."

"Sure. But I'll see you tonight."

Somewhere on the other side of the campfire, they heard

the rattle of a metal spoon inside a kettle. Each morning Myrtle Higgins rode her mule around the camp and awakened everybody with kettle and spoon.

"No! You can't see me tonight!" Emmalee protested.

"Why not? Are you going to be kissing Randy Clay, or what?"

"Don't be funny. You can't see me at all." She softened slightly. "Unless you do something to prove to me that you're . . ."

". . . a better man than you think I am? That won't be hard. Just give me a couple of days."

"What are you planning?" she asked, suddenly alarmed. What if he killed Red Cassidy as he'd allegedly slaughtered Brutus?

"Time will tell," Garn said.

Fire-On-The-Moon

Three days later the wagon train was camped at the juncture of Ladder Creek and the Smoky Hill River in western Kansas.

Myrtle Higgins did not climb aboard Ned that morning; the banging clatter of spoon against metal was not heard. Pleased with the train's progress and relieved to find no evidence of Indians, Horace Torquist had decreed a half-day of rest. Lambert Strep would spend the morning filling the barrels on his water wagon; horses, cattle, and oxen would be allowed to drink their fill before moving on. Colorado, once unimaginably distant, was now within striking range.

Emmalee rose before dawn and bathed long and luxuriously in the river. She had laundered all her clothing on the previous evening, and now she put on her bright red-and-white gingham dress, brushed her hair until it gleamed like spun gold, and walked over to the Creels' wagon. The train was drawn up in the tip of an arrowhead-shaped pocket formed by the convergence of river and creek. A high, grassy ridge rose southwest of the camp, tall grass green as jade in the shining dawn, and it occurred to Emmalee how cozy and protected this campsite was. Feeling clean and glorious, she wondered where the Pennington party was camping. Their great pillar of dust hadn't been seen for several days. Poor Lottie, she thought, remembering Burt's sassy daughter. What a pity she has to travel in all that dirt!

Drawing near the Creels' wagon, Emmalee heard Bernice Creel moaning in pain. She ran the final yards to the Conestoga and clambered inside.

"Ohhhhh, Em." Bernice groaned. "I'm so glad you've come. The pain is worse than ever this morning."

Emmalee glanced about the dimly lighted wagon. Bernice was in her hammock, but Ebenezer's was empty. And no wonder. She saw the old man lying on the floor next to his whiskey barrel, which was poorly concealed by an old horse blanket. As always, he was wearing his thick moneybelt. After a moment of panic, Emmalee judged that his bony ribcage was going in and out. He was alive.

"Honey, you've got to give me some of that white powder real quick. Hurry. I can't stand the pain much longer. Lately Ebenezer's been giving me some in the middle of the night, but he had him a little too much of his own medicine last night, poor man."

Emmalee took the bag of opium powder from the bin in which it was stored and put a heaping spoonful into a mug of water.

"Hurry." Mrs. Creel was panting like a woman in childbirth.

Emmalee held the mug to Mrs. Creel's lips. The woman drank the elixir in gurgling desperation, then waited for its effect to take hold, grasping her swollen abdomen as she prayed. Finally, she felt the first rush of relief and relaxed a little.

"Ebenezer thinks I don't know what this is," she said, smiling thinly.

"Do you want some more?"

"No. We have to ration it. It's opium. I know. He tells me it's a kind of peppermint to settle my stomach. He's a dear man."

Emmalee covered the snoring Ebenezer with a shawl. "Shall I read to you?" she asked Bernice Creel.

"No. I want to talk to you. There's a favor I've got to ask. Honey, I don't want Ebenezer to know this, but I'm not going to make it to Olympia. I can't hold out that long."

"Oh, Mrs. Creel, don't be silly. You'll—"

"No. Save your breath. I can tell. And I want you to promise me this: that you'll take care of Ebenezer after I'm gone. Oh, I don't mean to wait on him hand and foot, you know, but just watch out for him. He could get hurt the way he carries on."

She gestured at Ebenezer with a limp hand.

"He didn't always used to drink this much, you know," she said defensively. "It was all that trouble he had during the war, and after."

"Did Ebenezer fight in the war?" Em asked. He looked much too old for it.

"He's always had this problem about picking the wrong side, the wrong man," Mrs. Creel went on. "And in the Civil War he thought Jeff Davis and the Rebs would win. We lived on the Union side of the Ohio and almost all of our neighbors was loyal to Honest Abe. Well, one day that Union general, Boris Spaeth, comes through town on his way to attack Jubal Early's troops in Tennessee. . . ."

Emmalee had read of the bloody exploits of "Mad Dog" Spaeth, most feared of the Union officers. "Go on," she said.

"Well, Ebenezer got it into his head to be a spy. He

tried to get news of Spaeth's progress to Jubal Early. Naturally, he was caught. Eb's been in jail till just two months ago. We were ruined, lost the farm and everything. We haven't a cent to our names."

Emmalee wondered how this could be true, since she'd seen very clearly that big hundred-dollar bill. She suspected that Ebenezer had a few secrets he wasn't telling *anybody*.

"It's just lucky that Horace Torquist is the strong, generous man he is," Mrs. Creel said. "He accepted us on his train, in spite of everything. And Ebenezer's enjoying himself for the first time in years. He's taken a shine to this handsome young scout. You know the one I mean?"

"I think so."

"Eb says this young man is really going to go places." Just like Jefferson Davis, Emmalee thought.

"And how *is* Mr. Landar these days?" she asked.

Emmalee hadn't seen Garn since that night underneath the wagon. He had gone off promising to do something that would, in a manner of speaking, redeem himself in her eyes. And he hadn't come back at all. She owed herself a kick in the posterior for thinking, even for a moment, that he'd bother. But she had to admit, too, that if anybody required such a display of personal worth from her, she would have a strong impulse to tell them off.

"Mr. Landar comes here at night?" she asked.

"Oh, yes. He and my husband have a snort or two. Then Mr. Landar goes off to do whatever he does.

"I think he gambles," Mrs. Creel added. "He was telling Ebenezer they ought to roll craps. But, of course, Eb's got no money."

Probably not anymore, if he gambled with Garn, Emmalee reflected. The man was *completely* unprincipled, to try to bilk a self-deluded old failure like Creel, and whomever else among this party of innocent farmers he could gull.

"I'll go over to the chuckwagon and get us all a little breakfast. . . ." Emmalee was saying, when, from the ridge to the southwest, there came a long cry of woe and warning. It awakened the camp more effectively than Myrtle had ever done, and by the time Emmalee had pushed open the canvas flaps of the Conestoga and jumped down onto the ground, people were milling in wonder and alarm outside their wagons. They saw a horseman coming at breakneck speed down the ridge toward the camp, leading a riderless horse by the reins. Emmalee recognized Randy Clay. He was heading for Horace Torquist's tent.

She ran toward the tent, as did dozens of people, and got there just as Randy was reining his mount in a cloud of dust. The second horse tossed its mane nervously. Torquist must have been awakened by Randy's cry, because he stepped barefooted out of the tent, buckling his belt.

"Clay! What is it?" he asked. The wagonmaster was trying to be calm, but Emmalee noted a flicker of panic in his question.

Randy made no bones about trying to appear composed. He wasn't. "J. C. Steele and I were out scouting today's trail," he said, speaking raggedly, "and we . . . and we . . ."

"Out with it, Clay, for God's sake."

". . . J. C.'s dead. He took an arrow right between his eyes. One moment he was talking to me, next minute there's an arrow in his head and he's on the ground, dead. I don't know where it came from."

"You didn't see any Indians?" demanded Lambert Strep, who had raced up in a nightshirt and hurriedly pulled on boots.

"Not a glimpse," replied Randy. Emmalee saw that he was trembling.

"Arapaho," said Garn Landar coolly, striding upon the scene. He was fully clothed: buckskin jacket, breeches, silver-banded hat. A rifle was slung over his shoulder. "Chief Fire-On-The-Moon. I told you."

The crowd, which was growing by the moment as more and more people came to see what was happening, now quieted to a hush.

"But Randy didn't actually *see* any Indians," Torquist said hopefully. "The arrow could have come from some lone brave out hunting."

"Really?" Garn smiled, his voice easy, eerie. "Take a look up at the ridge."

The people, hitherto preoccupied with Randy's news and Torquist's reaction to it, turned and cried out in unison. All along the ridge, from sky to sky, were the Arapaho, hundreds and hundreds of them on horseback, brandishing lances and spears, quivers of arrows and long, curved bows. An army of painted savages poised above the encampment, conveying a sense of ominous, hideous power, but motionless and absolutely silent. Emmalee heard a collective gasp from the people around her, part of which was her own terrified exhalation.

"What are you going to do now?" Garn asked no one in particular.

"We can't fight them," mourned Strep. "We're peaceable folk. We don't even have that many guns."

This was true. With few exceptions—rifles for rabbits, a couple of shotguns for pheasant—the Torquist party was unarmed. Torquist had seen no reason for it. "Our virtue is our armament," he had said on many occasions, "and the Lord is our defense."

"They don't seem in any hurry to attack," Torquist murmured in wonder. "Perhaps they'll just move on."

His voice had spirit in it, an effort of optimism meant to reassure his followers.

"They don't have to do a thing," Garn said, deflating Torquist's fragile hope. "We're trapped. The river and the creek are at our back and flanks. The ridge is in front of us. I couldn't have picked a worse place to camp if you'd given me ten years to figure it out."

His voice had the heat of whiplash and true anger in it now. Emmalee realized how ignorant she really was. Only a little earlier she had been thinking how cozy this spot seemed.

The other scouts now appeared—Cassidy, Ryder, and Mexx—fully clothed, grim, and jittery.

"Hey there, boys," Garn drawled. "Steele's dead, and you've got a little problem up there on the ridge. Which one of you dullards was bright enough to tell Horace to camp here?"

"This is no time for recriminations!" cried the wagonboss. "We have to decide what to do."

But Cassidy, to his credit, took the responsibility for error. "I figured it'd be better to ford the river last night, so's we wouldn't have to start today all wet."

"We might well start today all dead" was Garn's only comment.

The people in the crowd were regarding him in a completely new light now, a wholly respectful light.

"We have to plan what to do," said the wagonboss uneasily. Emmalee, who was close to him, saw pain in his expression, and realized the cost of the effort he was expending in trying to maintain a commanding air.

Suddenly the Indians on the ridge moved, just a slight shift of position. The center of their line parted and there appeared, riding up from behind the ridge, a figure of splendid but terrible wonder. On a pony white as snow, in a headdress of feathers three feet high, wearing bands of gold on his arms and legs, face and body painted vividly, sat a brave whose very bearing suggested ruthlessness, mayhem, and peerless contempt.

"There he is," said Garn quietly, in a voice that did not try to conceal awe. "Fire-On-The-Moon."

"Oh, my God!" breathed Torquist. He stopped, aware that he was displaying not only doubt, but fear.

Then, intruding absurdly upon the scene, one of the Bent daughters, Priscilla, came running up, hollering, "Hey, everybody, there are two dead dogs down by the river!"

She looked around, as if wondering why everyone was gathered here. Then she saw the Arapaho and froze in her tracks.

"I have an idea," said Randy Clay. "During the war," he explained, "when Mad Dog Spaeth was beseiged in Fort Cuyahoga, he made it appear as if his troops had more cannon than they did by sticking stovepipes out of portholes on the battlements."

"I see what you're getting at," exclaimed Torquist.

"And the attackers thought he had more firepower than he actually did. They withdrew. Now, if these Indians were to think we had cannon—"

"But we don't have cannon," said Garn.

"We've got wagonwheels. And axles. We've got wagonpoles."

"I get you," exulted Lawrence Redding, blacksmith. "We'll take wheels off the wagons, and cut wagonpoles to cannon-barrel length. We can grease them black, to look like the real thing. At this distance, them redskins'll be fooled like nothing."

"I wouldn't bet on that," Garn said. "When it comes to putting mental pressure on an enemy, they're way ahead of us. Fire-On-The-Moon drove half a camp to suicide once just by circling around its wagons and, once every hour, shooting a flaming arrow down into their midst. He waits. Until we find out what he wants, the battle is all his."

"Enough of that talk, Landar!" admonished Torquist. "Clay has a good idea and the only one I've heard so far. I think it'll work."

The people, just minutes ago so favorable to Garn, now shifted behind their leader. They wanted to believe that Randy's ploy would save them.

"Women and children to the wagons," Torquist commanded. "Men, begin removing wheels from the innermost circle of wagons."

Emmalee walked up to Garn. She could not help but think of those wildly intimate moments beneath the wagon. Her body recalled the feel of his bare chest against her naked breasts and her mind remembered how difficult it had been to pull away from him.

"Hello, Emmalee," he said to her now, as if that incident of ecstatic conflict had never occurred. "Better find a wagon and crawl inside."

She realized that he probably knew more about the Arapaho than the other scouts, certainly more than anyone else on the train. She also understood, in a very direct way, that his knowledge might be their best defense.

"What's going to happen now?" she asked.

"I'm going to protect you." He smiled, but his expression showed real concern. "Just like I said."

Emmalee was not about to make a wisecrack or debate the issue. Suddenly she was very glad that he was there, whatever his faults were.

"What does that chief want?" she asked.

"Frankly, other than live women and dead men, I don't know what he wants."

"Do you think Randy's plan will work?"

"No," said Garn. "But don't worry. I'll take care of you."

For once, Em did not reject the offer.

* * *

The mock cannon, ten of them, did look reasonably authentic, even when viewed up close. Torquist's men, working frenziedly, had stripped wheels and axles from wagons, fitted them with long, thin, blackened sections of wagonpole, and when they were rolled out beyond the wagons onto the prairie facing the ridge, Emmalee could almost make herself believe that they actually *were* cannon.

The only problem was that she knew they weren't.

Three farmers took up positions, one trio per cannon, as if they were gun crews, and looked up at the Arapaho, still motionless, on the crest of the ridge.

Horace Torquist came out of his tent, fully dressed and confident.

"Now we shall triumph," he declared.

"Mr. Torquist," bleated Jasper Heaton, the Indiana farmer, "A calf musta got loose from the herd last night, an' she's drowned or somethin' down by the river."

"Not now, Jasper. Let us discuss it when the Indians disperse.

"All right, men," he ordered, his wild mane of hair like a burning bush beneath the red penumbra of dawn, "light your torches and prepare to fire."

The "gun crews" were equipped with torches, making it appear as if they were ready to fire the fuses and powder that would propel cannonballs. It was a colossal bluff. The torches were lighted.

Up on the ridge, the warriors nearest Fire-On-The-Moon drew their ponies next to him.

"They're thinkin' things over real hard now," gloated Ebenezer Creel.

Emmalee remembered a prayer she had learned at the Lutheran orphanage. She started to say it.

Ten warriors left their chieftain's side and began to ride slowly down the ridge toward the cannon.

Emmalee caught a glimpse of Garn Landar shaking his head and smiling bitterly. She stopped praying.

"If anyone fires a weapon at these braves," he said, "I'll kill him myself. Do *nothing*, or you're dead right now."

The Arapaho braves rode down toward the camp, growing larger and more distinct as they came. Emmalee saw the fierce daubs of warpaint across their high cheekbones and their bold, proud eyes, black and glaring. They rode bareback, powerful thighs gripping their horses. Emmalee was aware of the arrogance of physical strength: strong legs, bulging breechclouts, iron-hand stomachs, deep chests, and mighty arms.

"Hold your ground," Torquist commanded his "gunners," who turned and looked pleadingly toward him. The gamble was not working, and they knew it. The only question now was what the Indians would do when they got close enough to verify that the "weapons" were phony.

"Don't do a *thing*!" Garn warned again. "Don't challenge them in any way. Maybe they'll take this as some sort of a joke, although the Plains Indians are not noted for their sense of humor."

"I thought it was a good idea. . . ." said Randy in his own behalf.

"You tried," Garn told him. "That's more than most."

"Th-this is it!" faltered Torquist.

The ten braves fanned out, one to a "cannon," and halted their horses. They studied the wagonpole barrels carefully, then looked at one another with contemptuous grimaces that were terrible to behold. A warrior rode up to Mr. Torquist and raised his spear threateningly. The wagonmaster showed signs of coming completely apart.

"He wants the torches doused, Horace," said Garn.

No one was questioning Garn now; nobody else seemed to have any idea of what to do.

The torches, useless anyway, were extinguished; the Indians looked fierce, disdainful, triumphant.

Now the brave with the spear motioned Torquist to step forward. The wagonboss understood the signal well enough, but terror froze him to the earth.

"Get out there, Horace," ordered Garn, and in his voice was a register of authority Emmalee had not heard before. "Get out there, damn it. He's not going to kill you."

For a moment it seemed as if Garn were wrong. Torquist stepped forward and the Indian regarded him dispassionately for a moment. Then, suddenly, the brave's spear slashed down through the air, jabbed at Horace's shoulder. He cried out and fell to the ground. The Indians turned and galloped back up the hill toward their leader, yipping and shrieking.

Everyone rushed out to Torquist, who was on the ground, shaking and holding his shoulder. Emmalee saw blood seeping through his flannel shirt and onto his fingers. She could tell at a glance, however, that the wound was not deep.

"What the hell do you make of that?" Ebenezer Creel cackled. "That there redskin coulda kilt old Horace, but he didn't."

"That's because he didn't want to," explained Garn. "Blooding a man, as that brave just did to Torquist, is a sign that he could have killed but chose not to."

"Why not?" asked Torquist, clutching his wound.

"Because the man who has been spared is already at the mercy of the one who could have killed, and who could still do so at any time."

"How do you know so much about these things?" demanded Randy Clay, with considerable heat.

"I spent a lot of years out here. The high plains are my home."

Myrtle Higgins pushed her way through the groups of people around Torquist, cut away his shirt, and began to apply a bandage. "What do they want, anyway?" she asked, looking up at the ridge, along which the Arapaho were still arrayed.

"Well, they don't want to kill us, at least not yet. . . ." Garn began.

The wagonboss interrupted testily, threatened by Garn's steady and confident supply of comment and information, humiliated by the fear he had just displayed.

"All right," he called, "all right. If they can wait, so can we. Everyone stay calm. Women and children will remain inside the circle of wagons. Men, get to work and water the horses and the cattle. Drive them down to the river."

"Hey, Mr. Torquist, there's Indians down by the river too," shouted little Jimmy Buttlesworth, the miller's boy. He had taken a position high in a cottonwood and had a good view of the terrain.

"What do you mean?"

"Upstream," said Jimmy. "They're dumping sacks of stuff in the water."

Two dead dogs.

A dead calf.

"Poison of some kind," Garn said quietly.

But everybody heard him, and they understood what it meant. The animals smelled that water, needed it. They were restrained inadequately in makeshift corrals of rope and sticks and fluttering pieces of cloth. When the sun rose a little higher and the day grew a little hotter, horses, cattle, and oxen would push through those frail barriers and head for the river. And death.

"The Arapaho can't befoul a moving stream permanently," Torquist calculated.

"But they can do it long enough to cause us plenty of trouble," said Garn.

"Strep," asked the wagonleader, "what's the water situation?"

"Half the barrels full, boss. I was goin' to fill the rest this mornin'."

Torquist surveyed the Indians on the ridge, crossed his arms, forced himself to assume a stubborn stance. The people needed his wisdom, his will. He had to pull himself together. "We'll save a couple of barrels for use in camp," he decreed. "Men, take the rest over to the animals. It'll keep them in their corrals. Stay calm, everyone. I shall go to my tent and devise a plan of action."

Almost no one remained calm. The men busied themselves watering the animals, knowing full well that a few barrels would not long overcome the sweet lure of the river. The women and children debated the kinds of shelters they might create should the Arapaho attack, and decided that, short of a giant bird that would pluck them from the camp, nothing could save them. Up on the ridge, the Indians had dismounted now. They squatted in the grass in groups of four or five or six, eating cold joints of meat and casting aside the bones.

Emmalee could see Fire-On-The-Moon, still astride his white pony, patient, implacable, waiting. She realized how lucky she was to have gone to the river before dawn, and when she returned to the wagon and read Mrs. Creel the Twenty-third Psalm, she was very conscious of having walked in the valley of the shadow of death.

Ebenezer was out telling anyone who would listen what Robert E. Lee, Jeb Stuart, Stonewall Jackson, and Jefferson Davis would have done to these Arapaho, if they were there and if they had half a chance. Emmalee finished reading, gave Bernice a double dose of medicine—the poor woman was as alarmed by the Indians as she was tortured by pain—and sat down on the Conestoga's endgate, intending to catch up on her sewing. It did seem a little silly to darn her heavy trail socks when she might soon be dead, but the activity helped to keep danger from her mind.

Garn walked up just as she was getting a clump of yarn untangled.

"Emmalee," he said, "you sure look pretty in that red-and-white dress."

She saw him looking at her breasts and remembered how she had felt when he kissed them.

"Thank you," she said crisply, squinting in the sunlight, trying to get the darning started.

Garn took off his hat and used it to cast a shadow for her. The needle flashed.

"Ah, you're good at that sort of thing," he said. "Make some man a fine wife one day."

"That's what some people have told me."

"But you're not interested?"

"Not yet. It depends on the man anyway, doesn't it?"

"Well, it does depend a little on you too. But I didn't come over here to discuss a future you don't seem to be interested in. The fact is, we're in big trouble here with these Indians."

"Do you think I'm so stupid as not to know *that*?"

"I don't think you're stupid at all. A little bullheaded maybe, but . . . well, there's no time for that now. We're in deeper trouble than anyone suspects, and I want you to do me a big favor."

Emmalee ceased working and looked up. He was serious. "What is it?" she asked.

He put his hat back on. The silver pieces glittered in the sun. She saw the vacant spot where the missing piece had been.

"Go to Horace Torquist's tent," he said. "I need you to tell him what to do."

"But Mr. Torquist is perfectly capable of—"

"No, he's not. Torquist is an able man, but he functions well only when the world he sees before him matches an idea of a world he keeps safe in his mind. Those two worlds are pretty different right now. Falling apart in front of everyone, as he did a few minutes ago, hurt him badly too."

Emmalee was curious. Garn had, quite casually, rendered Torquist less puzzling. "Why don't you go see him yourself?" she asked.

"It's very difficult for a fellow like Torquist to take advice, especially from a man like me. But there's a chance he might listen to you."

"Even if he does, what do I have to tell him?"

"Pay attention," Garn instructed. "That's what I'm here to talk to you about."

A few minutes later, Emmalee stood in front of Torquist's tent and called his name. After a long moment, during which time she could hear the squeak of bedsprings, the wagonmaster came to the door. He had a faraway, almost distraught look in his eyes and his usually impeccable appearance was marred by a misbuttoned shirt.

"Miss Alden," he said, "I'm very busy. . . ."

Emmalee did as Garn had advised, ignored Torquist's protestation and pushed inside the tent. It was as neat as ever, except that the bed was unmade. The wagonleader had been lying down, worrying.

"Emmalee . . ." he started to say.

"I have an idea that might work," she interrupted, getting it out quickly. "Let's send an emissary up to see Chief Fire-On-The-Moon and see what he wants. You know how these Indians are. They hold themselves like kings. They want to be attended with diplomacy and respect.''

Torquist thought it over. ''I suppose I could do that,'' he mused. Emmalee's heart went out to him. He seemed so fragile in some ways, a mere husk of the man he appeared to be when he spoke to the people. His great dream of a perfect community beyond the mountains was threatened by the Arapaho, and he stood in double jeopardy. In the first place, he would lose his dream; in the second, he would lose the concepts of virtue and rectitude by which his dream was sustained.

''An emissary might work,'' he said in a stronger voice, as if the idea had been his from the start. ''We've got to do something, or we'll lose the advantage of time we've been able to gain from Pennington. Any ideas as to whom we ought to send?''

''What about that scout?'' Emmalee said. ''The one who's always doing all the talking? I understand he knows sign language and even a bit of the Arapaho tongue.''

''Good work, Emmalee.'' Garn grinned, mounting his black stallion. ''If I don't come back, it's been nice knowing you. Enjoy yourself in Olympia.''

Then he was riding up the ridge toward Fire-On-The-Moon. Emmalee could see the Indians get up from the grass and leap onto their ponies, watching alertly as Garn rode toward them.

Torquist and the scouts stood outside the wagonmaster's tent.

''I'll say one thing about Landar,'' said Red Cassidy, ''he sure is a hard man to figure out. It looks like he's out huntin' his own death.''

''I hear he's a gamblin' man,'' said Tip Mexx, poking Hap Ryder in the ribs. Hap had already lost half his pay to Garn in a series of poker games.

"What's this about gambling?" demanded Torquist, tearing himself away for a moment from his preoccupation with what would happen between Garn and the Indians.

"I said Landar is taking a gamble."

Emmalee was standing close to the tent, watching the ridge too. Torquist noticed her there. "Women and children to the inner ring of wagons," he scolded. "I swear, nobody obeys around here."

It was as if he had completely forgotten her contribution to this enterprise! With considerable irritation, Emmalee started back to join the women, then realized that she couldn't bear to miss out on what was happening on the hill. The men of the camp were crouched down behind the outer circle of wagons, armed with pitchforks, axes, and hammers. They were intent upon Garn's progress, so no one noticed Emmalee as she slipped inside the Conestoga nearest Horace Torquist's command tent. It was cool and dark in the wagon. She unfastened a couple of lashing and folded away a small section of canvas. She could see the ridge clearly.

Garn rode straight up to the Arapaho chieftain, holding his hands before him to show that he was not armed.

Arapaho braves on horseback immediately surrounded him and he was lost from sight. Emmalee could not deny a pang of fear for him, and explained it to herself by thinking that she would be just as afraid for anyone in that position.

Then the Indians moved away from Garn, their ponies dancing and sidestepping, and Emmalee saw him, still on his black, next to the chief. A few moments later, the two men were riding down towards the pioneer camp, trailed by at least two dozen warriors.

"I wonder what's happening now?" Emmalee heard Torquist fret.

"Be ready, boys," Cassidy instructed. "But don't go grabbin' for your guns until they make the first move."

Garn and Chief Fire-On-The-Moon reined their horses in front of Mr. Torquist and the scouts. The mounted braves fanned out into a circle around the men, protecting their chieftain, threatening Torquist's group. One brave took up a position right outside the wagon in which Emmalee was hiding. She did not dare to move or breathe. He was so close that she could smell the heat of his body, see the intricate diamondlike designs in the silver armbands he wore. This was an alien, and his eyes were sharp and savage. Emmalee held her breath, no longer disbelieving stories about people roasted alive over slow fires. The circle of braves could kill Garn, the scouts, Horace Torquist, and Randy Clay in the space of seconds.

But they had not as yet made any move to do so.

Then Emmalee looked at Chief Fire-On-The-Moon and knew that her own death, the deaths of all the others, was only a matter of time. The combination of a rangy, sinewy body, crown of eagle feathers, and lean, sardonic visage made the chief more animal than man, a prince of animals perhaps, but savage all the same. He looked down at Torquist with curiosity and a kind of arrogant amusement that Emmalee recalled having seen recently on the face of someone else.

No time to think about that, though. Garn was speaking.

"Mr. Torquist," he said, slowly and with great seriousness, "our visitor, great chief of the Arapaho nation, is here to partake of our hospitality and generosity."

Horace Torquist looked confused. Then he said, "It is our wish to have a peaceful visit with the chief. Tell him that, Landar. Tell him we're peaceable people. We don't even have weapons."

Emmalee, peering through the tiny opening in the canvas, saw Garn turn to the chief. Using a series of rapid hand gestures, with now and again a word strange to Emmalee's ears, he conveyed the wagonleader's message.

The chief snorted, speaking quickly to Garn, gesturing as well.

"Fire-On-The-Moon has no wish to harm us," Garn told Torquist. "But he and his people are very angry that the coming of the railroad, along with the depredations of the buffalo hunters, are making it difficult for his people to sustain themselves."

"I'm sorry to hear that," said Torquist, lifting his hands, letting them fall. "But what can I do?"

Again, Garn and the chief exchanged words and gestures.

"In return for the passage of white men across his lands," Garn translated, "the Indians have decided to exact a fee."

"Yes, yes," said the wagonmaster almost happily, "I have money. . . ."

Garn shook his head. "You don't understand," he said. "The Arapaho want our cattle, in replacement for the buffalo that have been killed. They need meat for food and skins for clothing and dwellings."

Emmalee saw Torquist's face turn pale. The precious cattle! They were to be the breeding stock of great dairy herds in Olympia!

The brave sitting on his horse in front of Emmalee suddenly jerked his head in the direction of the wagon, as if he'd heard something. She felt her heart stop for a beat, then it recovered, hammering away like mad. The Indian relaxed. Emmalee almost sobbed in relief.

"Ask him if there is anything else we might give him," Torquist was instructing Garn. "Anything except the cattle."

"I can't do that," Garn said. "It would insult him. He wants only the cattle. In return, he will leave us alone, unharmed, and let us go on our way."

Torquist hesitated.

Sensing difficulty, Fire-On-The-Moon sat up even straighter on his horse and made an abrupt gesture to his braves, who tensed for action.

Then it happened. Emmalee felt rather than heard someone slip into the wagon. Her poor muscles were already screaming from holding herself motionless all this time, and her nerves were screaming from the tension of the Indian just outside. So she screamed too.

"God, girl!" Myrtle Higgins said.

"What are you doing here?"

"Wanted to find out what was happening."

There was no more time for talk. The brave, startled by her scream, grabbed his knife and slashed a giant swath out of the canvas. There stood Emmalee for all to see, in her pretty dress and with her gold hair spilling down.

"Jesus Christ, Emmalee," she heard Garn say.

I'm sorry was in her mind, but her tongue failed to work. The Indian reached up, grabbed her, and swung her through the air. She landed stomach-down across the back of his pony, so hard the wind was knocked out of her. She was conscious of the horse moving. Even before she'd regained her breath, the brave jerked her upright. She found herself looking into the pitiless, sardonic eyes of Fire-On-The-Moon.

Fire-On-The-Moon said something in his language and laughed. All the braves joined in. So did Garn, sitting on his horse next to the chief.

"My compliments to you, Emmalee," he said dryly. "Arapaho don't laugh much."

Emmalee felt stupid and ridiculous. She was also angry, mostly at herself and her predicament, but also at Garn for laughing.

Fire-On-The-Moon was saying something to Garn. The chief reached out and ran his fingers through Emmalee's hair.

"Tell him to get his hands off the woman," Torquist said edgily. "I won't stand for anything like that."

"Shut up," Garn told him, smiling pleasantly, his voice so mild he might have been commenting on the weather. "Shut up. He's decided that he wants Emmalee."

Fully afraid now, Emmalee tried desperately and unsuccessfully to squirm free of the brave's grasp.

"If this feathered barbarian is so keen on letting us live," she said to Garn, "ask him why he poisoned the river."

"I already did. It is a sign of his determination. If his people do not get the cattle, neither do we. If they do not survive, we perish as well."

The chief had grabbed a big handful of Emmalee's hair. He didn't pull it but he held on tightly and made some gestures to Garn with his free hand.

Garn gestured back, smiling and easy, and patted Fire-On-The-Moon's magnificent white horse.

"What's going on?" Emmalee asked through her teeth.

Garn was nonchalant. "He says he wants you. I told him you're mine. I offered to trade you for his horse.

"His *horse*!"

"Emmalee, if you say another word, I swear I'll cut your tongue out," Garn said, smiling. "And how could you live without it? I just want you to know that it's going to cost plenty to get you out of this."

The chieftain counted his fingers, pointing in turn at his horse, Emmalee, then Garn, who responded by counting his fingers and gesturing too. Emmalee lost track of what was happening. Suddenly the chief grunted, the brave released her, and she fell to the ground, sprawling in the dust, dirty and trembling but otherwise all right. She was sure she'd never get the smell of the Indian out of her red-and-white dress.

The Indians laughed again, seeing Emmalee there in the dirt, but this time Garn did not join them.

"Well, Torquist," he told the wagonmaster, "the Arapaho will let us go without taking anyone or harming anyone. Fire-On-The-Moon holds all the cards, and you're losing time. He could keep us here under siege, if he wanted. You can buy new cattle out west, but if Pennington gets to the best land first . . ."

Torquist saw that he had no choice and yielded.

"Tell them to take the cattle." He sighed, a sad-eyed, wild-haired prophet astride the Kansas plains. He might have interpreted this outcome, unpleasant as it was, as a victory, because the lives and futures of his people had been retained. But his purity of purpose could not abide compromise, which he believed to be defeat. And so Horace Torquist retreated again to his tent, bearing a burden of disappointment and guilt that was to gnaw its way into his soul.

Purple Mountains Majesty

Death at Arapaho hands would have been relatively quick; the summer sun, the seemingly endless trail, showed less mercy. Hot June gave way to torrid July, each day more unbearable than the one before. Pioneers woke to searing dawns, their bodies soaked with sweat, and spent countless hours trudging beside the ever-rolling wheels. They gasped burning air, could not speak for the dust. From time to time great thunderheads appeared suddenly in the sky, to dump hail and driving rain on the plains. When the clouds rolled away, the sun beat down again, turning the rain-water into vapor. Moisture filled the air like steam; it was even hotter than before the storm.

August proved more terrible than July. Emmalee believed that she would never be cool again. Day by day, week after week, the wagon train rolled on, dreaming of Colorado, of icy mountain springs and wind in the high Rockies.

After each day on the trail, while his people made camp, Horace Torquist found the best vantage point in the area, climbed to the top of knoll or hill or promontory, and scanned the horizon. Always he descended in elation, the intensity of which increased as the wagon train neared Denver. Not once did he see any sign of Burt Pennington's wagons, nor the great cloud of dust they raised. To the wagonleader it meant that Pennington had held to a northern route, longer and less traveled, and that he therefore must have fallen far behind.

So when the Torquist company rolled into Denver on August 20, 1868—with plenty of time to re-outfit and all of September to cross the looming Rockies—the wagonmaster and his weary followers looking forward to celebrating their arrival were shocked and crestfallen to find their rancher rivals already encamped, prepared to break camp; in fact, sassy, rested, and ready to roll.

The arrival or departure of any big group of pioneers was always an event. Residents of Denver and members of wagon trains already camped there for re-outfitting and recuperation gathered around the Torquist people as they stumbled disconsolately onto the flats east of the city. Emmalee, riding with the Creels, immediately saw Burt Pennington, Lottie, and Otis, the savvy scout. Pennington's bald pate was brown as a nut from the sun; Lottie looked cool and elegant in a long pink dress with matching pink, patent-leather pumps; Otis wore a sidearm, high boots, and a belt of cartridges buckled around his hard belly. He was chewing on a weed.

"Hey, Torquist!" Otis goaded the leader of the farmers. "You boys might as well turn around and go back to Missouri. Ain't too many supplies left here for you."

"It'll be impossible for you to reach Olympia by the first of October for the start of the land rush," Pennington added cheerfully. "Just as well too. The land beyond the mountains is meant to graze longhorns, not to plow up for wheat and corn."

"We'll see about that," said Torquist, smiling without

spirit. "The only question I have is: If there aren't adequate animals and supplies to re-outfit here, how did *you* do it?"

"Just one of them there lucky breaks," Otis gloated.

"Yep," said Pennington. "We had to swing north to avoid them Indians. As luck would have it, we passed through Fort Morgan on our way here to Denver. They had *all kinds* of horses and oxen and mules. We could cross the Rockies five times with the grub and gear we got."

"I'm glad to hear it," Torquist said, trying to keep up a good front.

Lottie flashed Emmalee a dazzling smile as the wagon on which Emmalee was riding rolled by. "Seems I remember that dress from St. Joe!" she called bitchily.

"Who in the hell was that?" asked Ebenezer Creel in a snarling wheeze. He was riding next to Emmalee on the wagon seat.

"Pennington's daughter."

"Huh!" pronounced Ebenezer, taking another look at the spiteful Lottie. "I can tell she ain't never had to work a day in her life. Don't you pay no never-mind to her, Emmalee. You're a whole lot tougher than *she* is. Although I think you still ought to tie up with a good man who'll protect you from yuhself. Anyway, when it comes to hard times across the Rockies, I'd bet you against prissy Miss Pennington any day!"

Ebenezer was just trying to be nice, Emmalee realized. He was hoping to cheer her up. Ever since the morning at Smoky Hill River, when she'd thrown the whole train in jeopardy by disobeying orders and hiding in the Conestoga, Emmalee had been the butt of jokes, "the girl who almost ruined things for everyone."

"Hey, Em!" Myrtle Higgins had attempted to console her. "You didn't try to do anything but find out what them damn men was up to. That was my idea too. The only difference is that you got caught."

Quite a difference.

Since that morning, Emmalee's wounded pride wouldn't permit her to face Garn. Ebenezer had let drop, now and again, that Garn was "comin' over to the wagon for a little snort," but Emmalee always found an excuse to be elsewhere when he appeared. She was sure he would gloat about having saved her from the chief, tell her how comical she'd looked upside-down on the Indian's horse.

"That scout ast after you," Ebenezer always said. "I reckon he thinks yer avoidin' him."

"Maybe he's right," Emmalee replied ruefully. The trouble with pride was that it was pretty hard to live with after you'd gone and done something really stupid.

Randy Clay had come around too, and he was more than sweet. He told her that what had happened out there on the prairie hadn't mattered. "What matters is the future," he assured her fervently. And he *was* right. But then he proceeded to speak of the adjacent tracts of land that he and Emmalee would claim, and how someday . . .

Emmalee listened to him, appreciating his ambition and liking him immensely.

"Let's wait and see what it's like when we get to Olympia," she would say. Which was good enough for Randy.

"You an' me, Em," he'd say, in his manner that was at once totally direct and appealingly modest, "I just think good things're gonna happen to the two of us. I just feel it in my bones."

"I think so too," Emmalee always told him, but still she had the dream of *her* land, *her* home, *her* life. After she gained those things, gained them on her own, *then* she might turn her attention to other matters. Why did she feel this way? Emmalee had sometimes asked herself that very question. The answer was complicated, comprised partly of her God-given independence of spirit, partly of the trials she'd had to endure after her parents died, and partly of a compelling memory. She recalled, as vividly as if it were yesterday, the morning she and her father and mother had piled their worldly goods onto the wagon and driven away from their little farm in the Pennsylvania hills. They were caught up in a sense of adventure, Destiny sang in their hearts, yet when Emmalee had looked back for the last time at the small, square white house and the big red barn, when she thought of herself at play beneath the lilacs or hiking up along the Appalachian ridges, she believed in her soul that somewhere on the far side of America there waited a place as dear and sweet as that one had been.

Her great journey was a trek from home to home. Once a person had her patch of earth, her piece of sky, *then* there would be time for all the other things.

"Let's wait and see what it's like in Olympia," she'd told Randy Clay.

But Olympia was still beyond the Rockies. This was only Denver, a rude frontier town aswarm with all sorts of people bound for points distant, attempting to scratch from each day just enough to tide them over to another dawn. There were cowboys, employed, unemployed, or passing from one place of employment to the next. There were many Chinese, hired to do construction work on the cross-continental railroad. And there were hundreds of pilgrims and pioneers, like Emmalee herself.

To the west, beyond Denver, loomed the fantastic, implacable Rockies. They rose to the sky; they seemed to *hold up* the sky, bastions and bulwarks so mighty that the heavens could never fall.

Emmalee quivered in her soul and stood in awe before those mountains.

Yet others had crossed them.

And so would she.

* * *

Since leaving St. Joe, the Torquist farmers had lost all their cattle to the Arapaho. Fifty-six horses had died, along with twenty-nine oxen. Three dogs were dead, seven had run away, and twenty-one of the original 178 Conestogas had broken down irredeemably and been abandoned. The wagon train had come over six hundred miles. Fifteen people had died, and Bernice Creel was failing fast.

"I just don't know what we're gonna do now," mourned Ebenezer. He had given his poor wife a triple dose of opium, and still she writhed in agony, biting down hard on a piece of wood to keep from screaming.

The wagon train was bedded down for the night. Last rays of red twilight lanced through purple peaks and colored the camping plain with the brilliant hues of roses and blood. Emmalee stood beside Ebenezer in the cramped Conestoga, looking down at his wife, powerless to alleviate her agony.

"I'll go into town and find a doctor," she said. "He'll be able to do something."

"Oh, God, I hope so," said Ebenezer.

"No." Bernice Creel groaned. She took the piece of wood from her mouth, scarred with the indentations of her ancient teeth. "Carry me outside," she said. "I want to see the mountains."

"Awww, honey," said Ebenezer.

"We've come all this way and I want to see the Rockies, at least."

"You got a right," said Ebenezer.

He and Emmalee unhitched the hammock from its moorings and carried Bernice out through the canvas flaps of the Conestoga, laying her down gently on the endgate. Her body was incredibly thin and wasted; she couldn't have weighed more than eighty pounds. But her eyes were still alive, her mind still clear, and when she turned to look at the mountains, at the last rays of sunlight shining through the purple peaks, the old woman let out a faint cry of wonder and, yes, happiness.

"I have come this far, after all," she said. "Ebenezer, you go on. I want you to go on."

"What are you talking about?" said the old man gruffly, kneeling down beside her. "We're both of us crossing over to the other side."

"Yes, but in different ways, Eb. I have to cross first and go farther."

Emmalee felt a sudden chill in the air, which she attributed to the coming of mountain night. Then she knelt down beside Mrs. Creel, too, and knew differently. She was on the hard wooden planks of a wagon, but her knees were in the sod beside the Monongahela, in the earth of Springfield, Illinois. All over camp, people were talking and working and living, but an invisibile canopy of death was descending upon the Creels' wagon.

"You've been a good man to me, Ebenezer. . . ." Mrs. Creel was saying.

The old man knew what was about to happen, but he did not admit it. "I did my best," he said, taking her hand, "but don't talk like this. You'll only get yourself into a state. We don't want this kind of talk."

"Ebenezer!" exclaimed Mrs. Creel, in a gasp that was like a shout, a cry for help. A paroxysm shook her, as if her body had been seized and shaken by a gigantic hand.

"Bernice!" the old man wailed. "Hang on, Bernice, we'll get you some medicine."

But it was too late for medicine, it was too late for anything. Bernice died with her face to the mountains; the great blue peaks were reflected eternally in her gaze.

Later, as Ebenezer in his hammock slept the sleep of the abandoned and bereft, with the sound of coffin nails reverberating throughout the camp, Emmalee and Myrtle Higgins washed Bernice's body. Looking down sadly upon this withered husk that had once been a woman, Emmalee began to cry.

"I know," said Myrtle. "Here you took care of her all this time, brought her all this way . . ."

"It's not only that. I was thinking of everybody. We're all young once, but time passes so quickly. And this is how everything ends."

"No news in that, honey. You'll pardon me for being blunt. I don't talk no other way. Sure it ends like this. What matters is how you handle the time you got."

"Ebenezer's all alone now."

"So that's what's on your mind? Being alone?"

"Not really, I—"

"You can lie to yourself, honey, but don't lie to me. Everybody's alone in death. But in life nobody is, unless they want to be. Remember what I told you about choices? Life is your time to make choices. After that, it's too late."

They finished their task, sponging the body that had once cradled youth and dreams, love and lust and desire, all gone now. Emmalee found Mrs. Creel's dresses, picked the one that looked best, and put it on the body. The garment was too large for the shrunken woman. Myrtle used pins to give the dress an appearance of proper fit. Then she drew herself a cup of whiskey from Ebenezer's barrel, splashed about an inch of it into a second cup, and motioned Emmalee to follow her.

They sat down in the dirt alongside one of the Conestoga's big wooden-spoked wheels. Myrtle drank and grimaced. Emmalee sipped and coughed.

"Have some more," Myrtle said. "Just what the doctor ordered, believe me."

Emmalee's second sip went down more smoothly. Across camp, the hammering stopped.

"Carpenter'll be bringin' over the coffin in a minute. Funeral in the mornin'. Ain't nobody got much time to grieve. How you feelin' now?"

"Better."

Myrtle drank, smacked her lips, cleared her throat.

"I understand that Randy Clay's thinkin' of marryin' you?"

"Well, he's . . . he's been talking about getting land together."

Myrtle's laugh was a snort. "I don't see much difference, do you? Hey, honey, you should give it some real serious thought. Choices, remember. Chance for a good man like that don't come along every day. Bet I know what's really on your mind though."

"You do?"

"Sure. Garn Landar. You're just plumb flatout buffaloed by him now."

"I am not!"

"Like I said, don't lie to me. First you think he's some sort of a rake, could charm the snakes down outta trees. A gorgeous, reckless ne'er-do-well, and a man to stay away from. Then, when we all get ourselves in a big mess, way out beyond the high-water mark with them Indians, he ups an' saves our arses. And while he *is* savin' our hides, you go an' figure out a way to make a fool of yourself, an' to almost foul up the deal Landar is cuttin' with big chief Fire-On-The-Moon."

Emmalee said nothing. Myrtle was too close to the truth. She was, in fact, right on the truth.

"Why, honey, I bet you haven't even gone over and thanked Garn Landar for saving you. That chief is still ridin' his white horse 'stead o' you because of Garn, you know that?"

That, Emmalee had to admit, was also true. But how was she to thank Garn for what he'd done? *He* was the one who'd told her that he would do something to make her regard him in a respectful light. And he had. But her own ignominy was so intricately bound up with what he'd done that she was hesitant to face what she was certain would be his sardonic reception of her thanks. *She* had been the one posturing as an individual of maturity and common sense. Yet she'd been the one who'd hidden in the Conestoga: a reckless act of bad judgment no matter how you looked at it.

It was dark now, except for the light from a curved scimitar of moon above the foothills. Emmalee saw Myrtle shake her head.

"Honey, Garn Landar may be all you think him to be, or even worse, but you ought to go thank him for what he did. The man deserves that, anyway. You can do it. You got the stuff. I been watchin' you. A lot of people been watchin' you. You ain't been bellyachin' about that two-year deal Torquist made you sign, an' you took right fine care of poor old Bernice."

"But everybody thinks I'm an idiot because I almost provoked those Arapaho."

"Could of been me." Myrtle laughed. "Thank Landar first chance you get. You'll feel better."

"I will," Emmalee promised, remembering the time she'd spent in Garn's cabin on the *Queen of Natchez*. She'd thought she had seen the last of him *then*, with no regrets. She had thought she'd seen the last of him, too, after that intimate night beneath the wagon. But his handling of the Indians, along with relatively discreet behavior on the train, had pretty much set aright the suspicion with which he'd first been regarded, so it looked as if he was here to stay.

Every time Emmalee thought she might have seen the last of him, he kept popping up again, with a wink and a grin and a smart remark to put her in her place.

"Emmalee, I swear I'll cut your tongue out. And how could you live without it?"

"All right," she promised Myrtle again, "I'll thank him when I see him."

"Can't hurt," replied the older woman, belching. "Yonder comes the coffin now. Best we ditch these whiskey mugs."

Carpenter Juneus Peabody, blacksmith Lawrence Redding, and the Buttlesworths, father and son, carried the coffin over to the wagon and set it down on the endgate. Myrtle lit a lantern inside the wagon. She and Emmalee lifted Bernice Creel's body and laid it gently inside the plain, elongated wooden box for burial in the morning. Ebenezer did not awaken.

"I'll stay with him," Emmalee said. "I promised Mrs. Creel I'd take care of him."

When the others had gone, Emmalee put a second blanket over the sleeping Ebenezer. She was just about to blow out the lantern when she caught sight of Creel's big leather money belt hanging from a hook on one of the Conestoga's curved wooden ribs. Emmalee excused herself for being only human, yet she could not help but remember Ebenezer's offer of a hundred dollars for taking care of his wife. She would never have dreamed of taking money that was not offered to her, but she *was* curious. . . .

The belt had about fifty slots notched into its thick length. Emmalee ran her hands over its cool, supple leather and removed it from the hook. Glancing at Creel to make sure he was still asleep, she carried the belt beneath lantern light and slipped a finger into one of the slots, touching crinkly paper.

She thrust her fingers into a second slot.

More paper, crisp and rustling. Like money.

She checked three more notches and felt paper in every slot.

Emmalee's heart was beating fast. If there was a hundred-dollar bill in each of the slots she'd assayed, it was enough to buy her out of bondage to Horace Torquist!

Ebenezer's hammock swayed slightly as he shifted position. Emmalee started and hid the belt behind her. But the old man slept on. Carefully then, she grasped a corner of one of the bills and withdrew it slowly. The numeral "1" revealed itself. She drew the bill out a little farther. A "0" showed itself in the lantern light and a second "0" followed. Another small tug and a third "0" dazzled Emmalee's eyes. She yanked the bill all the way out of the slot. It was a *one-thousand-dollar note*!

Emmalee discovered that her heart was not completely free of larcenous impulses. She held the belt to her breast, clutched the bill tightly in her hand, and studied Creel. Did he count his money every day? Had he really been gambling with Garn? Had he been drinking too much? Might he have become confused about exactly how much cash he had?

Oh, Emmalee. Forget it. You can't do this. And you're always saying how you want to make your way on your own.

But . . .

"No," she said quietly, taking a last look at the money before slipping it back inside its notch. The digits glittered, $1000, but now Emmalee saw, printed proudly across the crisp paper, CONFEDERATE STATES OF AMERICA.

Not knowing whether to laugh or cry, she took all the bills out of the belt. There were tens and twenties, a lot of fifties, more hundreds, quite a lot of thousands, and even two glorious ten-thousand-dollar notes. All of it was Confederate currency. Ebenezer Creel held a king's ransom in worthless money. Maybe it had been his reward for spying on Union General Boris Mad Dog Spaeth.

Emmalee replaced the bills, hung the belt back on its

hook, got her bedroll, and spread it beneath the wagon. She'd be nearby in case Ebenezer awoke and needed somebody to talk to during the night. How silly she seemed to herself now. Bernice was dead in the coffin, Ebenezer was bereft, helpless, and asleep. Yet Emmalee, strong and young and healthy, had been standing there in the wagon, holding the belt as if it were the holy grail, dreaming of release from five-hundred-dollars' worth—two years' worth—of bondage.

Don't even think of doing something that idiotic again, she chided herself. Had the money been real, Torquist and the others would have known where she'd gotten it. Then she'd have been in a jam for sure.

She imagined Garn Landar laughing at her and quickly determined not to think about him.

She slipped into her nightdress, pulled blankets up around her neck—Denver was colder than the Great Plains had been—and thought of the Creeks, whose long life together had just come to an end. She thought of her own life, too, and of the things Myrtle Higgins had told her. Obviously Randy confided in the old woman, clever enough to know that Myrtle, in her own way, would pass along to Emmalee continuing word of his serious interest in her.

A man was definitely serious if he wanted to go partners with you in acquiring land. And he was *really* serious if he was thinking about marrying you.

Without difficulty, Emmalee conjured up a mental image of Randy Clay, with his guileless smile and strong, honest face, his golden, rough-cut curls and lithe, powerful body. The Bent sisters were always mooning over him. Every time they saw him talking to Emmalee, they would hardly speak to her for days afterward. Trouble was, Randy was sort of hesitant. He could talk about land and the future just fine, but dealing with actual feelings came harder for him, and he was awkward at it. Emmalee had wanted to kiss him the one time he'd asked. But his shy streak and his natural reticence, at other times so appealing, in retrospect made it almost seem as if she would have been kissing a favorite brother.

That was your own fault, she accused herself. The body she'd felt pressing against her own in the shadow of the Conestoga had not been that of a man intent upon bestowing a brotherly kiss.

What would she tell him if he worked up the nerve to make a forthright proposal? He might. Soon they would be *in* Olympia, actually claiming the land they'd been dreaming of for so long. What would her answer be?

Emmalee didn't know. She just didn't feel ready to decide, to make such a choice, Myrtle's peptalk notwithstanding.

But if she didn't match his seriousness of intent, assuming he came to her and minced no words, wouldn't he lose interest in her? Wouldn't he have a right?

Garn was a definite problem in this matter. He complicated everything. There was no doubt in Emmalee's mind about her bodily response to him, as if her physical being had a will in rebellion against propriety and good sense. Emmalee found it both irritating and dangerous to realize the sheer physical attraction he exerted upon her, even when she was only thinking about him. That kind of influence had to be watched carefully and guarded against. If a woman could remember the sensation aroused by the sweetness of a man's caress, remember it long after the caress had been bestowed, if she could feel the flow of tender fire elicited by his kiss, wasn't that perilous to her independence? Particularly if he was a man whom she could not trust?

Long months on the trail had afforded Emmalee chances to observe many different people in a variety of crises. And she had learned this: Human beings did not change very much. The bold stayed strong; the fainthearted and timorous remained so; complicated men like Horace Torquist were not suddenly transformed into straightforward souls.

Garn Landar was not about to change either. If—and Emmalee admitted it—if he made her feel like a woman and made her want him as a man, that was just a part of his dangerous charm. A stallion craves the mare, a buck his doe, and the rattlesnake loves to doze on warm rocks in the sun.

Emmalee forced herself to come to a conclusion so that she could get to sleep. *She* had the personal strength to forge a mighty future. Garn didn't and never would. After all, he'd even failed in his promise to get the wagon train to Denver ahead of Burt Pennington. A new adventure might present itself, and off he would go in pursuit of it. Some new girl would come along, to whom he would take a transitory fancy. . . .

Emmalee found it quite difficult to get to sleep.

Harbingers of Grief

Burt Pennington's men, preparing to leave Denver that morning, were busy hitching horses and oxen to their wagons during Bernice Creel's funeral. Cries of "Whoa! Back!" and "The goddamned harness is all snaggled up!" could be heard at the gravesite, absurdly punctuating the dry cackle of Ebenezer's sobs and the defiant phrases of Horace Torquist's eulogy. The old man, who did not trust ministers, had asked the wagonmaster to say words over Bernice's coffin, and Torquist obliged.

"Death is not an end!" he cried, his strong chin jutting toward the heavens, thick hair stirred by the mountain breeze. "It is the beginning of a new life. Even in the destinies of those of us who remain behind, events that appear to be disasters may be filled with hope."

To Emmalee's surprise, Torquist seemed to have acquired a new lease on his own personal hopes. His spirits, so much at variance with yesterday's heavy gloom, puzzled her. She could not imagine what had caused him to regain his fire. Bernice Creel had died, Burt Pennington was getting a head start over the mountains, and re-outfitting the train had scarcely begun. None of these events, in Emmalee's eyes, was cause for cheer, let alone optimism.

Emmalee stood next to the grave, holding a Bible. Ebenezer had asked her to read Bernice's favorite passages when the earth was cast down upon the coffin.

"Many long years of our lives pass by," Torquist orated, "and we view the world from a single window, as it were. But then we become aware that the world is not as we have seen it. So we change. There comes a time when we no longer see as children, we no longer speak as children. There comes a time when we put aside our childish things. . . ."

Emmalee watched him, listening carefully. Some inner transformation or a piece of welcome news, an obscure happenstance or a deliberate act of will, had wrought its effect on him. He was still Torquist of the troubled eyes and prophetlike demeanor. But he was indeed looking at the world through a different window now, and Emmalee was at a loss to know why.

The people noticed it, too, and in spite of the funereal occasion, there was little sense of tribulation, even less of defeat, in their collective bearing. The men were hatless but unbowed, the women bonneted and somber; there was an aspect of victory in their bearing. We are alive, they affirmed in the set of their shoulders, the steadiness of their eyes. We have survived. We have crossed the prairies and we shall conquer the mountains too!

Only Ebenezer showed the emotion of bereavement and loss, sobbing sporadically in the dry, hollow manner of the elderly. But even he stood erect, aware of ceremony and moment. "She made it to the mountains," he muttered now and then. "At least Bernice had a chance to look at the mountains 'fore she left."

Next to Ebenezer stood, to Emmalee's slight surprise, Garn Landar. He looked younger, almost boyish, without that broad-brimmed hat that always cast a shadow over the upper part of his face, an effect that sometimes made his gleaming grin all the more mischievous. Garn seemed sad today. He did not look Emmalee's way, but kept his eyes on Ebenezer, about whom he seemed concerned.

She also found Randy Clay among the people and looked at him until he felt her eyes. He gave her a brief smile but then, apparently thinking of decorum at a burial, frowned and averted his gaze.

"Ashes to ashes," Torquist concluded, picking up a handful of gravel and scattering it on the coffin, "dust to dust. Emmalee?"

Virgil Waters, Jasper Heaton, and Lambert Strep began slowly to spade earth upon Bernice's box as Emmalee stepped forward and read:

"The princess is decked in her
chamber with gold-woven robes,
in many-colored robes she is led
to the king,
with her virgin companions, her
escort in her train.
With joy and gladness they are led
along
as they enter the palace of the
king.
And as nothing are the tribulations
of the desert,
as nothing the woe of dun-colored
seasons.
The world of fallen shields
and rivenings
is cast aside.

And the people rejoice with
their queen, who is made whole
and through whom they are
healed.''

Emmalee closed the book. These words had brought joy to Mrs. Creel and must have had some significance to her, but they carried little meaning for the girl. Kings and queens were hard to find on a wagon train.

''Thank you, Emmalee,'' Torquist said expansively. ''But before we go about our labors,'' he went on, raising his voice so that everyone could hear him, ''Bernice Creel, a fine and loyal woman, would be glad to know—as you'll all be glad to know—that I have been able to make arrangements for all the supplies we shall require.''

Emmalee felt that, had this not been a funeral, with shovelsful of dirt still falling into the grave, the people would have cheered.

''So let's get back to work now,'' Torquist said. He pointed up at the Rockies. ''What are those mountains to us?'' he asked grandly.

''Amen!'' the people answered.

Randy Clay rushed up to Emmalee as the group broke up, drifting slowly away from the grave.

''Isn't it wonderful?'' he asked her.

''What's that?''

''How Mr. Torquist has made sure we get supplies. It's amazing how fortune turns. There are some horses and oxen here in Denver, and he bought them. But we needed more, and we needed wagons too. Well, there's a train here from Indiana that's not going on. They've given up and their people are staying here in Colorado. Mr. Torquist paid them a fair price for their animals and gear.''

''We're still behind Pennington though,'' said Emmalee,

pointing at the long column of wagons that, even as she spoke, was rolling out of the camping grounds.

"We'll overtake them. Mr. Torquist feels that the availability of new supplies, plus his ability to buy them, is heaven-sent. He thinks God is rewarding us for having crossed the plains."

"I hope so," said Emmalee. She caught sight of Garn and Ebenezer heading in the direction of Creel's wagon. This would be as good a time as any to thank Garn for having saved her from the Arapaho.

"Randy, I'd better be getting along to my work. Now that Bernice Creel is gone, I've been sent back to being a seamstress, and there's no end to the things that need patching."

"Sure, Em, sure. But I was just wondering . . ."

"Yes?"

"Well, I was just . . . just wondering if I could see you tonight? Maybe we should, you know, talk over some . . . things."

Randy had gotten up his courage and his hopes, which Emmalee certainly did not want to dash. Besides, after the thinking she'd done last night, she figured it would be a good idea to hear what Randy was prepared to say. Talking couldn't hurt.

"I'll be at the wagon," she said, watching his face light up.

"That's just great, Em," he said. "See you after supper. I got to help Lawrence Redding forge wheel rims all day."

He ran off toward the smithy and Emmalee walked over to Creel's wagon. When she arrived, the old man was sitting on the endgate, drinking coffee, but Garn was not in sight.

"Hey there, Emmalee," Ebenezer said. "Thanks for readin' them pretty words. It meant a lot to me. And, o' course, I can't thank you enough about carin' for Bernice."

He was wearing his big belt, but he reached inside a trouser pocket and pulled out a bill.

"This is for you, just like I promised," he said, holding the money out to her.

Emmalee stared. It was a one-hundred-dollar note, legitimate, bona fide, printed by the United States Treasury Department.

"Don't think I'd keep it in my belt when I'm supposed to be asleep, do you?" he rasped, winking at her. "It's the only one I got."

To her profound embarrassment, Emmalee realized he had not been asleep while she'd been ransacking his money belt. Yes, she remembered that he'd shifted positions, the hammock had swayed. . . .

"Take it, Emmalee," Ebenezer said, pressing the bill into her hand. "You did good work, you're an honest woman, no more curious than most. Take it."

"But you said it's all you have."

"Don't make no difference. When I get to Olympia, I'm gonna get plenty more. Me an' Garn's gonna get right rich in Olympia."

Emmalee defeated the impulse to ask whether he and Garn were going to open a gambling casino or a saloon together.

"Take the money and that's an order," he commanded. "It's yours. You earned it. And you gotta save up to buy your freedom from Horace."

Emmalee accepted the bill. "If you need it . . ." she started to say.

He waved away her offer, shaking his head. "It's yours. Just don't lose it."

"By the way," she asked hesitantly, sticking the money into her bodice, "have you seen . . . ?"

"Landar? Yeah, he went over to see Burt Pennington about something, 'fore Burt left."

Wondering why Garn would want to see the man who'd fired him, Emmalee hurried to the other side of the camping grounds, from which the Pennington train was departing. She'd known it was a huge company, but the actual sight of it moving off, wagon upon wagon into the mountains, struck her with fearful awe. Pennington had all of these people with him. They would be first on line, in the most advantageous positions, when the land rush began. Torquist might be optimistic *now*, but how would he feel—how would they all feel?—on October first, competing with this organized army of ranchers?

She thought she saw Garn a couple of times and called his name, but two other lean, tall, buckskin-jacketed young men turned to her with smiling anticipation. She was forced to disappoint them. Finally she heard his voice—no way to miss that singularly resonant sound—behind a Conestoga. Dashing around a brace of sullen mules, she found him.

Talking to Lottie Pennington.

Lottie was dressed strikingly in a pale-green, trail-worthy gingham dress, the skirt of which ended at the calves of her intricately ornamented western boots. Around her head she wore a scarf that matched her dress and set off her shining rust-colored hair. Lottie looked beautiful, smiling coyly at Garn, one hip cocked to better display the lush curves of her body.

Emmalee wore the sober calico she had chosen for Bernice Creel's funeral. She'd swept back, pulled tight, and pinned up her hair into a bun of mature severity.

Garn's back was to Emmalee, so Lottie saw her first.

"Why, Emmalee!" the redhead called, as if she was her dearest friend in the whole wide world. "It's so good to see you again! And I was *so* glad to learn that you'd reached Denver safely."

Emmalee gaped. What was going on here, anyway?

"Garn, I'm sure you've met my good friend Emmalee Alden? After all, you *did* travel on the same train."

Garn turned to give Emmalee an ironic smile, one corner of his mouth lifted slightly. *He* knew what was going on. "I think I've seen her," he said.

"Em and I met in St. Joe," continued Lottie, with exquisite sweetness. "I just know we're going to be such close, *close* friends in Olympia. Aren't we, Em?"

Now Emmalee knew exactly what was happening. Lottie was trying, with no lack of skill, to charm Garn Landar. She wanted to say, "Garn, don't be deceived! Lottie Pennington is not sweet at all!"

Instead she said, "Yes, Garn and I have met, thank you." She was thinking that Ebenezer had been wrong, or misinformed. Garn had come over here to see Lottie, not Burt. She decided not to thank him at all for saving her from Chief Fire-On-The-Moon.

"What are you doing over here, Emmalee?" he asked, looking boyish and virile and candid without his big hat.

"I was just . . . just walking around. . . ."

"Emmalee did a very nice job reading the Bible this morning," Garn told Lottie.

"Oh, I can imagine," the redhead replied. "She *is* so gifted, don't you think. I wish *I* were."

"Lottie, you have many attributes," said Emmalee, wishing she'd had the sense to bite her tongue.

Garn just smiled, enjoying the exchange immensely.

"Lottie!" called Burt Pennington from the wagon seat of a Conestoga. "Lottie, we're leavin'. Either climb on now or get left behind."

"Oh, I really *must* go," trilled Lottie. "But I'll see you both in Olympia, won't I?"

She climbed aboard the wagon, swinging her behind much more than was necessary, Emmalee thought.

"Bye-bye," called Lottie, waving.

The wagon rolled away.

"Clever girl, isn't she?" asked Garn, turning to Emmalee. He was smiling wickedly, but his eyes searched hers in the old way.

"Oh, very."

Why am I feeling so spiteful? she asked herself. Garn *deserves* Lottie. They're two of a kind.

"You really did read well at the funeral," he said. "Why those particular passages?"

"Bernice Creel liked them."

"I'm disappointed. I was intrigued at the idea of a princess being taken by a king and . . . what was the wording? Being 'made whole' by him? I thought maybe you'd selected the passages."

"No."

"Sorry. My mistake. Just hoping, I guess. I've had the feeling that you've been avoiding me since our little encounter with Chief Fire-On-The-Moon. Gettin' into a situation like that could be a blow to anyone's pride. No matter. It's good to see you've finally come around to thank me for saving you from the chief. Does that redeem me in your eyes? Have I finally done something that is not totally reprehensible?"

"I was just . . . walking here. But, yes. Thanks."

"You don't sound very grateful to me."

"*Thank* you."

"Good. It was a difficult negotiation. Also costly. I thought I performed splendidly. Speaking of which, may I see you tonight? There are some things I want to talk to you about."

"Why not speak to me now? Here I am."

"I would, but what I have to say might take a while. I've got work to do and so do you. See you tonight."

Emmalee watched him stride away, noting the powerful,

fluid grace of his movements, knowing that this, too, was a danger to her.

"I'm afraid we don't have anything to talk about," she called after him.

"I disagree," he called back.

Damn, she thought. I can deal with him perfectly logically, but only when he's not around.

Emmalee was too busy sewing, darning, patching, and stitching to think about Randy or Garn for the rest of the day. At twilight, when cooking aromas from the chuckwagon drifted her way, Emmalee's eyes were fuzzy and almost crossed from concentration and her stomach burned with hunger. Thin strips of fried mountain goat, purchased in Denver, assauged her emptiness, along with fresh-baked bread. There was even dessert, to make the blessing full: mountain berries with cow's milk. Emmalee felt satiated, sanctified. She returned to her wagon—she was back with the Bent family again—to find Garn leaning against the Conestoga.

"Moon's coming up," he said. "Too many people around. Let's take a stroll."

Two of the Bent girls, Cynthia and Darlene, poked their heads out from behind the Conestoga's canvas flaps disapprovingly.

Garn took her hand as they walked away from the wagon. Emmalee tried halfheartedly to pull free of him, but, as he'd done on the deck of the *Queen of Natchez*, he held on. "It's all right," he said. "We're old friends, aren't we?"

"Where are we going?"

"Away from camp. Maybe up there in the boulders on that pine-covered hill. Good place to watch the moon rise."

"What if I don't care to watch the moon rise?"

"You will. It's easy to see that you're a person who relishes beauty."

Emmalee realized that he was working his usual magic upon her. She felt excited, despite her better judgment, for such a feeling, with him, was dangerous. She would think matter-of-factly and dwell upon concrete things. She saw that he was wearing freshly polished boots, dress trousers, and a white silk shirt. He wore his hat too. It seemed different to her for a moment, until she perceived that his headband of silver pieces was missing.

"Wagering again, were you?" she asked wryly.

"What do you mean?"

"Your headband."

"Oh, that. It was nothing. I didn't want the silver anyway. Only a feather to replace the one piece I gave you in Cairo."

"And I'm the feather?" Emmalee found that she was enjoying the turn of the conversation. She ordered herself not to. Badinage like this was one of his tricks. After all, he'd never change. He had gambled away his precious hatband again. She wondered who had it now.

"No, you're my good-luck piece, remember? But I always seem to lose that hatband when you're around."

"Can't blame me for the second time," she said.

He laughed. That was just like him, to treat everything she said as a joke, especially when she was trying to be serious.

"I don't want to get too far from camp," she said, after they had climbed a short distance. "What do you want to talk to me about?"

"Don't you know?"

"You're probably going to tell me that business about needing me, and everything."

"I guess you wanted to hear it. Here you are."

The hill above camp was not especially high, but it was

fairly steep. From the bank of boulders upon which they stood, Garn and Emmalee could see the wagons circled below like a necklace of grayish-white pearls. Denver lay in the distance, a few lights beginning to twinkle here and there as night fell. Garn, still holding her hand, eased Emmalee carefully down from the rocks. A narrow, grassy meadow separated the rocks from pine trees that covered the top of the hill.

"I didn't expect to hear anything in particular," Emmalee said. "From you."

She saw his gleaming, mocking smile. "I'm just curious, that's all," she added. "Besides, you were holding my hand too tightly. It would have made a scene in camp to jerk away from you."

"Must watch our reputations, mustn't we? Torquist could still dump us in Denver for upsetting the innocent pilgrims. Don't worry, I can get you to Olympia."

"Why do you even want to go there?" she asked him. "Are you interested in farming or ranching?"

"No, but something profitable is likely to turn up."

"Just as I thought. You're not interested in anything."

"False accusation." He grinned lazily, leaning toward her. His eyes were warm and sparkling. Emmalee realized that she was smiling too. He was the same Garn Landar, all right, but she felt at ease with him this time. Watch it! she warned herself.

"You've led poor Ebenezer along, haven't you?" she asked. "Letting him think he's going to get rich!"

"It's a possibility."

He was very close to her now, his eyes holding hers. She did not feel like moving away. I'm completely aware of what's happening, she told herself. There is no chance of my losing control. If he grabbed her and pulled her close, she'd be prepared. He wasn't going to catch her unaware this time, nor bewitch her body before she had a chance to think.

"The only thing you're interested in is yourself," she said quietly, still smiling, teasing him really.

"Not true . . ." he murmured, lifting his hand and resting his fingertips against her cheek. Emmalee felt pleasant warmth, but not the usual jolt his physical touch engendered. I've overcome his charm, she thought. I'm strong enough to resist him now.

"What did you want to talk to me about?" she asked again, making her voice crisp and businesslike.

"I guess it can wait," he said.

His lips were inches away. She felt the softness of his breath against her mouth.

"But this can't," he whispered.

Then he came forward the final measure and his lips met hers, a very gentle kiss, hardly a kiss at all, not at first. There was no need to struggle, or to try to twist away from him, because this was different from the time under the wagon and Emmalee was totally in command of her emotions. It was a wonderfully languorous kiss, and in her confidence she even let herself kiss him back. Yielding to that first wave of pleasure felt quietly voluptuous, especially since she knew that she wasn't really going to yield at all. Emmalee felt sensation stir from deep within her being rise and flow. Garn's music surged through her, the symphony of his body and his tongue, and she pressed herself close to him, feeling every hard inch of him straining against her. His mouth sought her and his voice was sweet. "Emmalee, Emmalee." His voice was music, all shimmer and dazzle and glow. The music rose in her body, then in her soul, as he touched her with stunning kisses, pulled away her shirtwaist, his lips upon her breasts now, as with his hands he keyed the fragile, glorious notes of ultimate desire. She felt her skirt sliding away, all clothing gone. Night air tingled upon her bare and burning body. She was open to the sky, the stars, and Garn. He was not forcing her to do anything and so she did not have to resist. I can stop anytime I wish, Emmalee told herself, and I suppose I should stop pretty soon.

Garn drew her down upon the meadow grass, he prepared to take her, she prepared to give, rousing in her yet another tide of pleasure with the caresses of his hand, where the folds and petals of her body sang, abloom with rosy dew. Anytime I wish . . .

"I am the kind of man," he whispered urgently, "who will ask but once for what he truly loves."

She heard his words, but as from far away, dulled by the vast waves of pleasure he was giving and by the greater ecstasy he was preparing to bestow. She felt him poised between her thighs, where she was open with desire, the long, dark shape of his body over her, heard him whisper the one crucial question he would pose but once.

Anytime . . .

"Will you come with me and always be mine, no matter what?"

"*Iiiiii . . .*" She gasped, feeling the shape of him, big as a fist, at the portals of her emptiness and need.

But the words of his question resounded slowly within her consciousness, like an echo: *Will you come with me and always be mine, no matter what?*

Come with me.

Always.

Be mine.

The exclusiveness, the finality of those words startled Emmalee back to awareness.

What was that question again? What had happened? How had she let things get this far?

"Always?" she asked, her voice hoarse and strange.

He hesitated above her, seeming to desire an answer

before he continued. Emmalee was fully alert now. But she did not struggle to get out from beneath him.

"Not yet," she heard herself say. "I don't think . . ."

Then they heard a sound, a scratching, grating noise. Someone was climbing toward them over the boulders below.

They leaped up and began pulling on their clothes.

Oh, my God! Emmalee was thinking. What I almost did! Garn had changed his tactics. Instead of approaching her in his overwhelming, cavalier manner, he had insinuated himself tenderly and had almost possessed her. She had been on the verge of surrender, completely witless. Her flying fingers managed only to get her shirtwaist half-fastened and Garn was still shirtless, buckling his belt, when Randy clambered to the top of a boulder and looked down at them.

"Emmalee!" he cried, his voice full of pain. Then his eyes rested on Garn. "I demand an explanation, sir," he said.

He lowered himself carefully from the big rock and moved cautiously toward Garn, his fists at the ready.

"Don't be a fool, Clay," Garn said quietly.

"I want to know what's going on here!"

"Nothing, anymore," answered Emmalee, her voice tight.

"What did happen, then?" Randy amended, circling Garn warily.

"*Nothing,*" cried Emmalee.

"The lady's right, Clay," said Garn, following Randy with his eyes. "Emmalee and I came here to talk. It was my idea. I take full responsibility. I made her a proposal—"

"Oh, I'll bet you did!"

"—which she declined, and then—"

"And then," Randy interrupted, "you tried to have your way with her, didn't you?"

"Well, yes," admitted Garn, in his easy, candid manner, "but I assure you that the fault is all mine."

"And so you shall pay the price," vowed Randy, leaping forward, his fingers closing around Garn's throat.

"Pleasssssee!" cried Emmalee. "Please stop."

While it was certainly true that Garn had wanted her, it was also true that she had done nothing to resist him. Whatever his motives were, and however honeyed his words had been, he was not completely at fault.

It was too late to explain these ambiguities to Randy, though. He had forced Garn down onto the grass. Emmalee tried to pull the men apart.

But Garn gathered his great strength, jerked, twisted, and tossed Randy into the air. Garn was on his feet instantly, crouched on the meadow grass. Randy rushed him. Garn dodged, swung to one side, caught Randy's arm as he passed, and with a sudden, deft, brutal movement, brought Randy's arm down across his bent knee like a stick of dry wood. The crack of broken bone was separated from Randy's cry of agony by an instant too small to be measured.

"Landarrrrrr!" Randy screamed.

Emmalee was aghast. "You didn't have to do that!" she cried.

Garn stood like a savage in the twilight, his teeth gleaming in the waning light. Emmalee thought with horror of what this man had almost persuaded her to do, just moments ago. It seemed as if she had been another person completely when under his influence. But she had been rescued, if not from Garn then from herself. Randy had rescued her, and now he stood holding his sagging, ruined arm, grimacing with excruciating pain.

"It was instinctive," Garn was saying. "I didn't mean to hurt the kid, but he came at me like a mad dog and . . ."

Horace Torquist, Lambert Strep, Jasper Heaton, and

several other men appeared on the ring of boulders bordering the meadow. There was a look of horror, mingled with disbelief, on the wagonmaster's face as he interpreted the scene: Emmalee disheveled; Randy, wounded in an effort of salvation; and Garn, looking for all the world like the last survivor of a wild, lost race.

"It wasn't Emmalee's fault," Garn said again. "It was mine. I forced myself on her but she didn't really . . ."

He'd meant to say "didn't really want me," but the wagonboss interrupted.

"You all right, Miss Alden?" asked Torquist nervously, as the other men formed a wary circle around Garn.

"Yes," she said, "yes," buttoning her shirtwaist. No, she thought. "Nothing . . . happened," she faltered.

"Get out of here, Landar," ordered Torquist, assuming a stance of rectitude and judgment.

Emmalee went to Randy, who was trying to keep from crying out. She winced at the sight of his savaged arm; a sliver of broken bone had pierced the skin. She realized how deeply he cared for her.

Garn gathered up his shirt and hat.

"Don't worry, I'm going," he told them, his voice perfectly calm and composed. "Sorry, Emmalee. I shouldn't have wanted you so badly. Guess it's for the best that I only ask once. But I can see you're in good hands with Randy."

The meaning of what had almost happened came down upon Emmalee when she returned to camp. All the men had been embarrassed, she herself had been mortified, and they'd had to carry poor Randy down from the hill since it hurt him too much to walk.

"I hope this will be a lesson to you, Emmalee," Torquist could not resist preaching. "You owe Darlene Bent a profound debt of gratitude."

"Darlene?"

"Yes. She and her sister, Cynthia, said they saw you literally being dragged away by Landar. When Randy Clay came to the wagon after supper to talk to you, as the two of you had apparently planned . . ."

"Yes, that's so."

". . . they told Randy what they'd seen. He instructed them to tell me and then he set out looking for you."

Emmalee said nothing. A series of closely woven happenstances had led to disaster for everybody. She felt responsible, especially toward Randy, who would now have to cross the Rockies with a cast on his arm. Yet if he had not come in search of her, she would certainly have given herself to—and been taken by—Garn Landar. And who knew what might have happened then?

But was she better off the way things had turned out? Emmalee guessed so. Garn had revealed his real savagery by what he'd so expertly and unthinkingly done to Randy. A man who fought that well did not have to hurt an opponent so badly, Emmalee reasoned. Garn could have subdued Randy with less violence. It was in his nature, beneath the charming facade, to conquer. A man like Garn was out to conquer women, too, in whatever way he could. She knew it fully now.

Again she had let herself fall beneath his spell. She had almost surrendered. No—*face it, Emmalee*—she *had* surrendered. There just hadn't been time for him to claim the booty that belonged to the victor. She'd lost her mind, and because of it she'd almost lost her body too.

It was something that wouldn't happen again.

"This *has* been a lesson to me," she assured Horace Torquist, who believed she had almost been raped.

"I'm glad, Emmalee. The world is a harsh place. People are cruel. I myself was fooled by Landar for a time. We must watch out for men like him. Nobody is blaming you. A girl who can attract a fine man like Randy Clay is the kind of girl I want standing beside me in Olympia."

"Thank you, Mr. Torquist," said Emmalee hollowly.

"But you *were* with Landar, you know," he chided. "It wouldn't have happened at all if you hadn't been with him."

Oh, true. Hindsight is wisdom incarnate.

But hindsight could not blot out the knowledge that she had been absolutely in Garn's power and that she had *wanted* to be.

He had been thrown out of camp not solely as a result of his own recklessness but because of their commingled passion, utterly beyond thought and raging with desire.

In the final analysis, however, after admitting the depths of her own complicity, Emmalee could not forgive Garn for what he'd done to Randy. It had been manic and unnecessary. Even his charm, even the unerasable memories of the ecstasy he'd given, could not excuse gratuitous brutality.

"I'm glad he's gone," she said aloud.

"Hey! Who's that?" called Ebenezer Creel. "Oh, it's you, Emmalee. How you doin'?"

"Not terribly well, I'm afraid."

"Hey, what's the matter now?"

"There was a fight."

"I hope you kicked the dickens out of her . . . or him."

"No, the fight was between Randy and Garn."

"Garn was in a fight?" asked Ebenezer, concerned. "Garn knows how to kill guys. Is the other feller all right?"

"It was Randy Clay. His arm is broken."

"Hmmm. Got off easy. What was they fightin' about?"

Emmalee fumbled for an answer.

"You, huh?" Ebenezer guessed. "Well, I don't know Clay all that much, but I can tell you that ol' Garn, he loves the ground you walk on. I told him, just like I told you once, that you ain't his type, you're too sweet, but he said you're the one he wants."

"He says a lot of things."

"I know that too. Most men do, when it comes to women. But he loved that silver hatband, and that's what it cost him to keep you outta Fire-On-The-Moon's clutches."

Emmalee started in surprise. She'd known that the chief had asked to have her and that Garn had demanded the white stallion in return. She'd believed that the bargaining had ended in a stalemate. Now she remembered the chief pointing at Garn and counting his fingers. Counting the pieces of silver?

"Yep," said Ebenezer, "Garn had to hand over that hatband, all on accounta you. But he didn't mind."

He never even told *me*, Emmalee fretted, thinking of Garn as she spread out her bedroll and prepared for sleep. Having so recently assigned him to perdition, she was now forced to reconsider the man.

But I didn't know! she told herself.

The whole thing was a disaster and, anyway, he was gone.

She noticed that the one-hundred-dollar bill Creel had given her was missing when she undressed. Frantically, her mind flashed back over the day's events. She remembered tucking the bill into the bodice of her calico dress that morning.

Just before supper, she'd washed and put on a shirtwaist and skirt. She recalled holding the bill and wondering what to do with it. Put it in her bedroll? Keep it with her? The Bent sisters were always interested in what she was doing, so, operating on the theory that practicing busybodies are potential felons, Emmalee had . . .

. . . put the bill back into her bodice.

Which Garn Landar had loosened behind the boulders on the hill.

Next morning, she went up the hill to search, taking care that no one would see her and think her depraved for returning to the scene of what they believed to have been heinous ravishment so narrowly averted.

No one saw her.

She didn't find the money either.

Promised Land

Emmalee saw Olympia for the first time while riding behind Randy on his dapple-gray. The Torquist train had been struggling down the western slopes of the Rocky Mountains for a week. Cresting the last range of foothills on a golden late-September morn, shimmering clouds of mist parted suddenly, prophetically, and there for all eyes to see lay the promised land of dreams and destiny.

There were others on the train who may have seen their destination before Emmalee, but she was the first to cry out.

"That's it! That's it! There it is!" she shouted in jubilation, dabbing at tears with the back of her hand. She could not have been any less exultant than Columbus when he heard the watch call "Land!" and saw from the prow of the *Santa Maria* the fresh green shore of a new world.

I've made it! she said to herself. *I've come all this way!*

"We've made it, Em!" said Randy with quiet joy. He turned in the saddle, a bit awkwardly because he still wore a splint and sling on his arm, and kissed her gently on the cheek.

"Yes, *we* have," Emmalee affirmed. She put her arms around his waist, pressed her cheek against his broad back, sharing his happiness. Since the fight behind the boulders and Garn's subsequent departure from the train, Randy had been more and more forthright in his courtship of Emmalee. She did nothing to discourage him either, thinking that she had finally learned the difference between a man with promise and a man without. He had, as yet, made no direct proposal, but it had become common for the people on the wagon train to see them together.

As the wagon train drew nearer and nearer to the frontier village of Arcady, a small cluster of rude buildings in the middle of the Olympian plain, Emmalee and Randy surveyed their new home with a mixture of anticipation and apprehension.

The setting itself elicited a quiver of elation from even the most skeptical, matter-of-fact heart in Torquist's party—which probably belonged to Myrtle Higgins—and caused in Emmalee a sensation similar to that of a big mug of beer drunk quickly on a hot day. Behind her, to the east, were the purple mountains through which she'd just passed, and to the north rose the rugged Sacajawea range, named for the Indian woman who'd guided the explorers Lewis and Clark through this region and onward to the Pacific. Down from the Sacajawea flowed the twin tributaries of the Big Two-Hearted River, named for the dual nature of its boon and bane: On the one hand, it watered the vast Olympian plain, making the land rich and productive; on the other, melting snow and sudden mountain storms sometimes swelled the Big Two-Hearted, flooding the plain. The lush promise of the land, however, far outweighed the possibility of intermittent floods. The settlers were undeterred by the prospect of disaster in the face of all this natural beauty and promise of well-being. If they could claim land, if they could hold onto it, no tempermental river was going to rob them. Never!

Emmalee felt a flicker of apprehension, though, when she perceived the formation of Olympian topography, the manner in which God and nature had arranged the land. Bordering the foothills of the Sacajawea Range and sweeping down into the valley to the village of Arcady were low, rolling hills and little groves. The hills were covered with jade-green grass, the soil beneath the grass almost blue with glistening vitality, so fine and fertile that not even Iowa's best could compare to it. These hills, bisected by the river, would be perfect for Torquist's farmers. South of Arcady, on both sides of the Big Two-Hearted, the tributaries of which joined to become one deep blue channel on the plain, were fields of tall grass waving in the wind, perfect for ranching. Even now Emmalee could see Pennington's ranchers and their wagons spread out on both sides of the river, set to race out and claim that land when the rush commenced.

True, the farmers might have desired those broad, flat fields, which would be easier to plow and till, beneath whose primeval sod lay fine and fertile earth. But they could claim the groves, the hills, and still be content. No, the problem for the community that Olympia hoped to become lay with the river, which Emmalee understood at once. The ranchers, who meant to claim the prairies south of Arcady, would rely on the river to water their herds of cattle. The farmers upstream would need the water to irrigate their crops, should rainfall be scarce.

Burt Pennington had thought of that too. As Torquist's train came down out of the mountains and crawled its last slow miles toward Arcady, Emmalee saw here and there, behind bushes, partially concealed beneath groves of trees, the outlines of Conestogas in the hills along the river, north of the village. Pennington had men in position to claim the grazing lands he wanted *and* the riverbanks in the areas to which the farmers would be drawn, in order to exert control of water rights in all of Olympia.

"It's not fair!" she said aloud.

"What?" asked Randy, who'd been drinking in the awesome landscape.

She explained, and he understood at once.

"Pennington can't be that callous!" he exclaimed, in a pained voice. "We all have to live here."

He touched his spurs to the flanks of the dapple-gray. The big horse trotted toward the head of the train.

"Where are we going?" Emmalee asked.

"To see Mr. Torquist."

They found the wagonmaster driving his horses from the seat of his Conestoga, conferring earnestly with scouts Ryder and Cassidy. Torquist had also noted and interpreted Burt Pennington's strategy. There was a certain gimlet-eyed concentration to his visage that Emmalee had not seen before in precisely this way and that seemed as atypical and foreboding as his burst of optimism in Denver. Torquist was no longer—not exactly—the man of pure ideals she had met in St. Joe, but what he was now and where he was tending Emmalee did not know.

"This is outrageous!" he was telling the scouts. "This is absolutely beyond the pale! As the Lord is my witness, I'm going to do something about it."

"What?" asked Cassidy. "It's a land rush. First come, first served. All's you can do is try and get in position and claim the land you want and hope for the best."

"You fellows want to stick around and give us a hand, case there's trouble?" Torquist asked.

"Nope. Me an' Hap is scouts and guides. We get nervous thinkin' about bein' in one place any too long."

"I could make it worth your while," Torquist pressed.

"No, sir."

Then the wagonmaster caught sight of Randy and Emmalee on the horse.

"What is it, Clay?"

"I guess you already know. The wagons up along the river."

"Intolerable. I'll speak to the claims agent about it as soon as we get to Arcady. We'll all have to register our intent to claim land anyway. Rush starts day after tomorrow. We don't have much time to get situated. What are you two planning on doing?" he added, with an air that might have seemed avuncular or even paternal had Emmalee not realized that Torquist was reminding her of the two years servitude to him.

"We've been talking it over," Randy told him forthrightly. "We'll let you know what we decide."

There were many decisions to make but finally they were in Olympia, with the wagons forming their three great circles one last time. Emmalee slid down from the dapple-gray and looked around. Compared to Cairo and St. Joe, Arcady was a toy town. Yet it was a town, with a couple of rickety clapboard houses, a stable, a tiny church, and a sprawling general store that seemed to house a lot of different activities. Telegraph wires, running down from the mountains, threaded through a hole bored into the wall of the store. A big sign, LOANS, hung from a sign beside the door, and a massive, hand-lettered notice was tacked to the side of the building.

U. S. LAND CLAIMS AGENT
INQUIRE WITHIN
ALL PROSPECTIVE CLAIMANTS MUST
BE PROPERLY REGISTERED OR RISK
DISQUALIFICATION

This was it. She was there now. Her future had arrived and things had to be decided. Today, registration, without which she could not claim land at all. Then the land rush itself. *This land. My home.*

Torquist's people came to a halt outside little Arcady on the Big Two-Hearted River, awestruck by the colors of this promised land. Its hues were new as a new world, new as time, still fresh and luminous from the palette of God. The sweeping sky, a glittering, dancing blue, reflected the darker blue of the river, spotted with foamy white rapids that poured over boulders, the rocks pearly white on one side, thick with forest-green moss on the other. Grass grew rampant, brilliant green along the river, turning to darker green and gold in the rolling hills. A soft, late-September wind came in over the plains from the Pacific. The air was hushed, but expectant. The end of one journey, the beginning of another.

"Randy, maybe we should talk now," Emmalee said, looking up at him on the horse. "You're right. It's time for some choices."

Very soberly, conscious of the importance of this moment, Randy dismounted. "Let's walk down to the river," he suggested.

A crowd of Pennington people had come out of the store to watch the arrival of the Torquist train. They stood in the dust shouting halfhearted welcomes to their rivals. Skirting them, Randy and Emmalee walked quickly through the village toward the gurgling river and sat down on its grassy bank. It was about twenty yards wide and deeply channeled, a river that knew floods and fast water, although now it was no more than three or four feet deep.

They spoke at the same time. "I've been thinking . . ." Emmalee began. "I've been meaning to ask . . ." said Randy.

They laughed. Randy reached out and touched her hand. "Let me say this?" he asked. "I've been wanting to for a long time."

Emmalee nodded.

"I've learned quite a few things on the way west, Em. And I think you have too. When I almost ran you down beside that wagon back in St. Joe, we were just kids, more or less. But we've had to face things, and we're more than just a few months older now. We've grown. And I think we've grown together. You've learned—I think—not to be duped by . . . well, you know what I mean. And I've learned that I'll never have what I want unless I get right up on my hind legs and ask for it."

Emmalee waited.

Randy paused, holding her gaze. "I want us to get engaged, Em. That's what I'm asking for. It's because I'm in love with you."

His eyes, usually so sparkling and bright, were darkened with intensity. His strong, handsome face seemed drawn and even pale in spite of trail sunburn. He leaned toward her.

"I've been thinking things over too," she said.

His words and his presence, the very strength and goodness of him, combined with the euphoria of journey's end to produce in Emmalee not only a feeling of tenderness toward Randy—a tenderness more acute than ever before—but also a vivid sense of promise. It was as if a time had come to draw a line, to make one's mark, to stake a claim upon the territory of her soul.

"I want to make a life for us," Randy was saying. "A life together. You and me. Because I love you, Em."

"Randy, I'm—"

"Don't answer yet if you're not sure."

"It's not that, I'm—"

"I have it all planned," he went on. "I know I don't have much to offer right now," he said, ducking his head, "but time will take care of that. I'll work hard. We'll both work hard. I intend to get the best farming land there is and have the best darn farm around. You'll claim land right next to mine—we'll see to that—and right after the first harvest we'll get married."

"After the first harvest?" asked Emmalee.

That wouldn't be until next fall, a year away.

"Em! Does this mean . . . ? Dos this mean you're saying yes?"
to support them. I wouldn't feel right about it. I think it'd be better to wait until we have a harvest in the barn." He looked a little worried. "Of course, if you'd really like to go right ahead . . ."

"No, Randy, you're right, of course. And I still have to settle things with Mr. Torquist, but otherwise . . ."

"Em! Does this mean . . . ? Does this mean you're saying yes?"

Emmalee paused a moment, trying to sort out emotions, impressions, ambitions. Myrtle had been right, back there on the Kansas prairie, when she'd said it wasn't good for a person to be alone. She'd also been right about finding a good man, if you were lucky enough. Emmalee had grown up sufficiently to judge the truth of Myrtle's advice, and she'd been lucky enough to find Randy, or be found by him. Emmalee had no fear that, by getting engaged to Randy, she was surrendering her independence. I can have land, home and love too, she realized. Randy is not like some other men who would demand to own you, body and soul.

And there was a year to get used to the idea.

I'm doing the right thing and the good thing, Emmalee decided.

"Em?" Randy was asking, his voice at the ragged end of hopefulness.

"Yes," she told him. "Yes, I will be your betrothed. I'll marry you whenever you say it's time."

"Oh, Em!" he cried with sudden, wild delight, scarcely

able to believe what he perceived to be such extraordinary fortune. It was as if the skies had parted and suddenly vouchsafed him a miracle. "Oh, Em, I promise I'll make you so happy," he said, taking her into his arms as best he could with the splint.

Then he kissed her and Emmalee responded, lost for long minutes in the commingled excitement of their mutual promise and future. She felt the hunger of his need, sensed also his restraint, and thought that she was glad of it. He was treating her as a lady ought to be treated; she felt safe with him, and wanted.

Their betrothal kiss was long and very sweet, tasting just faintly of salt. Although they were both too distracted then by happiness and future resolves to think consciously about it, the salt was a reminder that men and women alike are made of perishable flesh, which must struggle to survive, and whose great dreams are as permanent as the dust on a butterfly's wings.

Horace Torquist stood on his wagon seat and called "*Whoooaaa!*" one last time. The proud but ravaged train lurched to a halt. Horses sagged in their traces. Oxen showing ridges of bony rib all but fell beneath their yokes, and the pilgrims climbed down from wagons, from the backs of weary beasts, and faltered toward the general store. Randy and Emmalee, holding hands, walked up from the river and joined the others just as a thinnish man with a shrewd face and a fine black suit came out of the store. He wore a flat, low-crowned black hat. Some kind of pin or badge was attached to his lapel. He surveyed the gathering pilgrims with a look that managed to be bored yet cannily appraising at the same time.

"Name's Vestor Tell," he drawled. "Claims agent here. You deal with me. Treat me good, I do the same for you.

Likewise the opposite. Simplest way to do business. Who's your wagonboss?''

''I am,'' answered Torquist, stepping to the front of the crowd. His hair was as wild and unruly as ever, but his fervently righteous prophet's eyes were marked by that strange new light that Emmalee could not interpret. ''We're here to register for the right to take part in the land rush.''

Vestor Tell shrugged and nodded. ''It's a free country,'' he said. ''Sort of got beat out by these ranchers so far, but that don't make no never-mind to me. Got your passenger list handy?''

''Passenger list?'' asked Torquist, standing there in the dust in front of the general store. His clothes were covered with dust, his boots full of dust, trail grit coated his tongue. Yet the claims agent ignored his discomfort, ignored the fatigue of them all, to pursue this detail.

''Right,'' said Tell. ''Maybe you don't understand. I got to keep track of things. Can't have more parcels of land claimed than you have eligible people to claim them, if you get my drift?''

''Of *course*,'' said Torquist, understanding. He turned to Randy. ''Clay, run back to my wagon, will you? Beneath the seat there's a metal chest. In a gunnysack. Inside you'll find a tablet with a list of names on it.''

''Yes, sir.''

Randy hurried away. Tell watched him go.

''That boy hurt his arm, eh?'' he asked, making small talk. His eyes swung to Emmalee. ''That your husband, ma'am?''

Before Emmalee could respond, Torquist interrupted. ''I see that Pennington's people are positioned to get land all along the river.''

''So?'' said Tell.

''Do you think that's fair? We're farmers. Crops need water just as badly as longhorns do.''

Tell shrugged. "So grab the river land first. That's your job. Mine's just to handle the claims you do make. Oh," he added, as if it were an afterthought, "I also loan money. Case any of you need it."

Emmalee stored this information in the back of her mind. She certainly needed money—she needed five hundred dollars, to be exact—but she wasn't prepared for a decision of that kind yet. Borrowing money was a very risky thing if you'd never done it before. Besides, Vestor Tell did not strike her as terribly trustworthy. He was too confidently lackadaisical, almost arrogant, and his casually sleepy look was just a little too carefully affected.

Randy came back with the tablet, which Torquist took from him and handed to Vestor Tell, who proceeded to go over the list slowly, name by name.

"Oh!" Tell exclaimed then, looking up at the crowd. "No need for you all to hang around here. Can't deal with you but one at a time anyway. Get yourself a drink, find some shade. You can start formin' up a line in ten, fifteen minutes or so."

Some of the pioneers drifted off, others slumped down beneath the big cottonwoods that grew around the general store. Randy took Emmalee's hand again.

"Let's go in. Bet they've got sarsparilla in this store."

"Just a minute," Emmalee said. Her instinctive mistrust of Vestor Tell, combined with a formless but increasingly powerful premonition regarding Horace Torquist, compelled her to remain within earshot.

"Em, you've made me so happy. . . ." Randy said, as they leaned together in the shadow at the side of the general store.

Emmalee heard him and was glad. But she also heard the exchange between Torquist and Tell. It was unsettling.

"How many'd you lose?" Tell asked, running his finger down the list of names, counting.

"Only two," Torquist replied. "Little girl named Petunia Petweiler, couple of days out of St. Joe. And an elderly lady, Bernice Creel. Lost her in Denver."

Emmalee was so amazed that Torquist would tell a lie that she did not immediately understand his reasons. This complicated man, a leader by the strength of his will and the power of his purse, had turned away from what he thought was corruption in Galena, Ohio, to form a better community in this new land, Olympia. But the rigors of the trail, the thievery of the Arapaho, and Burt Pennington's ability to come out ahead time and again, these factors were bringing forth dark features from the depths of Torquist's soul, in spite of himself. Bernice Creel had been the *sixteenth* member of Torquist's train to die. . . .

"That all you lost?" asked Tell, with some surprise. "Even Pennington had nine fatalities, and he had along a doc and plenty of medicine."

"Just those two," maintained Torquist.

"No men at all?"

"Didn't lose a one," said Torquist.

". . . and we'll build a big stone house . . ." Randy was saying, "with this huge fireplace. . . ."

Emmalee heard him, but she continued to follow the conversation between wagonboss and claims agent. Now she understood what Torquist was up to. Seven men *had* died on the trail. Five of them, two almost as old as Ebenezer Creel, had succumbed to natural causes. Young Teddy Barnstable's horse had fallen on him, and Dolph Beidermann had slipped off a cliff in the Rockies. The ages of these men, however, didn't matter. They would have been eligible to claim land, And Torquist was working on a scheme to pretend they still *were* alive and somehow claim land in their names!

"You wouldn't try to pull any fast ones with me, would you?" Tell demanded drowsily.

"Sir, I resent that," Torquist declared in answer, his big chin jutting toward the heavens.

Emmalee resolved to speak to Torquist at the first opportunity. She was worried. Stress and defeat seemed to have dangerously cracked the wagonmaster's rigidity, and he was on the verge of compromising everything. True, there were hundreds of ranchers and farmers ready to claim land. A small number of false claims might be concealed for a time. But eventually the truth would be known. It could not be otherwise.

Certainly Torquist must be aware of this? He would not threaten the future of his community for the sake of seven parcels of land.

Would he?

"All right." Tell shrugged, handing the tablet back to Torquist. "Get your people lined up. I'll register them one man or one couple at a time, depending on their status. My office is inside."

With that he ducked into the general store, leaving Torquist with Randy and Emmalee.

"Yo!" called Torquist to his pioneers. "We're about to register. Form a line here next to the store. I'll go in first and learn the procedure." He glanced around nervously, then added: "Uh . . . Japser Heaton, Strep, Redding . . . and a few of you others there . . . you hang back. I got to . . . ah, discuss details with you before you boys register."

Emmalee was sure that this conversation would have something to do with Torquist's apparent scheme. He would *never* get away with it! He was about to enter the store, but Emmalee had time for a discreet remark that might serve to restore his good sense.

"Don't these land claims papers eventually become permanent government records?" she suggested, calling up the images of Olympia's territorial government and Washington, D.C., where the Homestead Act had originated.

Torquist understood that Emmalee was warning him. Shifting moods passed quickly across his broad, strong face: surprise, offense, anger.

"You have your own problems, Miss Alden," he snapped. "I suggest you tend to them. I . . . we . . . did not come all this way to be beaten by Pennington and his ranchers. The soil is sacred, meant to be tilled. The Lord will understand what we have to do."

I just hope the government does, thought Emmalee.

Torquist went into the store.

"What did you say to him?" asked Randy. "He looked mad."

Emmalee hesitated, uncertain whether to tell Randy or not. *Tell him, of course! He's going to be your husband!* She was very new in the role of betrothed; it was hard to think of herself as someone's wife.

"I think," she said quietly, "that Mr. Torquist lied to the agent about the number of people who died during the trip."

"Oh, Em! Nonsense!" Randy said. "Horace Torquist would never lie. You didn't accuse him?" he asked worriedly. "Was that why he looked mad?"

"No, I didn't accuse him." Emmalee sighed, feeling a burden of unwanted knowledge and responsibility coming down upon her. No one in the train would believe that Torquist was capable of the least moral lapse. She alone had strong reason to suspect that the wagonmaster was contemplating a strategy that would jeopardize all their destinies. Yet there was nothing, just now, that she could do about it.

"I wonder what kind of duties he'll assign me," she mused.

"I don't know. But I promise you this, Em: No wife of mine is going to be beholden to another man. We'll find a way to pay Torquist off before we're married.'' He put his good arm around her waist and squeezed gently. ''I can't wait *two* years, my God!''

Torquist went inside, registered, and reappeared in the doorway of the general store. ''You just sign your name, is all,'' he said. ''Make your mark if you can't write. Every able-bodied man has the right to claim a hundred and sixty acres. Likewise every couple.'' He glanced at Randy and Emmalee, who were close to the head of the line, just behind Festus Bent and Willard Buttlesworth. ''Pretty crowded in there,'' he said enigmatically. ''Place does a lot of business of various kinds.''

Then the wagonmaster went off to talk to Heaton, Strep, and the others beneath a cottonwood. Emmalee hoped he'd given up his scheme.

Festus Bent, his wife, Alma, and their three daughters went in to see Tell. Buttlesworth hung back.

''Come on, Willard,'' Randy said. ''Let's go in. Might as well have a look at the store and wait where it's cool. They can't do nothin' but kick us out.''

The sawmill operator shrugged and entered the store. So did Emmalee and Randy, as the line of people behind them shuffled closer to the door. Once inside, Emmalee looked around. The place was unprepossessing, constructed of unpainted wooden beams and flat wooden planking with plenty of knotholes. Piles of dry goods, some brightly colored, some plain, were stacked at one end of the store, and from the beams hung scores of cured hams and rows of farming implements: hoes, forks, shovels, and axes. There were even a few precious posthole diggers, spadelike devices used to make the deep, narrow holes in which the wooden posts of fences could be set. Farmers fenced their land.

Just beyond the space in which these goods were arrayed for inspection and purchase, a squat, black stove crouched coldly on a stone slab in the center of the floor. A trio of tables occupied the floor on the far side of the stove, at which men and women were seated, talking, eating, and drinking mugs of cold, pale beer. Emmalee saw a barrel of beer at the far end of the store.

Then her eyes were drawn back to one of the tables. Familiar people there, bent toward one another like conspirators, talking. Myrtle Higgins, Ebenezer Creel, and a strange woman with hair of a bright-orange color not found in nature.

And with them was Garn Landar. His back was toward Emmalee, but it was Garn, all right.

Emmalee felt something very much like a shudder pass through her body. Her hands grew moist and her heart beat faster. She felt betrayed. Myrtle and Ebenezer knew what had happened between herself and Garn up there on the hill in Denver. Everybody had heard. Yet here they were, talking to him as if nothing had happened. Well, to be fair, they also knew that Garn had saved her from Fire-On-The-Moon, but still . . .

Before Randy could catch a glimpse of Garn, Emmalee positioned herself so that her betrothed's back was toward the table. She didn't want Garn to see her or Randy; she didn't want even the hint of an incident.

Moreover, she did not want to face Garn at all. She had no idea what her reaction to him might be.

Vestor Tell's desk was in the corner of the store, next to the telegraph machine, which rested on a long, low table against the wall. Tell sat on a spindly-legged stool, entering names on a long roster in front of him. Festus Bent had already registered—he and his wife and girls were examining dry goods—and Willard Buttlesworth concluded his business as well.

"We could sure use a sawmill in these parts," Tell told him, "but the high ground is rugged.

"Next," he called, motioning Randy and Emmalee to approach his desk. "Name?" he asked, taking up pen and preparing to write.

"Clay. Randolph Anthony."

"Place of birth?"

"Galena, Ohio."

Tell glanced up at Emmalee. "Man and wife?"

"No, she's my fiancée," declared Randy, loudly and proudly.

Out of the corner of her eye, Emmalee saw Garn Landar turn around. She also caught glimpses of Ebenezer and Myrtle staring at her.

"Congratulations," oozed Tell, bending to write. "Name?"

"Emmalee Anne Alden. Lancaster, Pennsylvania."

"You're a lucky man there, Clay. So the two of you want to claim a piece of land together?"

"No," said Emmalee, "we both want plots."

Tell shook his head. "No can do. Couples are only entitled to one portion of land."

His voice had risen slightly. He was not used to being challenged in any way. Emmalee was aware of conversations ceasing in the store as people turned to listen.

Emmalee could not believe that her enduring dream of owning land was going to end so abruptly, so pointlessly. Randy, who had counted on her claiming land, too, was staring helplessly at her, realizing the damage he'd done with his proud proclamation.

"Wait," she said, "if we're not married yet, then we aren't a couple. You said that *couples* were entitled to one portion. That means married couples, doesn't it?"

"Well, now . . ." Tell began.

"It must be written down somewhere," Emmalee persisted. "Let me see the rule."

Tell glared balefully at her for a long moment.

"Won't be necessary to read the law on it," he growled. "The point doesn't come up much, but I recollect, now that I think a bit on it, that you're right."

He entered Emmalee's name in the space beneath Randy's.

"Now here's the rules," he told them, with an amused glint in his eyes as if he had the final joke. "When the land rush starts, day after tomorrow, you two got to put wooden stakes with your names on 'em in the four corners of the land you want to claim. According to the rules and regulations of the government of the United States of America, the land is yours free. However, *if* within one year you have not tilled and planted one fourth of the arable acreage on your claim, and *if* you have not constructed a domicile on said claim, you forfeit your right to the land and it goes up for sale to the highest bidder."

Tell grinned.

Randy and Emmalee looked at each other, startled and bewildered. It was quite likely that he could meet these requirements, but if she had to devote most of her time to Torquist . . .

"I never heard of anything like that in the Homestead Act," Emmalee protested.

"This is a land rush," Tell drawled. "Strict provisions of the Homestead Act don't apply. Under the act, you'd have to pay a buck an acre for the land. Here you're getting it free. Territory of Olympia requires tilling and domicile to prevent shiftless exploiters from claiming land merely for speculation, get my drift?"

Emmalee understood, although she failed to see how it would not be speculation to buy up land from the unfortunates who were unable to meet the requirements.

But she'd won her point, to Tell's displeasure. She would be able to claim her own plot . . . if she got to a chunk of good land before some other pioneer did.

A canny gleam flickered in Tell's eyes. He lowered his voice and spoke quickly. "This is just between you and me, but I can arrange for you to have, shall we say, an *advantageous* position when the land rush starts. . . ."

He rubbed thumb and index finger back and forth, back and forth, the ancient money-counting gesture.

"We don't have any money," Randy blurted.

"How can you arrange something like that?" demanded Emmalee.

Tell, conscious that he'd made the wrong suggestion to the wrong people, retreated with an air of assumed levity.

"Hey!" he said. "Just a little joke. You two must have been out on the trail too long, can't appreciate a little joke."

"I guess not," said Emmalee. She was doubly angry now, and impotent to do anything about it. The land rush was being stacked not only in favor of Pennington's ranchers, who'd gotten to Olympia first, but also for the benefit of those who could—and would—offer Tell a bribe.

Emmalee and Randy, their registration concluded, turned away from Tell. Lambert Strep was behind them in line, looking more jittery than usual. Emmalee understood why when she heard him declare to Vestor Tell that he was "Barnstable, Theodore, of Kalamazoo, Michigan." That was the young man who'd died beneath his horse. Horace Torquist was proceeding with his plan, which Emmalee was certain would bring nothing but trouble upon them all.

"Well, as long as we're in here," suggested Randy, taking Emmalee's arm, "let's have a look around. If they don't sell sarsparilla, I wouldn't mind a beer."

"Oh, let's come back later," said Emmalee, trying to guide him toward the door before he saw Garn.

Her tactic might have worked had it not been for Ebenezer Creel, chock full of beer and good humor. "Em! Randy!" he cried happily. "Come on over and guzzle a snootful of brew! We got to celebrate our getting here and my getting rich!"

There was no way to avoid the situation. Randy, turning with pleasure toward the table at which Ebenezer sat, recognized Garn Landar immediately. He took a few fast steps toward Garn, almost as if preparing to assault him, but allowed himself to be restrained by Emmalee's hand and his own good manners. There were ladies present, Myrtle and the one with orange hair. Fighting with only one good arm was also ill-advised. Nevertheless, it was a very tense gathering at the table. Even Ebenezer perceived the extent of his faux pas. Only the orange-haired woman was immune to the stress of the moment. She had no idea what was going on.

"Have a seat," she invited cheerfully. "Let's get you both a mug of beer. Just engaged, are you? I couldn't help but overhear. Well, I do declare. That calls for a celebration. . . .

"Doesn't that just call for a celebration?" she asked, doubtfully now, her eyes reading the wary, grim faces around her as she tried to figure out what had so suddenly gone wrong.

But she forced a smile and plunged on. "Do sit down," she said again to Emmalee and Randy. "I'm Hester Brine. Pleased ta meet cha. I run things here at the store.

"You're just gonna love it here in Olympia," she said, making one last try.

"What the hell is going on here?" she demanded bleakly. Then she fell silent.

There was a long, long pause.

"Well, here we are," said Myrtle Higgins.

Garn Landar stood up. Emmalee had been trying not to

look at him, but it was impossible to avoid it. His eyes met and held hers, and in his gaze was a depth of seriousness, a searching intensity that she had not seen before. He was Garn but he was, somehow, *different*. Then she understood. Gone was the lighthearted cavalier swagger, replaced by a detachment that was cordial enough but oddly wrong, as out of place on him as a derby hat would have been. This was the man who had said to her: "*I am the kind . . . who will ask but once for what he truly loves.*" This was the man who had stripped her to glorious nakedness and opened her for loving upon sweet mountain grass, by which love he would have owned and conquered her. This was also the man who had conquered Randy by shattering his arm and who had bargained, shrewd and cool and grinning, with a murderous Arapaho chieftain.

But, looking at Garn now, Emmalee found it hard to believe that he was the same man who had said and done those things. His reckless spirit, which she had always criticized, was nowhere in evidence. She was aware that she missed it and simultaneously puzzled that she should. His ironic, high-spirited enjoyment of the absurd was likewise gone. Just a few months ago, in Cairo or in St. Joe, he would have loved this situation, this triangle: himself, and a woman he had wanted, and his rival for her affections, all standing in a public place with an audience looking on.

Now, however, he seemed neither to be enjoying the situation nor, particularly, regretting it. It was as if there were a blank place in his being, a portion of his energy deliberately shrouded from view.

Emmalee's heart was hammering away, although she did not quite know why. Everyone else was extraordinarily calm.

"Congratulations on your engagement, Miss Alden," Garn said in a resonant, sincere voice, absolutely without mockery.

Emmalee remembered the taste of his kiss.

"I hope you'll be very happy."

She felt his lips on her breasts, felt his kiss trailing down over her taut and quivering flesh. . . .

"At the risk of bringing up a subject best laid to rest . . ."

Emmalee felt his body poised above her, her own body hungry for the surging power and length of him.

". . . let me say that I regret what happened in Denver."

"You *regret* it?" snapped Randy Clay. "You're saying that you *regret* it? If that isn't a batch of hogwash, I don't know what is."

Emmalee said nothing, uneasily aware that her body was betraying her again.

"Clay," Garn was saying, in a tone that was business-like without being unsympathetic, "I know you're at a bit of a disadvantage temporarily, what with that arm. I'll gladly pay whatever you judge to be a proper reparation."

"I don't want your money, Landar. I don't want anything from you."

Everyone in the store was watching and listening now.

"Stop it, both of you," said Emmalee.

"You tell 'em, honey." Hester Brine stood up at the table. "I don't give two hoots and a holler what happened to you in Denver or wherever. This here's my place and you better act your age in it. Now, sit down like civilized folks and have a beer.

"That's an order," she added.

"Took the words right out of my mouth," said Myrtle Higgins. "We *all* gotta live here."

Hester brought mugs of beer over from the barrel and business in the store recommenced. Tell went back to registering land claimants; Emmalee sat down next to Randy, vowing to chat pleasantly for a few civilized minutes; Cynthia, Priscilla, and Darlene Bent launched a hissing squabble over a bolt of cloth, an argument resolved when Festus, their pa, threatened to buy a razor strop and use it on their rumps.

"Reckon even an old sharecropper like Fes Bent has him a good idea on occasion," Ebenezer commented, trying to lighten the mood at the table.

"Are you going to try and claim land, Ebenezer?" asked Emmalee, to keep the conversation going.

To her surprise, the old man exchanged wary glances with Hester, Myrtle, and Garn. Emmalee recalled how the four had been leaning together conspiratorially when she'd entered the store.

"Well not in a manner of speaking, not exactly. . . ." he fumbled.

Emmalee was amazed. Ebenezer Creel was hardly the type to falter over words. Some promised land Olympia was turning out to be! Horace Torquist was already embarked on a dubious ploy, the purpose of which was unclear, and these four people—including Myrtle, who was no-nonsense honest and hard as nails—were privy to another scheme, most likely Garn's. In spite of his newly bland manner, Emmalee decided, he must have retained a streak of his old tendency to look for sharp angles to play.

"You know," Hester said to Randy, "I got farm utensils here you might want to buy. I can extend credit too."

Emmalee studied the woman. She seemed to be about fifty. Her hair was tinted and her teeth were false, but she had a good, strong figure and a bold gaze. Her eyes showed a lot of experience and more than a hint of wisdom.

"Well, thanks," Randy replied. "I brought a few tools with me. First thing I'm going to have to do is find chickens and cows to buy, and seed for corn and oats."

"Seed I can order for you from Sacramento. Best place for livestock is Salt Lake. Burt Pennington's already sent men down there to buy longhorns and bring 'em back north."

Randy's expression darkened at the challenges: money, credit, stock, equipment, seed. He hadn't even staked his claim yet.

"How much," asked Emmalee, "for a milking cow?"

"Goin' rate was six bucks as of last week," Hester informed her.

Randy gulped. Emmalee tried to seem cheerful.

"Like I said, I do give credit on purchases. And I loan money."

"Against what security?" asked Emmalee.

"Have to be your land, I reckon. Unless you got something else."

"Is that your loan sign outside the store?"

"Naw. That belongs to Vestor Tell. He's fixin' to do real banking. Big sums. I don't have that much. But," she added, squinting up her eyes, "some folks like to know that all the cards are on the table."

"Are you saying . . . ?" Randy began.

"Anything against Vestor? Son, I don't say nothing against nobody. Just keep your eyes open, is what I advise. And remember that old Hester might be able to work out something to our mutual advantage in case the necessity arises."

"I'll do that," Randy said. He finished his beer and stood up. "Emmalee?"

She took a final swallow, rose, and left with him. She did not look at Garn. The tension of seeing him again dissipated slowly, and she knew that his presence in Olympia portended future meetings and—because of Randy—future conflicts. Why did Garn have to be there, anyway? Once more, just when she'd thought he was gone for good, there he was again. During the trek through the mountains, she'd almost convinced herself that this time she'd seen the last of him. Well, she would turn her hopes and energies toward a new life.

"Six dollars a cow!" Randy mourned. "I can't even afford one spavined heifer!"

"Don't worry. We'll make it somehow."

He put his good arm around her and kissed her on the cheek. "That's what I love about you," he said. "We'll make it. I hate to borrow money though."

"We'll think of something." Emmalee had never regretted quite so keenly the bargain she'd been forced to strike with Torquist. "I know! If Pennington is already bringing in longhorn cattle, maybe he'll need extra land on which to graze them. We could rent him part of our farms for pasture. . . ."

Randy was astounded. "Why, Em! How can you *say* that? In the first place, we don't even have any land yet. In the second, we're here to farm. Torquist would never permit it."

"But we need money and Pennington might pay."

"It's out of the question. A pipe dream."

Emmalee was a little irritated. She hadn't thought her idea was that bad, and she'd never quite understood Torquist's detestation of the ranchers. Land was land, after all. To be used as the men and women on it saw fit.

"Might as well sit around dreaming about getting rich like Ebenezer Creel," Randy scoffed. "I do wonder, though, what he and Landar are up to. Mark my words, they'll get into trouble. And when they do . . ."

"Let's not talk about it."

"You're right. Let's not. I'm going to mount up and ride out into the countryside. Do a little scouting around so when the rush begins I'll know exactly what to claim. I'll find some good acres for you too. I only hope the land's not too hilly."

* * *

The long line of Torquist's pioneers, waiting to register with Vestor Tell, snaked once around the general store and wavered off down toward the river, where children frolicked and some of the women had begun to do laundry. Emmalee was surprised to see Lambert Strep in the line again, since he'd already registered as Theodore Barnstable. Strep was hatless now, he'd shaved and changed clothes. He looked like a different person.

Emmalee drew him off to the side. "Lambert, excuse my prying, but didn't you register already?"

Strep had a sheepish, hangdog look. "Yup," he muttered.

"Then why are you standing in line again?"

"I'm not the only one," he replied defensively. "Jasper an' Virgil an' the others is doin' it too."

"How come?"

"Mr. Torquist said t' keep it under my hat. Even though it's perfectly all right an' we deserve it."

"Deserve what?"

"The extra plots of land that would have gone to the guys who died. Mr. Torquist says that they paid for that land with their lives, so some of us are gonna claim two spreads, if we can . . ."

". . . and register it in their names?"

Strep nodded in dull embarrassment.

"But, Lambert, you're signing falsely. You're bound to be discovered sooner or later. Your *own* claim might be disqualified."

Strep swallowed hard. "Mr. Torquist will take care of it. I trust Mr. Torquist. Don't *you*?" he demanded, taking a feeble offensive. "You wouldn't even be *here* if it weren't for Horace Torquist."

Emmalee gave up. There was nothing she could do about it now. Yet her suspicions were confirmed, and there was something unspeakably sad about a good man's fall from grace, to say nothing of his taking others over the precipice with him.

She spent the rest of the day setting up Torquist's tent and unloading his wagon. The wagonmaster had gone out to reconnoiter possible plots of farmland, and Emmalee was glad of his absence. She felt morally compelled to speak to him about the dangers of his scheme, and she also had to discuss with him the nature of her duties here in Olympia. If, somehow, she could arrange to work for him part of the time, leaving the remainder of her days free, then she might have a chance to make some progress on her own. Obviously, money was going to be a real problem.

First things first: get the land.

By late afternoon Torquist had still not returned. Seeing no sign of Randy either, Emmalee decided to take a look around for herself. She left Arcady, walking south along the banks of the Big Two-Hearted. The slow, mournful murmur of the river put her into a peaceful, dreamy mood and she strolled along happily, conscious of little but gentle sun, easy wind, and the perfume of flowers and tall, waving grass. Looking up, she saw a thick grove of willows in the distance, a wild cluster of trees growing along the river, and caught a glimpse of Conestoga canvas behind the leaves. Some of Pennington's people she figured. Approaching more closely, she heard the sounds of many axes and the occasional instructions and comments of people at work.

Were the ranchers building shelters already? They hadn't even claimed land yet. And willow was hardly sound construction material. The wood was too soft.

Curious, Emmalee left the riverbank and ducked into the tall grass, bending down and making her way toward the grove. She slipped into the trees and edged toward a small clearing. There she saw a group of women cutting branches from the willows and stripping them of bark. The branches were white, wet and slippery when stripped. Emmalee was puzzled. The branches were too wet to be used as kindling and too weak for construction. Moreover, several other women were chopping the branches into yard-long lengths and sharpening one end of each length into a point.

Weapons or spears of some kind? Was Pennington counting on a fight over the land claims?

Then, behind one of the wagons, Emmalee sensed movement, saw the prancing hoofs of horses, and into her line of sight came three riders.

Otis, Pennington's rangy head scout.

A small, mean-looking man whom Emmalee did not recognize.

And Lottie Pennington, dressed in a pink frock and a matching pink bonnet. She was mounted sidesaddle on a magnificent black stallion.

It was Garn Landar's horse!

Emmalee was as astounded by that as she was puzzled by the activity taking place. Would Garn have gambled or sold his horse? Or would he have . . . *given it to Lottie*?

Lottie looked demure and, as usual, faintly bored. Otis and the other man sat tall in their saddles, surveying the working women with the air of impatient supervisors. Whatever was happening was something of considerable importance. Emmalee edged closer to the clearing to see if she could find out what it was.

"Is this all you've got done?" the small man was demanding of one of the women. She was solid and sunburned, holding a hatchet in one gnarled hand.

"You don't like it, get down off that horse and lend a hand," the woman retorted with spirit. "We're doing the best we can."

"Come now," said Otis conciliatingly. "We're all in this together. It's just that we're going to need over a thousand stakes."

Stakes. The word touched a chord in Emmalee's memory but she didn't have time to think about it just then because Garn's horse caught her scent, neighed anxiously, and Lottie cried out: "There's somebody in the trees! There!"

Emmalee turned to run, but she didn't get far. The little mean-faced man, moving fast, leaped from his horse, dashed into the willows, grabbed Emmalee, and dragged her back into the clearing. He had snaggly teeth and a very hard hand.

"You're hurting me," Emmalee said, trying to pry his fingers from her arm.

"Well, I do declare," said Lottie, laughing, as she recognized Emmalee.

"Let her go, Alf," ordered Otis. "What are you doing here?" he asked casually but without amusement.

"I was out for a walk," Emmalee flared, rubbing her arm and glaring at Alf, who grinned malevolently back at her. "Anything wrong with that?"

"You're pretty far from Arcady," Lottie pointed out. "I should think you'd have had enough walking in Kansas and Colorado."

The women who'd been cutting branches stared suspiciously. Emmalee was sure she'd stumbled upon something of importance. Something that she ought to be able to figure out.

"You like this horse?" Lottie smirked. "I see that you're looking at it."

"These are serious days for us," Otis told her sharply. "Business first, pleasure later. Your father's warned you."

The Pennington girl flushed, frowned.

"Miss . . . Alden, wasn't it?" Otis asked smoothly. "Let me give you a ride back to town."

"You sure, Oats?" the small man asked.

"Yeah, Kaiserhalt, I'm sure. Shut up."

Alf Kaiserhalt seemed disappointed, giving Emmalee a glance that said, *Well, your luck, you got off easy this time.*

"The rest of you get back to work now," Lottie told the women, who scowled at her contemptuously. They didn't like her any better than Emmalee did. These rough-hewn, hardworking women, Emmalee realized, were much like herself. Although they regarded her as farmer and enemy, they knew as well as she, without having to express it, the shallow nature of Lottie Pennington's soul.

And they probably wondered, as did Emmalee, how Lottie had come by such a fine horse. Emmalee's mind flashed back to the time she'd seen Lottie and Garn talking behind the wagon in Denver, on the day of Bernice Creel's funeral. She also recalled that Garn had promised to get Torquist's train to Denver before Pennington's party arrived, a guarantee upon which he had not delivered. Perhaps he had never planned to deliver! His remote manner now, his conspiratorial attitude, were more than grounds for suspicion.

Had it all been some vast scheme to defeat the farmers from the beginning? Garn's "getting fired" in St. Joe, his fortuitous presence on the Torquist train, the little cabal around the table in the general store, and this puzzling scene in the willows?

But Myrtle Higgins wouldn't be involved, would she? wondered Emmalee.

Otis rode a glossy chestnut roan, upon which he pulled Emmalee with scarcely less harshness than Alf Kaiserhalt had shown. He spurred the horse lightly, guiding it out of the grove and back upriver toward Arcady.

"So you made it over the mountains?" he asked, quite friendly now. "What did you come poking around for? Looking for dogies, or what?"

Emmalee remembered her humiliation by Pennington in the Schuyler Hotel in St. Joe.

"What's the big mystery about cutting a few branches off trees?" she shot back.

Otis laughed. "There's a lot at stake. Every small advantage might count."

Suddenly Emmalee pieced things together. *Stakes*. Those women had been fashioning name stakes for markers on the day of the land rush. Tell had mentioned having stakes to place on the four corners of each plot of land that was claimed. Pennington's people would have their markers ready; Torquist's might not. He and his men were out surveying the land now, while the women were busy unpacking.

I'll have to get them started making stakes, Emmalee realized. Nobody's even thought of it.

She was a little apprehensive. A lot of the women were envious of her for having been able to ride a good deal of the way to Denver in Ebenezer Creel's wagon. Many of them were not entirely convinced that the incident behind those boulders had been Garn Landar's fault.

And Emmalee had to admit that they were not completely wrong.

"You know, you sure are one purty little gal," Otis was saying.

"I'm happy that you think so."

"Are you? Well, you caught my eye that first day in St. Joe and I figured, 'Yep, she's got a lot of spunk, she'll make it.' "

"Did you?"

"Sure. I can tell. Whyn't you leave them plowboys an' come with us? Give us a year, maybe two, an' we ranchers'll be runnin' this whole territory."

"You seem pretty certain of that. But there are a lot of dedicated, determined people on the train I came here with."

Otis laughed again, scornfully this time. "Hard work ain't gonna have a whole lot to do with it," he said.

"What do you mean?"

"That's for me to know and you to find out. You just come over and join us. We'll take care of you. *I'll* take care of you. You don't have a beau, I hope?"

"I'm engaged to be married."

Otis turned around to look at her, as if judging the truth of her statement. He had a hard-planed face and domineering, wide-spaced wolf's eyes. The whites of those eyes were exceptionally large. He had a hard stare to meet but Emmalee met it.

"Who you gonna marry? I know him?"

"I don't know. Randy Clay is his name."

"Big blond boy?"

"Yes."

"Farmer, of course. Tough luck for you."

"Why do you say that?"

"Because I know what's gonna happen in this territory."

"If you tell me, we'll both know."

"And ruin the surprise?" Otis guffawed.

Emmalee knew that he was not about to tell her anything of consequence, but, even so, she already knew about the stakes and she guessed that Burt Pennington had afoot a scheme more intricate than Horace Torquist would be likely to imagine.

"There's an awful lot of land out here," she tried, as they rode easily along the river. "It seems enough to satisfy all of us."

"And here I thought you was smart. Don't you know that one hungry longhorn needs at least ten acres of grazing land per season? A lot more than that if there ain't a lot of rain. Can't make money ranching cattle less'n you have a *lot* of longhorns, roamin' free an' eatin' to their hearts' content. Then here come you farmers with your dinky little crops an' your fat, stupid milkin' cows an' them damn fences to cut apart an' chop up God's free earth. An' this here barbwire, that cuts the hell out of grazin' cattle.'' He was getting angry now, thinking of barbwire. ''Tell you what, if I ever see me a stretch of barbwire fence in these here parts, I'm gonna loop a length of it around the neck of the nearest farmer, so he can get his throat slit and strangle at the same time.''

''Well, I hope I'm not that nearest farmer,'' said Emmalee.

''Hey. You don't have to worry. You just do like I say an' come on over with us.''

In spite of his crude frankness, or maybe because of it, Emmalee found that she did not dislike Otis. He was hard and unlettered but not malicious; she did not think he would actually attack a fellow human being without provocation . . . although she had to admit that she did not know the many things Otis might regard as provoking, barbwire excepted.

''There's a nice girl in *your* train,'' she suggested. ''Lottie. You could ask her to be your girl.''

''Hah! The boss's daughter.'' He sounded as if he were talking about farmers again. ''She'd suck a man dry in ten minutes an' leave him dyin' in a ditch. Besides, she's taken.''

''She *is*?''

''Yeah. By that scout the boss canned back in St. Joe. Landar. Lottie goes into town one day an' she comes back on Landar's horse. He gave it to her. She's his girl now, looks like.''

Emmalee sat there behind Otis, jouncing along as the roan neared little Arcady. One part of her treated Otis's news quite matter-of-factly. After all, she had already seen Lottie upon Garn's stallion. Emmalee felt confused, because she felt that something of hers had been taken away.

Yet how could that be, because Garn was not hers and she didn't even want him? She was engaged to marry another man.

But then she figured things out and understood: She felt as she did because she was simply reacting to Lottie Pennington's spite. That was all.

"Here we are," Emmalee said, as they rode into Arcady. She bounded down from the horse in front of the general store. "Thanks for the ride."

"My pleasure," said Otis. "Now, come callin' any time you want, hear? But don't come snoopin' around. Folks is pretty antsy an' you never know . . ."

Otis touched his hatbrim, wheeled the horse around, and spurred away. Emmalee watched him go, then turned to find Myrtle and Hester Brine watching her from the store's entrance.

"Where've you been?" Myrtle asked.

"Quick," said Emmalee. "Are the men back yet?"

"Nope. What's up?"

"We've got to get started right away."

"Started on what?"

Emmalee explained about the stakes. "We're way behind. Pennington has hundreds of markers cut already."

"Slow down, girl," said Hester. "The job'll get done."

"That's right," Myrtle agreed. "Don't go gettin' yuhself all agitated."

"Don't go getting myself all . . . ? Whose side are you on, anyway?"

"*What!*" Myrtle snapped.

Emmalee faced the old woman down. "A lot of things are funny around here!"

"That's true, an' right now you're one of 'em. Instead of standin' there, get goin' and round everybody up. *If* they'll listen to you. I seen people watchin' you ride in on Otis's horse. How you think *that* looks, huh?"

"I thought of that myself, believe me. Come with me, Myrtle. Please. They'll listen to you."

"I'll be around if you need me, but whyn't you give it a try on your own? You never know. One day a whole lot might depend on whether the folks listen to you or not. Try your wings now."

Most of the women were at the chuckwagon helping prepare fire and food for the evening meal. They'd observed Emmalee returning on Otis's horse and they scrutinized her warily as she approached.

"Listen, everybody," she began. "There's something very important that we have to do."

"Says you!" Alma Bent, Festus's wife, grinned. "We been workin' our fingers nigh on to the bone while you been bouncin' yo' bottom . . . on a rancher's horse, anyways."

Elvira Waters, Florence Buttlesworth, and Stella Strep, along with quite a few others, thought this was very funny. They laughed and laughed.

"No, really, this is important," Emmalee persisted. "Downriver, Pennington's women . . . the women, mind you! They're getting the name stakes ready for the rush. They have hundreds already. We haven't even begun."

"Why should we listen to you?" inquired Elvira Waters. "Mr. Horace Torquist is the boss of this here train. If he figures we ought to be cuttin' stakes, he'll tell us."

"Right," agreed the others, more or less in unison. "We'll wait an' do what Mr. Torquist says."

Emmalee realized two things: One, they weren't about to listen to her; two, they would never believe that Torquist was capable of wrong. She excused them their first lapse; it was the second that was truly frightening.

Myrtle intercepted Emmalee, who was on her way to the river.

"How'd it go?"

"They didn't listen to me."

"It ain't surprising. I'll have a little chat with 'em. Where you going?"

"To cut some stakes of my own. I don't need to wait for Horace Torquist to tell me what to do."

Randy and the other men came straggling back into camp at nightfall, subdued but tense. Emmalee showed him the stakes she had fashioned, with their names, ALDEN and CLAY, carved into the wood and accentuated with bootblack so they would be easily discernible. He was delighted. They went over to the campfire, where Emmalee got him a tin mug full of coffee and a plate of cornbread and beans. Emmalee sensed in the men who had returned, including Torquist, a kind of edgy, bitter resolve. Randy did not want to discuss it.

"What you women don't know won't hurt you, Mr. Torquist said."

"Forget Horace Torquist for a moment. I'm going to be your *wife*! If there's danger, we're in it together. That's how things are."

Randy thought it over and reckoned that she had a point. "You know those wagons Pennington has positioned upriver? Mr. Torquist has decided to challenge the men in those wagons for water rights north of town. Pennington's already got a tremendous advantage south of Arcady. But even he hasn't enough people to get a monopoly upriver."

"What do you mean, 'challenge' them," asked Emmalee.

Randy glanced around and lowered his voice.

"We'll fight if we have to," he said.

"Fight?"

"Shhh. Lower your voice. The women are not to know."

With difficulty, Emmalee stayed calm. "Not to know? Not to *know*? This group has always prided itself, perhaps unduly, on being peaceable. Now we've just arrived in Olympia, where Mr. Torquist wanted to found a peaceable community, and on the very first day he's planning violence. . . .''

''That's not the way it is,'' Randy tried to protest.

''And he doesn't want us women to know? What if something is going to happen to you? Don't you think I have a right to know about that?''

''Shhh! Em, please be quiet. Nothing is going to happen. Mr. Torquist feels that if we fight them right away, this once, over the water rights north of town, well, then we'll never have to fight again. If you show that you're strong, your enemies will want peace. That's the way good Christians have always conducted themselves. And Em, when we claim land, all you women are going to be back here in camp.''

''*This* woman will not be.''

''Em . . .''

''No.''

They stopped talking and looked at each other, self-consciously aware that they were quarreling.

''I've found us two good plots on a creek near the river,'' Randy said quietly. ''I'll claim them both for us. If I can. It's one of the sites that Pennington's men have their eyes on.''

''So you think there'll be a fight over it?''

''Likely.''

''Then I'm going to be there.''

Randy did not quite know what to make of this obduracy. ''Mr. Torquist,'' he pronounced, ''is going to order *all* of you to remain in Arcady on the day of the rush.'' In his voice was a note of unchallengeable finality.

''It's just possible that not everyone will obey him,'' Emmalee said.

Randy frowned but said no more about it, especially when Torquist arrived to speak to his people and, in passing, praised Emmalee by name for sounding the warning about preparation of the name stakes.

Emmalee was staying at the Bents' wagon again, until such time as Torquist should have opportunity to contemplate her immediate fate, and Randy walked her there with his good arm around her waist. Their little spat was all but forgotten now—he expected that she would have the good sense to remain in Arcady; she was determined to claim her own land—and when he pulled her close to him in the soft shadow of a whispering cottonwood, their kiss was full-hearted. Lost in the kiss, conscious of the fire building in their bodies, Emmalee had a fleeting sensation of the speed with which time was passing. Events of long ago mingled and melded with this very night, one kiss recalled all kisses, and the hungry, voluptuous warmth spreading throughout her body in slow, spasmodic waves suggested past pleasures of a dangerous kind. Randy's hand caressed her breast through the calico. His mouth was ravenous, kissing her. . . .

Suddenly he pulled away. "This isn't right, Em. We oughtn't to do this yet. But you make me forget. . . ."

She heard herself panting, gasping. His kiss had left an emptiness that was greater than his kiss could have filled, a fact that she knew to be true even as she understood that it did not seem to make sense.

"Hey! Who's that smoochin' underneath that tree? Get out into the moonlight so's I can see you better."

"It's Ebenezer." Emmalee giggled.

"Caught in the act," Randy said.

"Just who I been lookin' for." Ebenezer cackled as Emmalee and Randy stepped out of the shadow. He reached into his trouser pocket—he no longer affected the big, slotted belt—and withdrew a piece of paper. Emmalee couldn't see it clearly but she knew what it was as soon as

Ebenezer said, "Em, Garn Landar said for me to give you this. Said he found it an' it's yours."

The one-hundred-dollar bill. Garn must have picked it up that night behind the boulders in Denver

Randy misunderstood. "I told that bastard I didn't want anything from him," he cried, grabbing furiously at the money.

Emmalee, fearful lest he destroy it, clutched at the note too.

There was a clean, dry, ripping sound as they tore the bill in half.

"J-just as well," faltered Randy, as he squinted at the note in the moonlight and perceived its denomination.

"That there is Em's money," said Ebenezer. "I paid it to her for taking care of Bernice. It just got lost an' got found, is all."

"It's still tainted. It passed through Landar's hands," Randy said, thinking of seed corn, cows, chickens, and farm implements, thinking of Emmalee's freedom from Torquist. "Nothing good can come of tainted money."

"It *ain't* tainted," protested Ebenezer. "That was all I had left of my past, after the Yankees got through with me. An' it's still good. The two parts are clear and identifiable. You can read the serial number. Give it to me if you don't want it."

Gently, but firmly, Emmalee took Randy's half of the bill. "I'll keep it for now. We'll spend it on what we need most. That can't hurt."

"I don't like it," Randy maintained. "Everything Landar touches turns bad. He was going to get us to Denver before Pennington. He didn't. Now he's in Olympia, corrupting this land with his presence, just as he dirtied the money with his touch. I tell you, everything he gets his hands on turns bad."

Randy had, in his anger at Garn, let his tongue get away

from him. Now, realizing what he'd said, he ceased talking and stared at Emmalee in anguished and apologetic horror. She was looking at him with hurt in her eyes, as if he'd struck her. The fact was there between them: Garn Landar's touch had also been on Emmalee, on the most secret and sacred places of her body, those Randy himself had not yet touched or seen.

The twin fragments of the torn piece of money seemed almost to represent Randy and Emmalee themselves, distanced by Garn Landar's effect on both of them.

Rush

Emmalee awoke very early on the day of the land rush, rolled up her bedding, gathered towel, soap, and brush, and walked down to the river. She'd finished washing and was slowly brushing her long hair, sun-bleached now from months on the trail, when Hester Brine appeared. The orange-haired woman nodded in a friendly, matter-of-fact way, set a hairbrush and small covered container down on the riverbank, and began her ablutions. In bearing and manner, Hester reminded Emmalee of Myrtle, except that Myrtle did not use artificial hair coloring, which Hester began to rub vigorously into her scalp from the little container.

Emmalee realized that she was staring.

"Don't be alarmed," Hester said, grinning with her false teeth. "A little vanity never hurt anybody. Your turn'll come some day. Sure, you're a stunner now. Got a fine man who wants to marry you and another one who'd have you if he could. . . ."

Otis! thought Emmalee. Some man gave you a ride on his horse and half the world had you pegged as lovers.

"Are you from Olympia, Hester?" she asked, changing the subject as she folded her towel.

"Naw. Casper, Wyoming. You?"

"Pennsylvania."

"Honey, that is so far east I can't hardly imagine it exists. Vestor Tell's from there."

"From Pennsylvania? Are you sure?"

"Absolutely. He's always sendin' or gettin' telegrams from Philadelphia. That's where he's gettin' money, I figure. Money to loan the settlers."

"Is he allowed to do that? He's the claims agent. It's a government job."

"He's also the chief—and only—law enforcement officer in this part of the territory. If settlers need money, you think they're gonna care who they get it from? By the way," she added, "you don't have to be proud. I been down and out in my day, too, so if you want a loan, see me quick. I don't have all that much, but I can help you out. I *like* you, girl."

"Thank you, but Randy and I will manage."

Hester shook her head, began combing out her orange hair. "You remind me of me when I was your age. Hope you don't have to do the things I did to make ends meet. Good luck to you today, and just remember, I offered."

Vestor Tell rode down the line on an Arabian gelding that could have cost more than any ten of Torquist's Conestogas combined. Watching him, Emmalee was reminded of something out of its element, an entity superficially superior to its immediate surroundings, yet unsatisfied. Tell was subtle and keen. He would betray neither edginess nor anxiety, because he did not suffer from either of these. But he was very lean, in form and visage, and hunger he could not conceal.

But hunger for what?

"I'll fire the starting pistol shot at nine A.M.," Tell told everyone, "and if you don't know what to do then, neither God nor Andy Johnson can help you."

Mention of hapless President Andrew Johnson brought laughter from both farmers and ranchers, no matter that they would soon be locked in struggle to see who grabbed the choicest land. Abe Lincoln's successor had narrowly escaped impeachment. The forthcoming presidential election, however, did not directly affect the pioneers. As citizens of a mere territory, such as Olympia was, they were not permitted to vote. But in time Olympia would become a state, and every man present on the day of this great western land rush knew that immeasurable amounts of future power might be won by the judicious choice of land today. Upriver? Downriver? Close to the mountains or farther away? Land was the future and land was money, but which was the wisest choice of land and where did the greatest power lie?

Torquist, Emmalee recalled, had spoken of Thomas Jefferson's faith in the land and in the goodness of the people who lived on it. Perhaps this would always be so. Sitting next to Randy on his dapple-gray, waiting for Vestor Tell to fire the pistol that could begin the land rush, she wanted only for future generations to remember this day. *At one time*, she thought, her eyes tearing a little, at one time on the face of this earth it was possible for someone like me, who had lost everything, who had nothing, to gamble life and time against fate and fortune and let the chips fall!

"One minute!" bellowed Vestor Tell.

Had there been an observer situated in a high place overlooking Arcady today, he would have seen arrayed on both banks of the Big Two-Hearted, north and south of the village, a veritable army of men, women and children, animals and wagons. Just as Torquist had feared, the

Pennington ranchers were in the most advantageous positions. But this morning, with the starting gun imminent, the sheer expectant energy of the farmers seemed to offer them an edge of their own. They were ready, and some of them were ready to fight if need be. Emmalee and Randy had already fought.

"Well, this is it, I guess," he'd said, while saddling the dapple-gray after breakfast. "Wish me luck."

"Good luck," Emmalee had said, pulling on her riding boots.

"What are you doing?"

"What does it look like? I'm putting on my boots."

"Why?"

"Because I'm coming with you."

An expression of alarm replaced the initial disbelief on his face, alarm over what might happen to her combined with shock that she was going to persist in defying his wishes.

"Em, I thought we settled this yesterday."

"I thought we did too. I'm going."

"The rest of the women are staying here in camp."

"Some of them are, but not all. Take a look around."

Randy did, and he was as surprised as he was displeased with what he saw. Here and there throughout the area, a husband stood with hands on his hips watching in consternation his wife or, in some cases, his mother readying herself for the rush.

"Some of the women got to talking about it last night," Emmalee explained. "Our point is that there'll be less chance of violence with women present. Don't you think so?"

Randy was flabbergasted. "I can't believe you're doing this! This is not the way things are supposed to be!"

"How are things supposed to be? You or Willard

Buttlesworth or even old Festus gives the orders and womenfolk obey?''

''Well . . . well, yes, but only in important affairs. Em, you know I'm no tyrant, but . . . I'm worried about what might happen out there today. Please stay here in Arcady.''

''No,'' Emmalee said. Her boots were on now. She stood up and faced him.

''I don't have room on my horse for you. I have to pack the stakes, and a shovel, and some wire.''

''Oh, that's all right. I'll go borrow Myrtle's mule.''

Myrtle didn't need Ned anyway. She intended to claim just a few acres outside town for a garden. And she strongly encouraged Emmalee's plan.

''A man is sort of like a mule or an ox, Em,'' Myrtle said. ''If you stand in front of them and bang them over the head, nothin' will happen. But if you get behind 'em, they'll wonder what you're up to and they'll usually move, at least a little.''

''Em,'' said Randy when she arrived beside him aboard the mule, ''I guess there's nothing I can say to stop you. But listen. I've picked out land upriver and everything depends on me getting there quickly. You'll never be able to keep up on that mule. So this is what you have to do. When you reach a place where a small stream flows into the river—you can't miss it; it's the only stream on the east bank—ride upchannel for about a quarter of a mile. You'll see three white pines on a low hill. I will have placed one of my corner stakes there. You do the same. I'll have headed north, you go south. Pace off a square of land, don't forget to drive your markers deep in each corner, and we'll meet back at the original stakes, all right?''

''It sounds exciting.''

''I hope it's not more exciting than we've bargained for.''

Vestor Tell rode his horse to a place in front of Hester's general store, took a pistol from his holster, and raised it into the air.

"Prepare to stake your claims," he called. "No man's marker, once set in the ground, is to be touched by anyone else. First come, first served. I will officiate in case adjudication is required, and all claims are to be entered upon my map at the end of the day. Understood?"

A low, anxious hum of assent answered him. Drivers tightened reins, braced in saddles, readied their whips.

"All right . . ." said Tell, and fired the pistol into the air, a thin, sharp crack beneath the sweeping sky. Drivers lurched forward, hooting and shouting; women and children yelled and squealed encouragement. The animals, startled by the suddenness and frenzy, bolted forward from the riverbanks and onto the plain.

Randy stole a moment to lean from his horse and give Emmalee a quick kiss, then he was gone, galloping into the distance, his marker stakes jouncing against the horse's flanks. Emmalee kicked the mule furiously for half a minute. It finally deigned to move into a slow, ambling lope. The race had barely begun and already she was far behind.

On both sides of the river, as far as the eye could see, pioneers rushed to secure a piece of the living earth, so that they and their children and their children's children might have hearth and home.

Festus Bent, his wife, along with Priscilla, Cynthia, and Darlene, rattled by in their wagon, going hell-for-leather into the hills. Festus did not intend to be a sharecropper any more.

"Yo, Em!" called Priscilla. "I saw Garn Landar. He's back there in town."

For a moment, Emmalee was nonplussed. The Bent girls hadn't let her forget what had happened between her and Garn, nor had they ceased speculating as to whether or not it would happen again.

"What are you doing here then?" she shot back. "He told me he was looking for you."

But, in truth, Emmalee wondered what Garn was up to now. If he had any big schemes connected with claiming good land, sitting around Arcady while the land rush was under way could hardly be considered a likely start.

The pioneers scattered pell-mell at top speed all over the plain, and even Myrtle's mule got caught up in the excitement and increased its speed a bit. Not fast enough, though, to outdistance a shouting, cursing Pennington man in a red bandanna, who streaked past Emmalee and gave her a loutish leer. It was Alf Kaiserhalt, who'd yanked her out of the willows yesterday. His presence north of town did not augur well for a peaceful day; Kaiserhalt, scrawny bantam that he was, left a palpable aura of meanness in his wake. The sight of him made Emmalee want to wash herself all over, rid herself of the residue of malevolence he left in the air.

Riding north, Emmalee kept her eyes peeled for evidence of the Pennington men claiming water rights along the river. She saw, with considerable pleasure, that Torquist himself had driven his stakes into a rich swath of land just north of Arcady, and that Virgil Waters and sinewy Elwood Bliss of Iowa had done likewise right across the Big Two-Hearted. So the farmers would have at least some access to the precious water. This fact, however, did not content Emmalee for long. She remembered the false claims Torquist was undertaking today and also that there were miles of riverbank which Pennington and his men might readily seize.

By the time the mule had carried her as far as the small stream that Randy had mentioned, Emmalee's hopes for the day had broken down. In spite of intentions, the presence of women was not preventing trouble. Emmalee heard yelling and shouting near the river and in the hills, and saw with a sinking feeling that a scuffle had broken out between Festus Bent and Lambert Strep. If the farmers could not refrain from fighting between themselves, what hope was there in the long run? Lambert wrestled Festus to the ground as Bent's wife and daughters danced around like idiots, trying, apparently, to crack their father's attacker on the skull. Emmalee made a mental note of the scene, in case it should be important later. She wondered how Vestor Tell would resolve contested claims.

Bent was on top of Strep and his women were cheering wildly when Emmalee turned upstream and rode into the hills. At first she was disheartened. The land rose abruptly from the river and the hills through which the little stream flowed were steep, almost rugged. She saw very few pioneers surveying this section, having been discouraged by the comparative severity of the terrain. But beyond the ring of hills, revealed to her suddenly as she urged the mule over the crest, was a small, high, sweet plain, a rolling expanse of gentle hills and shady groves. Immediately she understood why Randy had chosen this area: The land was rich and sheltered; the stream would provide water, all but eliminating dependence upon the Big Two-Hearted. Then she saw the three white pines he had named as a landmark and rode toward them happily. He was driving his initial stake into the ground beneath the pines. She thought he ought to be farther along by now, since he'd gone on ahead, but it didn't seem to matter because there was no one else around to vie with him for the claim.

Randy began to look a little funny to Emmalee as she rode nearer.

Then he looked very strange.

And when she got right up close to him he looked exactly like Alf Kaiserhalt, who was pounding a stake that read A. K'HLT into the dirt. He looked up at her and grinned evilly.

"Well, lookee who's here, would ya? If it ain't that snoopy little spitfire from yesterday. Did Otis get what he wanted off'n you?"

Emmalee pulled Ned to a halt and looked around. This had to be the place Randy had meant; he really ought to be there, she hadn't seen him anywhere else. And she didn't see a sign of him there either.

Kaiserhalt was holding a mallet in one hand and looking up at her, his head cocked to one side like a fighting rooster set to attack.

"Otis just gave me a ride home yesterday," Emmalee said, almost civilly.

"Heh-heh. Shows what you know. Otis got a real bad case for you. Trouble with him, he's a gentleman. I ain't."

"That's obvious," said Emmalee. She started to dismount.

"What're you doin'?"

"Well, I'll tell you. I'm getting off this mule."

Randy had told her to plant a stake and then go south. Kaiserhalt was there, and there was nothing to stop him from making a claim, but there seemed no reason for Emmalee not to go ahead with her plans.

"I'd advise you to stay in the saddle," said Kaiserhalt edgily.

Emmalee tensed. She saw the vile glint of angry determination in the little man's eyes, saw the ripcord muscles bulge beneath his faded shirt.

"You can't claim this whole area," she told him. "Nor can you tell me what to do or not to do."

Emmalee knew now for certain that something was amiss. Alf wore a gun; Randy didn't. Had something happened? But if Kaiserhalt had harmed Randy in some way, where was the dapple-gray? Kaiserhalt could have driven it off, of course, but . . .

"You stay on that mule, or I'll teach you a few things. Warm you up for Otis, so to speak. . . ."

Emmalee studied the ground where Kaiserhalt stood. She saw his marker, half-driven, and the scuffled earth around it. A lot of dirt had been disturbed just for one wooden stake.

"You haven't seen Randy Clay here, have you?"

"Honey, I haven't seen *anybody* here. I got here first and this is gonna be *my* land, right along this stream."

Emmalee understood. Pennington had sent Kaiserhalt to claim land along the creek. The ranchers weren't missing a trick.

"Then I guess we'll be neighbors," said Emmalee, and climbed down from the mule.

Alf Kaiserhalt swung the mallet. "Now you're gonna get what's comin' to you, one way or t'other."

Emmalee ducked the blow, realized she had no time to get back up on Ned, and ran for the shelter of the pines. Kaiserhalt studied the hills for a moment, saw no riders, and advanced slowly toward her.

Good God, thought Emmalee, shrinking behind one of the pines, I've done it now. Maybe if I feint and run for his horse, get away . . .

"Some of you women just got to learn the hard way." Kaiserhalt grinned, coming toward her with the mallet poised.

Emmalee was about to scream, for whatever good that might do her, when her foot struck something. She looked down. It was a wooden stake and it bore the name CLAY.

Randy *had* been there. He'd driven his corner marker and then ridden off to place another. Alf Kaiserhalt had taken it out of the ground and was in the process of replacing it with his own stake. In the distance, Emmalee saw two riders come over the top of a hill, but they were too far away to help her. Kaiserhalt was right on the other side of the tree, weaving, bobbing, ready to attack her with the mallet.

"You'll never get away with it," she told him, trying to buy time.

"Get away with what? You fell off your mule and cracked your skull on a rock. Shouldn't be out here anyway. Got no business. I came across you an' got you back into town soon's I could, but unfortunately, I was a little too late."

He swung the mallet in a sharp, downward motion. Emmalee ducked down and to one side. The mallet tore away a strip of bark when it glanced off the tree.

Emmalee could tell that the riders had seen her plight, had begun to gallop toward her. But the distance was great, and meanwhile Alf Kaiserhalt came around the tree and lifted the mallet again.

"Like to do you another way"—he grunted—"but this'll have to fill the bill."

He struck again. In desperation, Emmalee grabbed Randy's stake, swung it upward in an arc toward Kaiserhalt. Stake and mallet collided with the ugly, crunching sound of wood on wood. The marker flew from Emmalee's hands and the handle of the mallet cracked like a stick. The ram-shaped head went flying.

Kaiserhalt laughed. "Hell, I enjoy a piece that puts up a fight." He leered. "Makes it better, see. You gonna get it, honey."

Emmalee wanted to run but forced herself to back slowly away from him. If Kaiserhalt overtook her from behind and forced her down, she wouldn't stand a chance. Once he got her on the ground, his wiry strength would keep her there.

She looked up, seeking deliverance from the approaching horsemen, but to her horror both of the riders had disappeared. How could that be? Down into a slight dip between hills? *Please, God . . .*

"Someone's coming!" she told Kaiserhalt, pointing toward the horizon anyway. If she could just distract him in some way.

But he wasn't buying. "That trick's as old as the river." He grunted, so close to her now, darting, crouching, that she could smell his breath: onions, bile, and spoiled meat.

Out of the corner of her eye, Emmalee thought she saw the riders again, coming over the nearest hillock, but she couldn't be sure because Alf Kaiserhalt made his move, springing toward her in a manner that she had seen somewhere before and which her subconscious mind had salted away. She saw him coming and responded without thinking, acting with a series of movements she did not know she possessed, but which she had also observed once before in Denver.

She ducked down and to one side, catching his clutching arm as he flew past, twisting his arm and bringing it down across her upraised knee. Alf Kaiserhalt's howl of agony rose to the sky. He stood there before her, grabbing at his devastated arm. Angry white slivers of rent bone sliced through his shirtsleeve; welling blood matted in the cloth, which stuck to his skin.

The two riders drew near and reined in.

"Not bad, Emmalee," said Garn Landar. "I guess you learn a lesson well."

"You all right, Em?" Ebenezer Creel cackled nervously. "What are we gonna do, Garn? What are we gonna do?"

Garn looked at Kaiserhalt and smiled slowly.

"Seems," he said, "that Emmalee has things well under control. I think we can count on her to do what she wants, as always. You *are* all right, aren't you?"

Emmalee nodded, biting her lip.

"Then I wouldn't think of interfering. Get his gun, though."

Kaiserhalt was suffering too much to care that Emmalee removed his weapon from its holster.

"All right, Ebenezer, we've got some ground to cover," said Garn. He tipped his hat to Emmalee.

"See you, Em," said Ebenezer, who seemed a little worried about leaving her there.

The two men rode away then. Emmalee noted that Garn was riding his black stallion. Maybe there was something in Lottie Pennington's moral code that prohibited her from using a man's horse on the day of a land rush. Emmalee also saw that Garn and Ebenezer were riding toward the rugged foothills of the Sacajawea Range. She almost laughed in spite of herself. If the two men intended to make a fortune out of inhospitable, unproductive mountain land, they had rocks in their heads. Emmalee felt a little sorry for Ebenezer, though. Obviously Garn had sweet-talked him into some fool ploy that tantalized the old man's imagination.

Well, there wasn't time now to think about that. She had her own problems. Alf Kaiserhalt had slumped down beneath one of the pines. Pain and hatred had turned his eyes red. Emmalee held the gun on him and tried to decide what to do.

"You are gonna pay for this, lady."

"If you don't shut up, I'll shoot you and put you out of your misery."

"Hah! You ain't got the guts."

Emmalee pulled the trigger. She wasn't especially familiar with handguns, but she had fired rifles and shotguns in the past. Both types of weaponry required fairly strong pressure on the trigger before they discharged. But she barely touched the trigger of Kaiserhalt's revolver when it barked and jumped in her hand. The bullet slammed into the ground in front of the wounded man, raising a small cloud of dust.

"Hey!" he yelled, terrified. "That thing's got a hair-trigger! You'll kill me."

"That's the general idea, if you don't stay put. After I stake my claim, I'm taking you back into town and having you arrested."

Where was Randy? She hoped he'd return soon. Kaiserhalt was peering around, judging the lay of the land, looking for some way to escape. Emmalee saw several riders and a wagon on the hill now. If she didn't get started and place her markers, she'd be out of luck, Randy's plan ruined, the day lost. She couldn't waste another minute guarding Kaiserhalt.

"What're you doin'?" the man asked suspiciously as Emmalee walked toward his horse.

"You'll see."

She took the looped lasso from his saddlehorn, carried it back to him, and began tying him to the pine tree.

"Owwwww! Careful of my . . . God damn it . . . my arm! You can't leave me like this."

"Don't worry. I won't be gone long. I have to drive my stakes before those people riding this way take the land I want."

Kaiserhalt laughed maliciously. "You ain't gonna beat anybody on that mule."

"That's why I'm going to borrow your horse."

"*What?*"

"Besides, Randy Clay will probably be back soon. I suggest you treat him with respect. He's not going to like it when he learns that you removed his marker."

Then Emmalee yanked Kaiserhalt's stake out of the earth, replaced it with Randy's, and drove her own into the ground too. Mounting Kaiserhalt's horse, she galloped southward and managed to place her second marker before the group of pioneers came down from the hill. She saw that they were from Torquist's party—Leander Rupp, formerly of Elkhart, Indiana, and a whole passel of his pale-eyed southern Indiana hillbilly cousins. She was barely familiar with the Rupps. They'd always had difficulty getting started in the mornings and usually they'd brought up the rear of the wagon train. "Leander Rupp carried a ton of dust across Kansas," Randy'd joked once. Apparently Rupp had had another late start today.

After driving her second marker, Emmalee turned east. When the official survey occurred, there'd be time to measure exactly, but Emmalee tried as best she could to gauge the distance covered by the horse and calculate accordingly. An acre was a little over forty-three thousand square feet, and she was allowed a hundred and sixty acres by law. Setting her third marker, she turned north and found to her considerable satisfaction that she was only yards away from Randy's easternmost stake. Then she headed back westward toward the three pines.

Randy was waiting for her.

"Em! We did it! We've claimed three hundred and twenty acres of gorgeous land."

"Where is Alf Kaiserhalt?"

"Who?"

"The man I told you about. The one who grabbed me in the willows. And where's Ned?"

In his excitement, Randy hadn't even noticed that Em was riding a horse instead of Myrtle's mule.

Quickly she explained what had happened.

"And he tried to kill you with the mallet?" cried Randy. "What did you do?"

"I broke his . . . I broke his arm. It was . . . luck, I guess. We struggled . . ."

"Did anyone witness this? Are you sure he pulled out my marker and replaced it with his?"

She did not want to mention that Garn had been present. It would only be an unnecessary complication. "I don't think anyone saw it up close. The Rupps were too far away at the time. But Kaiserholt did take your marker."

"And he also took the mule. Probably back to town. I'll deal with him when we get there. But meantime, Em, just think! This is all ours. We'll call it Three Pines. What do you think? And can't you just see the richness of that loam? One good harvest will be enough to get us on our feet. I'm going to get started and build a house right away. We'll put up a little cabin or something on your place. That'll satisfy the domicile requirement Tell told us about. I'll borrow a little money from Hester—I guess there's no other way—to buy some seed and a few cows. . . ."

Randy chattered on. He was happy. He was euphoric. Emmalee herself was more than pleased. She already had a hundred dollars. Using her land as security, she would borrow from Hester, borrow enough to pay off Torquist and get some seed and stock of her own. It did not seem, at that moment, as if she could possibly fail. The land was so rich.

They got on the horses and rode back to Arcady, which was already jammed with farmers and ranchers waiting to let Vestor Tell know the location of their claims. Dismounting, they joined the line standing in front of the general store. Arcady was abuzz with the news of the day, and very quickly Emmalee perceived a pattern. True to the fears of Torquist and his farmers, Pennington's ranchers had taken the best land. A palpable tension filled the air, rife with conflict, the disappointment of some just as intense as the triumphant satisfaction of others. Burt Pennington himself had taken a long swath of territory along the west bank of the river, not far from Torquist's claim, and his cohorts had managed to commandeer vast, contiguous sections on both sides of the Big Two-Hearted. It was a veritable empire of connecting tracts. The farmers, by contrast, were scattered all over, their holdings patchlike and faintly ludicrous when Tell penciled them in on his big map of Olympia. Some farmers were surrounded on all four sides by ranchland.

But even these farmers were not the most unfortunate. Some people had failed to claim land at all. These hapless men, Festus Bent among them, hung their heads and slouched against the walls of the store, beyond hope. Their women had already retreated, weeping, to the wagons, which seemed at this moment like the only homes they would ever have. There were two choices for those who had failed to make claims: They might go back east from whence they came, the burden of failure dogging their every step, or they could attempt to hire out as field hands to the newly propertied settlers. Within the space of a day, Olympia had added to its farmers and ranchers a third group, a bitter underclass of penniless men whose last great dream had been shattered. Such a situation did not augur well for tranquility in the Promised Land.

A big crowd of Pennington's people were celebrating raucously around the beer barrel when Emmalee and Randy entered the general store. There were plenty of farmers inside, too, but the two groups kept their distance as much as possible in the din and press. Emmalee saw Burt Pennington's ruddy, bullet-shaped head, saw Lottie beside him, beaming in demure, self-satisfied triumph. Lottie spotted Emmalee and her full, lush lips formed a brief, spiritless smile.

"How'd you two make out?" inquired Hester Brine, coming over to say hello to Emmalee and Randy. "Heared you had a spot of trouble."

"What?" asked Emmalee, puzzled. "Oh, Kaiserhalt. It was nothing. . . ."

"Watch your step," warned Hester in a low voice.

"Next!" bellowed Tell from behind his desk. "Step

along lively there. We haven't got all day. Well, now look what we have here!"

Emmalee and Randy turned toward Tell. Alf Kaiserhalt, his arm in a sling, sat on a chair beside the claims agent, regarding the young couple with his small, evil eyes.

"Seems we have a little problem here," said Tell.

"What's that?" Randy asked anxiously.

"Both of your claims are questionable, due to accusations made by Mr. Kaiserhalt here. I'm gonna have to adjudicate."

The people in the store quieted, pressing toward Tell's desk and the big map he had spread out before him.

"There's nothing amiss with either of our claims," said Emmalee, fighting to keep a quaver of uncertainty out of her voice. Kaiserhalt had returned to town first and she had no idea what tidings he had related.

"You," said Tell, pointing to Randy, "show me on the map the sections that you and your . . . ah, fiancée claimed."

Randy picked up a pencil, bent to the map, studied it for a moment, and then drew two rough squares in the uplands east of the river.

"Em and I staked these fair and square," Randy began. "We—"

"I'll be the judge of that, son," retorted Tell. "Alf, you go ahead and state your case now."

Everyone in the store was listening intently. One could have heard a blade of dry grass fall upon the plank floor. A bee buzzed near the beer barrel.

"Much obliged, Vestor," drawled Kaiserhalt, as if he and Tell were the best of friends. "You see, the whole thing's pretty simple, really. I was up by the three pines, driving in my first stake, when these two"—he gestured toward Randy and Emmalee—"came riding up. He was on a horse an' she rode a mule."

"That's not true at all!" cried Randy. "We weren't even together."

"Pipe down, Clay. You'll have your chance to talk when I say so," Tell commanded.

Kaiserhalt grinned. "They both jumped me," he continued. "I didn't have a chance. Broke my arm, they did, an' tied me to a tree. It was pitiable, I tell you. Then they put in their own stakes and rode off in separate directions to claim the land I'd figured on choosing. The gal took my horse too. Reckon she ought to learn what happens to horse thievers in this here country."

"You're a liar!" Emmalee spat at him.

"If that's so," drawled Burt Pennington, standing in the crowd that was watching these proceedings, "then how come Alf rode back into Arcady aboard a decrepit mule?"

"Don't you call my Ned any names!" blurted Myrtle Higgins, who was perched up on the cold stove for a better view.

The tension lessened for an instant as people laughed, but the levity did not last long.

"Did you take his horse or not?" Tell demanded of Emmalee.

"Yes, but I didn't *steal* it," Emmalee cried. "I only took it because I wanted to"—she realized how weak her explanation sounded—"to make my claim as fast as possible. Randy wasn't there at all. Mr. Kaiserhalt tried to kill me with a mallet. It took a while to fight him off and tie him up. I saw some people coming toward the land I wanted, so I—"

"Took the horse?" Tell grinned.

"Yes."

"And you alone, all by yourself, broke Alf's arm and tied him to a tree?"

"Ain't no woman born could do that to me." Kaiserhalt snorted. "See? I'm the one that's telling the truth."

Emmalee noted that Tell did not chide the scrawny rancher for interrupting.

"It is a little difficult to believe your story, Miss Alden." Tell smiled. "You licked a *man* singlehanded?"

"Emmalee's telling the absolute truth," Randy put in. "She did it herself. I wasn't even around. I'd gotten there first, you see, had driven my stake, which Kaiserhalt tore out of the ground, by the way, and—"

"Your testimony's got to be discounted." Tell shrugged.

"And why is that?"

"Well, you and the girl are tied up together. Naturally, you'd stick up for her."

"But—"

"Quiet. That's my ruling, and I have the sole right of adjudication in this territory. Do I make myself clear?"

"All too clear," said Emmalee, glaring at him.

There was no doubt in her mind that Tell was completely on the side of the ranchers. She wondered what cash had changed hands, what promises had passed lips, and how the future of Olympia would be affected thereby. She vowed to find out before it was too late.

But right now she had other problems.

"You mentioned that some people were coming toward you at the time you absconded with Alf's horse," Tell was addressing her. "That means there were witnesses. Who are they? *Where* are they?"

Emmalee looked around the store. She saw all those eyes upon her, waiting to see what would happen, what she would do. Taking the horse had seemed a good idea at the time. She hadn't given it a second thought. But taking a man's means of transportation, she realized, carried the same punishment as murder. Yet, she saw, most of the people were not against her. Oh, Lottie Pennington was enjoying every minute of Tell's nasty little charade, no doubt about it. But the women in particular, even the ranchers' women, seemed disposed to listen to what she had to say. Emmalee saw the suntanned, big-handed woman who'd exchanged harsh words with Kaiserhalt in the willow grove. That woman knew what Alf was like. And Otis, Emmalee noticed, seemed in no hurry to believe his mean-spirited comrade. Burt Pennington, however, pressed the issue.

"I hate to see a pretty little gal in trouble," he declared loudly, "but someone who'd take a man's horse could find it in her conscience to pull up his marker stake too."

"When we want to hear from you, we'll ask," shouted Horace Torquist. "Emmalee Alden is one of my people, and my people do not practice chicanery!"

"Ho!" Pennington shot back. "That's not what I've observed."

"Are you making accusations?" Torquist demanded, trying to move closer to Pennington through the crowd.

"Maybe I should. Maybe I *will*, when I get the facts," Pennington said testily.

Emmalee realized, with a sinking sensation, that Burt Pennington either knew or suspected Torquist's strategem involving the false claims. An angry rumbling rose from the crowd.

"I'm in charge here," bellowed Tell. 'We're conducting a serious inquiry and you all better shut up or get out, understand?" The people quieted but their tension remained, hanging in the air like bitter smoke. "You were saying," he reminded Emmalee sanctimoniously, "that there may have been witnesses?"

Emmalee thought it over. Garn and Ebenezer Creel had seen Kaiserhalt attacking her. But Garn and Ebenezer weren't there, not to mention the fact that she didn't want to upset Randy, which any word about Garn was sure to do. She studied the crowd some more and saw Leander

Rupp drinking beer at the back of the store. Rupp and his family hadn't seen much, but they *had* been there.

"Mr. Rupp may have seen something," she said, catching his glance.

Rupp looked stricken, the more so when Tell called him over to the desk. Rupp was a tall, wiry fellow with big ears and a hangdog look. He avoided Emmalee's eyes, but she saw Kaiserhalt grinning at the man.

"All right, what'd you see?" Tell demanded of the uncomfortable farmer.

"Uh . . . not too much."

"He's the one untied me from the tree," Kaiserhalt supplied.

"Look, what is this?" Randy asked. "When Em or I try to say something, we're told to hold our peace. When Mr. Kaiserhalt or anyone else—"

"Hold your peace or I'll disqualify your claims on the spot," Tell pronounced. "I'm the law here. Get it?"

"I think so," said Randy. "A law that takes sides." He stared unflinchingly at Tell, who glared right back. Emmalee had sensed the fact earlier, and now she saw again how Randy was being tempered and strengthened by challenge. He had the look of a young archangel about him still, but coming into his eyes, etching itself upon his features, was the steel and self-certainty of a seraphim.

Vestor Tell sensed it, too, averted his glance, and again addressed Leander Rupp. "Speak up, man. Your testimony could decide it all. What'd you see?"

Emmalee noted that Rupp's worried eyes immediately flashed to Kaiserhalt. He seemed to find some relief there, because he took a deep breath and spoke clearly.

"I saw the girl tie Mr. Kaiserhalt to the tree. I saw her take his horse. That's what I saw."

"She was alone when she tied him to the tree? That is, Mr. Clay was not around?"

"No, sir."

"He'd already done ridden off," Kaiserhalt pointed out. "Don't take nothin' for a able-bodied girl to tie me if I can't barely move on account of a ruined wing."

"So, Mr. Rupp, you saw her tie the man and steal his horse?"

"Yes, sir."

"I didn't steal it," protested Emmalee. "It's tied to the hitching rail right outside this store. He was trying to *kill* me."

"Heh-heh." Kaiserhalt snickered.

"And if Randy broke Mr. Kaiserhalt's arm," Emmalee persisted, "then why didn't Mr. Rupp see him?"

"I wasn't there for that," Rupp faltered. "I didn't see that."

"Of course you didn't. That's because Randy *wasn't* there."

"That's the truth," said Randy.

"I broke Mr. Kaiserhalt's arm all by myself," said Emmalee, turning so that she could address all the people in the room. "I did it because I *had* to do it. He attacked me. I saw him pulling Randy's stake out of the ground. Now that *is* the truth."

The tension between farmers and ranchers in the store edged to a dangerous new height. "Well, well," said Vestor Tell. "Seems we still have a passel of contradictions here. Looks like I'm gonna have to decide."

"No little bitty woman could break my arm," scoffed Alf.

Emmalee lost her temper. "I'm three or four inches taller than you," she told Kaiserhalt. "I'm not so little. Get up. Let me show everybody."

"What?" faltered Kaiserhalt.

"Get up. As a demonstration, I'll break your other arm."

The words took a moment to sink in, but the response was thunderous. Instantly Emmalee regretted her splenetic outburst. She had let her temperament play right into the hands of her enemies.

"Lookit how mad she gets!"

"I bet they did it, for sure."

"An' stealin' the poor guy's horse, to boot."

"Here's my decision," announced Vestor Tell. "Now, anybody with ears to hear has got to realize that we can't get no corroboration on the actual sequence of events out by the three pines. We weren't there. I'm inclined to believe Alf Kaiserhalt . . ."

Something much like a groan, followed by a suspiration of rage, rose from Torquist and his farmers.

". . . because Alf is clearly the wounded party in this. Just look at the poor man's arm. But . . . *but* like I say, I wasn't there."

"Nice of you to admit it," muttered Myrtle Higgins.

"So," Tell continued, "I don't know who pulled up whose stakes, nor how Clay and Miss Alden managed to crack Alf's bones. So what I got to do is I got to decide this matter on the basis of *in-con-tro-ver-ti-ble* evidence."

"You don't have any!" Torquist cried.

Tell grinned at him. "Sure do," he snapped. "The gal took Alf's horse. He can press charges on that matter if he wants to."

"I only care about them acres," Kaiserhalt replied magnanimously. "I ain't out to see a purty gal like that strung up from a cottonwood, even if she is a thief."

"But anybody who would steal a horse would lie. An' any man friend lookin' to claim land *with* her would lie *for* her. So the claims of Mr. Clay and Miss Alden are hereby disqualified, by the authority vested in me. I rule that Mr. Kaiserhalt gets both tracts of land, one to farm and the other to sell, such sale to be contracted within ninety days."

"No!" Randy cried.

Emmalee saw Leander Rupp bend toward Kaiserhalt. "Good man, Rupp," Alf said to the farmer. "Burt an' us boys'll take care of you. It don't matter you didn't get no land."

"Fraud!" shouted Emmalee. "I'm going to report this to higher authorities."

Tell just grinned at her, then he nodded toward the telegraph machine next to the wall behind his desk. "Go ahead," he said. "You cable Washington, D.C., and tell 'em all about how a horse-thievin' little spitfire took it into her head to steal a good man's claim."

He got no further. Randy reached over the desk, grabbed the claims agent by his shirt collar, and pulled him forward. The desk overturned, along with the big map that was on it. "Help!" cried Tell, as Randy drew back his fist. The imminent tension, the animosity and discord that had been building in the store came quickly to flashpoint, something Hester Brine perceived immediately. "Don't wreck my place!" she shouted, but it was too late. Otis leaped forward and grabbed Randy's arm before he could punch Tell. The claims agent himself escaped Randy's grasp and scurried for safety behind the toppled desk. Alf Kaiserhalt, fearing further injury to his arm, dashed toward the door. Burt Pennington, surrounded by several ranchers, tried to move through the crowd toward Otis, who now grappled with Randy. Their progress was hindered by Horace Torquist, who stepped in front of them, crossed his arms, and declared, "Let's have it out now. I think you ranchers are bribing Tell."

Burt Pennington swung from his heels, caught Torquist a fierce blow on the side of the head. The white-maned leader swayed backward into the arms of Virgil Waters and Willard Buttlesworth. But he did not go down. Pennington and his men advanced, fists ready. Women screamed and retreated behind stacks of dry goods. A shovel fell from its hook on the wall, striking Festus Bent on the head. Leander Rupp was slammed against the wall when Randy and Otis, wrestling each other, crashed into him. Rupp slid to the floor, his eyes glazed. "Stop it! Stop it!" Hester Brine shrieked. Horace Torquist threw a punch at Pennington, catching him just above the heart. "Daddy!" shrieked a terrified Lottie Pennington, as her father flew backward through the store and crashed into the beer barrel, overturning it. Torquist advanced on his downed rival, but was struck in the face by Lottie herself.

The whole store was in turmoil. Everyone in it was fighting or trying to escape or watching, most with enthusiasm and a few with dismay. The human animal has not come so far from caves and jungles that the sight of a snarling tooth-and-claw confrontation does not rouse the blood. Emmalee circled Randy and Otis, trying for a opportunity to separate them. Then Randy stuck his foot behind Otis's leg, twisted, applied pressure. The two men went crashing to the floor, Randy on top. Otis wore a revolver in a holster at his hip, and Emmalee saw him reaching for the weapon now.

She acted, grabbing the weapon before he had a chance to pull it and fire at Randy. The gun was cold and hard in her hand. She pointed it at the ceiling and fired.

Everything stopped, the screaming and the shouting and the punching. Emmalee climbed up on Vestor Tell's stool, holding the smoking revolver. All eyes were on her.

"Why did you stop fighting?" she demanded of them, the anger in her voice tinged with a mixture of bitterness and disgust. "Did you think the gunshot killed someone? Was that what made everybody quit kicking and gouging? Would a death have satisfied you?"

There was too much rage in the room to be dispersed by an admonishment, however sarcastic, but a few of the men looked faintly ashamed. "That's exactly what they're lookin' for," growled one of the ranch women. "Somebody dead. Ain't gonna be satisfied until they have that."

Otis and Randy got to their feet and stood in front of Emmalee. She handed Otis his gun.

"Take it."

He did. Randy watched him warily.

"Take it," Emmalee said again, "but put it away." Everyone continued to listen to her. Vestor Tell got up and set his desk aright. "There's no need to kill each other over what happened to my land claim," Emmalee said. "Randy and I are more than disappointed by what Mr. Tell has decided. But our problem—and all of the problems that I'm afraid we're going to face—can't be decided by violence. Because don't you see? If we begin fighting with one another over every trespass, real or imagined, there will be nothing left for any of us except bloodshed and mourning."

"You tell 'em!" cried Myrtle Higgins.

"That little gal's right," Emmalee heard a ranch wife telling her glowering husband.

Horace Torquist and Burt Pennington were on their feet now, standing side by side. Emmalee realized all too clearly that her words were not reaching them, but she continued to try anyway.

"Randy and I are going to appeal Mr. Tell's ruling," she said. "Legally. To whoever and wherever we have to make that appeal."

"My judgment's final, I told you that," muttered Tell. "Waste your time if you want."

"I don't believe you," Randy informed him. "I think something's crooked between you and the ranchers."

"Yeah?" bellowed Burt Pennington. "You better not

talk so quick. I'm a'goin' to find out some stuff on my own."

The situation seemed on the verge of breaking down again.

"Everybody out!" yelled Hester Brine. "You've done enough damage." She had managed to set the beer barrel aright, although a swarm of insects and somebody's hound were savoring the spilled brew.

"Nobody is going to take my land away from me!" Emmalee said. "But I'm not going to get it in a way that will destroy everybody's peace."

"How noble." Vestor Tell sneered. "Washington will back my decisions all the way, don't you know? But go on and find out if you like. It'll be a good education for you as to how the country works."

"Don't you talk to Emmalee like that," snapped Randy, stepping forward.

"I've had enough of this." Tell snarled. With a quick, deft movement, he reached inside his waistcoat and pulled out a small, mean-looking, short-snouted pistol. Emmalee saw Randy's eyes open wide in surprise and fear; she saw Tell's arm go rigid as he aimed and braced to fire.

The blast came suddenly, hurting Emmalee's ears, sounding and resounding within the store, a head-splitting explosion of immense force from so small a pistol. Emmalee could not believe that a miniature gun could produce such a report, nor that Randy was not hit at such close range. She was also surprised to see the tiny gun go flying from Tell's hand, to see Tell drop to his knees clutching his suddenly shattered, bloody fingers. The gun must have malfunctioned, exploded *in* his hand.

"Well, Ebenezer, it looks like I haven't lost my touch completely," observed Garn Landar.

He and the old man were standing in the store's doorway. Garn's big, long-barreled revolver smoked in his hand. He swept the store casually but thoroughly with his eyes, determined that no one there had the inclination to fire on him, and shoved the weapon into his belt.

Emmalee and the others realized, with some awe, that Garn had shot Tell's pistol out of his hand. The claims agent knelt on the floor, moaning. Emmalee and Randy realized, simultaneously, that Garn had probably just saved Randy's life and certainly prevented serious injury from a bullet fired at close range.

"Yep, Garn"—Ebenezer cackled—"you sure do have the touch."

"You all right, Tell?" Garn demanded of the claims agent.

Tell, realizing that he was in a legal situation far worse than temporary physical disability—he had pulled a weapon on an unarmed man, after all—chose discretion.

"I'm all right."

"Then get your map on the desk. I want to draw in the boundaries of my claim."

"Yep. The boundaries of his claim," seconded Ebenezer. "I want to draw in mine too."

The transition from violence to routine, almost as if it had been produced by Garn's easy attitude, calmed the people in the store. They pressed forward to see what Garn had claimed. Grimacing in pain, Tell picked up the map with his good hand and spread it on the top of the desk. Emmalee watched Garn as he stepped forward. He noticed her and smiled, but that was all. He offered Randy a casual nod. His behavior left her with a feeling that was quite like hurt. It was very odd. In the past, when he had teased and taunted her, when he had pursued her, even when he had attempted to seduce her, Emmalee had thought that she wanted him to go away and leave her alone. It would be far better, she had believed, if he paid no attention to her at all. It was true that the incident behind the boulders in Denver had been painful and embarrassing for both of them, but it had apparently resulted, on Garn's part, in a decision to treat Emmalee with detachment. That was what hurt. He had caused her all that trouble and . . . and this was the manner in which he'd chosen to deal with her. Actually, she oughtn't to have felt badly about it. She didn't care for him anyhow, so what was the point of regret, however faint? Wait a minute, she told herself, as a new insight struck her. I think he caused me a lot of trouble. Maybe he thinks I did the same to him.

But, even so, he didn't have to act so remote, did he? As if they'd never known each other at all?

"Better get that hand bandaged first chance you get," advised Garn, as he leaned over the desk and sought a pencil. "Don't want to let it get infected. What was going on, anyway?"

"Minor altercation," muttered Tell.

Garn glanced around, his gaze inquiring. His eyes rested on Randy.

"Thanks for what you did, Landar, but it's really none of your affair. It's all settled now."

"Like hell it is!" roared Torquist. "It's only the beginning." He addressed Garn directly. "Tell and the ranchers are in league with each other—"

"I wouldn't talk if I were you," threatened Pennington.

"—and Alf Kaiserhalt just swindled Clay and Emmalee out of their claims."

"Kaiserhalt?" asked Garn, astounded. "Last time I saw him, he was being tied to a tree by Emmalee. He tried to knock off her head with a wooden mallet but she grabbed his arm and snapped it as if it were a twig."

Garn saw Alf Kaiserhalt, who was trying to duck back into the crowd.

"You—you *saw* the incident?" faltered Randy, whose

glance went from Garn to Emmalee and back again. "Em, why didn't you?"

"Tell," pronounced Torquist peremptorily. "There *was* a witness. I think you better reconsider your decision."

"There was *two* witnesses," put in Ebenezer Creel. "I seen everything myself. Kaiserhalt attacked Em, but she beat him. Seen it all clear as day. She was tyin' him to a pine tree, last I saw."

Emmalee felt Randy's eyes on her. He was wondering why she hadn't mentioned the presence of Garn and Creel. Throughout the store, people were demanding that Vestor Tell change his decision and set the record straight.

"Kaiserhalt!" ordered Garn. "Quit hiding there. Come out here in the open. What's this about taking other people's claims?"

Virgil Waters got a hand on little Alf Kaiserhalt and shoved him toward Garn. "Well, she done took my horse," he whined, fully conscious of being defenseless and on the spot.

"You're lucky she didn't take your head off."

"Is it true?" Myrtle Higgins demanded of Kaiserhalt. "Is it true what you said earlier, about Randy breaking your arm? Were you lying?"

"Randy!" scoffed Ebenezer. "Randy Clay wasn't anywhere around."

"Change your decision, Tell," said Torquist, in a triumphant tone. "You've got that incontrovertible evidence you were looking for. From two witnesses who aren't even involved."

"Well, Leander Rupp wasn't directly involved either," Tell protested. "Why would he lie?"

"Rupp? Who's he?" asked Garn.

The feckless farmer lifted his hand slightly and looked sheepishly at Garn. "Here I am."

"Did you claim any land today, Rupp?"

"Ah . . . no, sir."

"What are you going to do in Olympia?"

"Well, uh . . . I suppose . . . something will come up."

"I expect it has already. Did one of the ranchers offer you a job, perhaps?"

Rupp flushed a dark red. "Ah, not in so many words. . . ." he managed.

"I expected as much," said Garn coldly. "Tell, I'd suggest you take these things into consideration."

"Yeah, change your decision. Give Randy and Emmalee their land," Torquist called out. He was supported by a rising tide of voices from his people. In contrast, the ranchers stood mute and scowling, having been made to look bad and angrily aware of their public humiliation.

"This ain't over by a long shot," Otis vowed, taking up a position next to his boss, Burt Pennington.

Tell, wrapping his hand in a handkerchief, said nothing at first. He seemed to be searching for a way out of the dilemma, a strategy that would not require him to back down.

"I expect I could find someone to listen to me now," Emmalee told him. "In Washington, D.C., or wherever."

"The truth is bound to come out," Randy added.

"Well, now," drawled Tell, after another moment of hesitant consideration, "I guess I was misled, wasn't I? Through no fault of my own, of course. It could have happened to anyone. Well, you know what we have to do in this territory? We have to give one another the benefit of the doubt. Poor Alf, in his pain, probably got confused, thought Mr. Clay might have attacked him. Things like that can happen. Oh, sure, they can happen. But . . ." He allowed himself a long pause. "But I got to bow to these latest facts that Landar and Creel came in with. So, yes, the claims up by the three pines will be entered on the map in the names of Miss Alden and Mr. Clay."

"Yaaaayyyyyyy!" cried the farmers.

"Thank you," Emmalee said to Garn. But he ignored her, bent over the map, and began to mark it with a boundary line. Emmalee could not make out, at first, exactly what area he had claimed, but she did see Vestor Tell's changing expression as the claims agent watched Garn delineate his territory. Tell's face first showed a kind of bewildered astonishment that changed to amusement and then, as Garn put down the pencil, to contempt.

Emmalee edged forward. She saw that Garn had chosen a site in the high country up along the Big Two-Hearted River, a remote and rugged area way up among boulders, stony ground, and trees. Land like that was good for nothing. Before she could register her disappointment that he could have made such a terrible claim—had she been right, after all, in assuming that he would never be a proper success?—Ebenezer Creel moved to the map. Gritting hard, the tip of his tongue between his teeth, old Ebenezer painstakingly outlined his claim: up in the high country, too, right across the river from Garn.

Vestor Tell was scratching his head with his good hand. "I reckon you fellows know what you're doing," he said doubtfully.

"Yup, sure do," said Ebenezer.

"Looks like sheer folly to me." Tell shrugged. "Nothing up there but a deep gorge, and hills, and rocks. Didn't make a mistake here, did you?"

"No mistake," Garn said.

People were crowding around the map now, noting what Garn and Ebenezer had claimed.

"Hey, that's up by Roaring Gorge," somebody said. "There's *nothing* up there."

"Rocks," snorted someone.

"In their heads," another added. "If that don't beat all."

"Threw away a chance to make a decent claim."

"Too bad, but if they're that stupid . . ."

"It is folly."

"Yeah, Landar's Folly."

Not a few people laughed.

But Garn didn't seem to mind at all. He turned away from Tell, his business concluded, and made his way to the beer barrel in the back of the store, trailed by Ebenezer. As Randy made sure his and Emmalee's claims were properly outlined on the map, she watched Garn. He took a long swallow of the cold beer that Hester gave him, then he embraced her lightly, affectionately. Myrtle came up to him, too, and Emmalee could have sworn, from the attitudes of Garn, Ebenezer, and the two women, that they were congratulating one another on some fine, mysterious coup that Emmalee herself didn't know anything about.

She felt left out, the more so because of the remote detachment with which Garn was treating her lately. Why, if she even tried to thank him for the testimony he'd just given, which had refuted Kaiserhalt and saved her claim, he'd probably just brush her off.

Jasper Heaton and Lambert Strep were laughing it up. "Sheee-it, ain't that Landar something!" Strep chortled.

"Yeah," came Jasper's reply, "he's the one was gonna get us to Denver ahead of old Burt. We all know how *that* turned out. An' now lookit that stupid claim he made."

"He ain't got the brains he was born with," Strep concluded, shaking his head. "Jeeee-zuzzzzz."

"Honey," said Randy, letting his hand linger briefly on her arm, "I'm going to try and see Hester right now about borrowing some money. I don't want to wait and be left out. I don't think it would be wise even to approach Vestor Tell about a loan, considering what's happened."

"Good idea, Randy."

"But there's one thing I have to know."

Emmalee had been expecting this. "Yes," she told him. "Garn and Creel were at the three pines. They saw what happened. But I didn't want to tell you Garn had been there because you might have—"

"Gotten upset? Maybe. And I don't trust Landar, anyway. It seemed to suit his purposes to stick up for us in the business with Kaiserhalt, but I wonder if that wasn't just to impress you."

His glance was accusatory. Emmalee felt a cold barrier between them, and she admitted to herself that she had, by withholding the facts, contributed to the building of that barrier.

"Even if I named him as a witness, I didn't know *what* he might say," she offered in her defense, recalling that Garn had once told her he never lied.

"Uhhh-hmmm," said Randy. "Em, you have to be honest with me."

"I *am* being—"

He shook his head. "No, there's something about this fellow, I don't know what, that exerts a strange hold over you. And if that hold's not broken, I'm afraid for our future."

"Oh, Randy," she cried, distressed. "That's not true. There's no hold, or anything like it. I just made an error of judgment, that's all. I should have told you he'd been there at Three Pines."

Randy seemed relieved. "All right, honey. Let's not worry about it anymore. I assure you that I can accept the fact of Landar's brief involvement in your life. *You* accept it, put it behind you, just treat him as you would anyone else living here, and we'll go on into the future. This is a great day for us, in spite of all the trouble."

He was right. She leaned toward him, and he touched

her forehead lightly with his lips. It was all right between them again, yet in her deepest soul Emmalee suspected that something awaited, something she did not want to see, but that already had a face and name.

Emmalee would have gone with Randy to ask Hester Brine for a loan, but Garn was still there, drinking beer at the back of the store. She saw Torquist leaving the place, and thought it would be wise to discuss with him now the duties he might require of her. But the crowd of pioneers was milling all about, and by the time she'd fought her way out the door and into the street, the wagonmaster was nowhere to be seen. Garn's black stallion was tied to the hitching post, and Otis leaned against the wall of the store, puffing on a lumpy, hand-rolled cigarette.

"Congratulations, Emmalee. You got what you wanted."

"Thank you."

"I'd be keerful, though."

"Why is that?"

"There's things afoot that you don't know about."

"Isn't that what you told me when you gave me the ride into town?"

"It's much more serious now," Otis said. "There was a lot of additional hatred created today."

"Don't think I don't know it."

"I'm not sure that you do. Tell you what. Say I come over for you after supper and we take a little ride and talk?"

"We can talk here. Right now."

Otis blew a blue stream of smoke and looked at her levelly. "I think you're wonderful purty," he said. "I could help you out a lot. Let's put it this way: I want to see you alone."

"I told you that I was engaged. I appreciate your honesty, but—"

"Clay." Otis shrugged. "Yeah, I seen him in there. He's a good, decent guy, but he's a farmer. He's already lost. You've *all* lost already. The deck has been stacked and the deals *made*."

"And you would tell me all these things, would you? How can I be sure that you're telling the truth?"

"Well, I reckon you know that I'm Mr. Pennington's right-hand man. I know a lot of stuff."

"There is such a thing as loyalty."

Otis straightened up, holding his temper in check with difficulty.

"I don't think it's disloyal," he said coldly, "to try and protect somone you like when bad things are about to happen. Do you?"

"I—I guess not."

"Then I can come for you tonight?"

Emmalee was torn. She had seen with her own eyes the growing acrimony between Torquist and Pennington. She knew that Vestor Tell and the ranchers were involved in some sort of shady deal that meant harm for the farmers. Otis might be able to provide details about these matters. But she was engaged to be married! How could she possibly go off riding with a man at night, a man whose interest in her clearly extended beyond friendship?

"Well?" Otis prodded.

But *if* she did go with him, let's say for a short ride—he seemed, in spite of his rough exterior, nice enough—and *if* she did learn from him information that would protect Randy and herself and the farmers, was that not worth the risk?

What will Randy think, if he finds out?

He'll understand.

What'll you do if Otis tries something?

I can handle him.

Is it worth the risk?

It's worth the risk. If I learn even one thing that will help us, it'll be worth it.

"All right," she told Otis. "I'll go for a ride with you. But only for a little while and only as a friend. I appreciate the fact that you're trying to help me."

"Sure. As a friend," said Otis, grinning.

"I mean that."

"Oh, I mean it too. I'll ride over here along about sundown, how's that? Reckon we ought to be a little . . . ah, *careful* about this. Say we meet 'bout a quarter mile upriver?"

Emmalee agreed, feeling uncomfortably sneaky and a little unclean. If this was what it felt like to be a spy, she didn't know if it was worth the risk. She wondered how Ebenezer Creel had felt while spying on the movement of Union troops. And how he had felt when all his efforts came to naught.

Otis tipped his hat gallantly and sauntered away.

A Question of Honor

Even though she had promised Otis that she'd meet him at nightfall, Emmalee worried about her decision. The rendezvous was risky, and it was being made under false pretenses on her part. She wanted to relax and prepare herself for it, but events conspired to increase her tension.

First, Myrtle assigned her to the group of women in charge of preparing the evening meal. Myrtle, who had bossed, cajoled, and scolded everyone all the way across the Great Plains, treated her charges equally and responded to excuses or complaints unvaryingly.

"Sure, I know you've got other things to do," she said, when Emmalee pleaded, just this once, to be let off, "but it's your turn to work."

So Emmalee peeled potato after potato and felt time drag. She'd been on the verge of asking Myrtle why Garn Landar had seemed so pleased about claiming worthless land, but managed to suppress the impulse. After all that had happened, it wasn't quite seemly to show particular interest in Garn.

Then, after supper was finally over, a second unavoidable delay presented itself: Horace Torquist wished to see her in his tent. At once.

"Emmalee!" he cried, when she entered. "I can't tell you how proud I am of you!"

He was seated at his table, upon which flickered a kerosene lamp. A map of Olympia was spread out before him, a map similar to the one Vestor Tell had, with the boundaries of farms and ranches marked in heavy ink. Torquist motioned her to a seat.

"Yes," he said. "Not only did you get yourself a fine chunk of land, you also showed the spirit that is going to win this territory for our kind."

"Our kind?"

"You and I and the others, Emmalee." His eyes glittered and he swatted the map with a huge hand. "I know we're at something of a disadvantage territorially, but Kaiserhalt erred badly by trying to cheat you and Randy. I want you to press the matter. Telegraph a formal complaint to the land office in Washington, D.C. Pennington is on the defensive now, and if we can show a pattern to his actions—his attempts to get all the land along the river, for example—perhaps we can get an inspector out here. Some of his claims might be disallowed. I know Pennington and Tell have cooked up something tricky and I wish I knew what it was."

Emmalee realized, once again, the extent to which Torquist's singlemindedness had perverted his original purity of purpose. The knowledge made her nervous, knowing as she did that his own scheme involving false claims jeopardized the future. He did not seem to understand that, however. To those who are inveterately self-righteous, only their enemies are capable of wrong-doing.

"I hadn't . . . that is, I'd just as soon let well enough alone. We have our claims. I don't think contacting Washington would serve a useful purpose."

Torquist looked disappointed. "You don't?"

"No. I hoped that, after today, the fight in the store and everything, we could all go about our business in peace."

"I'm afraid you're very naive. I guess I shall have to pursue matters in my own way, then. Let us proceed to our agreement. I know it is going to be difficult for you to establish your farm while you're working for me, but a deal is a deal, is it not?"

Emmalee nodded. That was something she had learned all too well.

"I don't expect much heavy work out of you," Torquist went on, "maybe some plowing and extra help at harvest time. Mainly, I'll have you taking care of my house, which I'm going to build immediately, and seeing to my personal needs, cooking, laundry, shopping. Things like that. When your chores are finished, you're quite free, of course, to work your own land and set up the necessary domicile."

When your chores are finished! Emmalee had a feeling that Torquist would not stint in the assignment of work. She would be lucky to have a moment's free time.

"Things are not easy in this life, Emmalee," said the leader sanctimoniously. "But we are tempered by fire, are we not?"

"Or burned," murmured Emmalee.

"Pardon me?"

"Nothing. When shall I begin?"

"Tomorrow morning. You can help dig the cellar and haul rocks for the foundation. Willard Buttlesworth and the men are going up into the woods to begin lumbering. I hope to have my house raised before the snow flies. You will live with me, of course. There will be a room for you. That is, you will reside with me until such time as you are married. What do you and Randy plan, by the way?"

"We hope to be wed after the harvest. Next fall."

"Wise. Well, during the second year of your obligation to me, you may live with your husband and travel to my house for your work."

Emmalee said nothing, imagining the situation. The constant grind of chores for Torquist, while all the time her frustration would grow. Randy was going to have a difficult enough job setting up his own farm. She might *lose* hers if she could not build some sort of shelter and get the requisite amount of land under plow. This did not seem to bother Torquist, however. He had money. Perhaps, already, he envisioned buying her land.

I've got to buy my way out of this agreement, she realized. Borrowing money from Hester now seemed to be the only answer, in spite of the fact that Randy had already done so.

"I shall see you in the morning then, sir," she said, standing up.

"Fine. Fine. Do you have gloves? Bring them with you. Digging a cellar is hard work and the handle of a shovel raises blisters and calluses more quickly than you might think."

"I don't expect much heavy work out of you . . ." Emmalee griped to herself, repeating Torquist's words as she left his tent. If digging a basement and hauling rocks wasn't heavy work, she wondered what was!

It was getting dark now, time for her to go meet Otis, but just as she was getting up her nerve to slip out of Arcady, a third delay, in the person of Randy, presented itself.

"Em! I've been looking all over for you. Where have you been?"

"Talking with Mr. Torquist."

He noted her crestfallen expression. "Things are bad?"

"They could be better." She explained what Torquist had decreed. "I don't think I'll have a minute to myself."

Randy sighed, looking discouraged. "Just when I was feeling good too," he said. "I'm going to borrow two hundred dollars from Hester. That'll be plenty to start with. I can buy seed, equipment, and stock. Enough seed to plant some acres on your land, too, and two hundred is not so much that we can't pay some of it back next year, *if* the harvest is good."

"If it's good. Are a lot of people asking her for money?"

"Yes. Quite a few."

"Randy, I was . . . I was thinking. Maybe I should borrow four hundred, use the one hundred I have . . ."

He frowned at the mention of what he considered tainted money.

". . . and buy my freedom from Horace."

"Em, four hundred is a fortune. You'll have to put up your claim as security. What if you can't pay it back? You'll lose your land."

"What were Hester's terms?"

"She wants a hundred back per year, and three percent interest. Face it, Em. With both of us working as hard as we can, and assuming a good harvest, we'll be hard pressed just to pay back *my* loan."

Emmalee had to admit that he was right. Yet, if she spent all her time in toil for Torquist, she'd probably lose her land anyway. If all options are risky, which option is the least so?

"I guess I'll have to think about it some more," she told Randy.

I'm going to do it, she vowed to herself. I'm going to get free of Torquist and worry about the future when it comes. That way I'll have at least a fighting chance.

"Em," said Randy, putting his arm around her and squeezing her waist, "let's . . . let's go somewhere and be alone for a while."

She thought of Otis, waiting for her, and of the information she wanted to get from him. She was also aware of Randy's affectionate need, and felt guilty all over again.

"Could we . . . I'm sorry, but I'm just awfully tired. I think I'll get some sleep. Would you mind terribly?"

He looked disappointed. "Yeah, well, I could use the rest myself. I'm going out with Buttlesworth in the morning to cut lumber for our new home. . . ."

Emmalee felt truly dissatisfied with herself now, knowing what she was about to do and hearing him talk about their future house. But she had committed herself to seeing Otis, having already determined that the risk of doing so was very high, but not excessive.

"I'm sorry," she said again.

"It's all right, sweetheart. I understand."

He walked her to the Bents' wagon, beneath which she would be sleeping, kissed her a little shyly—the Bent girls were inside the wagon—and walked away.

"Well, Em," said Darlene Bent meanly, "you seem to have just about everything, don't you?"

Emmalee did not answer. Time was running. The moon was rising. What if Otis got tired of waiting for her to show up and came riding into Arcady? There might be a scene. She spread her bedroll beneath the wagon.

"My sister asked you a question," said Priscilla Bent.

"You got a man and land and a future," Darlene whined. "Our poor old pa ain't got nothin' an' he's gonna have to hire hisself out. It ain't fair, that's what."

"I'm sorry," Emmalee said. She lay down and waited, taut and tense, while they berated her some more. Eventually they grew tired of it and began quarreling among themselves while getting ready for bed in the wagon. Emmalee bunched up her blankets and sneaked away into the gloom.

Arcady seemed ghostlike and impermanent beneath the moon. Lights glowed from the windows of the general store. Emmalee skirted it, heard men and women laughing and talking inside, saw Garn's big horse in front of the place. Saddlebags bulged on the animal's sleek flanks. Garn had obviously stocked up on supplies. Well, if he was going to live way up in the hills of Landar's Folly, he wouldn't be around town much. That was probably good, anyway. No, it *was* good. Emmalee wondered briefly about Lottie having had Garn's horse, and had she not been in such a hurry she might have paused to look in the window of the store. Was Lottie in there? Was she preparing, maybe, to go with Garn? But Emmalee did not wish to entertain the thought and she did not have time to look in the window. She passed the general store and walked on.

Otis was waiting for her, just as he said he'd be. She saw the tiny red glow of his cigar in the distance. Walking closer, she made out the large, dark shape of his horse, then the outline of Otis himself. Standing next to him, she could see his face quite clearly in the moonlight. He was all washed up and had on a clean shirt and neckerchief. He tossed his cigar into the river, where it hissed for an instant, died, and went floating away. The Big Two-Hearted murmured soothingly. Emmalee wished she could let her tension flow away with it.

"There you are." Otis smiled. He was pleased to see her. "Have some trouble sneakin' away?"

"You might say that."

"I knew you'd come, though." He reached for her, took her by the shoulders, and drew her toward him. She averted her face at the last moment, and his fumbling kiss of greeting landed on her left ear.

"Let's sit down," he said hoarsely.

"I feel like walking. I'm—"

"Nervous, huh? All right, we'll walk. But you just relax. You're in good hands when you're with Oats

Chandler. Ain't nothin' gonna happen to you that you don't want to happen."

He grinned. She forced a smile. It felt uncomfortable to travel under false pretenses, so to speak, like taking a bath in a river for the first time, only a lot less clean. Otis took her hand and they began to walk along the riverbank.

"I really am damn happy you came," he reaffirmed. "You shore are purty an' as you must be able to tell, I like you a lot."

She had the feeling that he was going to try to kiss her again, but he didn't. Her problem now was to get him off the subject of romance and onto the matter of Pennington's schemes. There wasn't any easy way to bring it up, though, without seeming suspicious. She waited for an opening.

"You ever think about settlin' down?" he was asking her. "Well, I guess you have, on account of you're engaged, ain't cha? But that can't mean much, can it, on accounta you're here with me?"

"No, I really am engaged. I'm here to see you as a friend, just like I said."

He stopped walking and drew her to a halt beside him. "You an' me don't have to pretend," he said. He dropped to the grass and pulled her down next to him, still holding onto her hand.

Emmalee smiled. There didn't seem to be much else that she could do. "I'm not pretending," she said.

"Come on," he said, puzzled. "You're too much woman for a farmer. I figure your deal with Randy Clay is sort of a temporary alliance, a way to get started."

"I'm afraid you're wrong," she answered firmly. "I'm quite serious about my betrothal."

"Well, that's too bad." He was disappointed. Then he rallied. "When you gettin' hitched?"

"After the harvest next fall."

"A lot can happen 'tween now and then," he said hopefully.

"That's true. And one of the things that has to happen is my being able to get part of my claim under plow."

Otis released her hand, reluctantly, apparently realizing that he had misread Emmalee. But he was still there with her and he could talk to her. What he'd said was true: There was a lot that could happen before the first harvest.

"You did right proud for yourself by getting that claim, Em. I never did care much for Alf."

"Were you able to get good ranchland?" she asked casually, easing toward the information she needed.

"I shore did. Great grassland next to Burt Pennington."

"Isn't there going to be . . . some problem? You know, the difference between farmers and ranchers. It's already serious, and—"

"Trouble ain't going to last long. Because, a year from now, two at the most, there ain't gonna *be* any farmers in these parts."

Now she had him talking. Keep it going, she thought. "Well, I don't know if I'm slow-witted or something, but I just don't understand."

Otis laughed sympathetically and put his arm comfortingly around her shoulders.

"Vestor Tell has got some deal to take care of it," he whispered. "Got it all worked out with Burt."

"Some kind of deal? What is it?"

Otis paused for a moment and Emmalee feared that he wasn't going to tell her anything further.

"I don't know everything," he said then, "but it has something to do with people Tell knows back east. Yep. He's got access to big money back there. I understand from what he told Burt that he's sort of been a black sheep in his family. They sent him out here to make a success of himself."

"As a claims agent?"

"No, he got that job through politics. His uncle or his cousin was or maybe still is senator from Pennsylvania. No, the claims agent thing is just temporary. He's really set on banking and property."

Emmalee knew that Tell was prepared to lend money. But land?

"I don't think he even bothered to make a claim," she blurted, then realized that Otis was on the verge of telling her what she wanted to know.

"It's not his land now," the foreman drawled. "It's your land now. The areas you farmers claimed. *That's* what he's fixin' to get his hands on."

"How?" asked Emmalee, more forcefully than she had intended. "And what has that got to do with your boss?"

Otis laughed lightly. "You sure are a lady that loves to chatter away, ain't you?"

"Well, you know all these *interesting* things," she replied. "I was just wondering how everything works."

"Sure you was. Sure you was."

Suddenly Otis stiffened and looked around. "Somebody's coming, damnit," he whispered harshly.

Emmalee heard the soft, scraping sounds of a horse's hoofs in the sand along the river.

"I'd better hide," she said, getting up and looking around. There was a stand of trees fifty yards away and tall grass not far from the river. She decided to head for the tall grass, feeling disgusted with herself for getting into this mess. Otis had only given her the sketchiest kind of information. It meant very little, at this point. She would have to learn a lot more on her own before she knew what Vestor Tell was really planning. And now she might be seen in Otis's company by someone from Arcady, who wouldn't wait to blab it all around. . . .

She ducked down and started toward the high grass.

But Otis grabbed her ankle.

"Hey!" he said. "You ain't got nothin' to fear. Oats Chandler protects his women. That's my first rule. Just rest easy here. Whoever it is is gonna go right on by an' not pay us no never-mind."

A moment later Garn Landar rode by, heading upriver. The black stallion was moving slowly under the weight of saddlebags and supplies. Garn passed them, riding gracefully, easily.

"Evening, Emmalee," he said, touching his hatbrim lightly. "Otis, good to see you. Nice night, isn't it?"

"Real nice," said Otis.

Garn rode on.

"Well, if he ever tells he saw us," Otis said, "we can say we're only friends."

He did not sound especially happy with that fact.

Settling Down

In the fall of that year, Emmalee lived in a one-room lean-to that had been tacked onto the side of Horace Torquist's raw, new house. The lean-to, as well as the house to which it was attached, was constructed of pine planks ripped by Willard Buttlesworth from spruce and ponderosa in the Sacajawea range. First the great trees were felled, then their trunks divided into sections, finally wedges were driven into the trunks and mauled with sledgehammers until long sheets of wood planking were ripped from the slaughtered trees, which screamed like living things in the process. Buttlesworth was good; the planks he produced were thick and sleek. But the work went slowly. He had been used to a circular, steel-toothed saw in his former home on a fast-moving Wisconsin river, where falls and dams harnessed the power of water. Here in Olympia, however, the Big Two-Hearted flowed freely across the plain, making it good only for irrigation and drinking.

Houses and barns rose slowly in spite of frantic work in that fall of 1868. Everyone in Olympia was obsessed with the coming of winter. According to those who either knew or pretended to know about such things, the warm Pacific winds might hold off harsh weather until late December, or even January. But inevitably—it was said—the infamous blue northers would come howling down out of Canada, across the Rockies, mingling with the Pacific air to drop tides of snow in man-high drifts upon the land. Those without shelter were certain to suffer bitterly. Thus trees kept falling, to be cut into planks, hauled down from the mountains by ten or twelve-horse teams, and turned into small, square houses, barns, sheds, and corrals.

Slowly, very slowly, with the air growing colder each day, Arcady and the surrounding area began to look like a community. There were a dozen new houses in the village now, and a pine-smelling chapel too. Hester Brine was building a six-room hotel next to her store. A schoolhouse was planned, the frame of which had already been erected near the river. Every day the ranchers drove cattle from California, which were stronger than the Salt Lake stock, into the new corrals, and farmers came back from Salt Lake with milking cows, chickens, hogs. All of this furious activity prevented internecine squabbling between the two groups, and even the landless men were kept out of trouble while working for one group or the other. On some days Emmalee chopped firewood from morning till night, breaking off only to prepare Torquist's meals. Up in the mountains, Festus Bent reported seeing a bear "with a pelt on him thicker than ten layers of longjohns on a fat woman." This was interpreted to mean that the approaching winter would be rugged.

Emmalee worked hard and unhappily for Horace Torquist. From the time she rose in the morning to fix him a breakfast of coffee, oatmeal with molasses, eggs, and fried fatback, until the late hour when she fell into her cot in the lean-to, listening to Torquist conferring in a low voice with Waters, Heaton, Strep, and the others, Emmalee was on the run. She had to make soap, separate cream from milk, tend the two cows, bake bread, get water, build and maintain the fire in the stove, and carry out the ashes, which she used to make the soap.

And there were constant problems with Torquist. Nothing seemed to suit him. The soap was "grainy." The bread was underdone or "burned." The fire was too hot or not hot enough. He thought it took her too long to churn the butter, and that she ought to spend more time scraping and sanding the new wood floors. Torquist was preoccupied, of course, with the fact that many of his farmers had not been able to borrow money—he himself had done all he could for them—and that their chances of surviving in Olympia, even with a substantial harvest in the coming year, were perilous. He was preoccupied and irritable, and he took it out on Emmalee.

The farmers, and Emmalee along with them, had fallen prey to a sudden and unexpected shortage of available capital. Emmalee, who had planned on borrowing enough from Hester Brine to buy her way out of bondage to the wagonmaster, and the farmers who had counted on Hester, too, found that she had stopped lending money.

"I just can't, honey," Hester had told Emmalee on a blustery day in late October. The two were seated at a table in the general store, next to the glowing stove. "It's not that I don't want to. You know I've already lent Randy and some of the others quite a bit of cash. But I have to look out for myself too. I've had hard times in my life and I don't want 'em agin'. I'm going to use what I have left to build a hotel. With Arcady growing as it is, and talk of the railroad coming through in a couple of years, a hotel could put me on easy street."

Emmalee wondered a little about Hester's past, but she had her own problems. She thought of approaching Vestor

Tell, but he seemed reluctant to lend anything at all to farmers, and besides, she didn't trust him. The few farmers who had gone to him, practically begging for funds, found that he wanted total repayment within a year's time, plus a seven-percent interest. His loans to the ranchers, Emmalee had heard, were offered at lesser interest—how much less she hadn't been able to find out—and with a longer repayment period. Tell, however, refused to discuss the specifics of his business with anyone. "I make private deals with individuals," he said. "They take it or leave it. If I think farmers are a bad risk, which I do, that's nobody's business but my own. I don't have to loan to anyone if I don't want to."

What this amounted to, of course, was a pattern favoring the ranchers at the expense of the farmers, but Vestor Tell just shrugged and announced that it was his prerogative to do what he thought most sound from a business point of view.

People hated him, people loathed him, but no one spoke up to gainsay the enterprising claims agent. Black sheep he might have been to his Philadelphia family, but this was America in the year 1868 and money had vast, indisputable rights. Or so everyone thought. To Emmalee, however, Tell's procedures seemed innately unfair.

The day she'd been refused a loan by Hester, Emmalee congratulated the woman on her plans for the hotel, wished her luck, and headed for the door of the general store. Tell was hunched over the telegraph machine, keying the dots and dashes of Morse code, sending a message to someplace far away. His mastery of the machine gave him an almost magical aura, adding an element of inviolability to the power of his money. She wondered if he was wiring Washington, D.C., and, if so, what he was saying to them. Torquist had implored Emmalee, several times, to report Kaiserhalt's attack. But Emmalee hadn't wanted to start that business up all over again. Besides, the only person in town who knew how to telegraph was Vestor Tell! Mail deliveries were erratic at best and took a long time. Tell was the man to see if one wanted to get a message out into the world, and it seemed impolitic, not to say dangerous, to try to send a message that would make him angry.

Leaving the store, with the clatter of the telegraph keys ringing in her ears, feeling immensely discouraged over Tell's dominance and her own semislavery, Emmalee decided not to go back to Torquist's right away. Instead she borrowed Ned from Myrtle Higgins—the old woman was inside her new cabin, sewing curtains for the windows—and rode out to see Randy. Torquist generously gave her Saturday nights off—"Once a week with your fiance is enough," he pronounced. "I don't want to be responsible for you getting into trouble."—so she usually saw Randy at the general store. It was the public gathering place, so the only privacy they enjoyed occurred when he walked her home, held her and kissed her in the shadows outside Torquist's house, speaking of the future in a voice filled with labor, fatigue, and a fervent hope that better times were coming.

Emmalee urged Ned up over the hills and saw the three pines in the distance. The trees were still there, but on one side of them now was a house made of timber and stone, and on the other side the frame of a barn was rising. She felt a sense of optimism and adventure again. Things were happening; progress was being made; this would be her home. Randy's arm had healed perfectly and he was up on the roof of the house, nailing shingles. He saw her riding toward him, paused in surprise, then scrambled down the ladder and ran to meet her. She slipped off Ned. Their kiss was affectionate and long.

"Em," he said, leaning back to look at her. "What are you doing here? Is something wrong?"

"Nothing serious. Well, yes, a lot of things."

"What, honey?"

She dropped Ned's reins, and the mule started nibbling sullenly at the dry grass of autumn. Randy took her inside the house, the rooms of which were large and light, but empty except for the kitchen, which had a stove, a table, and two chairs. His bedroll was in the corner.

"I've got some coffee, Em. Want some?"

"Please."

She roamed around the house, imagining what it would be like when they got it furnished, admiring the big stone fireplace that Randy had fashioned himself. Then they both sat down at the table. The coffee was very strong, but she needed it.

"Hester can't give me the loan," she said.

He looked worried. After initial reluctance to go any further into debt, she had convinced him that getting away from Torquist was worth almost anything. Now, however, the goal was in jeopardy.

"Can't or won't?" he asked.

"Can't." Emmalee explained about the hotel.

"Now what?"

"I think I'm going to try Tell. Maybe I can work something out."

"Oh, Em, I don't know. I haven't even finished the barn. There's not a sign of activity on your land—I just haven't had the time—and it's too late in the year to do much plowing, either on your place or mine."

"That's why I've got to leave Torquist," she said. "The rules are clear. We have to put up a shelter and get in a crop by next year, or say farewell to everything."

"You're right," he admitted.

"And the only way we're going to be able to do that is for both of us to work here."

Randy stared at his coffee cup. "What if Tell won't lend you money? I doubt he will. He doesn't take much to farmers."

"Then I'm going to telegraph Sacramento or Salt Lake."

Randy's head lifted in surprise.

"There are other places to borrow from. This land is good security. I can get the money. *Damnit!*" she added, for emphasis.

Randy smiled. "I hadn't even thought of that! But how are you going to . . . ?"

"I'll telegraph for information."

"Do you think Tell will let you?"

"He'd better."

"But if—"

"I'll do it on my own, then. If he can learn Morse code, I sure can. We've got to rid people of the illusion that Vestor Tell is the be-all and end-all around here, don't you think?"

"But he pretty well is. A lot of the big ranchers owe him money. Being in debt to someone makes even strong men docile."

"Well, I just want the cash. Money is not going to change me any."

Randy laughed. "I surely do believe you, Em. Oh! I just remembered. I have something for you."

He stood up and walked to the cupboard. "It's a gift," he said.

"Oh, Randy, you shouldn't have. We can use every penny. . . ."

"Hush. It didn't cost a cent, but it's pretty and I shined it up for you."

He opened the cupboard and took from it something small and sparkling. It looked to Emmalee like a jewel, but when he brought it back to the table and offered it to her she saw that it was a small stone, a very extraordinary stone, beneath the carefully polished surface of which glowed a dozen colors, reds and yellows and golds and blues combined. It was like holding a piece of the rainbow when he pressed it shyly into her hand.

"Oh, Randy . . ."

A small tear came to the corner of her right eye and pearled on the lash. The little stone was gem and symbol. It evoked in her a sudden bittersweet rush of feeling for Randy, for herself, for all they did not have and all they wanted.

"Don't cry . . ." he began.

"I'm not. It's just . . . oh, thank you. . . ."

He pulled her gently up from the chair and held her close to him, pressing his cheek against hers. Then they kissed and Emmalee closed her eyes, kissing him hard, not caring where the moment led. She felt his hand gently on her breast, yes, yes, but then he took it away, ended the kiss, held her against him.

"Emmalee, Emmalee." He sighed. "It's so hard to have to wait, isn't it?"

Emmalee nodded against his chest, realizing that she didn't care to wait, hadn't wanted to, and would have followed his lead joyously wherever he'd decided to go. Once, she remembered, she'd believed that a man who wanted everything from her, body and soul, no holds barred and no questions asked, was dangerous. But now she was forced to admit—and the admission was not distressing—that she wanted to be taken. Just then. Right now. Body, soul, and everything.

But Randy looked at it differently. He was willing to wait for the prize of her purity. That was one of the beliefs that made him what he was, a man she loved. But they were sworn to each other *already*, weren't they? How would waiting make either of them more pure? They had made their promises and plighted their troth.

True. But she realized that they conceived of love and its prerogatives in different ways. That would change, of course, as they grew to know each other better. And someday Randy would come to learn that physical intensity was not something to resist but to seek. Time would take care of everything.

Yet there was a tiny gulf between them when he took her back outside and helped her mount old Ned. Emmalee felt incomplete, odd, unsettled as she rode back toward Arcady.

"I want to borrow some money," Emmalee said.

Vestor Tell laughed outright, a casual, good-humored laugh, neither mocking nor ironic. "How much?" he asked.

"Four hundred dollars."

His eyes widened. "What on earth do you want that kind of money for?"

"I made a bad business deal a while back. I have to buy my way out of it."

Tell was seated on the stool behind his desk in the corner of the general store. Emmalee stood before him. He placed his hands, palms down, on the desk and smiled at her. A bandage wrapped his right hand.

"Borrowing four hundred dollars might just turn out to be an even worse deal," he said.

"I don't think so. Will you lend me the money?"

"No."

"Why not?"

"I don't think I have to tell you."

"That's not fair."

"Fair. Unfair. Who's to say?"

"I have farmland, you know. I'd put that up as security.

It'll be worth a lot more than four hundred dollars. In not too long a time."

"We all know that, dear."

"Don't call me 'dear.' "

"Suit yourself. I'm just trying to be pleasant. Anyway, it's my policy not to loan to farmers. They're poor risks."

"That's true, if they aren't able to borrow enough for stock and cattle and equipment. They need a little help to get off the ground. But they're good people."

Tell grinned with satisfaction. In a flash, Emmalee understood that one of his basic goals was to see the farmers *fail*! Was this desire based upon some personal animosity that she didn't know about? What good would it be to Tell if the farmers failed? He hadn't loaned them money. He could not foreclose upon them if they defaulted on their repayments. Either he had a peculiar animus against the farmers themselves, or he had other schemes afoot. These had to have something to do with his biased loan policy.

"You've lent to the ranchers readily enough."

"They aren't poor risks." He shrugged. "What more can I tell you?"

"All right," she demanded, having decided to confront him forthrightly, "where are you getting the money that you do loan out?"

He looked startled, then suspicious. "Why do you want to know?"

"Is it from a bank back east? Or from a private source?"

"None of your business. Besides, what's the difference?"

"I've heard talk about you."

His eyes narrowed. "Have you, now?"

"Yes. Normally, I try and discount gossip. But what I heard leads me to believe that you weren't entirely on the up-and-up back east. Do you know what that suggests to me?"

He was getting angry, and his reply was clipped, cold. "I don't care what it suggests or does not suggest to you."

"I'll tell you anyway. I'm not very old, but I have learned this: People don't change all that much. If you were less than honorable back in Pennsylvania, you might be that way here too."

"My, my. What a smart girl."

"Mr. Tell, I want to know what the rules are."

"The *what*?"

"The laws. The rules that govern what you can and cannot do in your position."

A smooth mask of blandness came down over his face. He appeared perfectly self-confident now, but Emmalee could sense the effort he was expending in order to show her that oh-so-calm facade. "I don't know that there are any, particularly," he said.

"I don't believe that. There is a land office in Washington, D.C. It has a policy. Its claims agents must be subject to that policy. Banks are not totally independent either." She looked him directly in the eyes. "I'm just interested in the rules," she said.

"They wouldn't interest you because they don't apply to you," he said smoothly.

"Let me be the judge of that. I'd like to send a telegram."

Tell's expression changed. He still looked unruffled, but his eyes turned brighter, sharper.

"Where to? Washington, I suppose. Be glad to send it for you, of course, but it'll cost money."

"No. I want to wire Salt Lake City."

"Salt Lake? What in heaven's name for?"

This plan of action had been in the back of Emmalee's mind. She had already guessed that Tell was reluctant to get her information on the actual laws that applied here in Olympia. She would definitely have to acquire that data herself. Tell wasn't going to provide information that, she was sure, would threaten him considerably. But wiring Salt Lake City might solve her more immediate problem: money.

"I want to wire the Pacific National Bank," she told Tell. "Randy Clay told me it's the biggest bank there. I just wonder if they'd consider loaning me the money I need. With one hundred and sixty acres of excellent land as security."

Tell paused, thinking it over. His eyes were hard. Emmalee could see that she'd touched him to the quick. He didn't want her wiring the bank in Salt Lake. But she did not yet know the reason for his reluctance.

"Well," he said, affecting a drowsy air, "you certainly are persistent. I like that. I really do." His mien told her that he didn't like it at all, not one bit.

"Then you will send the wire?" Emmalee was unable to keep a measure of surprise out of her voice. She glanced behind Tell and saw the telegraph keys on the table next to the wall, the wires leading out of the store, connecting little Arcady with the larger world. She saw the drawers beneath the table. Perhaps directions for sending and receiving Morse code were in one of those drawers? It was a thought. . . .

"No need to send the wire to Salt Lake at all," Tell was saying.

Emmalee didn't know whether to be suspicious or angry. "There isn't? And why not?"

"Because I'll loan you the four hundred."

There had to be some sort of a trap here. Emmalee wondered what it was. Vestor Tell was not the sort of man who would capitulate so readily. "Yes, but why?" she asked. "And all of a sudden?"

Tell's smile was friendly and benign. "I was just testing you, is all. Had to see if you stuck to your guns, if you had the gumption to keep on pressing me for the dough."

He lowered his voice and glanced at the people who were shopping in the store. "Too many of those farmers," he said conspiratorially, "don't have the gumption to keep on coming back. That's how I judge who's worth a loan and who isn't. You are!" he added expansively.

Emmalee knew that this was untrue. There were farmers Tell had turned down three and four times. He was lending her money because he didn't want outside interference, from Salt Lake or anywhere else. It was highly useful information, and it proved what Emmalee had already suspected: Tell was engaged in activity questionable at best, and illegal at worst. She still did not know what it was but that fact was of less immediate importance than her loan.

"What terms?" she asked, bracing herself for another set-to over interest rates.

The claims agent showed her the palms of his hands. A small patch of dried blood showed on the bandage.

"Why, the same as for my rancher friends," he exclaimed, as if hurt by her mistrust of him. "Three percent, and three years to pay back. That all right with you?"

Randy and Emmalee hastily erected a log-and-sod cabin close to the new house at the three pines. The walls were pine, the roof sod, the chimney fieldstone. Dried mud blocked the chinks between the logs. Randy could not believe that Emmalee had been successful with Tell where so many others had failed.

"It was my charm, I think," she said gaily, kissing him. "Charm and the fact that he's afraid of something. And I aim to find out what it is."

"Now, Em. Go easy."

"Well, you're right I guess. But let's face it. We're lucky. But we shouldn't crow about it. Our luck doesn't erase the fact that a lot of us farmers are in trouble. Winter is coming fast. You can feel it in the air.''

Emmalee had brewed a pot of tea, which she served Randy in her new cabin. There was also a plateful of biscuits and fresh honey. The tea had arrived in Arcady via the biweekly supply train of wagons that now came regularly from Sacramento. Emmalee had made the biscuits herself. Willard Buttlesworth had provided the honey; he'd cut down a bee tree in late November, a hollow maple in which he'd found thousands of frost-numbed bees and a mountain of swollen, dripping honeycombs.

The cabin was snug but somewhat dark. It had only one window. Randy planned to cut a few more, but for now the place would have to do. The main point had been to get a shelter built on Emmalee's land, both to satisfy the requirement that a domicile occupy the claim and to give Emmalee a place to live.

This tea was a celebration of the cabin's completion, and Emmalee poured it into old china cups, gifts of Ebenezer Creel from his wife's things.

''To us,'' she said, taking a seat opposite Randy at a little carved table given her by Horace Torquist. The leader had at first been incredulous when Emmalee presented him with five one-hundred-dollar bills—one of them torn—and then shocked when he'd learned of her borrowing from Tell. But Emmalee was adamant. She would buy her freedom. Emmalee believed Torquist had eased his conscience by giving her the table. ''You'd be better off with me,'' the wagonmaster had said. Emmalee hadn't thought so, still didn't think so, and there she was serving tea in her own little house.

''Good,'' said Randy, sipping cautiously. ''I've never had tea before.''

It was only Emmalee's second time, the first having been at Hester Brine's store. Trade with the Far East was bringing the brew, practically unknown in the Middle West, to California ports, and from there to Olympia.

They drank in silence for several minutes. Randy spooned a huge dollop of thick honey on a biscuit and ate it slowly, savoring the taste. The day was cold and overcast. A sharp, steady wind blew down from the Sacajawea Range, but the logs in the cabin's little fireplace burned steadily. Emmalee felt warm and secure, then increasingly drowsy. She wanted to hug and cuddle.

"Hope it's an early spring," said Randy. "Then we can start plowing right away."

"I hope so too."

"Thought I'd sow some rye, first thing."

"Wouldn't corn be better?"

"What?"

"Corn is hardier," Emmalee said. "We don't really know what the weather will be like during the growing season out here. Corn can take more punishment, if need be, and still give a good yield."

"I've already asked Hester to order rye seed for me," said Randy, looking at her.

"You could change that. Besides, corn seed is cheaper, and the extra money might go to buy another cow."

"The cows I have will give us enough milk."

"We could sell the extra milk in Arcady."

Randy set down his teacup and stared at her.

"Who'll buy that milk?" he asked, a little sharply. "The farmers who haven't been able to buy cows don't have money. If we only hadn't run smack-dab into Fire-On-The-Moon out there in Kansas . . ."

"Ranchers drink milk, too, I suspect," said Emmalee. "They don't use longhorns as milking cattle, as far as I know."

"The ranchers? Emmalee, what are you talking about?

We're not going to sell anything to *ranchers*! It'd be like betraying our own kind. They hate us and we hate them."

"I just thought . . . that it'd be a good idea. If they want milk, we have it. And they can afford to pay for it, so we both come out ahead."

Randy laughed. "Don't be a goose, Em," he said. "The farther we stay from Pennington and his crowd, the better off we'll be."

She didn't like his laugh, or the easy manner in which he'd dismissed what she thought was a good idea.

"If they begin to realize that we can be of use to them and vice versa," she said, "why, I bet things'll begin to go much more smoothly around here."

"Forget about that. The die is cast."

"What do you mean?"

"I'm afraid it's a fight to the finish, Emmalee." She noted he had called her Emmalee; he usually said "Em" or "honey" or even "darling."

"I still think it doesn't have to be that way," she maintained. He poured himself some more tea, added a spoonful of honey, and stirred it in vigorously.

"I haven't seen any signs that it's going to be different, have you? Do you have any indication that Burt Pennington likes us any more than he used to?"

Emmalee had to admit that she had seen no such signs. Oh, Otis was friendly enough when she chanced to run into him in town. He always tipped his hat and stopped for a moment to pass the time of day, but he knew that Emmalee was really engaged. As for Burt and Lottie, they were seldom seen in Arcady. Their magnificent hacienda-style dwelling at the ranch was the talk of Olympia. There, with lovely Lottie serving as hostess, Burt planned strategy with his followers exactly as Torquist did with the farmers. No, there were few signs of amity coming from the other side of the river.

"Perhaps if we made some gesture of friendship," she suggested.

"Gosh, Em, what's got into you? I know you've said things like this in the past, but I thought you'd have learned different by now."

"There hasn't been one real fight since that big brouhaha in the general store."

"That's just because Pennington is biding his time. Mr. Torquist explained it all to us the other night, over at his place."

"You went to one of his meetings?"

"Yes. Is anything wrong with *that*?"

Emmalee studied his expression. He looked surprised and a little hurt. He even looked a little angry. She herself was aware of feeling a bit miffed over his attitude. He didn't like the idea of making money by selling milk. He didn't care for her suggestion of planting corn instead of rye. He thought she was naive about Pennington and the ranchers.

Well!

But Randy realized, as did she, that they were having a disagreement.

"Sorry, Em," he said sheepishly. "Our first fight, I guess."

"Just a few different ideas."

"It's not important."

"Sure, we'll work it out."

"I guess I'm just a little more cautious than you by nature," he said.

They leaned across the little table and kissed each other.

"Better than honey," he said.

"Let's forget all about it. Do you know what I think would be a good idea? It's almost Christmas. What if someone were to organize a big party and dance for everybody?"

"You mean for all of our people?"

"No, I mean for *all* of the people. Everybody in Olympia, farmers and ranchers alike. I just thought of it a moment ago, when it occurred to me that there hasn't been a fight in a long while. I know there's been hostile talk, but if we got everybody together . . ."

"Who's 'we,' Em?"

". . . maybe in Hester's new hotel—it's almost finished and she's got that big hall on the first floor—why, I bet there'd be enough good feeling started up there to see us through the whole year without a bad incident!"

"I don't know, Em. Maybe you'd better talk this over with Horace Torquist. He knows about things like that, politics and all."

"Fiddlesticks! He doesn't know about socializing at all! In fact, it would be good for him especially. He's got to stop holing up with Waters and Strep and . . . everybody. He's got to get out into the real world. That's it, then. We'll have a big Christmas dance and invite everybody."

"I don't know, Em."

"I'll speak to Hester the next time I ride into Arcady for supplies."

Emmalee was so excited about her idea that she could hardly sleep that night. And although she hadn't planned on going to town for several more days, she saddled Randy's dapple-gray the very next morning, rode along the stream to the river, and followed the Big Two-Hearted into Arcady. It was still very early. She saw farmers milking their cows, feeding their chickens and hogs. Thin smoke from breakfast fires rose from chimney tops and drifted over the town. Emmalee rode by the hotel, which had been painted a gleaming white, and tied the horse to the hitching rail in front of the general store.

The front door was locked. Emmalee walked around to

the back, which was the entrance Hester normally used. It was open and the rich smell of freshly brewed coffee rode on the air. Emmalee saw the big cast-iron coffeepot bubbling on the stove. Cups, saucers, plates, and several loaves of dark bread had been set out on a table.

"Hester?"

There was no answer.

She must have stepped out for a moment, thought Emmalee, entering the store. It was quiet and seemed much larger than it usually did with all the people talking and shopping and visiting. Emmalee poured herself a cup of coffee and looked around. Her eyes were drawn to Vestor Tell's desk in the corner and to the telegraph on the table behind his desk. She walked over to it and studied the device. It was quite simple and did not look complicated enough to send a message all the way across the country. By pressing and releasing a flattish-looking, leverlike key, a signal system of dots and dashes could send her words anywhere she might want them to go. But she did not know that system of dots and dashes. Feeling slightly nefarious, but much more curious, she checked to find Hester still absent and then tentatively jiggled the handle of a drawer beneath the telegraph key. The drawer slid open a fraction of an inch, then halted with a jerk. It was locked, but the clasp was old. A little jerk, a twist, a little pressure and . . .

Sure enough, the draw slid open.

Inside there was nothing that looked like a code, much less a code book, but there was a stack of papers. Upon cursory inspection, they seemed to be decoded letters that others had wired to Vestor Tell. Emmalee felt a little funny now, as if she were opening strange mail or peeping through a window into someone's house. But, even so, it would be true to say that the words leaped up at her just as determinedly as she gazed down to read them. Tell had apparently been keeping the messages he'd received as business records, in order to show what a good job he was doing. They were identical in salutation:

MR VESTOR TELL
US CLAIMS OFFICE
TERRITORY OF OLYMPIA

They were generally filled with praise for the fullness of Tell's reports and for the successful work he was carrying out:

COMMENDATIONS REGARDING EQUITABLE LOAN POLICY OLYMPIA STOP CONSULT TERRITORIAL BANKING CHARTER, 2 JUNE 1866 SHOULD NEED ARISE.

Another read:

CLOSE ATTENTION SHOULD BE PAID TO POSSIBLE GRAZERY-TILLER CONFLICT STOP SIGNS OF DISCORD ARE TO BE ADDRESSED AND REPORTED AT ONCE.

And:

REGARDING YOUR SUGGESTION THAT FEDERAL INSPECTION TEAM UNNECESSARY DUE TO HIGH LEVEL OF COMITY IN ARCADY STOP STATUTES MANDATE VISIT WITHIN TWO YEARS OF SETTLEMENT STOP HOWEVER PLANNED INSPECTION POSTPONED ON YOUR RECOMMENDATION UNTIL LATER DATE.

All of the messages closed:

UNITED STATES LAND OFFICE
WASHINGTON, D.C.

Emmalee wondered exactly how Tell had worded his messages to the land office. Those hadn't been kept, obviously. But she could determine from these filed telegrams, which he was apparently retaining as proof of his tremendous success, that he was being grossly deceptive in three main areas: first, in the loaning of money; second, in his reporting of the situation regarding ranchers and farmers; third, in attempting to delay if not cancel a visit by inspectors from Washington.

The whole thing made her *so* mad! She tried another drawer, hoping to find the code book. She was angry enough, just then, to sit right down and tap out a message that would inform Washington of a few things. . . .

Then a key rattled outside in the front door lock. *Tell!* thought Emmalee. She slammed the drawer shut—much too loudly: any nearby dead ought to have sat up immediately—and raced toward the table where she'd left her coffee cup. *Mistake!* she decided.

Then the door swung open.

Hester Brine. She regarded Emmalee with mild surprise. "Just openin' up for business. I take it you came in the back way?"

"I'm sorry. I thought you were here."

"Well, I was. Then I wasn't. And now I am again. Help yourself to the coffee. Oh, you have. Good. What do you want to send a telegram for, so early in the morning?"

"What? I—"

"How do I know? I saw you through the window when I was walking by the front of the store."

Emmalee felt embarrassed. Even worse, she felt stupid. "I was just—"

"Don't tell me. I don't want to know. Just a word to the wise. You're one up on Vestor since you got the money out of him. But be careful. He don't like to have people get the jump on him, an' he'll wait an' he'll wait to even things out. Get my meaning?"

"Very clearly."

"So unless you know exactly what you're dealing with, and unless the stakes are pretty damn high, don't rattle his cage any more just now."

Hester took off the heavy woolen shawl that she was wearing against the chill of that December morning, warmed her hands over the glowing stove, poured a cup of coffee, and sat down at the table. She motioned Emmalee to join her.

"You want to know what makes Vestor so strong?" Hester asked abruptly.

"He has the contacts back east. He has money."

"Yes. But more than that. It's us. It's everybody around these parts. He keeps the farmers and ranchers divided, plays them off one against the other, and draws strength from the hostility he helps to foster."

"But he's friends with the ranchers, he loans them money. . . ."

"Only seems that way, just seems he's friends with them. Nope, I think he's using them for some purpose of his own."

"That's the reason I came to see you," Emmalee said.

"Why? Because Tell is using the ranchers just like he's using the farmers?"

"No. Because there *is* hostility. Because the two sides are so far apart. You know, I had an idea. . . ."

She told Hester of her plans for a big Christmas dance and party. The orange-haired woman listened thoughtfully.

"What do you know?" she said. "Sounds like it might be fun. Maybe, it bein' Christmas and all, the menfolk will stay out of trouble."

Enthusiastically, they set about planning the event. Hester would make up a big notice and tack it out in front of the general store, where everyone would see it. The word would get around. There were plenty of people around who played various instruments, so there'd be a band for dancing.

"Randy knows how to call square dances," suggested Emmalee. "He told me he used to do it back in Ohio."

"Good. And there's a supply train due in today. I'll send an order back with 'em for a couple cases of moonshine."

"But Mr. Torquist is against drinking, I'm afraid."

"Honey, it ain't his party. He can stay home if he don't like it. Say, this is a good idea you had. Build up a little spirit around here. The place could use it. How are you and Randy getting along, by the way?"

"Oh, fine. I'm so happy to be on my own at last."

"On your own at last and you're planning on getting married?"

"Away from Mr. Torquist, I meant."

"Lot of talk about you and Randy, you know. Living out there all by yourselves and everything."

"People will always talk. In our case, there's nothing to talk about."

"That bad, eh?"

Emmalee looked at Hester. She was just about to ask what Hester meant when Vestor Tell entered, followed by some women who had come to buy flour, coffee beans, and rice.

"Time to go to work," said Hester, getting up.

"You'll have plenty more to do in about half an hour," Vestor informed her. "I just caught a glimpse of the supply train coming over the plains. Looks like they got at least half a dozen wagons with 'em this time."

"Hmmm," said Hester with interest. "Wonder what for? Two or three's usually enough to haul the stuff we need."

Emmalee finished her coffee, nodded to Tell—he'd finally removed the bandage from his hand, she noticed—and went outside to watch the wagon train arrive. It was an important event in the lives of settlers on this rich but relatively remote plain, and from all over the countryside people headed toward Arcady. On horseback, on wagons, and on foot they came, eager for news and goods from the west coast. (Emmalee had already begun to think that, as soon as she got her land paid off, a trip to the west coast would be grand.)

The wives of three ranchers pulled up in front of the store in a buckboard, a small, utilitarian wagon with four wheels, one seat, and a flat bed for hauling tools or supplies. The two-horse team was driven by Cloris Hamtramck, the big-handed woman Emmalee had first seen the day Kaiserhalt had nabbed her in the willow grove. Among the ranch women, Emmalee probably knew Cloris best. Mrs. Hamtramck had been particularly impressed by Em's speech against violence on the day of the land rush, and she was always ready with a grin or a bit of gossip when she saw Emmalee in town.

" 'Lo there, youngster," Cloris said now, climbing down from the buckboard's seat along with Mrs. Jacklinson and Ruth Rutkowski, wives of Pennington's close friends. "Hear you got yourself a new cabin. How's the love life?" She winked and spit tobacco juice next to the wagon wheel. The older, hardier women did not shrink from enjoying the pleasures of their men; Cloris knew how to drink from a moonshine jug too.

"Everything's going pretty well," answered Emmalee. "I just wish the ground hadn't frozen. Randy and I could be getting some plowing done before snowfall."

"Wish I had your energy." Mrs. Jacklinson groaned, trying to stretch away the kinks left by the wagon seat. She and Mrs. Rutkowski went into the store.

"Everybody is working too hard out here," Cloris said. "It makes us mean."

Emmalee told her about the plans for a Christmas party. "Hester is making up a sign to hang in front for everybody to see."

"Now you're talking," Cloris said. "It's about time we had some fun and let our hair down around here. Tell you what, I'll start spreading the word about the big shindig. Yonder comes the wagon train. Let's have ourselves a looksee."

The street was filled with people now, milling about and watching as the wagon train covered its last hundred yards. The extra wagons had evoked even more interest than usual. Everybody was wondering what kinds of goods and supplies would be in the vehicles. Hardy teams of ten mules apiece pulled the wagons, and the drivers were wiry, dour men in dark clothes and heavy capes. They rode on the wagons or walked beside the mules carrying long looped whips that they flicked and snapped when the beasts showed signs of faltering.

Just as the train was about to stop, two things happened. Ebenezer Creel came riding into town on Garn Landar's stallion. And Horace Torquist, along with five farmers, arrived too. They looked grim. Emmalee noted, to her amazement, that Torquist was wearing a big, long-barreled revolver in a holster on his hip. His dislike of weapons seemed to have been overcome.

The crowd cheered when the head driver called his final "Whhoooooaaaa!" and asked if anybody on God's earth had a smile, a kind word, and a long drink of good whiskey.

"We got the whiskey," called Cloris Hamtramck.

Almost everybody laughed. Except Ebenezer Creel, Torquist, and his little group of men.

"You got what I came for?" Torquist demanded of the head driver.

"Yup. Rear wagon."

"All right. My men and I will take it over to my farm and unload while you do what you have to do here in town."

"Suits me," said the driver. "You can unload as well as me an' my boys. Just see that the wagon and mules get back here by noon."

"Deal," said Torquist. His mouth was hard, his eyes were icy, suspicious slits. A big hat partially matted down his wild, white hair. In one sense, he seemed dominant and demonic, rather as of old but with a sinister aura added. Yet, looking again, Emmalee had the impression of a man embarked on a desperate endeavor. What, for God's sake?

She watched as Torquist, Waters, Heaton, and the rest surrounded the last wagon and guided it out of line toward the leader's farm on the river. It almost seemed, by the way they were acting, as if the wagon were fragile. Then Emmalee realized that Torquist had ordered something of great importance to him and that it had been delivered in the wagon. She also saw that she was not alone in this conclusion and overheard Alf Kaiserhalt muttering to a range hand, "I reckon that's what they've been waiting for. We better ride out and tell the boss."

Kaiserhalt was still wearing a cast on the arm Emmalee had broken for him. The fracture ought to have healed by now, but he'd been trying to rassle a dogie down to the ground in order to give it Pennington's Rocking P brand and the frightened little animal had kicked him in his bad arm, rebreaking it.

People were still wondering and looking after Torquist and the wagon when Ebenezer Creel spoke up. He'd ridden a long way down from the highlands of Landar's

Folly. Frost coated his new mustache and wispy beard, covered his coat collar with a glistening white film.

"You bring Quinn along this trip?" he demanded of the head driver.

"Yes, my good fellow, he certainly did."

The voice was cultured and clipped, rather high-pitched, and the few people who snickered openly upon hearing it were joined by quite a lot of others when the man about whom Ebenezer had inquired climbed haltingly down from one of the wagons. He was middle-aged, but slim and dignified. He had strong, capable-looking hands, but his fingernails gleamed. His face was pink and smooth. He wore a smart suit, a stylish cape, soft leather boots, and a derby hat. It was the hat that drew attention most.

"Looks like we got us a freakin' dandy in this town now," commented Vestor Tell, who'd emerged from the store to observe the scene.

"And you are Mr. Landar, I presume?" asked the man, approaching Ebenezer and extending his hand.

Ebenezer shook it. "No, I ain't. We work together." He observed the new arrival carefully and without great enthusiasm. "You *are* Jacob Quinn?"

"Of course I am, my good man. Mr. Landar hired me to—"

"In these parts, it's better if a man don't discuss his business in public."

Quinn turned and saw all the eyes on him. "Oh, I see your point. I quite agree."

"Glad you do," said Ebenezer. "Now, you got 'em with you?"

"Yes. They're in the wagons."

"I hope they can walk. We got a fur piece to go, up into them there hills."

Ebenezer pointed to the Sacajawea Range, north of Arcady.

"Oh, my," exclaimed Quinn, in a high-pitched tone that made people laugh, "that's quite a distance."

"You can ride with me," said Ebenezer.

"Oh, I'm not concerned about myself."

"Well, I figured your boys was tough enough, for what we have in mind for them."

"They are."

"Then what's the problem?"

"It's just that I brought my niece along with me. I had no idea this area would be quite so . . . bucolic," he finished.

The townspeople did not laugh this time, but stared at one another, wondering what "bucolic" meant. They were also wondering exactly what this fancy stranger with the funny hat was talking about.

He proceeded to show them. Walking to the lead wagon, he drew aside a piece of the canvas flap and said, "Delilah? Are you ready? We've arrived in Arcady. Come on out and have a look."

Emmalee and the rest were just beginning to take their measure of a lovely, dark-haired, dark-eyed young woman who stepped charmingly down from the wagon on her uncle's arm when Jacob Quinn turned slightly and shouted something in a strange tongue. Then the reason for the extra supply wagons was revealed. Canvas coverings were flung aside and dozens of alien-looking men leaped from the wagons and onto the ground. Jacob Quinn said something else, and the men fell into a column in front of Ebenezer Creel.

"Chinese!" exclaimed Vestor Tell.

Emmalee stared. She knew that Chinese were working on the expanding railroads in the west and in the ports along the Pacific coast. She had seen a few in Denver. The Olympians gaped at these foreigners, amazed as much by the visitation as by whatever new folly Garn Landar had apparently dreamed up in his head. The Chinese stared back, in a manner that was rather gloomily observant, sharp-eyed yet giving nothing away, no signs of interest or curiosity or surprise. If these were hired men, Emmalee thought, they were also hard and proud. One of their number, who wore a yellow headband, began speaking to them in abrupt, almost brutal tones, then ceased. He seemed their foreman.

"They're ready to march whenever you say," Jacob Quinn announced to Ebenezer.

"I'll have to borrow a horse for you and the girl," said Creel.

"I can walk," Quinn responded readily.

The crowd laughed. There he stood in his soft boots and fine clothes, next to his demure, sweet-looking niece. Emmalee envied her clothes: a woolen traveling suit of dark blue. Buttons that appeared to be of real gold ran down the front in two decorative rows. And Delilah Quinn wore the grandest hat Emmalee had ever seen, a three-cornered affair with ribbons, feathers, and a little silk chin-strap. Emmalee wished that Lottie Pennington was there to see how a *real* lady dressed. There was something so friendly, direct, and just ever-so-slightly vulnerable about Delilah that Emmalee liked her right away.

Delilah's large brown eyes widened apprehensively as Festus Bent took it upon himself to step out of the crowd and approach Jacob and his niece.

"Did I hear you say you was gonna *walk* all the way up to Landar's Folly?" Bent chortled, turning and looking at the Arcadians to make sure they got the joke.

"That's right," answered Quinn calmly.

"Hell"—Bent laughed—"you can't even stand!"

And with that he pushed Jacob Quinn to the ground.

"Tenderfoot!" he roared, laughing.

"Come on, Fes, hold up!" some said. But many more

laughed along with him. Disdain for the "tenderfoot," for the cultivated, civilized newcomer was born more of envy than actual animosity, but it was real. Pioneers whose lives were unvaryingly and often almost unendurably hard were simultaneously proud of themselves yet deeply aware of the crudeness that colored their lives. This awareness produced a complicated mix of emotions, among which scorn for the tenderfoot was one result.

"Oh!" exclaimed Delilah, stepping toward her uncle. "Are you hurt?"

Quinn shook his head, grinned, and began to get up.

"Stay down 'less you want to go down again," Bent barked.

"Stop!" cried Delilah.

But her uncle got readily to his feet. Bent wound up and got ready to throw a big haymaker, laughing at the newcomer's lunacy in taking on a pioneer as tough as he was.

Before his arm got halfway around, before he had the slightest chance of striking Quinn, the tenderfoot shot three straight left jabs into Bent's lantern-jawed face. One jab broke his nose, the next removed four teeth, and the third shattered the big hanging jaw itself. Festus Bent was unconscious before he hit the ground.

There was a collective exhalation of breath from the Arcadians. Emmalee felt like cheering. Quinn stood casually over Bent, massaging the knuckles of his left hand.

"I'll walk," he said to no one in particular. "Dee, you ride with Mr. Creel. Here, I'll help you up. How long is this trip, anyway?"

"Oh, three hours at least," said Ebenezer.

"Good. I could use some exercise."

Torquist's wagon, while not forgotten in the always well-heated atmosphere of Olympian politics, immediately dropped to a low second place beside Garn Landar's Chinese and their traveling companions, the Quinns. The rumors flew thick and fast, like sparrows to an open granary door.

"Niece, hah!" scoffed Alma Bent, busy trying to revive her husband. "That girl is a man's kept woman if I ever saw one. Did you see that dress she had on? It must of cost a hunnert bucks! Oh, Festus, you idiot! Ain't nothin' never goin' to go right for you?"

"Do you reckon that man was a prizefighter or something?" asked Leander Rupp of no one in particular. "What the hell would Landar want with a man like that?"

Emmalee, who overheard both comments, had to admit that the same questions were on her mind.

"The Chinese are helpin' with the Continental Railroad," mused Vestor Tell, "but Landar's Folly is hardly the best place on earth to lay track."

A small spate of laughter followed Tell's remark. But it did not last long.

"See the way that head Chinese boy looked?" asked Elvira Waters. "I heard once that them Orientals use a knife so good they can cut you right down the middle, head to toe, an' you'll walk on maybe another twenty feet before you realize it and fall apart."

"What *are* Creel and Landar doing up there in the hills anyway?" Cloris Hamtramck wanted to know.

So did a lot of other people, but the matter did not seem to affect them directly, and when life is hard things that have no immediate effect are pushed aside. Emmalee went back into the store, bought flour, yeast, and a little sugar, looked at the big sign for the Christmas party that Hester had made, approved it, and then went out to mount the dapple-gray and ride home. She saw Myrtle coming toward the store. It had been a couple of weeks since she'd seen the older woman, so Emmalee stopped to chat.

"You missed all the excitement," she said.

"Yeah? What happened?"

"The wagon train came and Ebenezer met it. There were over twenty Chinese. Also a man and a girl. They left for Landar's Folly."

Myrtle looked surprised. "A girl?" she asked. "I didn't know there was gonna be a girl."

She realized that she'd revealed too much, and stopped talking. But it was too late.

"Then what do you know, Myrtle?" demanded Emmalee, as pleasantly as she could. She remembered Myrtle, Hester, Ebenezer, and Garn leaning conspiratorially over the table in the general store.

"Just surprised a girl would come all the way out here," the old woman answered lamely. "That all right with you?"

"*I'm* out here."

"Hmmm," said Myrtle.

"What are Garn and Ebenezer up to?" Emmalee asked, having decided a frontal assault was as good as any and better than most.

"How the hell should I know?"

"But you do."

"Even if I do, it doesn't concern you."

Emmalee felt left out. And intensely curious.

"How's things with you and Randy?" inquired Myrtle, changing the subject.

"Fine."

"Remember what I told you way back there in Kansas? That it ain't no picnic to be alone? I guess you finally came to that conclusion."

"I guess I did."

"There's one other thing though."

"Yes?"

"The fit's got to be right."

"The fit?"

"Yep. In every way. So if you're planning on getting hitched, I guess the fit must be right."

Emmalee guessed that Myrtle meant the way that a woman and a man matched up, in ideals, dreams, ambitions, and desires."

"I think it is," she said.

"Good," said Myrtle. "I hear you borrowed money off Tell too. Why'd he go and get so agreeable all of a sudden?"

"I don't know."

"Then watch your step."

"I aim to."

Saying so long to Myrtle, Emmalee mounted the gray and headed back home. On the way, she met Torquist and the farmers taking the empty wagon back into Arcady. She waved to them and they responded, looking considerably less grim than they had in the village, as if a load had been taken off their minds. As she rode by Torquist's farm, Emmalee could not restrain her curiosity. She guided the horse past his big new house with the lean-to on the side, that lonely appendage from which she'd recently escaped, and down toward the barn. Its doors were closed and—Emmalee saw with amazement—padlocked. But she eased the gray right up next to the barn and stood up on the saddle, peering into one of the narrow ventilation slits that Torquist, always forward-looking, had installed.

And she saw them.

Great gleaming spools of barbwire stacked high, at least a hundred spools, to fence off the farmers' land from that of the ranchers. She recalled Otis's anger at the mere mention of barbwire, his fury at the way it cut up grazing cattle and ruined the lay of the land. And here it was, in Olympia, enough wire to fence all the farms around.

Emmalee sighed and rode back home to tell Randy.

It looked like trouble would be coming along with Christmas that year.

Deck the Halls

Hester's new hotel, designed to be the showcase of Arcady, was aglow with light and color. Olympians who approached it in the frosty, falling darkness on Christmas night, themselves recovering slowly from holiday dinners of roast pork, biscuits, and gravy, saw the gleaming whiteness of new paint in lantern light outside, and the great hall downstairs was festive with tree, streamers of colored paper, and Chinese lanterns. The memory of the *Queen of Natchez* had given Emmalee the idea for the lanterns.

Emmalee and Randy had exchanged gifts in the morning at the new house. He gave her a pair of delicate, gilded barrettes. She presented him with the posthole digger he wanted, and which she'd had to sell four of her ten chickens to afford. After that, they'd gone into town to help Hester decorate the hall for the evening dance.

"It looks great, even if I do say so myself," Hester pronounced. A row of tables along one side of the big room held bowls of fragrant punch and all manner of cakes, pies, and cookies baked by farm women and ranch women alike. Next to the area in the far corner, which was reserved for the band, stood a bar at which pioneers might partake of something a little more powerful than punch. There were chairs for those who might wish to be seated along the other walls, and the center of the room was open for dancing. The Christmas tree, cut and dragged down from the Sacajawea by a dozen eager children, stood near the entrance and colored streamers, along with the Chinese lanterns, hung from the ceiling.

"We might of got us a bigger tree," one of the boys had reported after coming back down from the hills, "but we saw this Chinaman with a yellow headband waving a gun at us, so we turned back."

His comment had been noted, discussed, and then set aside, like so many of the other inexplicable tidbits relating to Landar's Folly.

Members of the band arrived first. Otis was going to play the washboard, which he carried in under his arm. He put the washboard down in the corner, drew Emmalee off to one side, and presented her with a genuine silver snuff box.

"I know it ain't exactly what you might fancy," he told her, almost bashfully, "but I wanted to give you a little somethin'. Just to show we're friends."

Emmalee felt embarrassed. She had no gift for him. But she fixed him a big drink of lemonade and corn likker, which made him happy enough.

Accompanying Otis on fiddles were Bates Knell, rancher, and farmer Virgil Waters. Lambert Strep came with an old accordion and rancher Royce Campbell, who—it was said—had once been a seagoing pirate, brought his guitar. Randy told them the square dances that he knew, and the men went off to rehearse a bit before the crowd arrived.

A big group was expected. Emmalee's idea, supported by Hester Brine's indefatigable publicizing, had spread word of the party throughout Olympia. Only the bedridden or the very young would be absent. And the contingent from Landar's Folly, of course. The Chinese foreman came to town once a week on Tuesday mornings, regular as clockwork, entered the general store, pointed and grunted when he saw what he wanted, paid cash, and departed. Everyone called him Yo-Bang, which derived from the color of his headband, but they did not call him that to his face.

In a way, Emmalee was glad that Garn Landar would not be coming to the party. His absence eliminated the possibility that anything untoward would occur between Garn and Randy, or between Garn and Emmalee herself. Also—and Emmalee was a little surprised at herself for realizing it—if Garn was not present, he could not spend time with Lottie. In some vestigially possessive part of her soul, Emmalee did not care for the idea of Garn having anything to do with Lottie. She still had no idea why the Pennington girl had been riding Garn's horse that time, but every now and again she wondered just what was going on between them.

In another way, Emmalee was rather disappointed that Garn would not be coming. So many of their early encounters, whether they had been verbal, raising her ire, or hot and physical, raising her to passion, now seemed far away, incidents and events out of another time. She'd been much younger then, in attitude and demeanor if not in age, and her actions had been those of a girl. Now she felt much more grown up and womanly, and if he met her and talked to her now, well, he would see that. She was not the more reckless, impulsive Emmalee of last spring and summer. She could handle him now, she felt, put him in perspective. And she wanted him to see the relationship she had with Randy, which was so steady and considerate and . . . mature.

If Garn observed that relationship, Emmalee felt, then

he would understand once and for all how different from her he really was. He who once had the gall to suggest that they were like each other!

The only thing that bothered her, in these deliberate ruminations, was why she ought to be concerned at all with what Garn Landar thought. In the end, she ascribed her concern to the fact that things had ended so badly for them—that awful scene among the boulders above Denver—and that she was a sensible, forgiving sort of person who just did not want to see things end badly. She didn't care for the detached way he looked at her now. It probably meant that he had repented his transgression, she concluded, which was good. But there was no need for him to treat her so coolly, was there?

On the other hand—and this was the part she tried to keep herself from thinking about—Garn had seen her with Otis on the riverbank that night. Nothing had happened between her and Otis, but how was Garn to know that? What must he think of her now?

I don't care what he thinks, she told herself, pouring a glass of punch. That's just the point. She decided to forget all about it; she walked over to help Hester cut cakes and pies.

Country people always arrive all at once for a social event, as if to come either too soon or too late would somehow betray the uniqueness of the occasion and ruin the event itself. Also, they did not have all that many affairs to attend. At any rate, the hotel was practically deserted one moment and jam-packed the next. To their credit, the opposing camps appeared to be trying to honor the occasion, if not each other, with an appearance of civility. Even Horace Torquist managed to smile, although he contrived to avoid Burt Pennington and both the corn likker and mild, wine-flavored punch.

Talk came more easily to the women of the two groups than it did to the men, but a drink or two helped, and when the small band started up the mood in the place lightened considerably. The members of the band had never played together before and their opening number, "God Rest Ye Merry Gentlemen," was a little shaky. Yet it was recognizable, and the people applauded, which gave the players confidence. They launched into a rousing version of "Oh, Susannah!"

"Guess I'd better get on over there and get ready to call a square," said Randy, who'd been standing next to Emmalee and drinking punch.

He left to join the band. It occurred to Emmalee that she didn't have a partner for the dance. Even worse, she saw Lottie Pennington coming toward her through the crowd. Lottie wore lavender, which suited her exquisitely, setting off that shining red hair. For once, Emmalee was not distressed. She knew she looked good in a long-skirted gown she'd sewn herself, powder blue with gold piping to match the barrettes Randy had given her.

"Why, it's Emmalee Alden, what a surprise!" exuded Lottie. She inspected Emmalee carefully. "I must say, marriage agrees with you. When is the baby due?"

Emmalee smoldered but held her temper. "I'm afraid you're mistaken. I'm not getting married until next summer."

"Oh, my goodness. I've offended you." Lottie looked cheerful.

"Of course not. Think nothing of it. Have you a beau these days?"

Lottie averted her eyes cagily, then looked back at Emmalee. "Isn't it bad luck to say? It's a jinx to put your mouth on it."

The expression meant that a person ought not discuss a bit of luck or a fond desire, lest a dream go glimmering.

"So some say."

"Did you organize all this?" asked Lottie, feigning awe and looking around the teeming hall. "All the work! I'm so impressed. And there's your fiancé getting ready to call a square dance, isn't he? He's most attractive."

This sentiment was genuine on Lottie's part, but she managed to convey an impression of surprise that Emmalee had managed to snare such a man.

"I hear that you're living in the same house with him," she hissed.

"It's not true. I have a cabin on my own land."

"I do hope you keep it."

"What do you mean by that?"

"Nothing. Can I ask you a personal question?"

"By all means."

"Do you think you're . . . well . . . right for Randy Clay?"

"*He* seems to think so," replied Emmalee coldly.

"Oh, don't be upset. It's just that he seems so warm and friendly and, you know, sort of old-fashioned."

That's why I'm so fond of him, Emmalee thought.

"And you seem like such a go-getter—so capable and everything."

"It's nice of you to say so."

"Oh, I know. It is, it is. But I just meant . . ."

The band ended "Oh, Susannah!" and Randy called out, "Everybody ready for a try at a square?"

He was answered by an affirmative din.

"Get your partners then, form up, and let's give it a go."

The fiddles whined, accordion, guitar, and washboard joined in, the sound of the washboard accentuating rhythm as a drum would have. Along with everyone else, Emmalee clapped her hands to the beat and could not keep from tapping her foot. The rough music filled the hall, people whirled, and Randy called the dance:

"... promenade and around you go,
gonna marry the girl with the pretty red bow ..."

If Randy called all night, Emmalee reflected, she wouldn't have a chance to dance at all. Even Lottie had someone; she was dancing with her father. Burt's bald, bullet-shaped pate gleamed in the light. She checked around, looking to see if there might not be a prospective partner.

"... all join hands and go to town,
gonna marry the girl in the calico gown ..."

And then, to her surprise, she caught a glimpse of Garn Landar. He was taller than most of the other men, and she saw him making his way slowly through the crowd to the bar. He was formally, elegantly dressed in an expensive suit of blue serge, gleaming white shirt collar, and a cravat of maroon silk with a golden tie pin. But he looked tired and rather preoccupied. Nevertheless, he greeted those he passed in a friendly manner. She saw heads turn to follow him. *What's* he *doing here?* Garn had become a mystery and he drew the attention accorded to one.

She was wondering if he'd seen her or not—he didn't seem particularly interested in the party—when she heard somebody behind her say, quietly but effervescently, "Oh, my goodness! Isn't he adorable?"

She turned to see Delilah Quinn standing beside her uncle Jacob. She looked fresh, ingenuous, and very pretty. She was watching Randy call the dance.

"Oh, hello!" she said when she saw Emmalee looking at her. "You're one of the town girls? I'm Delilah. I've wanted to come to town since *forever*! How I envy you living here!"

"Jacob Quinn." Her uncle bowed, smiling. Emmalee extended her hand and Jacob took it for a moment into his own. Emmalee gave her name.

"We've been keeping Delilah up in the hills too long, I'm afraid," he said, smiling again and inclining his head slightly toward his excited niece. "She wanted to have some fun and here we are."

Emmalee liked them both immediately. Jacob was strong, straightforward, confident. Delilah seemed forthright as well and attractively guileless.

"What kind of a dance is this?" she asked, watching the whirl.

". . . Swing your partner, do-si-do,
gonna marry a girl who won't dance too slow . . ."

"It's called a square dance."

"And that cute man who's saying the words?"

"He's the caller."

"I meant what's his name?"

"Randy Clay," said Emmalee. "Don't you have square dances in . . . where are you from, if you don't mind my asking?"

"San Francisco."

"Of course we have square dances there," interjected her uncle, "but Dee's been in private school for some years. She wasn't exposed to—"

"Oh, Uncle Jake! I want to forget about those times. How dreary. I want to have some fun now. Where are you from?" she asked Emmalee.

"Pennsylvania."

"Oh, my! How did you get here?"

"Oh a wagon train across the country."

"Really? How I *envy* you! I've never done anything. And now they have me up in those hills. . . ."

"It's only temporary, Dee," said her uncle.

"And they're always *working*," Delilah went on, which removed from Emmalee's mind the chance thought that Delilah and Garn might be . . .

"Do you have a beau?" asked the girl, in her frank but thoroughly inoffensive way.

"I guess you could say I do. I'm—"

"You're so lucky. If I had a beau I think I'd like *him*."

She meant Randy.

"Why aren't you dancing?" she asked Emmalee. "Oh, Uncle Jake. Do you suppose anyone will ask me? Will you dance with me if no one else does? But please try not to look like my uncle, all right?"

> ". . . Go back to your partner,
> Swing her around,
> Gonna marry that gal and settle down."

With that verse, the dance came to an end. Everybody cheered and applauded. "What'll we do next?" Randy asked.

" 'Turkey in the Straw,' " called Myrtle Higgins, hoisting a mug of applejack. The squares of dancers readied themselves. Band members tuned their instruments for the new song.

"What are you doing up in the Sacajawea?" asked Emmalee, as casually as she could. Since Delilah and her uncle were so friendly and open, it seemed a shame not to inquire.

"Oh, it's very exciting," said the girl. "You see, the river—"

Jacob took her arm. "Look, Dee," he said. "There's a

square that needs another twosome. Would you excuse us, Miss Alden? We'll chat some more later, I'm sure."

Emmalee was sure, too, sure that Jacob had not wanted his pretty niece to talk about what was happening on Landar's Folly. But she had learned, maybe, that whatever it was had something to do with the Big Two-Hearted.

Watching the second dance was worse than watching the first. Everybody was having fun, and Garn Landar was dancing with Lottie Pennington! Emmalee saw the shameless way that Lottie pressed against him every chance she got, and she did not care either for the manner in which Garn smiled down at her. Emmalee decided she needed a breath of fresh air and went outside into the lantern-lit chill. She heard the music end and the cheer that followed. The band started playing "Ora Lee." I'd better go back inside, Emmalee thought. She was beginning to feel a chill.

Then Garn emerged, alone, from the hotel. He was smoking a thin cigar. His posture, his alert glance, told her that he'd come outside for a purpose. She attempted to brush past him but he caught her arm and held on.

"Yes?" she asked coldly.

"Will you accept a 'Merry Christmas'?"

"Yes. Merry Christmas."

He didn't release her. "Em, can I talk to you for a moment?"

He had that same cool, detached air about him, yet she sensed a seriousness of intent toward her. She didn't know if she liked that or not.

"If you think we have something to talk about," she answered noncommitally.

"It's possible," he said. "I just wanted to say once and for all that I'm sorry about the way it ended for us in Denver. Since you arrived here, I've tried to treat you properly when we've seen each other. I don't think I've embarrassed you or imposed myself upon you. Would you mind if I began to show a bit more friendliness now?"

"As you wish," she said coolly. "But I must go inside."

Still he did not release her. He tossed away his cigar.

"Come on, Em." He smiled. "Friendship is a two-way street. I said I was sorry."

Emmalee felt herself softening, exhorted herself to stay on guard. "It's too late to be sorry. Everything worked out fine. Forget about it."

"Do you really mean that?"

"I'm like you in one way, maybe. I never say what I don't mean. Why do you care, anyway, when Lottie Pennington rides around on your horse?"

The words were out before she knew it. She saw his gleaming smile. It infuriated her.

"Does that bother you?" he asked.

"No," she lied.

"Good. And I certainly don't care what you and Otis do at night along the riverbank. But how does Randy feel about it?"

There was a faint trace of mockery in his voice now, a part of the Garn she'd known. She was about to respond in her old manner as well, by flaring at him with a taunting retort, but then she put herself in his position for a moment. What *was* he to think? He'd seen her, a woman engaged to be married, in a highly compromising position with another man. If she'd once thought *him* reckless, hedonistic, and selfish, what must he now think of *her*?

"Otis Chandler," Garn was saying. "He's all right, I suppose."

"At least he got his people to Denver like he promised!"

Garn laughed. "That's the spirit," he said. "Keep it up. Myrtle and Hester told me you'd changed. I didn't believe a word of it, and now . . ."

Myrtle and Hester talked about her with Garn? Emmalee was surprised and insulted.

"And for your information, angel, Lottie's horse went lame in town one day and I loaned her mine for a few hours. Is that all right with you?"

"A likely story. And don't call me 'angel.' "

"I've told you before, I never lie. Now tell me how you and Otis ended up out there listening to crickets."

"I'm not going to waste my time. . . ."

Emmalee tried to twist away from him. She did not succeed. He spun her away from the hotel doorway, forcefully but not harshly, drew her along the hotel's brightly lit facade, around the corner and into the darkness. She felt his arms around her then, but before she had a chance to struggle his mouth came down on hers and he kissed her. At first, she tried to resist, to pull away, but the insidious power he'd always held over her was still alive. Her mind dimmed, a surge of heat rushed through her body, colored lights flashed behind her closed eyelids, and inside the hotel, behind this wall against which he pressed her, the band began to play, very sweetly, "Greensleeves." That ancient, haunting melody, the darkly irresistible power of Garn's kiss, took her out of herself, loosed the sweet nectar of love inside her, and she began to drift beneath a spell she believed to be unwanted, undesired. . . .

Instinctively she'd closed her eyes during the kiss, but some remnant of sixth sense alerted her from deepening reverie. Still in Garn's embrace, she caught a glimpse of Randy. He was standing out in front of the hotel, looking up and down the street. Looking for her? She twisted away from Garn, and pulled him more deeply into the shadow. Randy went back inside the hotel. Garn saw what had happened.

"You'll never cease causing me trouble," she flared at

him, her voice a husky whisper in the darkness. "Look what you almost did this time!"

She went back toward the hotel entrance by herself. Garn's words followed her.

"It wasn't just me, Emmalee," he said.

Randy was talking to Delilah Quinn when Emmalee came back inside, or rather it was the other way around.

". . . and you've claimed land here?" Delilah was saying in her wonderfully enthusiastic manner when Emmalee walked up to the two of them. "That's so adventurous! I'd just love to do that, to stay out here forever and live off the land."

"It's not all as easy as that," Randy said, thoroughly flattered, charmed. "But every year things'll get better. I hope."

"Of course they will. Hi, Emmalee. Where've you been?"

"I went out for a little fresh air."

"You should dance. Randy and I just danced to 'Greensleeves.' It was fun. Isn't it amazing what a little band like that can do? Oh, I'm sorry, have you two met? Emmalee, Randy. Randy, Emmalee."

"Well, yes," said Emmalee, as Randy toed the dancefloor with his boot, "actually, we're—"

She was interrupted by a sudden commotion at the doorway. The people inside the hotel were laughing, drinking, and making a lot of noise, but the newcomer's howl attracted everyone's attention. Heads turned to see Alf Kaiserhalt, stumpy, half-drunk, but triumphant. He still had one arm in a sling but he held his other arm high above his head. And in his hand was a looped length of barbwire.

"Hey, everybody!" he called. "Lookee what I found

over at Torquist's place. And there's a whole lot more of it, let me tell you!"

There was a short silence filled with tension. Barbwire. The symbol of division between farmers and ranchers, reflecting, as nothing else could, the difference in the way the two groups viewed freedom, survival, and the land. Was the countryside to be open, as it had been for thousands of years, with men and animals roaming freely? Or was it to be fenced into plots and tracts, with one man's destiny and domain set apart from that of his neighbor?

"My barn was locked!" roared Horace Torquist, rushing toward Kaiserhalt. "You broke in, damn your soul!"

He was blocked and seized by Royce Campbell.

The evening, which had produced an amity unknown since the settlers had first arrived in Olympia, disintegrated completely, instantly. The thin veneer of civilization, so hard-bought, so prized, spun away utterly as the two groups remembered the roots of their enmity.

"Don't you say a word about your precious barn," shouted Burt Pennington. "You fellows knew all along how we feel about barbwire. Just let me tell you this: First farmer who sets up a fence gets it torn down. Second farmer who does gets his barn burned. Next one, barn and house. Take it from there."

The ranchers gave a brutal cheer. The farmers shouted in angry horror.

"Then your longhorns are gonna be found dead on the range," bellowed Torquist. "Dead on the range, do you hear me?"

"Next to every dead cow of mine," Pennington shot back, "there'll be a dead sodbuster." He used the cattlemen's derogatory term for farmers.

Hester Brine's voice rose above the din.

"You all get out of here," she shouted. "Every one of you. I'm ashamed to live in the same town with the lot of you. Here Emmalee and I went and tried to make things better, and now look what you've gone and done. It's a pity. It's a damn crying shame. Now just get out."

There was no war that night, but its seeds had been planted in fertile soil.

"Well, you tried," said Cloris Hamtramck to Emmalee sensed a seriousness of intent toward her. "These goddamn men. Look, if there's anything I can help you with, let me know, hear?"

Barbwire and Barbarians

The sod had lain upon the land for millennia, a rich carpet of grass whose matted roots twisted thickly, deeply into the earth. Emmalee attacked it bravely, armed with an iron-bladed plow drawn reluctantly by Myrtle's Ned. She had to work at least as hard as the mule, constantly pressing the wooden handles of the plow so the tip of the blade would stay in the ground. The sod had to be turned over so that seeds could be planted in black earth never before warmed by the sun. It required all of her effort and half a morning to plow one furrow a hundred yards long. Ned halted of his own accord and Emmalee looked back at her narrow, shallow furrow. She sat down on the grass and wiped dripping perspiration from her face with the sleeve of her shirt. "I'll never be able to do this," she moaned aloud.

Ned gazed at her dolefully. He agreed.

Across the fence, Randy plowed his land alone. He was only Emmalee's neighbor now.

Spring had finally come, after a long, hard, troubling winter. In Emmalee's estimation, the only good thing about it had been the snow, which prevented farmers from putting up barbwire fences. Burt Pennington had had no cause to make good his threats; a shaky half-truce existed in the territory.

Emmalee wanted to forget all about winter. She shuddered at the very memory of isolation and loneliness. During the short, harsh days, Randy had worked at building his barn, had hewn fenceposts to be set when spring came, had tended his cattle. Emmalee saw to her little cabin, cooked, cleaned, mended, and sewed. They met for the meals she prepared, which they ate huddled near the kitchen stove with the wind howling outside. It had seemed rather like an adventure way back in January, the two of them holding out against wild nature, but the shattering *sameness* of the days had a dismal, cumulative effect upon them. No matter how Emmalee tried to be cheerful, no matter how hard Randy sought to dwell upon future dreams, workaday concerns intruded. Along with those matters, such as the relative merits of corn versus rye, or the continuing question of barbwire, came conflict. At first their disagreements were cloaked in a lighthearted, teasing manner, as if the question of fencing was really not *that* important, as if it didn't matter whether corn or rye would be planted in the fields come spring. But gradually their differences of opinion were expressed more forcefully, as on the night in late February when Randy said, "That's it, Em. I'll plant rye and you plant corn. We don't have to talk about it anymore."

And they hadn't. As time passed, there were fewer and fewer things to talk about.

To make matters worse, their moments of tenderness, attenuated as they were, merely built up the tension of desire without offering the pleasure of release. Even a sweet kiss, a light embrace, left in its wake the frustration of unsatisfied need. At night, alone in her cabin, Emmalee would stand by the window, looking out at the fields of blowing snow, hugging herself for warmth, feeling her heart grow as cold and lonely as the distant hills. Only a year ago she had cuddled next to Val Jannings in the sleigh; how fine it had been to bc warm and beloved, and how she longed now to be held and caressed, kissed and stroked, yes, and how much she wanted to be taken. She remembered, during those long, long nights, every kiss she'd ever had, every touch, and how she had felt receiving them. And she imagined, with a vividness that sometimes made her gasp, what it would feel like to be utterly shaken by passion, breathless in the dazed and dazzled splendor of her flesh.

Only once each week was there anything really to look forward to. She and Randy would ride into Arcady together on Sundays, to sell a little milk and a few eggs to Hester and to attend services at the new church. They would ride on Randy's dapple-gray, negotiating with difficulty the ruts and drifts on the windswept prairie. Sometimes it snowed as they rode along, the wind-driven flakes cold and stinging on their cheeks. But the trek was always worth the trouble because there would be people at the church, company, conversation, and these were necessary to stave off the assaults of cabin fever during the rest of the week.

On the second Sunday after Christmas, a new face appeared among the worshippers: Delilah Quinn, who rode Garn Landar's big black stallion down from the Sacajawea in the company of Yo-Bang. The somewhat frightening foreman, with his long knife and unblinking gaze, would wait in the vestibule while Pastor Runde conducted services, would wait still longer while Delilah drank coffee and visited, and then would escort her back into the hills, to return again on the following Sabbath.

Emmalee appreciated seeing Delilah, who was funny

and candid and lively, characteristics not easily found among the general lot of churchgoers. Myrtle and Hester, who, it was rumored, had had a colorful past, spent Sunday mornings drinking coffee and brandy at the store; Cloris Hamtramck didn't come to church at all. But after a very few Sundays, Emmalee realized that there was a definite pattern to Delilah's appearances. She would arrive a bit late, after Pastor Runde had finished reading the gospel and while the choir was nearly through "A Mighty Fortress Is Our God." She would remove her cloak in the vestibule, stand at the back of the little church for a moment, and then try to get a pew as close to Emmalee as she could. After the service concluded, she would laugh and drink coffee and talk with Randy and Emmalee until it was time to leave. Delilah never mentioned anything specifically about Landar's Folly, or about Garn himself, and it would not have done to inquire either, because the girl was full of bright chatter, little adventures she'd had that week, her impressions of Olympia, a new way she'd found to broil a joint, bake a cake, fire the stove.

It did not take long for Emmalee to realize that Delilah had eyes for Randy. She also saw that Randy was torn. He brightened as soon as he saw the Quinn girl and always followed her conversation closely. He laughed at every single witticism she uttered, and never failed to fall into a gloomy, shamefaced silence when he rode with Emmalee back to three pines. One Sunday, after a week of particularly heavy snow, Delilah did not show up for church at all. Randy was clearly beside himself but trying not to show it, looking out the church window time and again, even getting up in the middle of the service—to Pastor Runde's disapproval—and going outside to check for a sign of Delilah Quinn. Her very presence gave him pleasure, her absence dismay. Afterward he was elaborately attentive to Emmalee.

Almost as soon as she saw what was happening, Emmalee felt herself accepting it, and she knew that it was over between Randy and herself. If I really cared, I'd fight, she understood. So she waited for him to realize the truth.

On a bright Sunday in early March, when warm Pacific winds again moved across Olympia, melting the snow and caressing the newborn buds of trees and plants, Randy Clay and Emmalee Alden, bethrothed, became Mr. Clay and Miss Alden, neighbors. It was a Sunday that felt and smelled like Easter, still three weeks hence. Delilah was at the top of her form. Randy laughed and laughed as she described Yo-Bang's attempt to explain American ways to his countrymen. Her uncle Jacob had overheard the foreman telling his men, among other things, "To understand Yankee, it is first necessary to realize he is by nature very tricky and complicated. He does not say what he means, nor does he mean what he says, and he does not appear to know the difference. If he tells you to do something, wait, for he will soon change his mind. Chinese be simple and direct. Yankee be inscrutable."

To her credit, Delilah tried to bring Emmalee into her conversations. But this was an afterthought. Her performances were clearly for Randy. After church, she and Yo-Bang rode with Randy and Emmalee, separating where the surging stream ran down into the bucking, rolling, roaring Big Two-hearted.

"See you next Sunday," called Delilah, in a voice that suddenly lost its cheerfulness and became wistful, lonely, a little sad.

Randy was gloomy, too, as he guided the gray up over the hills toward Three Pines.

It was time.

"Randy, please would you stop the horse," Emmalee said quietly.

Randy did so. Emmalee dismounted and so did he. They

gazed spiritlessly for a moment across the land they'd claimed, which had such a short time ago held for them the hope of a glorious future together. Hope for the future it still possessed, but something had happened, something wholly natural but irremediable, to end the togetherness.

Emmalee waited.

"Oh, Em. I feel so awful about what's happened," he said at last.

She went to him and they held each other for a long moment.

"I didn't mean for it to be this way," he said. "I just felt betrayed at first, and then when Delilah came along every Sunday . . ."

What was this? "Betrayed?" Emmalee asked.

"I wish you would have told me why, Em. Then maybe Delilah wouldn't have begun to mean so much to me."

"Told you why? You wish I'd told you why what? I don't understand."

He looked directly into her eyes. "You and Garn Landar. On Christmas night outside the hotel. If you'd just explained it to me, told me why . . ."

Randy *had* seen her kissing Garn Landar that night, and it had preyed on his mind ever since.

"I couldn't help it . . ." she started to say.

"Don't, Em."

"Garn Landar means nothing to me. . . ."

"I don't think that's true, Em. Whatever you might think you feel. All I know is that Delilah is beginning to mean something to me. It's tearing me apart inside, because I gave you my promise. . . ."

His voice trailed off.

"Randy," said Emmalee slowly, quietly, her face pressed into his chest, "I want you to be happy. And I've seen how much you respond to Delilah. She makes you happy. There isn't much more to say. You're free."

It was a difficult moment for them both, a time of tears and regrets on the windy hill. But after the moment was over, Randy walked upon the earth as if a great burden had been lifted from his shoulders.

Emmalee strode—and plowed—her fields alone.

Feeling guilty about resting when there was so much work to be done, Emmalee got up off the grass and returned to her plow. She had better get to work, what with the problems she faced. Foremost among them was the fact that she owed four hundred dollars to Vestor Tell, the first payment of which fell due in September, only six months hence. If she defaulted, her land would be lost. She did have the cabin, a domicile, but there were all those acres to plow and plant and she and Ned were having trouble enough gouging a couple of furrows out of the sod. She had purchased the plow from Festus Bent for a dozen eggs and half a gallon of milk. It was a rickety old thing, brought out all the way from Arkansas. He hadn't been able to claim land and now worked for Horace Torquist as a hired hand; he didn't need the plow. In spite of its age, it did have an iron blade. Some plows were made entirely of wood, blade and mold-board alike. These were quickly ground to pieces in the age-old sod.

Emmalee urged Ned forward, bent to the handles of the plow, and began another furrow. Suddenly the plow lurched in her grasp and a grinding metallic crack of rending metal sounded from the earth. Ned stopped of his own accord. Emmalee leaned down to see what had happened.

The plow had struck a rock buried in the sod; the precious iron blade had cracked jaggedly in two. Emmalee felt like crying. But she compromised and cursed instead. She ought to have ordered a new plow from Salt Lake for twelve dollars, but she'd wanted to save the money. And now look! She would have to buy a new plow anyway, and it would take at least two weeks to arrive. Two invaluable weeks during which she might have gotten at least a portion of her corn crop planted. (Emmalee was putting in corn; across the way, Randy had opted for rye.)

There was nothing else to do but go into Arcady and place an order for a new plow with Hester. She was thinking that maybe she could borrow someone else's plow and work at night when she rode by Torquist's big new farm on the river. He and several hired men were out putting up a fence. She saw the posts driven out across the prairie, and the spools of barbwire waiting to be unstrung and nailed to the posts. She also saw horsemen in the distance watching the proceedings. They were ranchers and that meant trouble.

Myrtle Higgins was out spading her big garden when Emmalee rode by the old woman's cabin. Catching sight of Emmalee, Myrtle gestured vigorously. Emmalee went over and stopped. Myrtle stroked Ned affectionately and gave him a once-over.

"He don't look like he's being overworked."

"That's because not much work has been done."

"How come, honey?"

Disconsolately, Emmalee explained about the plow.

"Too bad. Shows to go you, never beg, borrow, or buy anything off an unlucky man, an' Fes is that, in spades. Get on down from Ned and join me in a cup of tea. You look plumb tuckered.

"You also look like you lost your last friend on earth," Myrtle added, when she and Emmalee were seated with teacups in the shade of a cottonwood behind Myrtle's cabin. "Having some of those before-marriage doubts, or what? How's Randy making it?"

"Randy's doing fine. It's me I'm concerned about."

Surprising herself—she thought it rather unseemly to dump problems on somebody else—Emmalee poured out the whole tale: Garn on Christmas night at the hotel, Delilah Quinn, everything. She felt like crying, felt a need to let go. But a girl who crossed the Great Plains wasn't about to shed tears over bad luck or a man!

"Sounds like you and Randy mignt not have made it work anyway," Myrtle said, after Emmalee had finished her recital.

Emmalee was a little hurt. When a casual observer seems able to interpret your life easily, you're bound to feel dumber than a cootie in heat.

"Oh, I had my hopes for you there for a while," Myrtle continued. "You gave it your best shot, I know. But I guess the fit just wasn't right."

"You mentioned the 'fit' once before."

"Shore did. It's mighty important. *Mighty* important. Guess you and Randy just didn't have it. Wrong kind of signals. Wrong kind of responses."

"And Randy fits with Delilah?" Emmalee felt wronged in an obscure way, although she realized that she had no right to feel that way.

"I don't know. That's something the two of them got to find out for themselves. Just like you do."

"Me? With whom? How?"

"Full of questions today, ain't cha? I don't know who with. That's your problem. But I do know how. By taking a chance on somebody. By taking a risk. Can't think of it like you're surrendering your soul. It's more on the order of gambling a piece of yourself to win a hunk of happiness down the road. And if it don't work out, well, it hurts but you live."

Emmalee sipped some tea. She smiled in spite of herself. "Myrtle, are you trying to make me feel brave, or what?"

"Hell, no." The old woman laughed. "You're brave enough for the both of us, and then some. It's just that I can tell you where I think your heart is tending, but that won't do no good. You're just going to have to admit it on your own. You've come a long way. Be a shame if you was askeerd to go the final mile."

When Emmalee entered the general store to see Hester about ordering the plow, Burt Pennington was angrily addressing Vestor Tell. Otis looked on.

"Damn it, Tell, them sodbusters are out there stringing that unholy wire all over God's earth. Aren't you going to do anything about it?"

Tell shrugged and showed his palms. "What would you have me do? It's not against the law to build a fence."

"Yeah, I know." Pennington sneered. "You're a real stickler when it comes to the law. We all know that, don't we?"

Tell just grinned. Pennington stalked furiously out of the store.

"How you makin' out, Em?" asked Otis, touching his hatbrim gallantly. "How about I buy you a cold beer?"

They sat down at a table with two large mugs of brew.

"Well, how's everythin', Em?"

"Not so good. My plow broke and I have to order a new one. I'll lose a lot of time waiting for it to arrive."

"In fact"—he leaned toward her and began to whisper —"in fact, you need more than time, you need help."

"I couldn't agree with you more."

"No. Listen. Are you planning on stringing that there barbwire?"

"Mr. Torquist has been after me to do it."

"Well, don't you do it. Burt is serious. If those fences go up, there's gonna be trouble."

"If he attacks farmers, Burt is the one who's going to be in trouble."

Otis took a long swallow of beer and looked carefully

away. "Lots of things can happen at night," he said significantly, "can't they?"

He wanted to buy her a second beer, but she demurred.

"Gettin' advice from Oats Chandler?" asked Hester, after Pennington's foreman had left.

"Yes, but I need more than that." She told Hester of her latest misfortune, and the storekeeper agreed to order a new plow and even extend the twelve dollars' worth of credit, to be paid by Emmalee's customary deliveries of eggs and milk.

"You're a good risk, honey," Hester said, "and besides, everybody seems to think this is going to be a good growing season. Weather's been perfect so far. Besides, I can manage twelve bucks."

Indeed, the weather was one of the marvels of that spring. All through April and May, the days were bright and sunny. Gentle rain fell at night, two or three times a week. Pastor Runde attributed this fortuity to the prayers he offered up in the church each week, but whatever the reason, grass grew tall for the cattle to graze upon, wheat, clover, corn, and rye all thrived. The rain softened the sod, too, and when Emmalee's new plow arrived from Salt Lake, she went to work and managed to plant an entire section of her land with corn. It took root quickly and deeply in the marvelously rich soil, and by the first of June the stalks were growing green and high.

Behind their new fences of barbwire, the other farmers prospered, too, and in Arcady on any afternoon, the sense of exuberance could not be missed. Torquist's farmers, who had spent weeks carefully watching to make sure Pennington would not make good his promise to retaliate, let down their guard a little. Patrols no longer rode the fencelines every night; it no longer seemed necessary to be so determinedly vigilant.

Behind his own string of barbwire, Randy's rye grew

thick and green. Emmalee had warned him about the fence, telling him what Otis had said, but he was unconcerned. "Em, it's all talk," he told her expansively. "It's 'fate accomplished,' or whatever it was that Mr. Torquist said at our last meeting."

Torquist still met with a small group of farmers each week, to keep track of the situation and to make plans for the future. Emmalee was never invited but Randy, in an attempt to be friendly and to keep her informed, usually told her the gist of what had occurred at the meetings. Tell had been heard to say that the inspection team from Washington was not going to show up at all this year, so the excess claims made by Virgil Water, Lambert Strep, and the others certainly wouldn't cause any problems. It seemed that the white-haired leader had succeeded—so far, at least—in his clever ruse.

Hearing these things, Emmalee felt again as she had a long time ago: Something had gone seriously wrong in Torquist's plans for a perfect community. Something had gone voluntarily, willfully wrong, and there would be retribution.

One day in early June, when Emmalee was out in the field hoeing weeds from her corn, Randy came out of his new house and sauntered over to the fence that separated their two farms. He carried a tin pail and in it was glorious lemonade. She was soaking wet with perspiration and only too aware that the dampness made her dress cling to her body, but it could not be helped. He crawled carefully through the strands of barbwire and offered her the pail. She sat down, leaning against a fencepost, and took long, long swallows of the cold drink, finally breaking off to gasp her gratitude.

"Hester got the lemons in from California," said Randy. He seemed nervous. "Came on the last supply train."

"Nice. Thank you. They must be very expensive, though."

Now he seemed even more nervous.

"Good crop of corn you got there," he said. "What are you planning to do with it once the harvest is in?"

"I'll keep what I need for flour and for my own animals and sell the rest to whoever wants it. Pennington's cattle can't graze in winter. They're going to have to eat something."

Randy didn't reply. He and Emmalee continued to disagree on how farmers and ranchers ought to deal with each other. Like Torquist, Randy wanted an absolute barrier between the groups. Emmalee thought that idea was silly, and impossible to boot.

Randy cleared his throat a couple of times. Emmalee perceived that he wanted to tell her something but was having a little trouble getting it out. Since the March Sunday on which they'd decided to end their engagement, they hadn't spoken about personal things. The closer a relationship has been, the greater the tendency to avoid any hint of intimacy after the relationship ends.

At length, Randy found his nerve. "I hope you'll attend the wedding, Em," he said. "Delilah and I would both feel badly if you didn't."

It was the unexpectedness of the announcement, rather than the news itself, that shocked Emmalee. Naturally, she had thought that at some future time Randy would marry, just as she figured she, too, would wed one day. She had even considered the possibility that Randy would marry Delilah Quinn. Someday. Maybe. But this suddenly? Already? Right now?

"On the Fourth of July," Randy was saying. "In the church in Arcady. I've already made the arrangements with Pastor Runde."

"I'm happy for you both," said Emmalee. Now she

really felt alone. "I guess you decided to get married before harvest after all. Well, everybody says the crops can't fail. . . ."

"That doesn't really matter anymore." Randy did not meet her eyes. "I never thought about it, of course, but, you see, Delilah has some money of her own. We'll be all right, and there's no need to wait."

"Some money of her own . . ." Emmalee repeated hollowly.

"Yes. It's a tragic story, really. Dee's parents were lost at sea while on a trip to the Far East. Her father was a businessman. He wanted to establish regular trade with Hong Kong and Singapore. Her uncle Jacob has been her guardian ever since. He's an engineer."

Emmalee put aside the matter of the wedding. She drank some more lemonade. No wonder Randy had seemed a bit nervous when she'd mentioned how expensive the lemons must have been. He could afford them now. He could afford a lot of things now. She couldn't.

"What's an engineer doing at Landar's Folly?" she asked.

"Doing some building for Garn, I guess. Delilah told me she's not supposed to talk about it. Will you come to the wedding, Em?" he asked again. "You haven't said."

"Of course I will," answered Emmalee, finding it hard to smile. "In fact, I'll be right up at the front of the church."

Randy seemed relieved—he was not a man who endured disharmony readily—and leaned tentatively toward her, kissing Emmalee on the cheek.

Somehow that made her feel worse than ever, and after he had crawled through the fence and gone back to his work, she sat there, glum and spiritless. In spite of all that had happened since she'd left Illinois, in spite of all her effort, struggle, and accomplishment, there she was, dismal and alone.

It's time to think some things over, she decided, returning to her hoe. Randy's announcement had stunned her—yes, she admitted that—to a new degree of clarity, and her relationship with him, with Garn Landar, too, stood out in bold relief. What had happened, really? There had been, with Randy, the lack of something she needed, a lack that, unspoken though it might have been, had introduced a note of emptiness. Once she'd thought that she didn't want to be possessed, body and soul, by a man. Yet, she discovered now, perhaps that was exactly what she wanted. And needed. The very brand of quicksilver passion Garn evoked in her, an undeniable exultation that fired her soul and shook her body with its power. But do I really want Garn? she wondered. Or do I think I do now because, having lost Randy, I realize how alone I am?

"The fit's got to be right," Myrtle had said.

"You got to take a risk," Myrtle had said.

Emmalee went on hoeing, thinking, mulling things over and getting nowhere. I've always come through before, she told herself. I've always been strong. I've stuck to my guns. I've been brave.

But these truths did not make her feel any better this time. Her earlier challenges had always come from other people, from situations or events, which she'd been able to meet by relying on her inner strength. This time the challenge, the problem, was coming from within herself. She was unhappy with the way her life was going, and she could not make up her mind what to do about it. She would not make a strong soldier, she realized, while at war with herself.

Dark clouds rolled in over the mountains. A storm was coming, but Emmalee barely noticed. She went on hoeing, seeking in physical activity relief from her own torment and indecision. By late afternoon the temperature was falling fast. Emmalee looked up when the first drops of rain struck her. Utterly exhausted, she was faced with having to run back to her cabin to avoid getting soaked. All over Olympia, people had seen the approaching thunderhead and had found shelter. Only Emmalee was left out in the fields, in the rain, alone.

The force of the storm struck when she was scarcely halfway home. Wind-driven sheets of rain soaked through to her skin. The sheer power of the deluge bent her over. She struggled to keep her footing on the slippery ground. It seemed as if she would never reach sanctuary, or know the slightest warmth or peace. It was suddenly all too much for her to bear: Randy, Garn, Tell, her farm, money, the storm, everything. Tears filled her eyes, clouded her vision. She stumbled onward, sobbing in grief. Sorrow and loss were no strangers to her, yet never had she been stricken with such a desperate sense of her aloneness. Blinded by rain and tears, she slipped and fell into a deep furrow of mud and running water and lay there for long minutes, howling in helplessness and grief, feeling only half-alive, wondering what to do. She couldn't think of a single thing.

Even so, she staggered to her feet and started again toward home. It was, at least, her own.

Finally she reached the cabin, fumbled with the doorlatch, and fell inside. For a long time she lay on the floor as the rain pounded down on the sod roof, a muffled, droning sound. Then she got up, stripped off her sodden clothing, put on an old robe, and stood by the window. Murky clouds of rain slashed down across the fields of her promised land, mocking both the future and the past. She thought of the tender roots of corn, washed away by flood, each delicate tendril missing forever the opportunity to live and grow strong in the fullness of the seasons.

Just hold on! she thought, picturing the tiny plants bent beneath rain and wind. Just hold on until the sun comes out!

She was praying, really, although not completely conscious of it. And out of the prayer came a flicker of her old strength.

I'm going to hold on too! she vowed. When she realized that, Emmalee knew she was all right. She started to feel better.

I'll go on from here, she told herself. I don't want to be completely on my own anymore. I'm going to find someone. She knew just who he was.

There was, of course, a chance that he would no longer want to have anything to do with her; she hadn't responded carefully when he'd asked his ultimate question. She'd barely been civil to him since.

There was even the danger that he would laugh at her. "I don't care," she said aloud. "I'm going to see Garn again. I'm going to find out what went wrong between us before."

But what if he did scorn her? After all, it was no secret that Randy had cast her aside. Wouldn't it appear that she was desperately in quest of a man to replace the one she'd lost? What if he just gave her his mocking grin, told her she'd already had her chance with him. What if he just plain told her to go away?

Well, as Myrtle had said, "It hurts, but you live."

"*You got to take a risk,*" Myrtle had said.

"I will," said Emmalee.

At first it appeared as if the storm would depart as quickly as it had come, just a ferocious summer shower sweeping out of the mountains, over the plains, to blow away into the west. But it poured all through the waning afternoon and into the evening, so heavily that in the dismal gray twilight Emmalee could not even see the horizon. The plain was covered with water, a glassy sheen upon the earth, and still the storm went on. Thunder crashed above Olympia, resounded off the slopes of the mountains, and came roaring back to sound again. She prepared a supper of porridge and biscuits in flickering lamplight, and fell into a troubled sleep. Great jagged forks of lightning turned the interior of her cabin bright as day. The darkness that followed was eerie and premonitory.

She awakened sometime after midnight. Her blankets were wet and water dripped steadily down upon her. Springing up, casting away her sodden bedclothes, she swung her feet over the side of the bed. There was water on the floor. The rain had soaked through her sod roof, and even as she wondered what to do, a section of the roof collapsed, leaving a ragged hole through which wind and water blew. Her cabin was useless as a shelter now. After debating the situation a moment, she decided the hell with pride. She would go to Randy's house.

But with her cloak pulled tightly around her, standing in the open doorway of the cabin she was about to abandon, Emmalee saw horsemen in the illuminating blasts of lightning. The sight made no sense to her at first. Why would men be out in weather like this? Then an especially bright flash tore across the heavens and she had her answer. They were pulling down the barbwire fence that Randy had so painstakingly erected and driving his animals out of the enclosure. She saw cows and pigs start across her field of corn, saw the horsemen gather for a moment, then ride away into the falling shroud of rain and night.

Burt Pennington had struck.

It rained, off and on, for two more days and nights. The Big Two-Hearted showed its dark side, flooding the low-lying farms, washing away barns and new houses that had been built too near the channel. Horace Torquist's barn was washed completely off its foundation and lay, like a shipwrecked vessel, in the slowly receding pool of water that had once been his yard.

Whole fields of rye and wheat were washed away. Wisps of surviving stalks poked out of the water here and there, and when the water finally seeped into the ground or ran in eroded ditches down to the river, the stalks looked like fugitive hairs on the head of a bald old man.

Most of the barbwire fences were down, and farm animals roamed the countryside as freely as longhorns. Agonized, udder-swollen cows stood on the prairie, waiting to be found and milked. Hogs rooted in gardens; chickens ran everywhere.

When Emmalee rode into town to make her outraged report, Vestor Tell demanded that she identify the men she *thought* she'd seen tearing down Randy's fence. She couldn't, of course.

"A rain like the one we had will easily wash out a fenceline," he pronounced.

Everyone knew that the rain hadn't wreaked the dirty work, but there was nothing to be done about it. The farmers, bedraggled and impotent, dreamed savagely of revenge.

The ranchers tried not to show their jubilation. Before the growing season was even well under way, it looked as if their rivals, the farmers, were ruined. And for the ranchers, the deluge proved a godsend. In its aftermath the grass on the prairie had never been so rich, so green and thick, perfect for cattle to graze and grow fat.

"God didn't mean for the sod to be plowed up and turned over," Burt Pennington was reported to have said. "I see His hand in this."

Now the turnabout is complete, thought Emmalee.

Pennington is invoking the Lord just as confidently and familiarly as Torquist once did.

There was only one bright spot. The farmers who had planted corn, Emmalee among them, did not lose their crops. The corn was hardier, better-rooted in the soil than rye. So when the rainwater ran or seeped away, the stalks grew even faster than before. Randy, busily replowing and replanting, looked across toward Emmalee's fields with what, in a lesser man, would have been envy.

In his case, it was respect.

Two weeks after the flood, Vestor Tell approached Lambert Strep and offered to buy him out. "You're going to fail anyway," Tell pronounced pleasantly. "Sell now. Don't wait. I'm doing you a favor. I'll offer you less—and you'll be desperate enough to take it too—later on."

Strep refused and angrily spread word of Tell's arrogant offer throughout Olympia.

Tell didn't care; he could wait.

And now Emmalee knew what the claims agent had had in mind all the while: His so-called loan policy and all of his actions, including his efforts to keep an inspection team from visiting the territory, were designed solely to ensure that he ended up with the farmers' land. No wonder he had gazed with such a wry, uncaring eye upon the individual one-hundred-sixty acre claims; he had intended all along to own the whole shebang.

Bitter Harvest

"Do you, Randy Clay, take this woman, Delilah Quinn . . ."

Pastor Runde was a jovial, heavyset man, temperamentally more disposed to baptisms and weddings than to sick calls and funerals. He stood in front of the altar beaming at Randy and Delilah, who held hands before him.

". . . to have and to hold, for richer, for poorer, in sickness and in health . . ."

"I do," said Randy, in a strong, deep voice.

"And do you, Delilah Quinn, take this man . . ."

Emmalee sat near the front of the little church, in the second row of pews. She would gladly have been elsewhere—almost anyplace elsewhere—but she was damned if she'd let the snickering spiteful gab behind her back get to her ("No, Em simply couldn't face it. He jilted her, you know?").

Still, she'd gotten to the church early and taken a seat in front so she wouldn't have to face a whole roomful of eyes observing her entrance. Pride had its needs, but there were some limits to its spirit.

"I do," said Delilah Quinn.

Pastor Runde's round face was almost split by a joyous grin. "In the sight of God and our friends and neighbors," he intoned, "I now pronounce you man and wife."

Randy and Delilah kissed.

Emmalee managed to smile and keep her eyes open.

It was the Fourth of July, 1869, and a festive occasion in the territory. By a miracle of splendid weather and rich soil, the second plantings of the farmers who had been washed out had thrived, and it seemed as if they could expect a fairly decent harvest after all. Morale was good, if guarded, because there never was a farmer who confessed to feeling optimistic about a crop, not even if his corn grew ten feet tall or his wheat yielded a hundred bushels to the acre. So the weather, the holiday, and the wedding combined to put everyone in a celebratory mood. The church was crowded with people who knew Randy, and, even as the wedding progressed, Emmalee could hear the sounds of other farmers and ranchers arriving in town to shop and socialize, to take a respite from their everyday labors.

When the wedding was over, and Delilah Quinn was Mrs. Randy Clay, the newlyweds turned from the altar and walked up the small aisle between pews full of wellwishers. They were trailed by Delilah's uncle Jacob, who had given her away, and by the pastor. Jacob Quinn looked pleased but extremely tired. Whatever engineering he was doing for Garn Landar, it was certainly taking a lot of energy from him.

As the wedding couple walked past her pew, Emmalee turned to watch them go. Randy did not seem to see her, but Delilah smiled, although there was something vague about the smile, as if the bride, caught up in her own happiness, did not really see any of the individual faces that smiled back at her.

Then Emmalee saw Garn Landar. She'd assumed that he

would attend, since he obviously knew Jacob and Delilah as well as anybody except possibly the Chinese. He was sitting in the middle of the church, on the aisle. As Emmalee turned to follow the passage of the newlyweds out of the church, she caught him looking at her, ignoring Randy and Delilah completely. His eyes widened slightly when her eyes met his—he'd been surprised by her sudden turn—but he did not glance away. Instead he seemed to increase the intensity of his gaze, almost as if he were asking her a question, attempting to communicate with her through the very air. Emmalee could guess that much, but she had no idea what he was trying to tell her. Nor did she want to look away, lest the growing spell being woven between them disintegrate and go spinning away. It was a terribly intimate glance, as well as a puzzling and unsettling one, and in a sense it was as personal an exchange as she had ever had with him.

"Are you gonna stand here all day, or what?" hissed Myrtle Higgins, who was next to Emmalee in the pew.

Suddenly conscious of the fact that the church was almost empty now, that only she, Garn, Myrtle, and a few other stragglers were still inside, Emmalee finally broke off the glance. Garn seemed to smile slightly—Emmalee couldn't tell for sure—and headed for the door.

"What the hell was that all about?" Myrtle wanted to know.

"What? I have no idea what you mean."

"Come on," Myrtle said. "I may be uneducated but I ain't dumb."

By the time Emmalee got outside and made her way down the line of people waiting to congratulate Randy and Delilah, Garn was nowhere to be seen.

Emmalee kissed Delilah on the cheek. "I hope we can grow to be true friends," the bride confided. And Randy kissed Emmalee on the cheek. "Thank you for coming. It means a lot to me."

"We're neighbors," she replied as cheerfully as she could, wondering why the sight of the married couple vaguely depressed her.

"I know you'll find what you're seeking," Randy said. "You always have before."

Was that true? Emmalee wondered, walking away from the church. She had wanted to come west, and she had. She'd desired a farm, and she had it. She'd needed a domicile and a crop in the ground. These were hers—with even a new shingled roof on her cabin. But she had also come to realize that those things, while she would never give them up, were not enough! She needed something more. And if that something was love, was its price surrender? Was that what she'd read in the faces of the bride and groom? If so, it was not the kind of union she was looking for.

In honor of his niece's nuptials, Jacob Quinn threw a big party for them after the ceremony. Picnic tables were set out beneath the spreading cottonwoods behind the general store. Cakes and pies of every kind covered the tables. The smell of fifty fried chickens was succulent on the air, and a side of beef browned on a spit over a slow fire. Six barrels of beer stood beneath the trees, and there were a dozen earthenware jugs of hard liquor for those who wished it. While the wedding itself had been by invitation, Jacob did not care if the whole territory came to the party. "We've all been working too hard," he was heard to say. "Everybody come. Share the feast and raise a glass."

Most did, including Festus Bent. His jaw had healed but the four front teeth were gone. Still, he did not hate Jacob. Bent was the type of fellow who instinctively respected any man who could beat him.

Emmalee had just drawn herself a glass of beer from one of the barrels. She stood next to the general store, watching the people arrive, sipping the beer. Priscilla and Darlene Bent sidled up next to her, looking happier and more satisfied than Emmalee had ever seen them.

"Hi, Em." Priscilla giggled. "Bet *you* don't feel s' hot today, huh?"

"Bet you feel pretty bad, huh, Em?" echoed Darlene. "You lost your man."

"It wasn't anything like that," said Emmalee, realizing that she ought to keep her mouth shut and ignore these frivolous scatterbrains.

"You know why?" taunted Priscilla. "Our ma done told us. She said you lost Randy and you'll always lose men because you want things on your terms all the time. That's why."

"Tell her thanks for the information," said Emmalee, walking away from their spiteful snickers. She knew that she hadn't lost Randy, but she confessed to being a little startled by the phrase "on your terms." What, after all, was wrong with wanting important things in one's life on one's own terms? If those things—dreams, desires, property, love—were on *someone else's* terms then they wouldn't really belong to one at all, would they?

She was munching on a chicken wing when Otis and Lottie strolled by, hand in hand.

"Hello, Emmalee," Lottie gushed. "Did you go to the wedding?"

"Yes, I did."

"That must have taken a lot of nerve. I give you credit."

"Pipe down, Lottie," Otis said.

The crowd grew and grew, getting noisier all the time. One barrel of beer was emptied to a great cheer, then a second. Half the side of roasted beef was consumed within ten minutes, the men stuffing thick wedges of the tender, dripping meat between thick slabs of fresh-baked bread, the women eating more decorously with plates and forks. Emmalee made herself a sandwich. Someone gave her a glass of applejack, strong but good. Cloris Hamtramck, herself feeling no pain, came over to pass the time of day.

"Haven't seen much of you lately, girl," she said. "What you been up to?"

"Hoeing corn, mostly."

"Should be able to find more to do than that." Cloris winked. "Say, did you catch the latest on Vestor Tell?"

"Not that I know of. In fact, I haven't seen much of him lately. What's he up to?"

"Well, he's around, that's for sure. He met with my husband and a bunch of the ranchers last week." She lowered her voice. "He offered to sell them a big chunk of farmland."

"What? He doesn't own any farmland." *Not yet,* she added to herself.

"That's what I thought. But he sure as hell is talking like he does. You know, me and some of the other women don't like the way things seem to be going. There's more trouble ahead, though we don't know what it is. But I can tell you for gosh-darn sure, we don't look forward to some of these men messing things up. Life is goin' pretty well these days. Our kids are growin', we're all eatin', an' we like it that way." She gave Emmalee a cagey glance. "You know if Torquist is up to something? I'm sure he didn't forget that business about the fences being 'washed out' and all."

"I don't know. I'm just a woman with a farm of her own. Sort of an oddity. No one tells me much."

"Think you could maybe keep your ears open a little wider an' let us know if anything comes up?"

"I'll try."

"Good. You want another drink?"

"I'd better not."

"Come on . . ."

Cloris started to draw Emmalee through the crowd toward the liquor jugs, but they halted when Jacob Quinn climbed up on top of a picnic table and raised his arms for attention. Standing next to the table were the newlyweds and Garn Landar. Emmalee was surprised. She hadn't seen him since he left the church. She thought he'd gone back to Landar's Folly.

"A moment of your time, please!" cried Jacob exuberantly. "I think a few words are in order to mark this happy occasion."

An affirmative cheer arose from the crowd.

"Yeah, but make it short," somebody called.

Everyone laughed. The mood was good.

"All right, I shall. As you know, today we honor and celebrate the marriage of my niece, Delilah, to Mr. Randy Clay. She's very happy. He's happy. And so am I. . . ."

Emmalee watched Garn Landar. His eyes were on Jacob Quinn. He looked as if he was enjoying himself too. Emmalee wondered where Ebenezer Creel was.

"Let me say this," Jacob continued, "before I get so I can't talk and you all get so you can't hear."

More laughter.

"I know there's been quite a lot of speculation going around as to exactly what's happening up on Mr. Landar's and Mr. Creel's claim in the Sacajawea . . ."

Emmalee noted that Burt Pennington and Horace Torquist were paying very close attention to Quinn.

". . . and I just want to assure you that you'll know before long. It will be a boon to all of you, to Olympia, and to the entire west."

"If that's true," interrupted Torquist, "why don't you just go ahead and tell us what it is?"

"I would, except then I'm sure we'd get a lot of visitors, and we're working too hard already to deal with an invasion. In due course, everyone will be able to come up and see what we're doing. If things progress as they have, I would expect we'd have the situation pretty well in hand by autumn. Then you'll be able to see what Mr. Landar has wrought for the welfare of Olympia."

"Yeah, an' I recollect how Mr. Landar got us to Denver ahead of Burt," shouted Fes Bent, in half-drunken high spirits. There was another kind of laugh now, and while it didn't seem to bother Garn, Jacob Quinn began to realize that his remarks weren't having the desired effect. Rather than continue, which might turn the situation in a direction he did not intend, Jacob gave a final, brief assurance that *folly* had never been the right word for Garn's claim and that everyone should go ahead and have another drink. The momentum of the celebration remained unbroken, and after some curious, disjointed murmuring, Arcadians returned to recreation. The band that had played in the hotel at Christmas launched into "Turkey in the Straw." The whine of fiddles filled the air and voices were raised in happy song.

On impulse, Emmalee went up to Garn Landar. She felt a little nervous and wondered why, since she'd been brave enough to risk many things, approaching him seemed so hard.

"Emmalee," he said, looking down at her with surprise. "It's nice to see you again."

The last time they'd spoken had been Christmas night, outside Hester's hotel.

She stood there for a moment, wondering what to say. At least he wasn't asking her how she felt about Randy and Delilah getting married!

"It's nice to see you too," she admitted, knowing as she spoke that it was true. "I have to say that Jacob's little speech made me curious. What are you doing up in the hills?"

"I'd hoped to reveal it today, but the situation didn't seem quite right. The people aren't ready for the news yet. It would only upset them. Jacob thought so too."

She gave him her biggest smile. "You could tell *me*, though, couldn't you?"

"After all we've been to each other?" he retorted, with a hint of his old, mocking grin.

Damn! He wasn't going to say anything.

"Maybe I'll ride up to see for myself," she threatened playfully.

"You can try. Yo-Bang and his men are pretty alert, though. They might not let you through."

"They would if you told them I was welcome."

"Emmalee," he said, after giving his answer a moment of consideration, "you've always been welcome."

She watched his expression carefully, heard again the low, intimate, husky tones of his wonderfully caressing voice. She did not perceive a hint of irony. And she was emboldened. Recalling her resolution to establish a relationship with him again, Emmalee decided to take the risk and press on.

"I'd like to talk to you. . . ." she began.

"About what?"

"Maybe . . . us."

"Us? I thought you didn't want an 'us.' "

She glanced around at all the people. Not a few—the Bent sisters, Myrtle, Cloris Hamtramck, even Otis and Lottie—were watching them. Garn noted this, too, and saw also how uncomfortable the onlookers were making Emmalee. "You must want to discuss something very confidential," he said wryly. "We could go somewhere else. But are you sure you want to go off alone with me? It's always gotten *us* into trouble in the past."

"This is just as . . . friends," she said lamely.

"Okay, Em. Want to walk down to the *riverbank*?"

She was sure now that he was mocking her about the time he'd seen her with Otis, but if there would ever be an opportunity to discuss her feelings with him, it was now.

"All right, let's go," she agreed.

They left the party, walked through Arcady, and soon came in sight of the river. Children were shouting, splashing, and swimming in it.

"Some people got here first," Garn said.

They'd just passed the new schoolhouse. Not yet painted, the square little building smelled fragrantly of pine. It was cool and quiet inside. Four rows of small desks were bolted to the plank floor. Portraits of Washington and Lincoln hung on the wall along with two maps, one of the United States and one of Olympia Territory. A globe rested on the teacher's desk in the front of the room.

"I hope no one saw us come in," Emmalee said nervously.

"Would it matter to you if someone did?"

"I—I guess not," she said bravely.

"Why not?"

"What?"

"You heard me. Why wouldn't it bother you to have been seen?"

There was a slight smile playing about his mouth, but his eyes were dark and serious, boring into her. It was the same way he'd looked at her in church.

"I don't know," she said.

He seemed disappointed.

"Did I say the wrong thing?" she wondered.

"Yes. You ought to have said that it didn't make any difference because you wanted to be with me."

For an instant, she wanted to flare up at him, as she'd always done in response to his similarly arrogant remarks in the past. But this time she held herself in check. She was above fencing with him now, too grown up for that kind of game at last. And she did want to talk to him, to tell him how mixed were her feelings about the way they'd behaved toward one another in the past. His closeness was having the old effect on her again, yet it was neither his appearance nor his physical magnetism that seemed to freeze her tongue.

What's wrong with me? she thought. All I have to do is say that I'm sorry for the past, I'm ready to set it aside. All I have to do is ask him if he'll at least think of seeing me again. That's what I decided to do on the day of the storm.

But the words would not come, even though she had prepared them, even though she was ready to say them.

Garn did not make it any easier. He stood before her, still smiling slightly, as if he knew the struggle she was going through and knew, too, the reason for the struggle.

"You're not too often at a loss for words, angel," he said finally.

The tender term of endearment, his use of which she'd protested so fiercely in the past, stirred her now. It showed, she thought, that he felt deeply for her. But she still couldn't put her mouth on the words she wanted, the words that would tell him that she cared.

"I've said all I wanted to already," Garn was telling her. "I've done all I could. So you see that it's up to you now. . . ."

Emmalee remembered the first time she'd seen him, on the docks in Cairo, Illinois, recalled her first suspicious impressions of his casually reckless indifference. He was a man of grand gestures and pronouncements, facing the world alone and unafraid. In her mind's eye, she saw him climbing aboard the roulette table in the swirling Mississippi current, temporarily bested but undefeated, not even needing to be defiant, totally undaunted. She remembered—her body remembered—how he could set her passions aflame, like a flash fire sweeping through the fields of her heart. And she hoped that she had the power to set a similar flame in his soul.

So she stepped forward, put her arms around his neck, and pulled his head down for a kiss. Her lips sought his mouth, found his lips, and in an instant she was lost. He would not need her words at all; he would be able to understand this kiss. She had never kissed him, nor anyone, so fervently before, never initiated the kissing, and it seemed as if every tender word she might be able to recall or invent would pass unhindered from her mind to his, every promise of physical sensation would be there to grasp and hold. Other kisses with other men had always left an emptiness greater than anything a mere kiss could have filled, but this was not true with Garn. She wanted everything from him, with him, and realized now that she didn't care one hoot if the price of having it would be the surrender of her body and soul. . . .

But, gently, he pulled away from her, looked down at her almost with sadness.

"I did love you once, Emmalee," he said, in the cool quiet of the little schoolhouse. "Perhaps I will again. You've come a long way, but not far enough."

"What?" She couldn't believe this!

"You've learned many things, but not the whole of the lesson. You see, you have to offer me as much as I once offered you."

"But I don't understand." What did he mean? That she had to prove Alf Kaiserhalt a liar? Disarm Vestor Tell? Trade a silver hatband in order to save him from Araphaho Chief Fire-On-The-Moon? It occurred to Emmalee that he had, indeed, done a great deal for her, quite selflessly for a man she'd so often accused to being self-centered beyond redemption.

"You know where to find me," he was saying, loosening her fingers from the back of his neck, pulling her arms away. "I'll be there when you understand my meaning, when you find the words. . . ."

It was hard to meet his eyes. They seemed so disappointed and . . . accusing.

Outside, over the sounds of people at their pleasure, Garn and Emmalee heard the sharp crack of a pistol shot. Garn bounded to the window. Emmalee followed. A lone horseman was riding across the prairie toward Arcady, waving a pistol in one hand. As they watched, the rider fired a second time.

At first Emmalee thought it might be someone who'd had a bit too much to drink, a plowhand or cowboy engaging in a bit of dangerous revelry. But then why would he be riding *toward* Arcady from the north?

"Trouble?" she asked, putting her hand on Garn's shoulder.

"Afraid so," he replied, turning abruptly from her and running out of the school. "That's Ebenezer Creel."

Ebenezer headed straight for town, reining his sweat-flecked beast to a stop under the picnic cottonwoods just as Garn and Emmalee arrived on the run. The pistol shots, along with Creel's agitated appearance, brought partying to a shattering halt. Music died, dancing stopped, glasses were set down upon tabletops. Another horseman, riding more slowly, could be seen coming toward Arcady. The old man glanced fearfully back toward him.

"What is it, Ebenezer?" demanded Jacob Quinn, who'd run up to see what the matter was.

"Big trouble, I'm afeerd."

"Well, out with it, man," demanded Garn.

The second horseman drew nearer and nearer.

"It was this way," babbled Ebenezer, scratching his head. "We had a few trespassers. They hid in the bushes for a while an' then fired on Yo-Bang and the boys."

"Fired on?" Hester Brine asked. "You mean 'shot at.' Why on earth?"

"An' Yo-Bang, he done shot back. He kilt one of 'em."

"Killed?" repeated Garn, as if he could not understand, as if a great dream had suddenly come tumbling down. "This is exactly the kind of thing I wanted to avoid, this was the reason for all the secrecy."

"I know, boss." Ebenezer moaned. "But that's what happened."

The second horseman, in the person of Leander Rupp, came into town now and slowed his mount. Behind Rupp, draped behind the saddle, across the horse like a sack of flour, was another man. He was obviously dead and he was just as obviously Alf Kaiserhalt.

Emmalee wondered briefly why one of the farmers and one of the ranchers would have been out together spying on Garn Landar's property.

"Oh, Jesus . . ." Jacob Quinn said.

Delilah, the bride, was white-faced. Randy, looking stricken and puzzled, stood beside her.

Rupp came up and halted his horse. He didn't exactly have tears in his eyes, but a lot of sweat ran down. Nor was he bothered that every eye was on him.

"They shot old Alf!" he yelled. "Me an' old Alf was up in the hills an' that Chinaman with the yellow hankie in his hair done shot him. Wouldda shot me, too, if I hadn'ta been so quick."

"I came as soon as I could," Ebenezer was telling Garn and Jacob. "I wanted to explain what happened before he''—the old man jerked his thumb toward Rupp—''got here with his version of the story.''

''There ain't but one version,'' yowled Rupp. ''Alf got shot and I wouldda, too, if they'd been able. You see, they're keeping something secret up there, an' it ain't gonna do none of us any good. It's gonna ruin the lot of us, farmers and ranchers alike.''

Kaiserhalt and Rupp, Emmalee reflected. Did their cooperation in this spying mission presage a realignment of forces in Olympia?

Garn Landar leaped onto a picnic table.

''All right, everybody,'' he said. ''There's been an accident here.''

''Alf's been shot through the head,'' observed Vestor Tell, grabbing the dead rancher's head by the hair and examining it. ''That doesn't seem like much of an accident to me.''

''He was a trespasser!'' shouted Ebenezer. Emmalee hadn't seen the old man so upset since his wife, Bernice, had died in Denver.

''They're buildin' a *dam* up there is what they're buildin','' yelled Rupp above the rising din of horrified and outraged commentary. ''Landar and Creel and Quinn and them foreigners mean to contol the river, the main thing that gives life to all of us in Olympia.''

''A dam?''

''A dam!''

''It's not that way,'' pleaded Garn, still up on the table. ''You don't understand. . . .''

But the Arcadians thought they understood all too well. He who controlled the river would subdue to a considerable extent the ravages of heavy rain and spring flood. But he who dammed the Big Two-Hearted would then be able to hold back or release the water at will, and upon such power would depend the welfare of the entire plain.

Emmalee realized that Garn Landar was on the verge of becoming the most powerful man in the whole region.

If he lived.

"Tell, I want Landar, Quinn, and Creel charged with complicity in murder!" demanded Burt Pennington, as the women dropped back and the men came forward toward Garn and the others.

"Yes," agreed Torquist. "It's got to be done."

Tell looked a bit hesitant. He had faced Garn's weapon before, and Garn's revolver hung right there on his hip.

"I'm going back up the mountain and ask Yo-Bang what happened," Jacob Quinn began.

"I already done *told* you what happened," protested Rupp.

Emmalee looked around, studying the situation. Ebenezer was still on his horse. Garn was atop the table and Jacob stood next to it. She saw Garn's black stallion tied to a cottonwood not far away, its great head high, ears perked, as if he sensed the tension of the moment. She slipped away from the crowd, ducked behind the tree, and untied the horse. Puzzled for a moment to find himself free, he backed away from her and reared slightly.

"Garn!" she called sharply over the noise of the crowd. She ducked back behind the tree, but he turned and saw his horse free and unfettered. The men were closing in on him fast. There was little time, so he stuck his fingers against his teeth and let out a shrill whistle, a summons. The black stallion lifted his head high, saw his master, and set off at a fast trot toward Garn. Nothing and no one would get in his way.

Emmalee peeked out from behind the cottonwood and watched. Garn saw the horse approaching, yanked Jacob Quinn up on the table with him. When the stallion passed, the two men leaped aboard. The crowd fell back. Ebenezer took his cue. Two horses and three men broke from the crowd, galloping out of Arcady, people scattering every which way as they fled. Guns were drawn and a few errant bullets were fired, but with all the women and children around no one could get off a good shot.

Emmalee didn't even know if Garn realized that she'd been the one to untie his horse and make his escape possible. She contented herself with the fact that, at least, she'd done something to save *him* for once, in partial repayment of all the times he'd gotten her out of hot water.

The Arcadians, farmers and ranchers alike, were livid in their rage and florid in their curses. There could be no dam, not now, not ever. No one man—or even two or three men—could ever be allowed such power.

And someone had been murdered!

"Now, I ain't all so sure that charge'll stand up," drawled Vestor Tell blandly. He was not about to go poking around in such an affair; after all, it didn't affect him directly yet, did it? "Trespassing's a pretty serious offense in these parts. A man's land is sacred. You all bring me proof," he told Pennington and Torquist.

"Come on, Horace," Burt Pennington said to his former enemy. "We got to consider this. I understand it's also a tradition in these parts for men to take care of their own problems."

Darkness Falls

The sun turned against them all in mid-July, just when the clover was beginning to blossom, the ears of corn beginning to form, the kernels of wheat and rye starting to grow full and fat upon the stalks. No one divined this great betrayal at first, because it came so insidiously. An ally may become an enemy overnight, but it usually takes a while longer before the victim realizes what has happened.

Each day the sun came up over the Rockies to the east, burning brightly, coolly at first, then rising in a proud, hot, merciless arc above the land. All day long it blazed down, sinking finally into the west and leaving the Arcadians gasping in hot, muggy twilights. Sleep came hard in sweatsoaked bedrolls. People rose tired and cranky, the high summer sun already hot on their faces.

Very soon, people began to awaken worried as well. As July wore on into August and there was neither breath of wind nor sign of rain, the once-green leaves of corn sagged pale and limp from their sun-blasted stalks. A faint smell of burning leaves rose from the fields of wheat and rye.

Even the prairie grass began to turn brown, and the ribs of hapless longhorns grew more visible every day.

Drought.

Garn had been all too right, Emmalee reflected, when he'd once told her that merely getting to Olympia would be the easy part.

She thought of him often now, but then so did everyone in the region. The level of the Big Two-Hearted dropped and dropped until only a sluggish, shallow stream flowed in the deep channel. Although it was clear to some Olympians that lack of rain was causing the river to dry up, more people thought the dam was at fault, as though Landar, Creel, and Quinn were responsible for this new devastation. When it became clear that the longhorns were barely getting sufficient water to drink, a group of Pennington's men had ridden up into the Sacajawea, only to be turned back by a dozen armed Chinese.

"We've got to do something about Landar," was a refrain heard more and more often throughout the countryside.

But what could they do about him, holed up as he was in a kind of natural fortress?

Emmalee herself wondered what to do about him, but her ruminations were more personal. Again and again she replayed in her mind their conversation in the schoolhouse. "You've come a long way, Emmalee," he'd said, "but not far enough. You'll have to offer me what I once offered you."

What had he meant?

It was as if she were a dull pupil called upon to recite a lesson she hadn't yet grasped.

Several weeks after the wedding, Delilah invited Emmalee over for dinner. She went. Randy seemed a little nervous, but very happy in his new life, and Delilah was radiant.

Their crops were burning like everyone else's, but it didn't seem to matter all that much to either of them.

"Something good is bound to happen," said Delilah, sitting down at the table and serving a succulent rabbit hash with garden greens, fresh biscuits, and beer. "It'll rain when it's ready to rain."

But talk turned inevitably to the situation in the territory.

"When will the dam be completed?" Emmalee asked the new Mrs. Clay.

"I think before spring. I never paid too much attention. It was something the men did, that's all."

"But what'll it be used for? Certainly not to keep water from us down here on the plain?"

"Oh, no. I heard Uncle Jake and Garn discussing milling, mining. Things like that. Garn has a lot of good ideas."

I bet he has, thought Emmalee, with a combination of pride and rue. Many ideas, and she was excluded from them.

"Bye-the-bye, I saw Mr. Tell in town the other day," said Emmalee. "He certainly looks the cock-of-the-walk these days."

Randy showed a flash of honest anger. "Yes. He thinks we'll all fail now. He offered to buy out Burt Pennington, if the drought continues. Can you believe it? He's offered to buy out a lot of people, farmers and ranchers both. And if people default on their loans to him, he'll have the land anyway. He can't lose."

"I feel so sad for them," said Delilah, who had her own money.

Emmalee had a question. "Let's say a farmer goes bust and has to abandon his land. How much would it take to buy his plot?"

"Fifty cents per acre," said Randy, chewing rabbit hash.

No wonder Tell looked so content, thought Emmalee.

He *couldn't* lose, no matter how he had arranged his scheme. If he'd gotten the money he'd loaned the ranchers from bankers back east, he *would* have to repay it sometime. But if he wound up owning or controlling most of the land in Olympia, he would become virtually a baron. He could pay off his backers readily enough and still be left immensely rich.

"I was right all along," she said. "Tell never cared for either group. Loaning to the ranchers was just a wise card in his private game."

"You may have a point there, Em," Randy admitted. "But Tell is only a nuisance. The real danger to all of us comes from . . . from that dam."

"Oh, honey," said Delilah, "I don't think so. . . ."

"And something's going to be done about it too. Mr. Torquist and Burt Pennington, and some others are holding a meeting later this week."

"Are you going, honey?" his wife inquired.

"You bet I am."

"Do you think you should? I don't want you to get in any trouble."

"What trouble? What will Tell do? He's the law? Ha! Alf Kaiserhalt is dead and in the ground and Tell didn't lift a finger."

"There was the business about trespassing," Emmalee offered.

"Don't get me wrong," Randy continued. "It's not that I grieve much for Alf, after what he tried to do to you and me, Em. But it's the principle of the thing. Murder can't be allowed. Something's going to have to be done about that, *and* about the dam."

"So that's the purpose of the meeting?"

"You bet."

"When is it? Maybe I'll come too."

Randy looked at her, hemmed and hawed a little.

"You don't want to get mixed up in it, Em," he said.

"I thought you said there wasn't going to be any trouble, honey," worried Delilah.

"There *won't* be. That is, only the necessary . . . only what's necessary to survive here in peace."

Emmalee wondered why talk of peace always seemed so closely related to the possibility of struggle and violence. She also recalled Cloris Hamtramck's suspicion that the men were planning something that would bring new havoc to the territory.

"Well, when is the meeting?" she pressed Randy. "Just in case I want to attend."

"You better not, Em."

"Randy, *when* is the meeting?"

He didn't look at her directly, sort of stared at the bridge of her nose, then said, "You have to be invited by Mr. Torquist."

"It's *men's business*, is that it?"

"Well," offered Delilah, innocently displaying a trait that made her a good wife for Randy, "I guess it *is* men's business, isn't it, Em?"

Emmalee didn't have to spend much time deciding that Horace Torquist was not going to send her an invitation. But she had an ominous feeling that the many currents alive in Olympia were beginning to converge. She had no intention of letting that happen without her knowledge. What one doesn't know can hurt an awful lot.

Both of her cows were pregnant, thus dry, so she didn't have milk to sell these days, but she candled and packed her eggs, mounted Ned, and rode into town. Myrtle, who lived right outside the village, had no use for the beast anymore. She'd agreed to sell it and Emmalee was going to pay for the mule as soon as she had the money.

Tell was not at his desk by the telegraph and there was

no one in the store except Myrtle and Hester, who were drinking coffee and listlessly fanning themselves.

"What? No customers?" Emmalee placed her eggs on the table and sat down.

"Too hot," said Myrtle.

"People are scared." Hester shrugged. "They don't spend money—assuming they got some—when any minute they think the prairie is gonna bust into flame."

"One spark and my cornfield would," said Emmalee.

"Help yourself to some coffee."

"It's too hot. Where's Mr. Tell?"

"He went out."

"Out where?"

"Dunno. He was all upset. He heard there was some kind of a meeting coming up that he didn't know anything about. I figure he's out trying to locate the information. You hear anything about a meeting, Em?"

"No," lied Emmalee. Whatever Torquist and Pennington were planning did not include Vestor Tell.

"Maybe he just slept late today," she offered, making conversation. Tell owned one of the new houses right in the village.

"Naw. I seen him ride away," said Myrtle. "He's gone all right."

"Too bad. What if I wanted to send a telegram?"

"Who would you send one to?"

"President Ulysses S. Grant. I figure he'd enjoy how things are going out here in this part of his country."

The two older women laughed.

"Well, the United States Land Office would, I'm sure," said Emmalee.

"They will, in time. That inspection team'll come next year."

Next year might be too late, thought Emmalee. "Say," she demanded, remembering her first sight of Myrtle,

Hester, Garn, and Ebenezer huddled around this table on the day she'd arrived in Olympia, "did you two know about the dam from the start?"

"Yep," said Myrtle.

Hester nodded.

"Why didn't you tell me?"

The other two exchanged glances. "You never asked," drawled Myrtle.

"Why did Garn let you in on his secret then?"

"Guess he liked me." Myrtle grinned. "I told him he reminded me of a cross between the two men I shouldda married but didn't have the brains to."

"I've known Garn since he was a little shaver," Hester said.

"You *have*?" This was news to Emmalee.

"Sure. Back in Wyoming. His ma died early on. She had had some bad luck and was in what is considered a real old profession, just like me. She was sweet. His pa got framed by some shysters and they hung him. Me an' the girls sort of raised Garn, you might say."

So Garn's story *was* true. Emmalee did not quite know whether to laugh or cry. Was it possible that she had misjudged almost *everything* about him from the start?

"He told me that story once," she said. "He didn't mention any names, though."

"True story, every word," Hester said. "Including about me and the girls who raised him."

"So, you seen Garn lately?" asked Myrtle.

"Not since the wedding."

"Why not? That man loves you, girl."

They were alone, the three of them, and Emmalee had been thinking about Garn. She decided to speak frankly.

"He told me that he did . . . once," she said. "I don't know about now."

"Huh!" said Myrtle. "You're just chicken, is all."

"Garn Landar is a proud man," Hester put in. "He's not about to ask for what he wants more than one time. Did you know that?"

"He . . . he told me," Emmalee realized.

"An' you didn't do nothin' about it?"

"Listen here, Em," Myrtle said, putting down her coffee cup and leaning forward, "a lot of things aren't as hard as they seem to be, nor half as hard as you've been makin' 'em out to be. What do you think you're gonna lose anyway if you admit that you love somebody? I keep tellin' you, love ain't surrender, girl! You don't have to run up a white flag an' say, 'It's over, I give up, I ain't my own person anymore.' But you sure do seem to think about it that way."

"I guess it's because I had to get used to being on my own, relying on myself, very early."

"So did Garn. Maybe you're two of a kind."

"Well, could be Olympia's a big enough place for both of 'em," Hester said.

The Hamtramck ranch was about five miles south of Arcady, and by the time Emmalee reached it, she and Ned were parched. She couldn't remember having been this thirsty last summer on the hottest days crossing Kansas. Three towheaded Hamtramck children were playing in a narrow wedge of dusty shade next to the Hamtramck's squat sod house.

"Is your ma here?" Emmalee asked them.

"Well, where the hell else would I be?" asked Cloris cheerfully, poking her head out the door. "Come on in and set a spell before you get sunstroke. What brings you way out here?"

Emmalee tied Ned in the shade, treated him to a basin full of water that Cloris said she could spare, and then followed the woman inside. The sod house was dark and gloriously cool, but plain in the extreme. Just one large, dirt-floored room, it contained a table, a few stools, and two beds, one for the children and one for their parents.

"Joe's out trying to dig a well," Cloris said, mentioning her husband. "If it don't rain in four, five more days, I don't know what we're gonna do for our poor longhorns."

"If they'll eat burned corn, I have plenty."

Cloris served tea made from hot water and the dried leaves of Queen Anne's Lace. It tasted fine going down but left a bitter film in the mouth that, oddly, helped to relieve thirst.

"Quite a social whirl here today," observed Cloris. "First Vestor Tell and now you."

"Tell was here?"

"He's still here, far as I know. He rode out into the field to talk to Joe."

"Do you know what it's about? Are they maybe talking about a meeting?"

"I never heard about any meeting."

"Does your husband know?"

"If he does, he ain't said. That man gets more secretive on me every day, I swear. Course he's holdin' a lot of things in these days, on account of we might go bust here if the drought don't let up. He don't want to talk about it, know what I mean?"

"I guess I do."

"When's this so-called meeting going to be held?"

"That's what I'm trying to find out. You told me at the wedding that you had a suspicion something was about to happen. I think that time is coming. I haven't liked the way that Tell has been operating since we arrived here, and almost everyone has come around to my way of thinking. The men are up to something that doesn't involve Tell, and knowing that is bound to make him more dangerous than he is already."

"Somebody ought to do something," Cloris said.

"That's why I'm here. I've got something in mind. It might work, but I'll need help."

"I'll sure do what I can."

"Could you invite Vestor Tell to stay here for supper tonight?"

"That's all you want me to do?"

"Yes. Just have him for supper and keep him here as long as you can. I need the time."

Cloris's eyes narrowed. "You ain't gonna go an' get yourself in deep trouble, are you?"

"Not if I can help it, Cloris. Believe me, not if I can help it."

Tell's house was grand by Arcadian standards, a two-story clapboard affair with many windows, a little porch, and even a decorative cupola atop the steep, shingled roof. It was located down the street from the general store, its back to the store. The porch faced the river.

Emmalee approached it shortly after nightfall, coming toward it from the river side. The town was hot and quiet. Emmalee had waited for a long time down by the river, growing increasingly nervous. She needed darkness, and Tell's absence.

Pastor Runde's choir was practicing inside the church, a much-needed exercise since "Swing Low, Sweet Chariot" sounded off-key and discordant on the evening air. Emmalee stepped up onto Tell's porch, sure that the creaking of his floorboards was more than sufficient to awaken the dead. The front door was locked, but she found a side window partially ajar to receive the breeze, had there been any. She hitched up her skirt, hoisted herself up on the sill, and swung inside. It was hot in there, and very dark.

She stood near the window until her eyes had adjusted to the gloom. There were several lamps on tables, but she was afraid of too much light. Instead she hunted around until she found a candle in the kitchen. After lighting it, she shielded the flame with her hand and took a look about. The stories about Tell having come from a monied family seemed to be substantiated. His furniture was massive, gleaming, and ornate. The walls were even papered, something unheard of out here in frontier Olympia. The lamps had shades, fine, fragile, elegant things. Paintings hung on the walls, large glossy oils of people and scenes Emmalee could not quite make out by the light of her candle.

She passed through a dining room, then a parlor, entering a smaller room behind the parlor. A little stone fireplace stood along one wall, and bookcases, crammed full of papers and volumes, loomed above a huge desk. The desk was bare, however, and its drawers contained nothing more than a couple of outdated newspapers from Salt Lake City.

Then she thought she heard hoofbeats. Blowing out the candle, she edged toward the window, wondering how to get out without being seen. She was cursing herself for her recklessness now, but when she saw that the horseman was only some cowboy heading toward the general store, probably for a brew, she relaxed, lit the candle again, and returned to her search.

It was fairly easy, once she had determined that Vestor Tell was a methodical, organized man. The Morse code book, a thin little volume, was next to a history of telegraphy and a fat tome dealing with modes of human communication down through the ages. As an added bonus, regulations regarding banking operations in the territory had been inserted between leather-bound volumes of finance and law.

Emmalee urged Ned homeward through the hot night, like an eager schoolgirl who cannot wait to do her lessons.

* * *

Vestor Tell was at his desk in the general store next morning, sipping coffee contentedly and telling rancher Royce Campbell no, he was *real* sorry, but he just could not see his way clear to lend him money for the purchase of a drill bit that might locate water beneath the prairie sod.

"It's too bad, but what can I tell you," Tell oozed. "Whyn't you go over to the chapel and say a prayer for rain? That might just do the trick."

Campbell stalked out, mute, angry and impotent.

"Hello, Emmalee," Tell called. "How you be?"

"Fine," she answered, stealing a second look at him. He seemed to have no idea that she'd been in his house last night.

Hester was a little surprised to see Emmalee. "You give up on farming, or what?" she asked. "You were just in here yesterday."

Em made a big fuss about needing material for a dress she planned to sew, and this pretext got her alone with Hester back behind the stacks of fabric and dry goods.

"Now here's some likely cotton cloth. . . ." Hester was saying, holding out the material for Emmalee to feel.

"No," Em whispered. "Forget about that. I've learned something very important."

The orange-haired woman was all ears.

"Tell loans money as a business," Emmalee said. "He's allowed to do so under the Territorial Banking Charter of June, 1866."

"What's that got to do with the price of tea in—"

"Everything. The charter states that, all along, he's supposed to have used a set interest rate for all parties and treated all applicants equally. Hester, he's lied about this to the land office. That's why he's been delaying the inspectors. He's *corrupt*!"

"Honey, *I* know he's corrupt. *You* know he's corrupt. Lots of people do. But he's got Olympia by the short hairs. What're *we* gonna do? The people makin' it on their own—and I confess I'm one of 'em—say live an' let live an' let a sleepin' dog lie."

"Well, I'm not going to do that anymore."

"Oh, Lord. More trouble. And exactly what kind of uproar have you got planned?"

"I'm going to telegraph Washington, D.C."

"Big talk. How you gonna do that? Vestor's gonna do it for you, huh?"

Emmalee reached inside her bodice and withdrew the thin book of Morse code. "No," she said, "I'm going to do it myself. All I need is for you to figure out a way to get Vestor out of here."

"Jee-zussss! All you need is—"

"Shhh!"

"Shhh, yourself!"

"Well? Will you help me?"

"It might seem exciting now, but it's gonna backfire on you."

"I'll take the chance. That man is a parasite of the worst kind. I know that the rich feed off the poor. That's nothing new. But Tell is even more vicious. He *savors* the suffering and defeat of others. . . ."

Hester Brine listened. She remembered who she'd been, what she'd gone through, the things she'd had to do in order to live her life.

"All right," she said. "I wouldn't have had him for any sum in the old days—even then I had my self-respect—but I'll get Tell out of here."

She did.

"Vestor, honey," Hester said, about fifteen minutes later. "There aren't too many customers now . . ."

" 'Bye," called Emmalee, going out the door.

". . . and I just had a sudden *hankerin'*." She walked over to him and rested her hand on the inside of his thigh, high up.

"You know what I mean, Vestor? Day like this, slow, I can afford to take a little time off."

"How little?" Tell said in a hoarse, surprised voice.

"Or how *long*?" responded Hester. "What do you say?"

Tell bought it. "I'll leave first," he said, panting. "Give me about five minutes. And make sure nobody sees you."

"Nobody but you, Vestor. Nobody but *you*."

Tell left, then Hester, locking the front door. Emmalee went around in back, came in through the rear entrance, and locked herself inside the store. She went to the telegraph desk, opened the code book, and unfolded a piece of paper. She'd already composed her message. She pressed the key, expecting to hear the clatter that Vestor produced, but nothing happened. What was wrong? Had he turned it off, or something? Had all of her effort gone for naught?

Then she examined the instrument closely and found a small switch. Moving it forward, the machine came into humming life. Emmalee stood in a country store on the prairie beyond the Rocky Mountains, scarcely believing that she was about to send her message, her words, herself, all the way back across the mighty country whose expanse she had trod, step by slow step. It was a feeling of power such as she had never experienced before. It cleared her mind. It made her heart steady and her hand sure.

UNITED STATES LAND CLAIMS OFFICE

WASHINGTON D.C.

WE NEED THE INSPECTION TEAM RIGHT AWAY

BANKING RULES HAVE BEEN BROKEN PEOPLE

WILL LOSE THEIR CLAIMS THERE ARE PLOTS

AND DANGER PLEASE HELP

Then she tapped: EMMALEE ALDEN

And, after thinking it over for a moment, she added: AND THE PEOPLE OF OLYMPIA

But there was no answer. No message came back, not a dot, not a dash. She wondered how long it might take. At that moment some women rode into town and knocked their fingertips on the windowpane, wanting to get inside to shop. Emmalee barely ducked away from the telegraph in time to avoid being seen there. She opened the store and made up a story about Hester having had to go out, that she'd be back in just a moment, and they should go ahead and shop.

Hester did return, too, not long afterward, in the company of Tell. He seemed very pleased with himself, and wholly content.

Finally Emmalee had to leave. Remaining any longer would have seemed very suspicious.

I must have done something wrong, she thought. I don't think my message went through. She felt like a failure. Perhaps I'd better write a letter.

Dispiritedly, she went back home to watch her corn burn.

Salvation

A hot wind burned down from the north that night, sweeping out of the Sacajawea. Sun by day and wind by night. The million leaves in Emmalee's cornfield rustled like dry parchment. A full moon had risen huge and brilliant, its cheerfulness mocking the plight of all Olympia.

Emmalee pulled a chair over to the front window in her cabin and kept an eye on Randy and Delilah's house. If Torquist's meeting was going to be held tonight, she wanted to be there. And if the meeting was tonight, she would know when she saw Randy leaving his home.

But an hour passed, then another. Midnight drew near. The last light was extinguished in the Clays' house. Emmalee yawned, fighting sleep, and wondered if she might not just as well go to bed herself.

Then she saw a lone rider coming over the crest of the hills to the west. The horse moved slowly and it seemed as if the rider was slumped over in the saddle. Emmalee felt a shiver of alarm, the more so when it became clear that the horseman was headed toward her cabin. She rushed outside and across the yard to find out what was wrong.

It was Hester Brine, or rather what was left of Hester Brine. Both of her eyes were blackened. Her nose was swollen out of shape. She was not wearing her false teeth, and the lower part of her mouth appeared hollow and collapsed.

"Emmalee." Hester groaned. "I'm so glad to see you. Thank God you're all right."

"*Me?* Of course I'm all right. But, my God, what about you?"

The older woman was on the verge of passing out, it seemed. Emmalee helped her down from the horse and half-carried her into the cabin, easing her gently down onto the bed. In lamplight, Hester looked even more devastated than she had outside. There were cuts and bruises on her wrists and even on her neck, as if she'd recently escaped lynching.

"Hester! You poor thing. What happened? Let me get some compresses. . . ."

"No. No! Don't. That can wait. I'll be all right. It's you I'm worried about. That's why I came."

"What?"

Painfully, Hester gasped out her story. "I kept an eye on Vestor all day," she said. "I knew you sent that telegram and I wondered if there'd be any return message. I figured if he got upset, somebody back east had responded to your wire. There were a couple of short messages that came in during the day, and a fairly long one about midafternoon, but he stayed real calm. By that time I figured nobody was gonna answer you and I was feelin' bad about that 'cause I knew you'd be disappointed.

"Then along about suppertime he sidles up an' says to me, 'Hester, you made me feel real good this mornin' an' in return there's somethin' over at my house you can have.' He's got real nice things, you know, an' I confess I wouldn't mind havin' some of 'em. So I left Myrtle in charge of the store and went with Vestor.

"I shouldn't have. Soon as we got inside his place, he jumped me and tied me up. I was a considerable scrapper in my day an' I mighta fought him off, but he surprised me. He'd received a return message to your wire. . . ."

"*Tell* received it?"

"Yep. From what he said, I gather they didn't refer to you, but somebody chewed him out right royal. A territorial officer is on his way up here from Salt Lake an' it won't be long before those inspectors from Washington show up too."

"Why, that's wonderful. But—"

"You mean why he worked me over? That was part punishment and part his way of finding out who'd sent the wire. Em, I had to tell him. I couldn't take the beating no more."

"It's all right. You should have told him it was me in the first place."

"But I was afraid that he was going to even it up with you. After he left, I got free of the ropes and came here as soon as I could. I was prayin' he hadn't gotten here first."

Emmalee raced to the door and locked it. But, as she did, she saw Randy leaving his barn aboard the dapple-gray. Damn it. The meeting was tonight!

"Hester, do you think you can walk a hundred yards? I'll help you."

"If—if I have to. Why?"

"There's something I've got to do. Now, I'm going to take you over to Delilah's. She'll take care of you. I'm sure she will."

"I don't think you better go anywhere, girl. Vestor's out there somewhere."

"I'll be all right, now that I know he's on to me.

"But he's mean. You gone and ruined his whole set-up out here. He's finished now."

"Don't worry. I'll be careful. The men are having that meeting tonight and I have a sneaking suspicion they're about to mess things up almost as much as Tell has."

"You got a gun?" asked Hester.

"No."

"I wish you did."

Emmalee didn't say so, but she wished she had one too. Slowly and with difficulty, she walked Hester over to Randy's house and banged on the door until Delilah opened it. She looked distressed.

"Emmalee! Hester, oh my . . . what is happening? Have you seen Randy?"

"Yes," said Emmalee. "He just rode off. You didn't know?"

"No. I don't know."

"It's that meeting, I think. Can Hester stay here?"

"Oh, look at me. What am I doing, standing here? Of course, come in, come in."

There were at least twenty horses tethered outside Torquist's big tent, in which he'd been living again since the flood had washed his house away. Thin shafts of lantern light filtered through small rents in the canvas and a triangular patch of light came from the folded-back flap in front and fell upon the ground. Emmalee tied Ned to a bush fifty yards from the tent and approached as quietly and calmly as she could, so as not to spook the horses.

Holding her breath, she edged up alongside the tent and heard Torquist speaking.

". . . time to deal with the foe before he destroys us all."

There was a chorus of affirmative grunts. Emmalee found a small tear in the fabric and peered inside. The leader stood in the middle of the tent, holding a lantern. Burt Pennington stood next to him. The other men squatted or sat on the floor of the tent. Emmalee recognized Otis, Randy, Virgil Waters, Royce Campbell. They all looked grim.

"There is a risk to this thing," Pennington said, warning the men. "If this leads to a big investigation, what we did to the fences is gonna come out. Likewise, you farmers can't keep it a secret forever that Horace here made those fake claims."

"Water under the bridge," offered Virgil Waters. "You don't charge us, and we don't charge you."

"Everybody in agreement with that?" Pennington demanded, looking around at all the men.

There were no complaints.

"All right, we're together then," said Torquist. "There's nothing like a common enemy to bring good men together."

Emmalee remembered how Torquist had once felt about the ranchers and realized how much his thinking had changed. For the worse, she felt, because whatever was being planned here smacked of evil. She thought the common enemy he'd referred to might be Vestor Tell, until Otis asked:

"What are we gonna do about Tell?"

"I saw him ridin' out of town, goin' like a bat out of hell," Virgil Waters informed everyone.

"Out of town?" asked Otis. "Which direction?"

"West."

The men mulled that over, but couldn't tell what it signified.

"Yep," said Waters. "I saw him leavin' his place, saddlebags jammed full, just after supper. Me an' the missus was ridin' through town about then."

West? Emmalee wondered. There would be no reason for him to go west, unless . . .

. . . unless he had run away from Arcady, fleeing the mess he's made for himself. Then maybe he wasn't coming after her for revenge at all! The black sheep was on the road again, heading away, toward California, anywhere. . . .

"The hell with Tell," said Pennington. "We ready to move?"

Assent was low-keyed but determined.

"All right, Otis has the explosives. You're all armed."

Emmalee saw Torquist nodding, his face dark, set as if in stone. His wild bush of hair looked red in the lantern light, hued by fire, a ferocious prophet who had forsaken a dream of heaven for the more immediate rewards of hell.

"The main problem," Pennington was saying, "is that we got to face those Chinamen before we can get close enough to plant the explosives in that dam."

Emmalee shuddered. Now she knew what this meeting was about. They feared the dam, but feared more the power Garn Landar would exert over them with it.

"Just shoot straight," Torquist said. "Everybody ready to ride?"

And they were going to blow up the dam this very night. *Garn!* she thought, gripped by the horror of what she'd just overheard. Garn was in danger. So was Jacob Quinn and all the men working up there in Landar's Folly. The great dream of Olympia had wound its way down to the bitter reality of mayhem and death. An image of Garn came to her, lying dead on the banks of the Big Two-Hearted.

Next thing Emmalee knew, she was on Ned's back, spurring the mule fiercely northward, up into the hills in the face of the burning wind.

"Oh, go. Go. Move, for God's sake," she exhorted the obstreperous beast, slapping it about the ears with the ends of the leather reins. The men were mounting up now, back at the tent. If they rode fast, she had no chance. They'd overtake her easily. Even if they proceeded slowly, they might see her ahead of them on a moonlit night like this and take her captive before she reached Landar's Folly with her warning. She looked over her shoulder. They seemed to be moving slowly. That was good. Ned trotted a bit, then slowed. She urged him on. Far ahead, she could make out the dark shapes of the hills toward which she rode. When at length she dared to look back again, she could not see the men at all, only the swinging light from a few lanterns they carried with them.

Ned quit on her when she reckoned herself to be at least a mile from the borders of Garn's land. One minute he was plugging along, slowly but surefootedly, and she was swaying on his back. The next he had halted and stood head down, looking stubbornly at the ground. Emmalee kicked him, lashed him, but he did not move. He had gone as far as he was going to go, and that was that. The hot wind sighed all around; dark wisps of clouds skimmed low over the mountains; a thin, forlorn gurgle sounded from the wasted riverbed.

Behind her, Emmalee heard the riders coming on. They'd find the mule for sure, and they knew—or quite a few of them knew—that it was hers now. Let them puzzle it out, she thought, jumping off Ned and scrambling up the hill. The land sloped steeply upward now and she didn't see how she could miss walking right into Garn's area. The problem was that she'd never been up there before and she didn't know what to expect.

Glancing backward, she saw that the men had extinguished their lanterns. The moon disappeared then reappeared from behind a thickening cover of fast-moving clouds. The air felt jittery, electric and tingling. Emmalee's sweat-soaked dress clung damply to her skin. She hurried on.

If Torquist and the men caught her, what would they do? If they didn't guess outright that she was trying to warn Garn, would they make her talk? Randy might try to protect her—she was sure that he would—but after all he was just one of many, and the stakes were high. To men bent on murder and destruction, men desperate enough to employ violence to protect their futures, how much would one extra death matter?

And then Emmalee realized the full extent of the risk she was taking for Garn's sake. A risk that he would never know about if she were caught.

Behind her, she heard a cry of surprise and knew what it meant. The men had come upon Ned. She could imagine their consternation, their speculation. And their anger. She continued on her way, panting, gasping, exhausted already but unable to stop. Just keep moving, she exhorted herself. Just keep on moving. Ten more steps, that's all, just ten. Good. Now ten more. That's it. Now just another ten, and then I'll let you rest. . . .

And then she saw a dark, squat building far up the hill, on the bank overlooking the side of the river. There was a light burning inside, a dim, distant glow. She started toward it but her foot caught onto something and she went sprawling. Gritty dirt and small stones scraped the palms of her hands. Her knees were raw and painful. Somehow she managed not to cry out.

But it made no difference. Before she could get to her feet, Emmalee was seized roughly from behind and yanked to her feet. Turning, she looked into a hard, alien face, from which a pair of black, suspicious eyes regarded her with a mixture of interest and amusement. One of the Chinese. Two of his mates stood behind him. They were all armed with rifles. The men looked at one another and arrived wordlessly at some decision. Emmalee found herself dragged along toward the whispering river. Cloud cover rolled in heavily now and blotted out the moon and the sky. She had a sensation of great height. A note of fear sounded tremulously in her heart.

"Take me to Mr. Landar," she said, trying to remain calm even as they pulled her along over the rocky ground.

They didn't understand her. Perhaps they didn't want to. She was a trespasser.

Up there in the high country, the Big Two-Hearted passed through a long, deep canyon, the slopes of which spread upward and outward in the shape of a ragged V. In a ghostly light that came partly from the whitish-gray rocks on the sides of the canyon and partly from an oil lamp carried by one of the Chinese, Emmalee could now see the outline of the dam, a thick stony band in the middle of the canyon itself, and a flat, shallow lake spreading back up the gorge. The dam was just completed and held back very little water, but she could see by the size of the dam and the depth of the gorge that, when completed, millions upon millions of gallons of water could be harnessed for limitless power. The view from these heights was awesome. Two of the guards dragged her to the edge of the abyss. Both of them were grinning.

Emmalee screamed. "Landar! Take me to Mr. Landar!" she shrieked. "Take me to Mr. Quinn!"

They had a good laugh at her panic, then dragged her to a small windowless wooden shack nearby, pushed her inside, and slammed the door. It was pitch-dark and smelled of oil and kerosene. She fumbled for the door with her hands, found it, but it was already locked. The Chinese were laughing outside.

"Please. Let me out. I must see Mr. Landar. He's in danger. You're all in danger."

The laughter ceased, but not because of her warning. Emmalee heard footsteps approaching, then a curt conversation in Chinese. The door was pulled open noisily and abruptly. She was staring into the inquiring eyes of Yo-Bang.

"Dan-ger?" he asked, pronouncing the word carefully. "From you?" She caught a glint of humor in his clever eyes. He recognized her from all of his trips to church with Delilah.

"I'm Emmalee Alden. You know me. I'm a . . . a friend of Mr. Landar's. Please take me to him. You're all in terrible danger. So is the dam."

"Dam?" repeated Yo-Bang, with a quick glance in the direction of the river. He did not seem to believe her. "You. You step on trip-wire, give alarm. You stay here for night. In morning we see. Go to Missah Landar in morning."

He started to close the door.

"Don't!" Emmalee cried, flinging herself against it. Yo-Bang, the good servant, did not wish to disturb his master now, and she, an unarmed and patently peculiar *woman* babbling about danger and the dam, posed no threat to anyone. Let her cool off in the shack overnight. There would be plenty of time for more amusement with her in the morning.

"Dam!" she shouted one last time, gesturing frantically with her hands. "Blow up! *Boom! Boom! Boom!*"

Yo-Bang understood. "We go see Missah Landar and Missah Quinn," he said.

"Jesus, Emmalee!" exclaimed Jacob Quinn, standing sleepily in the door of the cabin to which Yo-Bang had rushed Emmalee. He was wearing a pair of reddish-colored longjohns. "What in heaven's name are you doing here?"

Even as he spoke, Garn appeared behind him, similarly attired and equally surprised to see her.

Breathlessly, she blurted her message. "Torquist and Pennington and a lot of others are coming here to blow up your dam. Hurry. There's not a moment to lose. They could be planting the explosives right now."

"Explosives?" wondered Jacob incredulously.

But Garn did not hesitate. He barked a quick order at Yo-Bang, who ran off calling to his men. Garn and Jacob, ignoring Emmalee, pulled on the trousers and boots they'd brought from the cabin, grabbed rifles, and raced off in the direction of the dam. Emmalee ran after them.

Night was well along the way toward morning. The wind had shifted to the west and Emmalee registered its cool, pregnant dampness without joy. What good was rain if a score of Olympians were fated to lie dead in it? Running down the trail that led from the cabin to the river, Emmalee saw in gloomy pre-dawn haze all of Quinn's Chinese lined up behind concealing bushes on the riverbank above the dam. They were armed and ready to fight. She made out the structure of the dam now, too, a broad wall of boulders, earth, and masonry spanning the canyon. Jacob Quinn had built well. He, Garn, and the Chinese, whose sweat and toil had wrought the structure, were not about to let it be blasted to kingdom come.

A single shot rang out from the woods on the hills below.

Emmalee saw Garn standing on a rise of ground overlooking the dam. He was staring downriver, peering into the morning mists for the first glimpse of the Arcadians. Shyly she went to him.

"Get back," he said. "Get down."

"No," she said. "Not after I came all this way to be with you."

He looked at her closely for a moment, then reached out and pulled her down with him behind a thicket of hazel.

"Well, let me thank you now," he said, smiling and holding her face between his hands, "just in case I don't get a chance later."

"Then I have to tell you something now," she said.

"Can't it wait?"

"No. I've waited too long already."

Emmalee felt the words rising. She had learned the words now, finally, and she believed in them with all of her heart and soul, which she offered in joyous surrender.

"I came here because I love you, Garn," she said. "And I'll ask this of you once, or twice, or as many times as it takes to get the answer I want: Will you love me too?"

"That's a question you only have to ask once," he replied, smiling and kissing her. "The answer is yes."

The blast of a shotgun roared out, echoing against the canyon's rocky walls.

"For as long as we live, anyway," Garn said.

A Sweetness of the Flesh

"Landar? Landar, are you up there?"

"That's Torquist," whispered Emmalee. "He sounds nervous."

"He has reason to be." Garn had one arm around Emmalee and in the other he cradled a rifle. Buckshot from the shotgun blast had whistled near them and scattered in the dirt at their feet like tiny pellets of hail.

"I'm here," called Garn, in a clear, resonant voice that carried in the eerie morning air. "Put aside your weapons. Come on up and let's talk."

Jacob Quinn crawled belly down along the ground, coming to join Emmalee and Garn. "All our men are in position," he said. "And as closely as I've been able to determine, they haven't planted their explosives yet. It'll be terrible. We've got to head off a shootout. We could tear to pieces a battalion of the best soldiers in the world."

"That's exactly what we have to avoid," replied Garn cheerlessly. "If that happens, there won't be anything left in Olympia for any of us. Emmalee," he said, "you'd better go back to the cabin and wait there."

"No."

"Please. Do as I say."

"I might in some cases. But not in this one. I'm with you now."

"Well, I can see that you're still as unreasonable as ever," he said. But his voice was full of love.

"All right, here goes." Garn lifted himself carefully, scanning the trees below.

"Torquist, Pennington," he called. "Don't do anything foolish. You'll all be killed. We have firepower and the high ground. We don't want a fight. Come up and talk."

"Aha, Landar! You can't trick us."

"I'm not trying to trick anyone. I'm trying to get us all out of this mess. Will you tell me why you want to destroy my dam? It's no threat to you."

A burst of bitter laughter came from the woods below. But there was no immediate answer to Garn's question. Emmalee pictured Torquist and Pennington, old enemies become unlikely allies, conferring with each other. She remembered how desperate and determined they had sounded in the tent. She was also worried about Randy.

"How do we know you can be trusted, Landar?" Pennington called. "Speak your piece from there. We're listening."

"Fair enough," said Garn, his voice clear and commanding. "That's all I ask."

He stood up and walked out in front of the bushes, the better to be heard. A shot rang out, the sharp crack of a deer rifle. Garn dropped heavily to the earth. The bullet whined away into the canyon.

"Lying bastard!"

It was Otis.

"Lying bastard, Landar, that's what you are."

"Oats, for Christ sake!" Pennington yelled.

"The bastard hasn't said a word about Emmalee. He's

got her up there. We found her mule. She warned him, or some damnfool thing, an' we don't have the slightest idea . . ."

Garn, unharmed, was lying face down in the dirt, trying slowly to crawl back toward the shelter of the hazel bushes.

Emmalee acted. "I'm here and I'm fine," she called, standing up suddenly so that she could be seen. "It's all right, Otis."

"Em, get down!" shouted Garn. Jacob Quinn tried to pull her back into concealment. She ignored Garn and pushed Jacob aside.

"Shoot me, if you want to," she called scornfully. "What's the matter with you, anyway? Yes, I came here to sound a warning! Who wouldn't, if she had a right mind? Have you forgotten what it cost us to get here? Have you forgotten what it was like on the prairie last summer, when only the dream of *being* here kept us moving? Because if you have, then you don't deserve this place! How are your children going to feel when they see you carried back down the hill dead? How are your wives going to feel? Randy, are you down there?"

A moment's pause. "Yes."

"How will Delilah feel, Randy? If you ever loved me, think of that."

"Put the gun down, Otis," Randy could be heard saying. "Put it down now."

There were sounds of a scuffle, grunts and curses.

"All right," Randy called. "Landar, speak your piece."

Garn, standing up again, obliged. "You're afraid of the dam and what you think it will do to Olympia," he said. "But you're all wrong and I'll tell you why. What makes this land so rich is the river. But it is also the river that can bring destruction unless it is harnessed. If you people fail, what use is this dam to me? I want you to succeed. I want us *all* to succeed. And when the dam is completed, man, not the Big Two-Hearted, will control Olympia. Certainly I will charge you to mill your flour and saw your logs. Certainly I will find the ore that lies beneath these hills of mine. I admit that I did live for a time by the gun, but I have new ambitions now.'' He glanced tenderly at Emmalee, who was listening intently, admiringly. ''But I tell you all that I have not come to Olympia to bring ruin upon it, or myself, or anyone else. This dam is the first step in making our territory a promised land. We stand together, or we all fail. Now, that's what I have to say, and I've said it. You must make up your own minds. I'll fight, but I don't have the stomach for it. I hope to God that you don't either.''

He fell silent and waited. The sound of a rising west wind whistled in the high branches of pines. Emmalee felt a few cold drops of rain on her face, sweet as nectar with their promise of deliverance.

After what seemed a long time, there were sounds of movement down in the trees.

''What's your decision, Torquist?'' called Jacob Quinn. ''Pennington, what's it going to be?''

''We're all going home,'' Horace Torquist called back. ''Landar, we'll see you in town one of these days. Seems we'd better be making new plans for Olympia.''

''For all of us,'' Garn responded.

It was quiet in the woods after a time, and quiet on the rim of the canyon above the dam. The Chinese relaxed and began to speak softly among themselves. Jacob Quinn sighed and stood up. He and Garn shook hands, then Garn took Emmalee into his arms, looking down at her lovingly, getting ready to give her the kiss that would seal their new life with promise and wonder.

''Hey, why the hell is everybody up so early? Emmalee, what are *you* doing here?''

Ebenezer Creel, in boots and longjohns, came stumbling down the trail from the cabin.

"Did I oversleep, or what? Say, I think it's fixin' t' rain. Come on over to the cookhouse. I'll fix us up some flapjacks an' grits."

"Good idea," said Garn. "The rest of you get started on breakfast. Emmalee and I will join you a little later."

Then he took her by the hand and led her toward the cabin.

He kissed her for a long time, and her body remembered what it knew and what it wanted to know again.

"Let's," she said. "Let's now."

"I'm not sure we should," he replied, teasing her. "Every time we've been together before, something's always happened and it's turned out badly."

"That was then." Emmalee sighed, pressing against him, molding her body to his. "This is now. I didn't realize it clearly then, but you were doing most of the giving. It's not going to be that way any more. I'm going to pay you back. I just hope you can keep up with me."

"I'll try my best," he said, slipping off her trail jacket and unbuttoning her shirt. Emmalee felt the cool air on her skin while, kissing him again, she tore buttons in her haste to make him naked. They unfastened each other's belt buckles. He fell to his knees, slipping her riding breeches down, kissing sweet flesh, then stood again as she did the same for him. He was strong and throbbing in her hands, and when he pulled her back upward for an embrace, when her breasts met the smooth, bronze skin of his chest, she quivered and shuddered at the contact.

"Something wrong?" he whispered.

"Oh, my God, no!"

She felt the beat of his blood where the length of him pressed against her, each pulse enhancing her anticipation, each pulse promising the spasms she wanted inside herself. Need shook Emmalee; her legs trembled; Garn's entire body quivered in her embrace.

"Now I'm yours," she said. "I surrender."

All but overcome by passion, he managed the hint of a smile. "Angel, you know I don't ask that. I never have."

"Stop arguing. I just wanted to say it once."

She cut off his laugh with a kiss. He lay her down on his narrow cot in the mountain cabin, the cabin a palace and the cot a bed as wide as time. He kissed her throat where the blood beat fast, and her breasts and all of her, pausing to give her the further sweetness of anticipation, and she said "No, no," which did not mean stop but rather meant no, do not pause do not stop, and then she had him and felt him, over and over and over, as if a million lavender lights flickered in her very flesh. It was gorgeous, gorgeous, and she beat at the air with her arms, trying to escape an ecstasy that could not be endured or relinquished, until pleasure was so great that it consumed him and her and even itself. . . .

They came out of the cabin and walked to breakfast through sweet falling rain. The earth was reborn. Garn and Emmalee, their arms around each other, looked down from the mountains upon the living fields of Olympia, which would yet be paradise for them.

The Beginning

After the ceremony, Pastor Runde offered a special prayer of thanksgiving. For, indeed, there was much for which to be grateful.

"Lord," he said, "bless these thy children, Emmalee and Garn, as thou has blessed us in thine own way and time."

The harvest was in, barns and granaries filled, cattle fat on the range and in the farmyards, all of Olympia thriving. A bank officer from Salt Lake and a new land official from Washington had cooperated to straighten out the mess left by Vestor Tell. Tell himself was behind bars in Sacramento, where he'd been arrested.

At the wedding party in Hester Brine's hotel, Emmalee sought out Ebenezer Creel. "I have a bone to pick with you," she said. "Remember all those times that you told me I wasn't right for Garn?"

"Yep," he said.

"I never admitted it, but it bothered me to hear that. Why did you think such a thing?"

"Shucks," the old man said, hoisting a mug of corn likker to toast her, "don't a fellow have the right to be wrong *once* in his life?"